DOUBLE DECEIT

Publisher JB Uitgeverij in collaboration with Head of Zeus
Dutch cover design Fiona Dijkhuizen
English cover design Head of Zeus
Cover picture *Shutterstock* Ekaterina Jurkova
Translated by Julienne Brouwers & Sarah Fencott
Edited by Sarah Fencott
Copyright 2020 © JB Uitgeverij
ISBN 9789083034829

Julienne Brouwers

DOUBLE DECEIT

thriller

1

My eyes snapped open and I sat bolt upright on the sun lounger. "Where is Tim?"

Oliver looked languidly at me from behind his newspaper. He usually read *The Financial Times* on a Saturday morning, but here at the holiday park shop, *The Telegraph* was the only newspaper he could lay his hands on. "I saw him just a minute ago."

That couldn't be true. "You were supposed to be watching him," I snapped. My eyes scanned the seats skirting the pool. Where was my son?

"He was playing with his bucket and spade." Oliver said, sounding defensive. "I only just picked up my paper."

I jumped up and felt the painful ridges from the lounger imprinted on my thighs. "Tim," I cried, looking around. "Tim!"

I held my hand above my eyes and scrutinised the children's pool, but the huge crowds restricted my search. Everywhere I looked, toddlers were splashing around with their parents or siblings, their chatter echoing beneath the large glass dome that shielded the indoor tropical swimming pool from the cool air outside.

Oliver leaped up to join the search and threw his newspaper on the lounger. "I'll take a look on the terrace, you focus on the water," he ordered and strode off between the tables and sunbeds, over which the holidaymakers had draped their towels to claim them.

I hurried along the edge of the shallow pool, past the red mini slide and the blue elephant, which served as a water fountain, to make sure that Tim wasn't playing behind it.

I returned to my husband, swearing under my breath. He was standing by the loungers with an anxious frown on his forehead. My voice trembled when I spoke. "He's not in the paddling pool."

"Not in the seating area either," concluded Oliver. "I've searched everywhere."

I didn't know what to do. Fear clouded my thought process and seemed to incapacitate me. "Perhaps he went somewhere else?" Into the deep end, I added silently.

"I'll go and check the hot tubs and showers. You go search the main pool," Oliver said firmly.

I was relieved to be given instructions and promptly veered right, while Oliver dashed off in the opposite direction. I staggered to the other pool, muscling my way through the plastic palm trees. A voice boomed over the loudspeaker announcing the waves would be starting at any moment. Surely he hadn't ….?

My feet thudded with every step I took, while I repeatedly yelled Tim's name and searched anxiously around me, looking for a little blond head. I reached the shallow part of the main swimming pool and felt the warm water at my feet. Tim was probably just playing somewhere around here, I tried to reassure myself, but I could feel my heart pounding inside my chest.

I waded through the water as fast as I could, but the resistance of the water caused a slowness that only exasperated my nerves. I shouted out my son's name at the top of my voice, devoid of any embarrassment. Several children looked up in surprise, but I didn't see Tim among them.

After searching the entire shallow end of the pool, I realised he wasn't here either. I felt a wave of panic passing through me as the water began to thrash about in the pool. Where, for heaven's sake, was Tim?

Two girls, about ten years old, stood next to me and held their hands in the air, ready to dive into the rippling water.

My voice sounded tense as I spoke. "Have you seen a little boy with blond, curly hair?"

The girls lowered their arms and looked at me bewildered.

I held my hand at hip height. "He's two years old, about this tall and wearing an orange life jacket," I explained.

They looked questioningly at each other and then slowly shrugged.

I had to restrain myself from grabbing and shaking them.

"No?"

They shook their heads sluggishly.

"Okay, thank you," I muttered.

I pushed myself up on the side, climbed out and scurried across the wet, ribbed tiles along the pool, towards the deep end. I'd have a better view of the water here, I reasoned. I mounted a small step and kept calling Tim's name while I frantically scanned the heads, surrounded by teens plunging with violent splashes into the water. My eyes began to feel irritated from straining. Would his life jacket keep his head above the water in those waves?

I scrambled off the step and strode all the way around the pool until I arrived at the palm trees, near to where we last saw him. The artificial, stuffy heat combined with the pungent chlorine odour in this enclosed space was over-whelming, causing a tightness in my chest – I felt like I couldn't breathe anymore.

I pressed my hands against my temples and closed my eyes. Stay calm, Jennifer, I whispered to soothe myself, but the shrill and screams from the chil-dren playing seemed to only further impair my thinking.

I opened my eyes again and saw Oliver standing in the distance. He shrugged and raised his arms in a gesture of helplessness, his face pale and haggard.

I ran towards him, panting, "I've searched the entire pool! I can't find him anywhere." I felt panic starting to overwhelm me – the unthinkable had happened.

"I checked all the showers and the hot tubs behind them," Oliver responded. There was a look of anguish in his eyes that I'd never seen before. "I've been asking people everywhere. No one has seen him."

I starting pulling at my lip in desperation and felt my hands shaking. The fear seemed to paralyse me. "I don't know what to do anymore. Maybe we should alert the lifeguards?"

"Wait a minute," Oliver said suddenly. "What about the playground, we haven't looked there yet." He turned abruptly and ran off.

I went after him across the slippery floor as fast as I could, all the way to the entrance of the pool complex.

In the sandpit a toddler with blond curls was playing happily with his back towards us. I didn't need to see his face to know he was mine. A mother would recognise her own child in any crowd.

I lifted him and pressed his warm chubby body against my chest, my legs shaking with relief. I buried my face in his neck and breathed in his lovely familiar scent. "I am so glad we found you,' I said, which was obviously a huge understatement. "Tim, sweetie. Mummy and daddy were so worried." Tears were pooling in my eyes, as he wrapped his arms tighter around me.

"Tim make castle," I heard him say cheerfully. He probably didn't even miss us.

He clambered out of my embrace. I wiped my cheeks with the back of my hand and looked at him intently. "Will you promise never – and I mean never – to wander off from mummy and daddy again? It is very dangerous."

He looked at me with innocent eyes and nodded slowly.

I breathed a deep sigh, then I put him down. My heart was still pounding behind my ribs.

Oliver stroked the back of Tim's head. "Don't ever do that again, son," he said.

I took Tim's hand. "Come on, we're going back to our loungers."

He seemed to sense the serious mood and walked meekly by my side.

My feeling of relief gave way to anger towards Oliver. He seemed so light-hearted about the incident. "Do you realise what could have happened?" I hissed over Tim's head.

Oliver gazed silently into the distance, his jaw set.

"You were supposed to be watching him." There was a note of ridicule in my voice when I continued. "Which entails actually keeping your eyes on him and not reading a newspaper."

"Sorry," he said somewhat vexed. "I was only distracted for a moment. There's no need to go on like that."

I snorted with derision. Surely he didn't expect me to let him off the hook so easily? "That's not a valid excuse, Oliver." I said, almost shouting by now. "You promised me you were going to make an effort to work on things, but it's obvious to me nothing is going to change. Don't you see that?"

"Shhh!" Oliver said, nodding his head towards Tim.

I swallowed my anger and felt a knot in my stomach, as we walked on in silence.

When we arrived at our loungers, I put Tim in his plastic high chair.

Just when I was about to ask Tim if he wanted some juice, I noticed Oliver was putting on his chinos over his swimming shorts. "I have to go," he announced, darkness crossing his eyes.

I looked at him perplexed. "What are you talking about?"

He slid his arms into his shirt and buttoned it up. "I just want to be alone for a while Jennifer,' he explained, avoiding my gaze. "I'm heading out for a stroll around the park. I'll see you back at the bungalow in a bit."

I stared at him in disbelief, then closed my eyes for a brief moment and shook my head. "Fine. Whatever," I retorted.

Oliver gave Tim a kiss on the head and walked away without saying a word.

I pulled myself together and turned to Tim. "Would you like something to drink, sweetheart?"

2

"Where are you?" I asked aloud. I stirred the red pasta sauce absent-mindedly with a wooden spoon that I'd found after a long search between the wine glasses. The contents of the holiday bungalow could be described as sparse at best. Tim was sat kneeling on a tattered rug in the living room playing with a toy car making humming noises. We'd brought a box of toys from home to keep him entertained during our weekend getaway.

I tried Oliver's mobile again as I doodled in the margins of a map of the holiday park we'd received at the reception upon arrival yesterday. It rang about five times.

"This is Oliver Smits' voicemail," I heard again. "Leave a message after the …"

I threw my phone on the counter and cursed loudly.

Why did he not just check in to let me know where he was? I hated not knowing what was going on.

Tim turned his head and looked questioningly at me.

"Sorry, pumpkin," I said in a loving voice. "You just go and play."

He didn't reply and returned to playing with his toy.

I stared into the distance, biting my lip. Oliver had been gone for hours. This wasn't like him at all. Was he angry with me? Maybe I shouldn't have exploded like that. Even though it clearly had been a bit careless, Oliver hadn't lost sight of Tim on purpose. I had to admit, something similar could have happened to any parent.

The sound of the kettle made me jump. Before pouring the boiling water into the pan, I automatically checked whether Tim was still at a safe distance from me. I tore open the packet of macaroni, the only type of pasta we could get our hands on at the mini store in the park, and shook half of the contents into the bubbling water.

While the pasta was gently cooking, Tim and I played together on the rug, but my thoughts were somewhere else.

After draining the macaroni, I took the blender I'd brought from home out of one of the cupboards in the out-dated, pale green kitchen. Purifying his food was the only way to get Tim to eat anything, he didn't seem to like any of the vegetables I offered him lately. I mixed the mashed sauce with the macaroni and placed the pan on a coaster on the oak table, which was, by the look of it, as worn down as the rest of the interior.

I decided to make a final attempt to get hold of Oliver, but my call remained unanswered yet again.

I lifted Tim from the floor despite his protest and placed him in the wooden high chair. "Come on, baby. Dinner is ready," I said, trying to ignore the knot in my stomach.

Tim looked at me with his big blue, innocent eyes. "Daddy?"

I went out of my way to sound as normal as possible. "Daddy will eat later." Tim was used to regularly having dinner with just one of us, so in that respect, nothing was out of the ordinary. As a high-powered lawyer, Oliver was swamped with cases, making long hours while I occasionally had to work evening or night shifts at the out-of-hours health clinic. We sometimes seemed to be leading separate lives.

I scooped a small amount of the hot food onto a plastic plate, cheerfully decorated with Disney characters. "Would Timmy like some yummy pasta? Mummy cooked it especially for you," I said brightly, but inside this whole situation was grinding me down. Something was terribly wrong.

After I put Tim to bed around eight, I couldn't help myself any longer. I immediately grabbed my phone and closed the door to the corridor to prevent Tim from overhearing, although these walls, which looked like cardboard, would probably not block out much noise.

I heard the telephone ringing as I paced up and down the room on bare feet across the cold tiled floor.

"Hello," sounded the familiar voice.

I could hear chatter and laughter in the background. "Lindsey. It's Jennifer," I said.

"Hey sweetie, how are you? Having a nice weekend getaway with the family?" she asked in a loud voice, sounding more animated than usual.

I ignored her question. "Where are you? Can we talk?"

"I'm in a restaurant. Paul and I are having a bite to eat." She remained silent for a moment as I heard the clickity-clack of her familiar, ultra-high heels against the floors while the voices in the background fell quiet. Since the time we'd first met at college, Lindsey always wore stilettos and despite my nervousness at the current situation – or perhaps as a result of it – I gave a jittery laugh.

"I'm in the hallway now so I can hear you properly," Lindsey continued moments later. "What's wrong?" Her voice sounded sober again, and hoarse, as was often the case.

I sucked in my upper lip and bit on it. "Oliver's gone."

There was a brief pause. "What are you talking about? You were on a weekend getaway, right?"

My gaze wandered outside, where a sudden autumnal shower made the branches of a row of elm trees sway. I really didn't like this time of year – the realisation that the days were getting shorter and the temperatures were dropping always filled me with a feeling of melancholy. "He's not answering his phone."

Lindsey seemed to sense my unrest. "Hold on," she appeased. "Tell me from the start what's going on. Where are you?"

I sighed. "I am in one of those godforsaken holiday parks somewhere in the south of the Netherlands," I said, wondering why I'd agreed to this. When planning our holidays, our destination was always the subject of debate between Oliver and I. I wanted to go camping, just as I'd done as a child and from which I cherished fond memories. Each year my parents and my aunt and uncle travelled with their caravan all the way to the south of France. My cousin and I would spend three weeks at our beloved campsite exploring the grounds and stuffing ourselves with French baguettes. My mother-in-law, on the other hand, had loved to select a luxury resort from The Marriot or Hilton. I knew deep down why I'd come to this park without grumbling – it had been a final reconciliation attempt on Oliver's part, which I'd seized with both hands.

"Oliver said he'd just go for a stroll around the block but he hasn't returned," I elaborated.

I walked to the television cabinet and grabbed the bottle of Merlot left over from last night. I poured a glass and took a gulp of the red wine, feeling the liquid slowly warming my body.

"How long has he been gone?" Lindsey asked.

"All afternoon." I glanced at the clock hanging on the wall and thought for a moment. After Tim's afternoon nap we'd decided to go swimming. "He left the pool about five hours ago."

"Oh no, I'm sorry. I'll move out of the way," Lindsey said, to someone else I presumed. Then she responded to me. "I don't understand. Did anything happen between the two of you?"

Should I confess to the umpteenth conflict that had arisen between us? It felt ridiculous and embarrassing. I took another sip of wine before coming clean.

"We had a falling out. Oliver was supposed to watch Tim by the pool, but when I looked up, he was absorbed in his newspaper. Tim was nowhere to be found."

"Timmy? Oh god, how awful," Lindsey exclaimed. "Is he okay? You did find him again, didn't you?"

"Yes, thankfully," I hurried to add. "We searched the entire pool complex, asked around everywhere until I was almost certain he'd drowned. You can't imagine the state I was in, I was beside myself." The overwhelming fear I'd felt came over me again. I shook myself out of it and pulled myself back into the here and now. "I naturally became angry with Oliver and nearly exploded, and then he just took off." I paused for a moment. "Lin, I'm terribly worried."

"Hmm …" muttered Lindsey.

I was expecting reassuring words – Lindsey's reaction only made me more nervous. "Where do you think he's gone?" He wouldn't leave me out here, not while we were trying one last time to patch things up … would he?

She spluttered. "Maybe he went back to Amsterdam. Have you already tried your landline?"

I felt stupid. "No, I didn't think about that."

"You know what? Why don't you phone home straight away. I'm sure he's just relaxing in the bath and left his phone in the car. Or something like that," she added. "You know what men are like."

"Yes, maybe you're right," I said despondently. I suddenly realised I hadn't checked whether our car was still parked at the entrance of the holiday park.

"Just try the landline, then call me back to give me the good news." The concern she'd expressed seemed to have disappeared from her voice, her speech was slurring again. She probably wanted to return to her dinner with Paul, her latest fling, back to her uncomplicated evening. I couldn't blame her.

I wasn't reassured, but I didn't want to take up any more of her time and spoil her date.

"Sure," I said complacently, putting my wine glass on the wooden coffee table. "I will."

We hung up.

I pulled myself together and tried our landline as I put my ear to the corridor door – everything was quiet. Tim was probably fast asleep by now.

The phone kept ringing, while the tension in my stomach grew stronger and stronger. "Pick up, Oliver," I pleaded.

Maybe he was indeed taking a bath and couldn't hear the telephone ringing, I thought, trying to calm myself down, or he was listening to his beloved jazz music with his head phones on while lounging on our couch, his loafer-clad feet hanging over the armrest.

I lowered myself onto one of the creaky wooden chairs with my phone pressed to my ear and waited and waited, but my call wasn't answered.

I gave up and flung my phone across the room onto the couch. I rubbed my eyes as the feeling of anxiety continued to grow deep inside. What was I supposed to do now?

I leaped up and went to the kitchen, trying to ignore the mess, which had resulted from preparing dinner in a tiny space. I grabbed a bag of crisps from the cupboard, ripped it open and took it with me to the couch in the lounge where I plopped down. I opened my laptop and whiled away watching an episode of my favourite series on Netflix – if Oliver wasn't here tonight, I might as well take advantage of it.

I stuck my hand inside the bag and mindlessly stuffed the crisps into my mouth. My gaze was focused on the small screen, where a handsome businessman in an office filing room loosened the buttons of his assistant's blouse, but it was hard for me to stay focused.

This wasn't going to work. I slammed the laptop shut and grabbed my phone again.

After only ringing twice, my call was answered.

"Lin, it's me. Still nothing."

This time I heard loud music playing in the background. Lindsey remained silent for a moment. "What do you mean, nothing?" she asked.

Where was her mind? "Oliver is not answering!" I shouted sharply. I kneaded my shoulders. "Sorry, my anxiety levels are through the roof. I've lost count of how many times I've called him – the landline, his mobile, nothing. I'm at a loss – I really don't know what to do anymore. Shall I call the police?" My gaze moved outside, where the lights in almost all the holiday homes had been switched off for the night.

"Let's not jump the gun. Damn it. Wait a minute, I'll go to the hallway."

I heard Lindsey mutter something to Paul. A moment later the music fell silent.

Lindsey spoke tenderly. "Hun, I understand you're upset. But if you ask me, there's no need to worry. You and Oliver are going through a rough time. Every couple has their ups and downs every now and then," she said as if she were an expert on relationships. "Give him some space."

I contemplated Lindsey's words for a moment. Was she right? I felt confused – Oliver had been the one to surprise me with a minibreak and had even specifically blocked his schedule for it. "This weekend was meant to breathe new life into our relationship," I responded. "It was actually his idea. I can't imagine him just leaving me out here all alone with Tim."

"I'm sure his intentions were all good," she spoke with confidence. "But you two unexpectedly had a row, which put a spanner in the works. Maybe he just wants some time to himself. You said yourself that Oliver has been occupied at the firm lately."

I thought back to the past few months during which Oliver often had to work overtime. When he did finally make it home as Tim was well asleep and I was sitting on the couch with a cup of tea, he often seemed deep in thought, his head buried in his phone. Whenever I'd confronted him about his behaviour, he'd reacted irritably and brushed me off.

I let out a big sigh. "Maybe you're right. He may simply want to recharge his batteries," I concluded. The feeling of anguish gave way to annoyance. "You would think he'd have had the decency to inform me rather than just sneaking off."

"It sucks, you're right. Quite inconsiderate."

Lindsey started laughing. "Make sure you give him a good telling off when he returns." She spoke in a calm and serious voice again. "Darling, don't drive yourself nuts. Have a nice bath, drink a glass of wine. Relax. I'll bet you anything he'll call tomorrow morning begging you to forgive him."

"You're probably right," I murmured without sounding particularly convinced.

"Of course I'm right," Lindsey said, with a tinkling laugh. "Babe, I'm going to pop back to Paul before he thinks I've bailed on him."

"Sure," I said and tried my best to sound jaunty. "Thanks Lin for taking the time."

"Any time, darling."

I followed Lindsey's advice, filled the tub, added a dash of lavender oil, and tried to get Oliver out of my mind.

3

When I went to bed around midnight, I put my mobile phone on the bedside table next to me with the volume turned up. I wanted to be absolutely sure I'd hear if Oliver were to call me. I jolted awake around three in the morning and immediately checked my phone, but the screen was blank. I opened WhatsApp and saw that he hadn't been online since the beginning of the afternoon. This wasn't like him at all.

I lay down in bed again and saw the moonlight cast a shadow on the white wall, revealing greasy finger smudges. No matter how hard I tried, I couldn't fall back asleep anymore. As I kept tossing and turning I loosened the fitted sheets, exposing the grubby mattress. Around five o'clock I got up and made myself a cup of warm milk, after which I must have dozed off.

Suddenly I heard a loud "mummy" from the adjacent room. The first sunlight trickled in through the plain, transparent curtains. I reached out next to me, but Oliver's side of the bed was still empty and cold.

After I got out of bed and headed for the small nursery, I felt a dull headache form behind my brow as a result of the restless night. I squeezed myself between the wall and the cot, which barely fitted next to the bunk bed, and lifted Tim up. I buried my face in his neck and breathed in his well-known, comforting scent.

With Tim in my arms, I walked the few metres to the living room of the single-storey bungalow and sank down on the couch. "Did you sleep well, sweetie?" I asked, unzipping his sleeping bag and freeing his arms.

He nodded and slid straight off my lap, then plodded barefoot to the box of toys and tipped it over. The sound made my head pound. I frowned as a sigh escaped my lips.

Tim pointed to the Duplo. "Mummy play?"

I nodded with little enthusiasm and lowered myself to the floor. Together we built a tower out of the colourful blocks, but after a while I started to feel antsy. "Pumpkin, you carry on playing. Mummy needs to do something," I said and went to the bedroom.

I took my phone from the bedside table, but much to my disappointment I had still not received a message from Oliver.

In a flash I remembered something. How could it have slipped my mind? I flung on the crumpled trousers that I'd tossed carelessly onto a chair last night.

I returned to the living room, where Tim was playing. Could I leave him alone for a few minutes? I grabbed my laptop. "Timmy, would you like to watch a movie?"

He immediately dropped the Duplo block he was holding and jumped up excitedly.

I put Tim on the couch and turned on an episode of Peppa Pig. "Mummy will be right back," I promised, but he didn't seem to hear me anymore.

I hurried to the front door where I put my coat over my nightgown and stepped into my ballerina shoes.

On the asphalt road I scurried past all the bungalows, most of which still had no lights on. The air was clear and crisp, creating the expectation of a beautiful autumn day. At the end of the road I turned the corner in the direction of the car park, which was less than a few hundred metres from the house. As I got closer, I slowed down my pace.

I leaned forward and rested my hands on my thighs to catch my breath, while scanning the full length of the car park, which was packed with cars.

My heart skipped a beat. Our Volvo was right where we'd left it on Friday night. A gnawing started in my stomach – it was evident now that something wasn't right.

I rushed back to our house, ignoring the bewildered look of an early brisk hiker accompanied by a Labrador.

Once inside, I saw Tim still sitting on the couch, his feet dangling over the edge, staring blankly at the screen. With trembling fingers I tried to press the buttons on my phone.

A sing-song voice sounded on the other side. "Good morning, police speaking. How may I help you?"

I bit my cuticle. "It's my husband. He left yesterday afternoon and never returned home."

"What's your residence?"

"Amsterdam."

"Hold on. I will put you through."

"No, wait!" I said. "We're not at home right now. We are in America."

It remained quiet for a moment on the other side. "America? You shouldn't be calling this number. The one you need is 911," the woman said kindly.

I swore under my breath. "No, I mean America in the Netherlands. It's a small village in the south of the country. We're staying at a holiday park for a weekend getaway," I explained.

She temporarily switched out of her role as a professional officer coming to my aid and laughed out loud. "Oh dear. How funny, America. I've never heard of the place. What a coincidence."

I muttered something meaningless. Just please connect me with the right person, I thought. I couldn't bear the thought of wasting anymore time.

"One moment. I'll put you through."

I let out a sigh and a few seconds later heard a male voice. "Good morning, this is Jennifer Smits speaking. I need to speak to …" I faltered. "It's about a missing person. I want to report my husband – he has disappeared. He's vanished, I mean gone missing," I rattled on.

Again I was reconnected.

Für Elise blared through the phone while I was on hold, the harsh, mechanical sounds hurting my ear. I rubbed my eyes, feeling exhausted.

My gaze moved to Tim, who still looked unperturbed as he watched the cheerful figures dancing across the screen.

"Department of Missing Persons," I suddenly heard.

I snapped to attention and introduced myself. "Yes hello. It's regarding my husband. Jennifer Smits speaking, by the way." I shook my head. "Oh I'm sorry, I already gave my name. My husband left yesterday and didn't come home. Something serious must have happened to him. This is unlike him. He's never been unaccounted for before," I blurted.

"Hold on, ma'am," the police officer hissed. He sounded like a man close to retiring, not easily impressed by anything. "Calm down, Mrs Smits. First, take a deep breath."

I rolled my eyes and sighed demonstratively. "Okay, I'm calm," I said to satisfy him.

"Very good." The officer spoke painfully slowly, with a local accent. "Tell me again. Your husband left home yesterday and didn't return?"

"That's correct. I'd like to report him missing. His disappearance is completely out of character." Admittedly, we'd had quite a lot of arguments lately, but he had never picked up and just left.

"What time did he leave the house?"

"We're not at home but we're residing in a holiday home in Limburg," I said, purposefully not mentioning the name of the village again. My nerves wouldn't be able to handle any more jokes being cracked. "He left around three o'clock yesterday afternoon and I have no idea where he went. He didn't take the car –

it's still sitting in the village car park. Something's not right."

"Aha." The policeman was still speaking at a snail's pace. "Do I understand correctly that your husband has been gone for less than 24 hours?"

I glanced at the clock, but I didn't actually need to do the calculation. Oliver had left in the afternoon and I hadn't yet had breakfast today. "Yes," I replied reluctantly. It didn't take a genius to see where this was going.

"I'm afraid, I won't be able to help you, ma'am. We can only officially register an adult as missing after forty-eight hours."

I felt the earth disappearing from beneath me. Wait until tomorrow? This was impossible – I'd never be able to make it through the day. "That's not an option." I thought of the crime series Oliver was a huge fan of, where the first few hours after a person went missing were portrayed as critical. "We're wasting valuable time here. You must do something." I appealed to his humanity. "We have a son, what should I tell him?"

"Madam, you …"

I interrupted him. "We can't wait that long to start searching! Something has happened to him." I felt desperate as I spoke of the unthinkable. "The longer we wait, the less likely we are to find him."

He sighed audibly. "Madam, eighty per cent of all missing persons return home within forty-eight hours. There is a solid chance he'll simply be back on your doorstep, claiming his car had a flat tire or he got caught up at work. You have no idea how often that happens," he said patronisingly.

I felt frantic. "That may well be, but that is not the case here."

The man was unimpressed and sighed again. "Has something happened between you and your husband?"

I could feel my guard rising. "What do you mean?"

"Perhaps you had a disagreement? You wouldn't be the first. Many people break up due to a fight and the next day they just continue as if nothing was wrong."

I paused for a moment and then decided to come clean. "Alright, so we did have an argument. I understand that it'd make you think he left on purpose and truth be told, I had drawn the same conclusion as well at first. However, now I'm completely convinced that his disappearance has nothing to do with our disagreement. He'd never leave his phone unattended for that long nor leave me completely in the dark as to his whereabouts. Besides, where could he have gone without our car? We're in the middle of nowhere," I said, cursing this rotten holiday park.

"Who knows, he might have taken a cab," the man suggested tediously.

I thought about his suggestion for a brief moment before rejecting it. I knew

Oliver detested taking cabs, he didn't like the idea of having no control of the vehicle he was in.

I shook my head. "I'm convinced something has happened to him, really." The thought of my husband, perhaps lying by the side of the road after a car had hit him, helplessly waiting for someone to come and rescue him filled me with dread.

"I want to believe you, ma'am," he said in a way that made it clear he didn't. "I'll make a note of your call. But as I said, it's only after forty-eight hours that I'm authorised to take any action on your behalf. I'm sorry, I really am. But until that time has passed, unfortunately, you're wasting your time," he added, but the way he said it made me think he was more concerned about his own time.

As the officer wrote down my name and number, I stared out of the small window, where two children were strolling along the road with a paper bag of fresh rolls under their arms. For a moment I considered the option of going out to search for Oliver myself. But I came to the conclusion that it wouldn't be wise to start aimlessly wandering the streets looking for him.

A feeling of hopelessness came over me. There was nothing else to be done. Only tomorrow afternoon would they be able to undertake steps to find him. I had no choice but to try to somehow make it through this livelong day ahead of me.

I heard the officer from afar. "Mark my words, he'll soon just walk straight back into the house."

4

There was a gentle knock at the door of the holiday home. That must be Lindsey, I thought with a sigh of relief.

When I'd rung her after the phone call to the police, she said she'd jump in the car right away. She didn't want to leave me alone right now and I was so grateful.

I glanced at Tim who was playing innocently with his toy cars. Then I hurried to the narrow corridor of the bungalow. Bright yellow stripes on a blue coat sleeve visible through the glass panel in the door stopped me dead in my tracks. My breath caught in my throat. I slowly opened the door with great reluctance, like a sheep being led to the slaughterhouse.

Two police officers stood solemnly in front of me, an expression of pity on their faces. They didn't look me straight in the eye but past me, seemingly distressed.

This couldn't be happening. I felt like I was about to lose it. My knees weakened and my voice squeaked. "Please tell me it's not my husband."

The male agent spoke in a hushed tone. "Mrs Smits, wife of Oliver Smits?"

I gave an almost invisible nod.

"I'm afraid we have some bad news for you."

All the blood seemed to drain from my head. I felt my legs sink away from underneath me; the female agent responded quickly by stepping forward and grabbing my arm.

I recovered and leaned against the doorframe. My heart started pounding again, pumping blood through my veins in a frenzy, trying to catch up.

I was vaguely aware of the fact that they were talking to me, but I was unable to translate the words into meaning. It was as if I was watching a movie that was being played in slow motion, distorting the sounds. I shook my head in an effort to wake up from this terrible nightmare.

"It's your husband," the male officer said. He swallowed visibly. "I'm afraid we have located his body. I'm sorry to inform you that your husband has died."

My shaking hands cupped my mouth, as if they were a plastic bag stifling the searing hyperventilation. But it didn't work, the panic took hold of me, leaving me completely numb. I looked at the man in disbelief, my eyes bulging. Everything around me seemed to freeze. I gasped.

I felt the woman take hold of me by my elbow, her voice sounding distant and muffled. "Come on, let's go and sit down."

She gave me a gentle nudge down the hall to the kitchen. I slowly shuffled forward, my legs feeling like jelly. The officer planted me on a chair.

My breathing became increasingly out of control. It felt like my throat was blocked as I was struggling for air, but my rapid respiration had the opposite effect – I felt utterly deprived of oxygen.

I looked desperately at the woman. Help me, I'm suffocating, I wanted to scream, but the words were stuck in my throat.

Her grey eyes calmly observed me. "Breathe deeply through your nose," she said in a soothing voice.

I tried to follow her advice, but it didn't work – I kept fighting for breath like a fish out of water.

The woman took the seat facing me and put her cool hands on my forearms. "Come on, give it a try. In through the nose, out through the mouth." She puffed effusively. "Two counts in, three counts out."

I repeated her words in my head like a mantra.

Slowly I seemed to get a grip of myself again and managed to get my breathing under control. As the balance between oxygen and carbon dioxide restored itself, my brain started functioning again. While the panic subsided, the questions starting whirling through my mind. Where was Oliver? What on earth had happened to him? Had he been involved in a terrible accident?

I pulled my arms back from under the hands of the female officer and gave a nod as a thank you. "What happened?" I finally managed to verbalise.

She answered in an empathic voice. "A walker found the body of a man in the forest located behind the holiday park. The lady was out for a stroll with her dog and saw a bright red shirt at the bottom of the hill, which caught her attention. As she looked closer, she saw that someone was lying there." I turned my gaze away and stared into space. The words coming out of the female agent's mouth whizzed past me.

"The walker called the emergency services right away," the officer continued. "When the ambulance arrived at the scene, they found that CPR wasn't an option anymore. We believe your husband already perished yesterday afternoon.”

I jerked my head towards the woman. Yesterday afternoon? So it happened not long after our fight. “Where was Oliver lying?”

The police officer looked at me with compassion through her round glasses. “Your husband was found at the base of a small slope. It looks like he stumbled or perhaps didn’t fully appreciate the depth of the slant. He presumably died as a result of misadventure.” The woman turned to her male colleague, who was standing and leaning back against the fridge, and spoke softly. “Peter, can you get Mrs Smits a glass of water?”

The man acknowledged her request and began opening the cupboards in search of a glass amidst the mismatched porcelain.

I rested my head in my hands. I couldn’t believe it. Oliver had been the victim of a dreadful accident. I had to know everything. “What was the cause of death?” My lips seemed frozen, making it difficult for me to pronounce the words properly.

Peter slid the glass of water in front of me and I thanked him.

“Unfortunately I can’t answer that question just now,” the woman replied. “We’ll have to wait for the coroner’s report.”

“The coroner,” I muttered, staring at the yellow diamond shapes on the plastic tablecloth. My hand reached thoughtlessly towards the glass. I took a sip of water, which left a cold trail as it made its way down my throat.

A trace of hope flashed into me. Maybe they were all mistaken. I rose to my feet. “Are you sure it’s my husband? There could be a mix-up of identity – it happens. It may be someone else.” It couldn’t be Oliver. It just couldn’t be true.

The male officer shook his head in pity. “The paramedics called us after they couldn’t find a pulse on your husband. When we searched his pockets, we found a wallet with an identity card in it. We were therefore able to conclude that it was your husband, Oliver Smits.” Peter exchanged looks with the female officer. “We’d like to ask you to come with us to formally identify him.”

Stupefied, I let myself fall back into the chair and nodded. The decorative pattern on the light green kitchen tiles was dancing in front of my eyes. I felt like I was having a terrible nightmare. Was this really happening to me?

I shook my head and refocused my attention on the female officer who was still sitting opposite me. “How did you know where we were staying?”

The woman pressed her glasses onto the bridge of her nose. “Since there are no houses in the immediate vicinity, it seemed most likely that we were dealing with someone from the holiday park. When we checked at the reception, they referred us to house number thirteen.”

I nodded.

Silence filled the room for a while, until suddenly I heard a loud humming from the lounge. Tim hadn't made an appearance all this time, so I'd completely forgotten that he was sitting on the floor in the semi-open living room. "Tim," I cried and jumped up.

I walked the few steps needed to be able to see him and then looked at my oblivious son, who was still playing with his toy cars. My son, whose life would never be the same from today onward. I turned around to look at the female officer and stammered. "My child no longer has a father."

The woman refrained from replying, she simply bowed her head.

I walked back to my seat and thoughtfully picked up on what the policewoman had said. An indefinable feeling came over me. "How do you know for sure this was the result of an accident?"

The woman looked up and exchanged a glance with her male colleague. "We haven't ruled anything out," Peter replied. I hadn't noticed the man's lisp until now. "Our colleagues are currently working hard on an extensive forensic investigation. The coroner will examine your husband thoroughly. However, at first glance, it looks unlikely he'll find anything out of the ordinary, but we'll have to wait for the official results."

"Wait for the results," I repeated lifelessly. Should I not be screaming or balling my eyes out, I wondered. But I felt neither anger nor sadness. I just felt completely numb.

I abruptly pushed the chair back and leaped up. "I need to see him. Now."

The woman in front of me stood up and straightened her uniform with long strokes. "By all means. We'll take you to him."

The male officer came down the hall with Lindsey in his wake. Her face showed a mixture of concern and confusion. It took a few seconds for me to remember that she'd of course been en route to me when the officers had unexpectedly turned up on my doorstep.

"Oliver is dead," I yelled and ran towards her.

I could see Lindsey's eyes open wide in disbelief before I fell into her arms. Only after a while did it dawn on me that the loud, lamentable screeching I heard was coming from my own throat.

Lindsey stroked my hair. "Oh, sweetheart. Bless you, sweetheart."

I leaned against my beloved friend like a rag doll and cried uncontrollably. The news was starting to sink in – Oliver was dead. My world had come crashing down. Life as I'd known it until now would never be the same again.

Lindsey was giving gentle pats on my back, rocking me back and forth. "Everything will be all right. Really, trust me. You'll be okay," she kept repeating, but we both knew it wasn't true.

I thought about Tim. I couldn't bear for him to see me so distraught. I let go of Lindsey and wiped away my tears with the back of my hand. I looked around for my son and saw through the window that Peter had taken him outside. Tim was playing animatedly with Peter's walkie-talkie on the grass in front of the bungalow, the wind whirling through his curly hair.

Lindsey stared at me with a look of horror on her face. She stammered. "What in heaven's name happened?"

I shook my head. I didn't have the strength to explain the details to her. "I want to go to Oliver, I need to see him. Can you watch Tim?"

She nodded. "Of course. Don't worry about him. I will stay here."

5

During the twenty-minute drive from our holiday home to the police station, the female officer sat next to me on the black, slightly tired leather seat. She'd told me to call her Allison. My gaze drifted outside. While life stood still for me, it seemingly went on undisturbed for the rest of the world. I registered children playing on a lawn, a car honking loudly for a cyclist who turned abruptly, trucks transporting their freight from place to place.

Just before we'd left the holiday home I'd explained to Lindsey that Tim needed to eat a sandwich and take his afternoon nap. She shouldn't forget to turn on his musical bear – otherwise he wouldn't be able to fall asleep. I'd briefly spoken to my mother on the phone, she'd promised to drive to us right away. I couldn't bring myself to call Oliver's parents yet. It was ultimately inescapable, but I decided to delay the conversation until it was absolutely final. It would by far become the hardest phone call I was ever forced to make.

My thoughts were interrupted when the policeman suddenly turned off the engine. Allison got out of the vehicle and gently opened my door. "Thank you," I mumbled before sliding over and exiting. My muscles felt stiff and it wasn't until now that I realised I'd been in the same rigid position throughout the entire ride. We mutely walked up the three steps to the police station. The building, constructed of large blocks of grey concrete, looked desolate and dreary, forming the appropriate backdrop to the harrowing movie my life appeared to have become. Allison asked me to wait in the hallway while she consulted a colleague in one of the adjacent rooms. Two other officers down the hall spoke to each other in hushed tones and seemed to be glancing in my direction, although perhaps I was only imagining things. It was hard to make sense of everything that was going on around me.

Allison swiftly returned from the room and turned to me. "Please follow me." She opened the door of the stairwell and we descended one floor. We walked silently across a long, fluorescent-lit corridor in the basement, where no natural light seemed to reach the space.

We stopped at a heavy, stainless steel door. "Your husband's body is through here," Allison said as she examined me. "Are you ready, or would you like to take a moment?"

I ignored the pain of my pounding heart and nodded.

Allison held her police badge against the card reader and I caught a glimpse of her picture, taken in better times. The massive door opened sluggishly and automatically, presenting a view of an almost empty space. In the far corner of the room was a metal table with a white sheet draped over it.

I held my breath as I followed Allison into the room, a blast of cold, airconditioned air gushing in my face. I still felt like I was dreaming and could wake up at any moment.

When we were standing next to the table, Allison held the two corners of the sheet in her hands and, after giving a short bob of her head, slowly lifted it until a face became visible.

I put a hand to my mouth and gasped. I could only see the forehead, but I knew enough. A mixture of panic and despair swirled through me. I couldn't ignore the obvious anymore. This was actually happening, Oliver was dead.

I wanted to hurl myself at him and never let him go, but I resisted the urge and spoke the definitive words. "This is my husband. This is Oliver Smits."

The policewoman gave a formal nod. "I'm sorry for your loss."

"Thank you," I responded in a monotonous whisper, my arms dangling lifelessly by my side. I turned my gaze from Oliver to the officer. "I need to be alone with him right now."

Allison put her hand to her mouth and coughed, visibly uncomfortable. "I'm afraid the pathologist needs to examine your husband first. Only then will his body be released."

I winced at hearing those cold words. Surely she didn't expect me to wait for that man to finish his job? If anything, her refusal made me more determined to spend a private moment with Oliver. "I don't care what the pathologist needs to do. I just want to be with my husband. Alone," I said bluntly.

She bit her lip. "I'm very sorry. Unfortunately, according to internal protocol, I'm not authorised to release a body – any deviations are subject to deputy approval," she recited, taking refuge behind lawful procedures. "You'll have all the time you need to be with him soon," she added, trying to soften the situation.

I emitted a mocking sound. As if they dealt with sudden deaths of young people here in this rural place on a daily basis, I thought to myself. "Deviate from the protocol?" I hissed with clenched jaws. "You're talking about my husband here."

The officer had a tortured expression on her face. To my relief, she buckled under the pressure of my insisting. "Alright then. Five minutes. That's all I can give you."

"Thank you," I said, feeling flustered and like I could burst into tears. Despite my angry outburst at the policewoman, I was keenly aware of the power she held at this moment.

Allison walked towards the exit and pressed a button, which opened the massive door to the corridor. "I'll be waiting for you outside."

I nodded and looked at my husband again. Oliver's cheeks were pale, nonetheless his face was virtually unscathed, which made it almost seem as if he were sleeping. I gently pulled the sheet further down, revealing his bare chest. I wondered if they'd discovered him like this or if they'd stripped him of his clothes. I felt an almost irrepressible desire to hold him tight, hug him and kiss him, to breathe in his scent and to never let go, but I knew it was pointless – he was not coming back.

After a moment's hesitation, I put my left hand on his shoulder, leaned forward, and rested my head on his chest. It felt odd and familiar all at the same time. With my other hand I reached for Oliver's and entangled our fingers. His chest hair tickled my face, and I smiled. Where I used to hear the pumping of his heart and wondered if it was his or mine, it now remained hauntingly quiet. My beloved husband felt cold and stiff, and I knew from my professional experience that he probably died some time ago. I closed my eyes, deeply inhaled his wonderful smell and resolved to never forget it.

"Oh, sweetie," I whimpered. "My poor baby. I love you so much. So much. I'm so terribly sorry about our fight." It dawned on me that we'd never be able to reconcile – the painful awareness weighed down on me like a heavy burden. I felt tears slowly gliding down my cheeks and dripping onto Oliver's chest.

My mind wandered back to the start of our relationship. We'd met in a pub, and in the beginning we'd spend days in bed together like this. Me lying with my head on his chest, which wasn't as hairy back then as it was now, his arm protectively wrapped around me, his hand gently stroking my cheeks. Spending hours together talking about all our plans for the future, laughing and making love. When we would finally roll out of bed around noon, I'd put on his boxers and shirt, much to Oliver's amusement. In recent months, those intimate moments never seemed to happen anymore. It was as if we were unable to connect like we used to. I couldn't remember the last time we'd fallen asleep lying closely, our bodies entwined with each other. Most of the time it was a quick 'goodnight', after which Oliver would roll over and turn his back on me. Otherwise he'd work at the office into the wee hours, only to quietly sneak into the room at night, careful not to wake me up.

After a while I stood up and studied his face, looking for clues. I spotted a nasty scratch that marked his right cheek. "What happened to you?" I asked, gently running my finger down his nose. I stroked his wavy hair tenderly, until all of a sudden I felt something wet and sticky. I shrank back and looked at my fingers. Blood. My gaze moved back to Oliver. I now noticed his beautiful, blonde curls were coloured red at the back of his head. He must have landed on his head as he fell.

I jumped when I heard a knock. "Mrs Smits," Allison called from behind the door. "We ought to head back upstairs now."

My hand rested on Oliver's chest as my eyes were full of tears. I didn't want to move yet. It was as if leaving this space would be the first step in letting Oliver go. I just wanted to stay with him, reminisce about the old days and all the fond memories we'd created together. "If only we'd had more time. Then everything would have worked out, for sure."

There was a long silence, until I heard the door swing open. "Mrs Smits," a voice behind me said. "I'm sorry, but we really have to go now."

I answered without looking back. "I'll be right there."

The door closed again.

It was agonising leaving Oliver behind in this cold, heartless room, but I had no choice. I leaned over and gently kissed my husband on the cheek. "Goodbye my love. I will see you soon."

I carefully pulled the sheet to cover him and left the room.

6

"Lindsey, I'm so grateful you came over to help me. I don't know what I'd do without you." A dull tiredness was lingering behind my eyes. In the past few days I'd probably slept no more than ten hours in total. It reminded me of the months following Tim's birth when he was suffering from colic.

"No problem," Lindsey responded, waving my gratitude away with her hand. A whiff of perfume flew by and I wondered when I'd actually showered for the last time. She had a faint smile on her lips. "A friend in need is a friend indeed."

After breaking the tragic news to Oliver's parents, they were – to put it mildly – not happy that I declined their offer to arrange the funeral. I desperately wanted to keep matters in my own hands. It bothered me insanely that they wanted to take over, although actually this wasn't any different to their behaviour when Oliver was alive. It sometimes seemed as if any opinion differing from theirs didn't count.

"Come on, we need to go to the study, we have to find these insurance details," I said in a half-hearted attempt at decisiveness. My parents had picked up Tim yesterday so that I could take care of things. He didn't seem to comprehend any of what was going on yet, the poor child.

Lindsey glanced at the grey sweatpants fitted loosely around my legs. "Babe, have you eaten anything today?"

I trudged up the first steps towards the upper floor with Lindsey in my wake. "Sure," I replied, although I couldn't recall what exactly.

"What did you have?" I heard persistently behind me.

I reached the landing and found myself gasping from the effort. A feeling of exhaustion overwhelmed me. "I really can't get anything down my throat at the moment."

"You have to eat something. C'mon, I'll prepare a sandwich for you," Lindsey insisted with a concerned smile, and started descending again.

I put my hand on her arm. "No, really, thanks." My voice sounded listless. "I don't want anything."

"I won't take no for an answer," she said in a perky tone. "Why don't you head to the study. I'll be right back."

I didn't have the energy to protest anymore so gave in. I entered the study, my eyes straying to the robust mahogany desk, an heirloom from Oliver's family, and could almost picture Oliver working his socks off on a lawsuit late into the night. Since he'd made the dream move last year to become a senior lawyer at the international firm in Amsterdam's financial district, where he'd been working for years, the workload had only intensified.

I felt my heart sink. Why had I always left the administration to Oliver? If only I'd been a wee bit more involved, I wouldn't be in such trouble now. I didn't have the faintest clue whether Oliver had arranged funeral insurance for us or if he'd even prepared a will.

I sank down on the black leather office chair, lowered my face into my hands and promptly burst into tears. There were just a few days to arrange his funeral – I'd never be able to get it done, there wasn't enough time. What kind of a hopeless wife was I?

I heard Lindsey come into the room. She put a plate of sandwiches on the desk and knelt beside me. "Oh, you poor thing." She wrapped her arms around me and gently rocked me back and forth. "Hush. Look at me. You're not alone. We're going to do this together, you and me. I'm here for you. You know that right?"

I usually took pride in being an independent woman and didn't like to lean on my friend like this, but I had to acknowledge that her aid was a necessity at the moment and nodded gratefully.

She released me and wiped the tears from my face. "Alright. Enough of that. We have to go through all the papers to find the insurance policy."

I pulled myself together and tapped on the desk. "It will undoubtedly be in one of these drawers. We'll need to go through all the documents one by one."

"Okay, let's get to it." Lindsey opened the top drawer, took out a stack of papers and handed them to me. "Why don't you start with this pile, while I work my way through the second drawer."

I offered her the office chair and nestled myself on the floor in a cross-legged position, on the thick, cream-coloured carpet.

We went through our piles in silence. Telephone bills, education certificates, concert tickets – these papers showed glimpses of the life I'd shared with Oliver. Yet so far, there were no signs of a funeral insurance policy.

Lindsey handed me a folder. "Here, this might be something."

With hope I glanced at the paper, but soon realised that it was a travel insurance policy I didn't even know we had.

I shook my head despondently.

"Too bad. No problemo," Lindsey said upbeat. "We'll just carry on. I'm sure we'll find what we need. How about I put on some music?" She seemed uncomfortable bearing the silence.

"I'm sorry, I'd rather you didn't," I said, my head bowed. Every stimulus seemed one too many. I was aware of the fact that I was terrible company at the present time, but I couldn't help myself.

We continued to plough on, silence filling the air, and not much later, Lindsey started working on drawer number three.

"Ah, how cute," Lindsey said all of a sudden, holding something up in the air. "A postcard from way back. It appears to be a love letter from an ex-girlfriend, sent to Oliver."

It was against my principles to snoop through my husband's private items, but I was curious. "Is it really? From who?"

Lindsey quickly read on. "Girl named Sandra."

Sandra? The name didn't ring any bells. Oliver had told me that before we'd met, he'd had just one serious relationship with a girl named Miranda, which he'd broken off after a year. There had been a few flings here and there afterwards, yet never anything too significant.

"May I see?" I asked.

Lindsey handed me the card. On the front was a corny picture of a couple on a beach at sunset. I turned it over and read out loud.

"Dear Oliver. Thank you for your wonderful gift and the great night together. I can't wait to see you again! Love, Sandra."

Love, Sandra? I felt queasy. This didn't sound like a fling at all. I stared ahead, at the blank wall with the classic embossed-pattern wallpaper. Oliver's mother had, without being asked, interfered in the decorating of our house, which we'd never have been able to afford without the financial aid of my in-laws, despite our two healthy incomes. The prices here in Amsterdam, especially in the southern part of the city, were outrageous. To accommodate Bernadette, we'd allowed her to design Oliver's study. "I find it odd that he never shared this with me. I thought I knew all about his former love life," I mumbled. It stung a bit.

Lindsey seemed to sense my uneasiness. "Ah, well you can't share everything with each other, can you? I also never confess to how many guys I've been with," she giggled.

"You're comparing chalk and cheese. This is my husband we're talking about. Not just another boyfriend," I lashed out.

Lindsey didn't seem to be affected by my verbal swing and shrugged her shoulders.

I drew in a long breath and calmed down. After all, what difference did it make who this girl was? I'd never get Oliver back anyway. Would it matter that much if he hadn't confided in me about all of his exes? Perhaps the relationship with this girl had turned sour, which made him decide to keep it to himself. I laid my hand on Lindsey's arm. "I'm sorry. I'm so sensitive right now."

"Don't worry about it," Lindsey responded, patting my hand.

It wasn't until I threw the card on top of the pile that Lindsey had already gone through that I laid eyes on it – the stamp on the card.

I gasped. "Oh my goodness." All the blood seemed to drain from my head.

Lindsey looked at me puzzled. "What's up?" Her gaze moved to the stack of papers. "Forget about that card, will you. It doesn't mean anything," she said, waving her hand casually.

I felt completely frozen. "He cheated on me."

"What are you talking about?" Lindsey laughed. "Of course he didn't cheat on you. You're letting your imagination run away with you. It's just an ex from the past. Don't start thinking such crazy things."

I shook my head in horror. "Look," I cried and pointed to the stamp, on which our monarch looked majestically back at me. "Oliver and I have been together for more than ten years. Well before King Willem-Alexander ascended the throne. It would be Queen Beatrix on the stamp if it was a girlfriend from the past."

Lindsey looked at the stamp, then at me, and then back again at the stamp. "Shit," she muttered, visibly blanching.

We stared at each other in shock for a moment. Until Lindsey's gaze changed into one of pity and I looked away, humiliated to the core.

I rested my elbows on my knees and cradled my head in my hands, staring into the deep-pile carpet and feeling baffled. What on earth had been going on here?

I heard Lindsey get up from the office chair and sit down on the floor next to me. "Babe. I'm sure there's a perfectly good explanation for it," she said and laid her hand gently on my shoulder. But we both knew it was an optimistic assumption.

I shook my head. "I don't want to talk about it anymore," I said resolutely. I had too much on my mind. "We have other issues to resolve."

Lindsey let go of my shoulders and spoke softly. "I understand."

I grabbed the bundle of papers and started frantically rifling through them. "We need to find that insurance policy."

Lindsey got up from the floor and went back to her chair. "It might do you good to blow off a little steam later over a bottle of wine or take a stroll together. Any time, okay?"

I felt a painful lump in my throat and nodded. Then I picked up the next pile of documents and started flicking through them.

It was fast becoming clear my life was a complete mess.

7

Slowly I awoke from an unsettled sleep. A glance at the alarm clock on my bedside table told me it was almost eight o'clock. I felt completely drained, as if I'd been out partying late into the night. My hand reached to my eyes, which felt swollen and puffy. Then it came back to me how I'd cried myself to sleep last night.

I had no idea how I'd managed to get through yesterday. The church where we'd celebrated Oliver's life served as a gesture to his parents rather than being my own or Oliver's choice. My mother-in-law was a complete wreck and had taken a number of her 'powdery little friends', as she called her Xanax pills. She never left the house without a box in her pocket. Under normal circumstances I wouldn't resort to any type of medication unless absolutely necessary, but this time I'd been seriously tempted to self-medicate. I'd held back though, because I didn't want to go through the funeral like a zombie and consequently remember everything as if in a haze.

Many people attended the service where Oliver's cousin had sung beautifully *Amazing Grace.* Tim had placed a rose on his father's coffin in a poignant ceremony, skipping through the church in a little grey suit my mother-in-law had bought for him. Throughout the day I'd received condolences and acted as a worthy wife, our family, friends and colleagues giving voice to their sadness in sincere but hollow words. It had been truly special – at least, that's what everyone assured me. Or perhaps people just said those things for a lack of anything more appropriate – after all, what meaningful comments could be made about a young father dying so suddenly?

Miraculously, Oliver's parents had managed to behave, sparing me any dramas. Against all expectations, my mother-in-law had even given a wonderful speech about Oliver as a small child, as photos of him taken during his childhood were projected onto a white screen behind her. Maybe those powdery little friends were good for something after all.

For nearly a week, I'd pulled out all the stops like a robot to organise a memorable farewell for my husband, deprived of any opportunity whatsoever to reflect or feel anything. Now that this hectic period was behind me, harsh reality hit me in the face like a sharp stick – going forward I'd have to do it all on my own. All that remained for me was a life without Oliver. I had no choice but to raise Tim without his father around.

I sat up in bed with a jerk. It felt like a plastic bag had been pulled over my head, taking my every breath away. My lungs filled up faster and more superficially, nevertheless I didn't seem to be getting any air. I felt my heart pounding inside my ribcage. I knew I was hyperventilating, but I wasn't capable of regaining control.

With eyes wide open, I stared into the semi-darkness, gasping for air. Don't lose yourself Jennifer, I said aloud. Two counts in, three counts out, I repeated the police officer's words I'd heard in the bungalow last week. Come on, you can do it, I encouraged myself. Slowly but surely I felt the panic ebbing away and began to relax.

I fell backwards onto the bed and my gaze went to the alarm clock, the red neon letters dancing before my eyes. I only wanted for sleep to claim me and never wake up again, but I knew that wasn't an option. I couldn't give in to the feeling of fatigue, I had to get up and carry on. Tim needed to be picked up, he'd been staying with my parents for days.

I threw off the duvet and swung my legs over the side of the bed. It was time for my son to return home.

8

Two months later

On a whim I took the phone out of the study. Oliver had been practically glued to the thing while he was alive, so if any clues about this woman were to be found anywhere, it would be on his phone. I leaned back on our grey sofa in the living room and heard Tim cooing through the baby monitor. It was well beyond his bedtime so he'd presumably fall asleep soon. I looked at the mobile device again and wondered if I'd find the name Sandra on it. Would he really have cheated on me?

It was now exactly two months since Oliver had passed away. After I'd arranged everything for the funeral, I'd turned my attention to Tim, seeking advice from the psychologist, who treated patients a few days a week in our GP practice, about how to explain Oliver's death to him. After two weeks I'd started bringing Tim to day-care again, where he was able to play carelessly with his friends. I thought it would be best to try to get on with life as normal – or at least as close to it – as possible. I'd intended to take some time off myself, but at home the walls came closing in on me and after a week I returned to work, where sorrow didn't consume me.

I couldn't say that I'd forgotten the card that I'd inadvertently stumbled upon, sent by the unknown woman. Rather, as the weeks had passed, I'd tucked it away in a small drawer, somewhere deep in my mind and had buried the key. But every now and then, the enigma managed to sneak out, tormenting my thoughts.

Tim was the one who had pulled me through the recent months. Although he was completely oblivious to the pivotal role he played, the little man made me drag myself out of bed every morning as he tightly clasped his chubby arms around me. I'd gratefully bury my face in his neck, easing my headache. His sleeping bag smelled of the night mixed with a hint of sweat – I had a tendency to cover him too much, because I myself was shivering so often in bed at night.

Part of me didn't want to believe that Oliver had been having an affair. Admittedly, things hadn't been too perky between us in the months leading up to his death. Tim's strenuous baby days had left a trail of deep wounds in our relationship, which had seemed too delicate and confounding to heal. In the evenings, when he was still toiling away at his desk in the study with only a table lamp on, I'd plant a kiss on the nape of his neck and he'd give a distant pat on my back in response. At one point, when Oliver had been regularly coming home late while hammering away at an important case, I'd jokingly asked if he had a mistress. He'd insisted nothing was going on and I'd trusted him. Nonetheless, I'd sensed a distance between us for quite some time, as if our lives had turned a corner from which neither of us would ever return, in spite of my efforts to try to rekindle our love.

I restlessly tossed and turned on the couch, the phone burning in my hands. I missed Oliver terribly. The months since the funeral had been excruciatingly tough. The neighbours who had no clue what to say, the well-intended suggestions from friends and the constant questions fired by Tim wanting to know when daddy was coming home – sometimes it became all too much to bear. Not too long ago, while in the supermarket, I couldn't stifle the tears as I walked past the croissants Oliver used to buy for us and bring upstairs to bed on Sunday mornings. There was no doubt he'd been a workaholic, but he'd spent the weekends with his family. The worst moment was perhaps the first seconds after waking up, during which I thought for a flash that everything was still all right, until the bitter truth hit me like a hammer to the head. Tim suffered from nightmares, and I sometimes brought him into bed with me. He probably needs it right now, I thought. But in all fairness, I might have needed the comforting more than him.

My eyes fell on the cardboard box under the kitchen island, which contained three empty wine bottles. Lately, the alcohol was flowing profusely, and as cutting it out altogether was a bridge too far, I set myself a limit of ten glasses a week. It was only Monday evening and I was already at three.

I clutched the phone between my hands. A sense of guilt came over me. Why did I not trust Oliver? Surely there was a perfectly reasonable, benign explanation for the card. There was no need to browse his phone to check his fidelity, right? Of course he was faithful to me.

In which case, I reasoned, there was little harm in simply confirming this by taking a quick peek. I decided that I was merely doing this to find peace and closure, to be able to move on. And so I put the phone charger into the port.

As I waited, my gaze wandered outside, where in the evening darkness the first flakes of sleet in December struck the restored stained glass window, only to instantly melt away again. Yesterday's forecast had been quite off as they'd predicted a blizzard. I stood up to close the curtains.

After a few minutes of charging, the device lit up and I entered Oliver's six-digit code with trembling fingers. I went to his contacts and immediately typed the first three letters of her name. A stab went straight through my heart – there it was. Sandra.

So it was true after all.

"That doesn't have to mean anything," I said out loud, trying to reassure myself. Sandra was a common name, it could just be an old acquaintance, a friend of a friend or a colleague.

I opened WhatsApp and searched for a chat session with Sandra. I soon spotted one, but to my disappointment it was empty when I opened it. The contents had been erased.

There was only one alternative to find out more. It would be bold and potentially harrowing but then again I didn't have much to lose. Being kept in the dark was worse than exposing the truth, even if it meant I'd been deceived by my husband.

I pressed the green button and heard the telephone ring.

There was a click – I nearly jumped out of my skin.

"Oliver?" I heard a woman say. "Long time no speak." I sensed sarcasm in her tone. "I didn't expect to ever hear from you again."

It became clear to me the woman had no idea of Oliver's fate.

"This is Jennifer. I'm Oliver's wife," I declared.

There was a short pause and then out of the blue I was cut off. This lady had some guts – she'd hung up on me.

Surely she didn't think she was going to shake me off that easily? I redialled the number and she answered again. "I'm sorry for hanging up like that. I was shocked, I mean … I still am." There was a short pause. "Why are you calling me?"

I didn't answer, wondering what I was hoping to gain from this conversation. I hadn't yet asked her any questions – even so, I knew everything. At least, enough to recognise it was true – Oliver had cheated on me. As the unsettling truth seeped in, I felt a numbing fatigue wash over me.

"I er …" I faltered. "I don't really know why I'm reaching out to you. I stumbled upon a postcard with your name written on it. A card addressed to Oliver." The words now came tumbling out of my mouth. "I had no clue of what was going on between the pair of you. Or actually I still don't know anything."

I eased myself up from the couch to pour myself a glass of wine hoping it would take off the rough edges of the painful heart-to-heart with this stranger.

"I'm so sorry," Sandra said again. This time it was a resolute apology. "I had no idea Oliver was married," she added, leaving me wondering whether she was being truthful.

I clenched the phone between my right ear and shoulder and with two hands I jerked open the heavy, stainless steel fridge-freezer door, which had been jammed for weeks. I resolved to have someone look at it soon. Lindsey would undeniably know a guy, who knew a guy. She had a way of taking care of those kinds of things.

"Although come to think of it, it doesn't surprise me," Sandra continued, while I poured the wine into my glass. "I'm afraid I can't help you though."

This conversation was far from over. "I wouldn't jump to conclusions." I pressed one of the buttons on the black display of the freezer and dropped an ice cube into my white Chardonnay. This old habit of mine had initially made Oliver smile – the plain, village girl he was dating put ice in her wine – but as the years passed, his amusement progressed into openly annoyed looks at my apparent lack of sophistication. Sometimes he'd resembled his mother more than he realised.

Sandra seemed to want to ditch me. "If you don't mind. I've got to go."

"Wait," I yelled, afraid she'd end the phone call again. "Hang on a moment. You don't understand. Oliver is … er … He has died."

There was the sound of a sharp intake of breath. "He's dead?"

I leaned my back against the fridge, took a sip of wine, and felt the cool liquid slide down my throat. Although completely wrong, it felt satisfying to shock her like that as well as having a trick up my sleeve to blackmail her with. Presumably she'd not dare to dismiss me again.

It stayed silent for a while.

She recovered. "How awful for you. I'm sorry for your loss. Honestly," she added softly. "But I really can't do anything for you."

I needed to push on. "I'm looking for answers. Please. My husband is gone and all of a sudden I find a postcard from you. A card that shouldn't have been sent to a married man. I don't know what to think about it. Your response speaks volumes, but I need to know for sure. Did you …" I took a gulp of wine and closed my eyes. "Did you two have an affair?" Saying it out loud made me feel sick.

"Yes," she admitted reluctantly after a few moments. "It ended some time ago. But … Yes, we were in contact for a while." She appeared to be downplaying whatever had gone on between them and it annoyed me immensely.

A range of thoughts and questions flashed through my mind. When had all of this happened? How could I have missed this? She was probably young, pretty and childless, I thought cynically. Did she also live in Amsterdam? I felt an almost irrepressible urge to know the down and dirty truth.

"Can we meet?"

"Meet? You and I? What good could come from this?"

I lost my temper. "You have no idea what this feels like. I need to know what happened between Oliver and you. Do you understand that I was under the assumption we were happily married?" For the sake of simplicity, I left out the quarrels we'd had recently. It was none of her business. "This is a lot to process. Please. Just a short talk from woman to woman." I felt tears welling up, but I pulled myself together.

She released her breath with a long, weary sigh and I imagined her shaking her head. "Alright then."

9

"Cheers."

"Chin, chin."

We clinked our glasses of gin and tonic and I pondered if this drink fell outside of my self-imposed quota. I decided it did, there was no point in torturing myself unnecessarily.

"To better times," Karen proclaimed.

I took a sip and felt the liquor burning my throat. I didn't particularly like the flavour, but then nothing seemed to taste right since Oliver had died. Lindsey had shown up on my doorstep tonight unannounced, declaring she was meeting all of our girlfriends in a bar called 'Home', but I questioned whether I'd made the right decision by joining her. Going for drinks with the girls wasn't where my head was at right now, but Lindsey was insistent – I had to get out of the house.

"How are you?" Frederique asked with eyes full of compassion.

I lifted my shoulder in a half shrug. "Alright, I guess. I'm constantly feeling tired though. I can't seem to get a good night's sleep. But I've just got to keep going, you know?" I tried to sound strong and upbeat – over the past few months I'd grown to despise the continuous looks of pity – but my attempts failed miserably. I sounded as convincing as a chocolate teapot.

"How are you holding up?" Karen asked.

I stared off into the distance. "There's no other option than to just put one foot in front of the other. I can't allow myself to fall apart. I need to stay strong for Tim, who simply doesn't understand what has happened, and for the patients at my practice." I didn't like to abandon the sick people relying on my aid and I'd feel awful if they thought their doctor wasn't there for them. I looked at my girlfriends. "It's remarkable how easily you can put on a front when needed."

Karen looked at me with a tormented expression on her face. It really wasn't her thing to talk about emotions.

Frederique touched my arm. "Ah you poor thing. You're so incredibly strong. I don't know how I'd cope if I were in your shoes. I can't believe out of all the people out there this has happened to you."

I turned away and smiled faintly. "Thanks darling." My eyes fell on my reflection in a mirror a few feet away and I realised that I hadn't looked this presentable in months. Upon Lindsey's arrival tonight, I'd flung on some clothes while she'd left the baby monitor with my befriended neighbour upstairs, after which I'd made a vain attempt to conceal the bags under my eyes with some makeup. Lindsey had entered the bathroom with a glass of wine in her hand, shaking her head with a smile as she leaned against the door. "You can take the girl out of the country, but you can't take the country out of the girl," she'd commented, looking at me from head to toe. My gaze had self-consciously descended. "Is there something wrong with this outfit?" Fashion had never been my strongest point, to be fair. Lindsey had firmly placed her glass on the washbasin and yelled back whilst walking towards my bedroom. "No need to worry. I'll find you something with a bit of oomph."

Frederique spoke again. "You know we're always there for you, don't you? Just a phone call and we'll come over. Bring you food. Or watch Timmy for a while."

"Or get you drunk," Karen added, with a mischievous giggle.

Everyone laughed with relief. I noticed Frederique had recently whitened her teeth again. They contrasted sharply with her cherry red coloured lips.

Lindsey gave me a wink and bobbed her head. "This is good for you." Lately everyone seemed to know what was good for me.

Lindsey resumed, waving her hand airily. "Getting out of the house, mingling with the girls." She was following the latest fashion trends as usual and wore an ochre-yellow oversized jumper with jeans that clung to her waist. Her long blonde hair framed her oval face. She looked radiant.

"How's Tim doing? Do you notice any difference in his behaviour?" Frederique asked.

Tim obviously sensed something had changed, but he wasn't able to comprehend what was going on, let alone verbalise his feelings. "He often asks for his father, like when we're eating. Or when I put him into bed, he'll say 'daddy kiss'." The pain of those words was almost unbearable.

Frederique's eyes filled with tears. "Sorry," she said, quickly wiping her cheeks. "I don't want to upset you anymore. This was meant to be a fun evening," she added and smiled.

I gave her a reassuring look, I genuinely appreciated my friends' efforts. "I try not to break down too often while he's around because it upsets him terribly," I went on, happy to be able to air my feelings. "But I haven't really noticed anything particularly unusual about him. I often let him kiss Oliver's picture. I framed one and put it in his room, to keep Oliver's memory alive."

"I'm sure he'll never forget him," Lindsey said sympathetically. "How could he? He was his father."

"I'm so worried he won't be able to remember him though," I said against my better judgment.

Karen ran a hand through her short hair and cast me a look of pity. "Hun, he's two. He's too young to have any vivid recollection of his father."

I found it hard to swallow. "Yes, I know that," I said miffed. "In any case, it feels better."

Lindsey shot Karen a warning glance, to which she responded by letting the subject rest.

The song *All I Want for Christmas* suddenly blasted over the speakers and reminded me of how Oliver and I had met in the weeks before Christmas. It had always remained 'our song'. The joyful tones made me reminisce about him so intensely that I couldn't speak for a brief moment.

"Isn't this a nice place," I heard Lindsey say.

I managed to respond flatly. "Yes, it is. Hadn't heard of it before."

"It opened just a few months ago, and it's become the place to be."

Over and above the buzz, I caught fragments of the chitchat at the table next to us, where a young man was boasting to his date about his performances in the gym, presumably to impress her. I wasn't quite sure why, but I burst out laughing and could hardly stop. I guffawed to the point of Lindsey looking at me questioningly.

I repeated his ridiculously pompous words quietly, afraid I'd insult him, but it didn't sound quite as amusing coming out of my mouth.

She smiled. "I'm delighted to see you laugh so freely again."

I realised that during those seconds of hysterical laughter it seemed for a fleeting moment as if nothing bad had happened and everything was the same as before, and it gave me a blissful feeling of hope. Hope of a future in which I could once again feel like the old Jennifer, something that had seemed impossible in recent months.

A waitress with a perpetual smile came to ask if she could be of any help to us.

"How about some nachos?" Karen suggested.

"Sure," Frederique said, but, knowing her, she wouldn't have many of them. She didn't want to ruin her slender figure.

"How's work?" Lindsey asked me.

"If I'm honest, I never feel like going in, but once I arrive it provides some distraction. On Wednesdays I still have my day at home with Tim, which is a welcome break during the week." I took a sip of my gin and tonic and wondered whose idea it had been to order this drink. "I've noticed though that I'm becoming increasingly irritated by the trivialities with which patients come to see me."

Frederique nodded her head supportively.

"You have no idea what kind of things people make appointments for." I resumed with a funny voice, "Doctor, you wouldn't believe the headaches I'm having. Doctor, my daughter has fallen in the playground and has a scrape on her knee. Doctor, my big toe is all swollen up." I got worked up again just thinking about it.

Lindsey and Karen looked up, a glint of laughter flickering across their faces.

"Darling, this does not sound like you at all," Frederique said, with a frown of concern. "You've always been so … so considerate and understanding of all those ailments."

The waitress brought the nachos, which Karen eagerly started nibbling.

I pondered Frederique's remark. It was indeed against my nature to pass comments on the daily worries that I encountered at work. Had I become so insensitive to the aches and pains of my patients? Was I no longer able to sympathise with them? It was as if my feeling of empathy had diminished, the whole situation had just chipped it all away. Perhaps Oliver's death had made me emotionally numb. I found it a sad and depressing conclusion.

"I'm sure it's just a temporary thing," Karen said, chewing on a nacho. "I think it's just a phase that will pass."

I flicked a lock of hair behind my ear. "I hope you're right. Either way, I seem to be struggling to focus and listen properly to my patients. I have to restrain myself from saying 'your big toe is supposed to be fat. My toe is fat too'," I tried to quip.

Frederique smiled.

My gaze fell on the Christmas decorations again, and it suddenly dawned on me that this year I'd be spending the holidays without Oliver and my heart sank. The last couple of years we'd spent Christmas Day with my parents, together with a single aunt, ploughing through the mountains of food that my mum would prepare. Boxing Day we usually celebrated with my in-laws and Oliver's sister, her husband and their two children. Although the tradition was quite nice, I couldn't bear the prospect of being there all by myself at the nothing-less-than-perfectly set table, the rows of cutlery announcing the various courses. Tim was at an age where he was unwilling to sit in a high chair for hours, for which Oliver's mother seemed to have little understanding, just like our choice of name for our son. When my parents-in-law visited us after giving birth, my mother-in-law had repeated "Tim" with an expression of disgust on her face. "I'm assuming his full name is Timothy," she remarked, clearly expecting a name with a little more grandeur. "No, it's just Tim," I'd murmured in discomfiture. "We like the name," Oliver had added to nip the discussion in the bud. I'd seen my father-in-law give Bernadette a poke. She'd pursed her lips together and managed to mutter "yes beautiful, indeed".

Lindsey pulled me out of my musings. "What's the matter, darl?"

I shared my doubts with her about how to navigate the Christmas period, after which she asked whether it was an option to skip dinner at the in-laws altogether this year.

"I can't do that to Bernadette," I replied. I'd learned from Oliver's father that she was still rather shaky. I didn't want to rock the boat by denying her time with Tim during Christmas. After all, he was the only tangible memory she had of her son.

Lindsey's eyes suddenly lit up. "What about if you take Tim to your in-laws and then come over to my place on Boxing Day? I'll arrange a decent bottle of wine and some comfort food. We'll hang out on the couch and spend the evening putting the world to rights." Lindsey hadn't been in a stable relationship for years and I knew she never had any plans for Boxing Day.

The idea filled me with relief and joy. This was the perfect solution. Tim could see his grandparents and I wasn't forced to muscle my way through a culinary spectacle, with Oliver's absence screaming in my face.

I gave her a warm hug. "That's a great idea, Lindsey. Thank you."

She took a mouthful of her drink and looked at me contentedly.

My gaze moved to the rest of our friends, who were sitting around the table, and then I suddenly recalled that Karen had recently lost her job as an orthopaedic surgeon after a long labour dispute. "How are you doing now?" I asked, feeling a sense of guilt. I'd been so caught up in myself over the last couple of months, I'd forgotten that I wasn't the only one going through difficult times.

Karen was always steady as a rock, but now she looked washed out, like a Dahlia after a summer shower, the head too heavy for its stem. "I'm fine," she said bravely, but her haggard eyes told a different story.

I stroked her arm. She felt brittle and vulnerable, despite the fact that she seemed to have put on some weight. "I'm sure there will be ample new opportunities for you ahead, you're such a champ," I said, and although I genuinely meant it, it sounded like a cliché.

Karen failed to respond to my well-intended comment. "Drinks, anyone?"

she asked.

I thought guiltily of all those bottles of white wine that I'd knocked back at home lately. I'd obviously never do anything stupid, I had to take care of Tim and look after my patients at work. Nonetheless, nearly every evening I'd consume a few glasses, otherwise I'd have a hard time falling asleep. "I'm still good," I answered.

I wasn't sure how to bring it up, but I had to get it off my chest. My recent discovery had been so incredibly painful that it felt like I would burst. I looked at my girlfriends – everyone seemed lost in thought – and decided, without hesitating any further, to drop the bombshell.

"He was seeing someone," I blurted.

Nobody said a word. Frederique blinked, looking appalled.

I felt anger welling up inside. "Are you listening? Oliver was having an affair. Involved with another woman." I punched the table with my fist and made Lindsey's gin and tonic almost spill over. "He had a mistress!"

Karen looked around uncomfortably, aware of the looks from the other tables.

"Oliver?" Frederique asked, seemingly in disbelief.

I nodded and felt tears welling up.

"You've got to be kidding. What a complete asshole!" Karen bluntly exclaimed.

"Hey, you're talking about her late husband, remember?" Frederique spluttered.

I started weeping.

"So what? No point in skirting around the truth, is there?" Karen countered uncouthly, but for once I was actually happy with her frank reaction.

Lindsey swore and wrapped her arm around me. "K, you can be really inappropriate sometimes, you know?"

The tears were now rolling down my cheeks, my shoulders heaving with each sob. I felt mortified.

"Oh my goodness. Jenn, how incredibly painful for you," Frederique said gently.

I managed a slight bob of my head and whimpered.

"I'll get you some water," Karen said, sounding relieved to be able to make use of herself.

Frederique rummaged through her Louis Vuitton handbag, and after turning out a load of makeup, she handed me a paper tissue decorated with pink hearts.

Gratefully, I took it and carefully began to dab under my eyelashes. Now I remembered why I hadn't worn any mascara during the last months. I probably looked like a clown now.

"I'm so sorry for you," Frederique said, gently stroking my back. Lindsey had already been in the loop of course, but I hadn't told her yet that I'd been in contact with Sandra.

Karen popped back from the bar carrying a glass of water. "Here you go, have a few sips," she said.

I followed her instructions and then took a deep breath. "I'm alright now."

"Do you want to share with us what happened?" Frederique asked.

I straightened my back, composed myself and then poured it all out.

10

I opened the door to Coffee Cups and was welcomed by their colourful rainbow logo. I looked around the place, which was filled with only a handful of people. I cursed, I had no idea what this woman looked like.

I had the assistant block the last hour of my morning clinic so that I could meet Sandra during the day. As it was fairly quiet, I soon laid eyes on a woman who looked questioningly at me. This had to be Sandra. She was different to how I'd imagined her to be. I'd subconsciously expected a blond bombshell with long, endless legs and a tiny waist and although admittedly Sandra was pretty, she wasn't in a conventional way. She had a petite figure and frail shoulders – there was something delicate about her.

I walked up to her and introduced myself.

"Hi, I'm Sandra," she said and responded to my handshake with a touch of her fingers. "I'm sorry to meet you under these circumstances," she added solemnly. I caught an expression of guilt on her face. "I felt terrible when I heard the tragic news about Oliver."

I nodded and remained silent for a moment. "Well then, I'll just go and get something to drink," I said coolly. I wasn't planning on going easy on her. "Would you like another?" I asked, gesturing at the cup she was clutching in her hands.

She smiled uncomfortably. "No thanks. I'm good."

I walked to the counter and ordered a latte macchiato. As I was waiting, I thought about how surreal it felt to have a coffee with my late husband's mistress – could I call her that?

I returned to the table with my order and took a seat facing Sandra, who was fiddling with her hands. My eyes fell on her long, red-painted nails and I imagined how she might have scratched Oliver's back with them. The thought made me sick to my stomach.

Then she looked me straight in the eye. "Before you start, I want to offer my apologies."

I stared at her in astonishment and could feel the anger starting to prevail again. "What exactly for?" I hissed. Did she fully comprehend what she'd put me through?

She was taken aback by my response and murmured something inaudible.

I leaned back on the soft, luxurious cushions and tried to calm myself down. By nature I had a fairly mild character, but lately I was flying off the handle more often than I'd like to. I raised my hand as a conciliatory gesture and sighed. "I'm sorry. We started off on the wrong foot. I didn't mean to snap at you like that. I just find this all very upsetting."

She shook her head. "It's okay. I can imagine. Well, I guess."

For a short moment I realised that under different circumstances we could have become friends and I felt a shift in my attitude.

I put on a brave face and decided not to beat around the bush any longer. "I didn't ask to meet you to be mad at you. I came here for some answers. Could you tell me what your relationship with Oliver was like? How did you two meet? How long have you been together? I need to know everything," I added, ignoring the little voice in the back of my mind that said I shouldn't be tormenting myself unnecessarily.

I took a sip from my latte, which to my annoyance was lukewarm. I considered for a moment going back to complain, but I had little interest in dealing with all the fuss.

The woman opposite me seemed to ponder my questions as I feared the possibly painful details that would emerge.

"We met almost four years ago at an event," she began.

I felt the anger flashing deep inside again. "Four years ago?" I blurted. That was even before we were married. Had my husband deceived me all this time?

"Calm down," Sandra soothed. "Nothing was going on back then." She bit her lip. "My husband, Roderick, works at Mason & McGant, just like Oliver did. Roderick is one of the partners in the office and I accompanied him to a party when the office celebrated a big win. I got talking to your husband."

I looked at her for a few moments. So her husband was in high places. Becoming a partner at a large, international law firm was pretty much the holy grail for every lawyer. Oliver had probably been flirting with her at that party, while I was sleeping ignorantly in our bed at home. I swallowed a bitter taste before I spoke again. "Carry on."

"We talked for a while and then went our separate ways. He never crossed my mind again until I bumped into him in a bar some time ago." Sandra avoided my gaze. "We drank a few glasses of wine and talked for a while. One thing led to another." Before I could even comment, she jumped up. "I'm going to get another drink."

I watched her defiantly sway her hips while she walked towards the other end of the restaurant, and I imagined how Oliver's gaze must have strayed to her buttocks. Clenching my jaws, I turned my head to look outside, where a cyclist raced past a stroller. The woman pushing it shouted at him and raised her fist, but the man carried on without looking back.

Moments later Sandra returned and plopped down opposite me again, with a glass of green-coloured super juice in her hand. "Just went to the gym," she explained.

I gave an insouciant shrug.

"Where were we?" she said light-heartedly, as if we'd just been catching up on the latest showbiz gossip.

"One thing led to another," I repeated her last words and wondered what people meant when they said that. In my life nothing ever seemed to lead to something else.

She must have noticed my annoyance. "Hey, I'm sure this is all very upsetting for you. But I can't help what your husband has been up to," she said brusquely. She started getting up from her chair. "I came here on a voluntary basis, so if you're going to continue to act like this, I'm out of here."

I mustered up a half-hearted apology and stammered, "I'm sorry. This is killing me," I said softly, opening my heart to this stranger in front of me. "You can't imagine what it feels like to find out your husband was having an affair, before having passed away so suddenly. My life has been turned upside down." I felt tears form in my eyes. "I can't confront him with this. You're the only one left who knows what exactly took place."

She sat down again and patted my arm.

"Fair enough," she replied. "What is it you'd like to know? I'll try to answer your questions as best as I can." Sandra took a sip of the green stuff and looked expectantly at me.

"How long did the affair last?" I started.

"Not long. About eight weeks, at most."

Her response pleased me. Perhaps this relationship was of less importance than I'd assumed.

I hesitated. I had to ask, but was dreading the answer. "Did you ever ... in our house?"

The question hung unanswered for a brief moment. She put her glass down in front of her. "No. Absolutely not. Not at his place, nor at mine. Only in a hotel."

Although the idea of Oliver and Sandra booking a hotel – for an hour? –

filled me with horror, I was relieved to learn that our house wasn't tainted. I'd been agonising over this for days.

"What you're saying explains a lot. In the lead-up to Oliver's death, he was burning the midnight oil at least three evenings per week. Or that's what he'd led me to believe. Now I know the real reason for his absence," I said dejectedly.

Sandra looked at me in surprise. "I don't know about that. We only saw each other about three times in total in all of those weeks."

"Really?" So had Oliver actually been busy at work then, I wondered. "He was very irritable and preoccupied in the last months before his death. He'd told me that he was slogging away at a complicated case and since I found out about you I'd assumed that it was a lie, but perhaps he was telling the truth after all," I reasoned out loud.

"Possibly." Sandra was tapping her teeth with her fingernail. "I suddenly remember something," she said. "Oliver once answered a phone call while we were together and during that conversation he was talking about a case at the firm about some guy named Van Santen. He kept repeating that name."

I shrugged, wondering where this was going.

"When he hung up, I laughed and told him that my maiden name happened to be Van Santen. You should have seen his reaction," Sandra said. "The serious look on his face scared me out of my wits. He furiously asked if I'd been eavesdropping on him. He made me promise that if anyone ever asked about it, I knew nothing."

I shook my head. It was completely out of character for Oliver to react so aggressively to something insignificant. What the heck was this violent outburst about? "Did you ever touch upon the subject again?"

Sandra rolled her eyes. "Are you kidding? I wouldn't dream of it. It clearly was a very sensitive matter."

I mulled it over for a while before I spoke again. "It might explain his behaviour in that period. Perhaps this Van Santen was a demanding business case. Although I find it strange that he didn't share it with me," I said.

Sandra was silent.

I finished my latte with a large swig. "By the way, who ended the relationship?"

"You could say Oliver did. He suddenly stopped responding to my texts. After a while I got fed up and got the message. He just wasn't that into me anymore." Shock crossed her face. "Or was that because he …?"

I sat up. "Oliver died on the seventeenth of October."

"Right." Sandra seemed to reflect on it for a moment. "That must have been around that time. I saw that my messages hadn't been received and had assumed that he'd taken a new number to cut me from his life. But now it actually appears …" Her voice trailed off.

I shook my head in disbelief. So if he hadn't died, then Oliver might have just continued this whole affair, I thought wryly. So why had he insisted on going on a weekend getaway with the three of us? Oliver had said he wanted to bring us closer together, but Sandra's words made me question his intentions.

My eyes fell on the golden ring on her left hand. She seemed to have picked up on it and spoke nervously. "My husband is still in the dark. I'd like to keep it that way."

I shook my head. What a horrible mess this was.

Sandra emptied her super juice in one gulp. "How did Oliver die?" she asked.

"We were on a family getaway for the weekend in Limburg. They found him close to the holiday park at the bottom of a hill. It looks like he may have stumbled or fallen while walking and tumbled all the way down the slope," I replied. I pictured him meeting his end and closed my eyes. Then I admonished myself and looked at Sandra. "He took a nasty fall and had a huge gash on the back of his head."

Sandra covered her mouth with her hand. "How awful."

I bobbed my head.

"How could he have landed so badly to the point of being killed?" she asked.

I shook my head. "I'm still waiting for the results of the forensic investigation, but in all likelihood he probably just had terrible luck."

"Was it a steep slope?"

I thought for a moment. We'd gone for a stroll with the three of us earlier that Saturday in the holiday park and had passed the scene where Oliver died later that day. "Now that you ask," I said, pressing my fingers to my lips, "actually, it doesn't make sense for him to fall down there. The slope next to the path is clearly visible and the passage is quite wide." I remembered that just after his death I'd found it odd that Oliver had taken a fall on that particular spot. He wasn't the type of person for rash behaviour and the accident had happened in broad daylight. But the feeling that something didn't quite add up had faded into the background in recent months. Now that Sandra had raised the subject, I realised again that the whole thing struck me as odd.

Sandra narrowed her eyes. "That's bizarre," she concluded.

I nodded.

We were silent for a while.

When I looked up, I noticed Sandra was sliding her arms into her jacket. "I hope I've been able to answer all of your questions," she said.

"Yes, thank you," I replied politely, but in reality our conversation had raised just as many new, unanswered ones.

She forced a smile and swung her handbag around her shoulder. "Take care."

11

I waved one last time to Tim, who was looking at me through the window. The letters "Care Bears" cheerfully decorated the façade above his head. Tim's day-care centre was located in a different neighbourhood to ours, which meant that I had to make a daily ten-minute detour by bike before continuing my journey to work. I put my foot on the pedal and cycled off to work in Amsterdam-West, which took me a good twenty minutes. While on the way home from work the streets were always crowded with people, Amsterdam was still asleep around this time of the morning. It was my favourite moment of the day as it was the only time I had to myself nowadays. No child, no work, no responsibilities.

I passed a number of canal boats and cycled all the way down the Prinsengracht. I raced over the next intersection and ignored the loud honking of the angry driver coming from the right. In Amsterdam cyclists have right of way no matter what, Lindsey always joked.

I glanced at the watch that my mother had bought me for my birthday last year. It was ten to eight, leaving me ten minutes before my first consultation as a family doctor would start. Although I always had the intention to arrive well in time, lately I was struggling to manage, which was unusual for me.

When I arrived at the practice, I parked my bike next to that of my colleague Hans, with whom I'd been working for a few years. Our family practice offered medical guidance to people with a variety of ethnical backgrounds, an aspect of my work I took much joy in. Hans had started in the practice about eight years earlier than I had and therefore had just the right experience. When we'd met we'd felt an instant connection.

The first patient was already seated in the waiting area as I entered the practice somewhat out of breath. I rushed into my consulting room, opened the connecting door between Hans's space and mine and called out "good morning." Hans sat behind his desk, his hair all tousled. I smiled and wondered if he'd even bothered to comb it this morning. 'He's a good guy, honestly, but he'd never get lucky with me', Lindsey had stated rather boldly when she'd met Hans once. I glanced at the framed picture of his wife, whom he'd met years ago at their

Church, and their two children.

I wanted to retreat again, but Hans called after me. "Today it's your turn to supervise Tom, remember?"

I closed my eyes for a moment and swore softly. I'd completely forgotten about that. "Of course I remember," I lied.

Tom was a first-year medical student who was doing his residency with us. He had his own consulting room on the other side of the waiting area and was seeing patients by himself, but with every ailment that was more complicated than a bruised toe or a wart that needed to be taken care of, he presented his diagnosis to us. I still vividly recalled how insecure I felt back then. You study hard for several years, work your socks off during two years of rotations, only to find out you still don't know anything.

While my computer was starting up, I rubbed my temples. I'd once again been struggling to fall asleep last night. The day had yet to begin and I was already feeling drained. I logged in, noted the time at the bottom of my computer screen and realised that only a few minutes remained to get a much-needed dose of caffeine.

I stuck my head around the door to Hans' room again and asked if he wanted a coffee as well.

"Thank you. Lots of milk please," he added, as if I wouldn't know after so many years. Hans looked at me thoughtfully and I wondered if I should have put on some makeup this morning. "Are you alright?"

I put on an expression of reassurance and nodded.

He swivelled his chair to face me and folded his hands in his lap. "Do you think you may have returned to work a little too early?" He was wearing the grey, woollen jumper that reminded me of a college student from the nineteen eighties. His green eyes looked at me gently through his round glasses. "After all, it's only been a month or two."

Two months and nine days, to be precise, since my life had changed forever. "As if I'd forget," I said, immediately regretting my sneer.

He generously ignored my comment. "Would it be a good idea if you were to take some more time off? It's no problem to hire a temporary employee. You see …" He faltered for a moment and an apologetic expression appeared on his face. "You look a wee bit tired."

I swallowed an unpleasant response and forced a smile. "That's a very kind gesture. But I'm fine. Honestly. It's actually quite nice to get some distraction at work," I added, which was only partly true. It was hard to admit that I was desperately trying to salvage my life and sanity.

"Two cups of coffee coming right up," I said breezily and swiftly left Hans' consultation room to avoid any more complicated questions. When I returned a little later, to my relief a female patient was sitting across from Hans. I set the mug on his desk, closed the door between our rooms and took a sip from my own coffee, after which I walked to the waiting area.

"Mr Visser. You're next."

A man of about seventy years old staggered towards me.

We shook hands. "Have a seat."

He lowered himself slowly onto the chair opposite me.

I put on a friendly expression. "How may I help you?"

"Doctor, it's the valve again."

I looked at him questioningly. "The valve?"

He pointed his finger to his chest. "Drives me nuts. My heart valve. I think the leak has worsened again." The old man's local accent led me to presume he'd lived in this neighbourhood all his life.

I opened his digital patient file and noticed that he indeed was suffering from tricuspid insufficiency for years.

"I used to be quite sprightly for me age, you know – was fit as a fiddle. But now ...I'm worn out all the time, can't even walk to the bingo room in one go. I need to stop at least twice on the way – I practically look like an old man."

I smiled.

"My ankles are all swollen up," he went on, looking at me with a glint in his eye. "How am I supposed to chase the ladies?"

I took my stethoscope from my pocket. "May I have a listen?"

The old man slowly unbuttoned his tiger print shirt and I slid the diaphragm of my instrument under his vest. I confirmed the heart murmur that was so typical of this disease. Then I took his blood pressure and saw that it was elevated.

"Right. You may button up again."

While he was getting dressed, I went through his patient file and noticed that he was taking medication for high blood pressure.

"Well, Mr Visser," I said, turning my attention back to my patient. "You're suffering from what we call a tricuspid insufficiency."

He looked at me in confusion.

"Also called a leaking valve, on the right side of the heart," I explained. "It shouldn't cause any serious problems, however it's important that we keep it under control. Your blood pressure has risen again. Are you taking your medication every day?"

He paused for a moment before answering. "Sometimes I forget about the pill."

The ringtone of my mobile phone suddenly sounded and I scolded myself for forgetting to turn the sound off. I noticed 'anonymous' on the display.

I turned away, raised a finger at Mr Visser and gestured: this will only take a moment.

"Jennifer Smits speaking."

"Good morning Mrs Smits, this is Detective Armstrong. My apologies for calling you at this time. I hope I didn't wake you up."

I thought of my morning routine of showering, waking Tim, changing his nappy and getting him dressed, trying to get him to eat his sandwich, Tim throwing up and me changing his jumper, luring him into his seat on my bike with sweets, three goodbye kisses at his day-care and cycling for half an hour.

"Not a problem at all."

"Good. I just wanted to update you on the investigation into the death of your spouse."

A knot formed in my stomach. I glanced at my patient, who was sat less than a metre from me. "Can I call you back later? I'm at work."

"Certainly."

After writing down the detective's number, I hung up and wondered if the coroner might have found something – something abnormal that shouldn't have been there.

"Hello?" I heard from afar. Mr Visser waved his hand in front of my face. "Doctor Smits, are you all right?"

I apologised and then gave my patient a friendly yet firm lecture on taking his medication, to which he promised to try harder.

In the following hour I saw a mother with a son who had burnt himself with an iron, sent a patient with a prolonged cough to the pulmonologist and prescribed antibiotics to a student with a throat infection.

Around half past nine, to my relief, I had a ten-minute gap in my programme during which I quickly got another cup of coffee.

Once back in my room, I sat down on my chair, took my mobile phone out of my pocket and dialled the number.

"Armstrong," he barked.

"Good morning detective. This is Jennifer Smits speaking. You called me earlier this morning. You wanted to have a word with me about the investigation into my husband's death, Oliver?" At first impulse I'd felt surprised that the police considered his death suspicious. However, I knew professionally that they were obliged to perform an investigation and after giving it more thought I was happy that they wanted to rule out any foul play.

He paused for a moment. "Yes, yes," he stammered, in a friendlier tone.

I heard the rustling of paper in the background as I took a sip of my coffee.

"We've received all the test results. I'm happy to inform you we've discovered nothing abnormal. The toxicology tests didn't reveal the presence of any drugs or medication. The autopsy on your husband's body was also entirely in line with our expectations." The detective coughed and then carried on summarising his findings. "No traces of violence were found. Neither on the body, nor at the location where your husband was discovered. Finally, no foreign forensic material was detected."

I hooked my feet around the chair legs and leaned backwards, mumbling a few words of relief.

"Your husband had a large wound on the back of his head that matched the rock he landed on. In all likelihood, he became unconscious almost instantly after his fall and died as a result of severe blood loss from his head injury. I feel therefore confident to conclude that your husband's cause of death was related to an unfortunate chain of events after an accidental fall. He just had terrible luck, to summarise it bluntly."

His words echoed through my mind. Unfortunate chain of events... Terrible luck...

How was it possible that he'd plummeted down the slope with such force that his injuries were fatal, I wondered. It was hardly the edge of a cliff or a steep mountainside. Perhaps he'd been all worked up by our argument to the point of becoming reckless.

"Mrs Smits, are you still there?"

I snapped to attention. "Yes, I am," I quickly said.

"Is everything clear?"

I closed my eyes and rubbed my face. "I guess so," I responded, although I wasn't sure whether to be relieved with this conclusion or not. Oliver's death just seemed even more senseless.

"So what happens now? Is this it?"

"Yes. We'll finalise our report, for which we won't need your help. You can come over to our office and collect your husband's personal belongings. I'll leave them for you at the reception. If anything else comes up, we'll contact you. Although that seems unlikely."

"Thank you so much for your explanation and efforts."

"At your service. I wish you all the best."

I was ready to hang up when Detective Armstrong interjected, "Oh yes, one more thing." After a short pause he continued, broaching an odd topic. "Well, it may be a bit of an impertinent question I suppose ... but were you by any chance aware of your husband preferring certain types of underwear?"

I wondered if I'd misheard. "Certain types of underwear?"

"Did he have a rather distinct, unusual taste in this area?" His voice sounded as if he felt as uncomfortable as I was with this conversation.

"Not a chance," I assured him.

"He didn't have, er … dare I say a fetish, as they call it nowadays?"

What was this man talking about? "He always wore normal boxer shorts. You know, typical men's underwear. Why are you asking?"

"Right," he mumbled and then paused for a brief moment. "That's peculiar. Your husband was wearing red, lace knickers when he died. They appeared to be ladies underwear."

I felt utterly gobsmacked. A long awkward silence filled the air as I took it all in. "This doesn't make any sense. He never wore anything like that." What was that man thinking? Was he taking the mickey out of me? Surely, he wasn't inferring that my husband wore my underwear, or worse, that he'd get turned on by it?

"I see. Perhaps your husband may have liked to wear your knickers. Or he may have bought a pair for himself to give it a try. Trust me, this seems quite normal compared to the situations I've encountered. You wouldn't believe the things I come across. Just when I think I've seen it all, a unique situation will present itself that knocks my socks off. There are a lot of weird people out there. Sometimes I wonder if I should quit and be done with the absurdity, or rejoice in the quirkiness of my job."

I felt lost for words. "But how …" I stammered.

"Very well. Not to worry. Mrs Smits, you take care now. I wish you and your son all the best. Goodbye."

Before I could even respond, he'd hung up.

My eyes strayed to the pile of post that lay on my desk that I just didn't manage to get around to sorting through. What in heaven's name was that all about? Why hadn't this detective brought this up sooner? Why would Oliver dress in women's underwear? I'd never seen him do such a thing before. I tried to remember when I'd last witnessed Oliver change, and came to the discomforting conclusion that it had been several weeks before his death. On weekdays in the morning I was already downstairs before he got up and in the evening I was usually asleep when he came to bed.

The phone on my desk rang, pulling me out of my thoughts. The number showed that it was our new assistant calling me on the internal line.

"Simone," I said.

"Yes. Right. This is Simone," she responded nervously. "Are you keeping an eye on the time? Mrs van Brock has already come to my desk three times asking when it's her turn."

I glanced at my watch and saw to my horror that I was running late again.

"I'll be right there." I hung up without waiting for a reply.

I wasn't even half way through the morning yet and I already felt utterly exhausted. Last night had been the third night in a row that I'd watched the hours go by on the alarm clock. Perhaps I should prescribe myself some medication to get more sleep. I couldn't keep this up much longer.

I swilled down the rest of my coffee and called Mrs van Brock from the waiting room. She dallied after me at a snail's pace.

After she'd taken off her coat with a lot of moans and groans, she flopped onto the chair in front of me.

"My oh my," she panted. "Would you believe that? Oh dear. I'm completely worn out. Isn't that something, eh? Exhausted by walking the short distance from the waiting room to here."

I folded my arms and smiled amiably. "Mrs van Brock, what can I do for you today?"

"I need a minute to recover." She took a paper tissue from her black lacquer handbag and wiped her damp forehead. Her full bosom rose and fell with her rapid respiration. She sighed once more and then commenced talking. "I'm alright now, thanks," she stated, although I'd refrained from asking. "You know what. Ever since my husband died, my condition has deteriorated so terribly. Isn't that odd? I used to be able to walk long distances. I'd stride to the grocery store and back without any problems." She looked at me with a face that was probably meant to impress me. "That's quite a distance, you know. I wonder how far that would be?" The old lady looked at the ceiling as if she'd find the answer up there. "It's two right turns, a long stretch straight ahead and a left turn and then you're nearly there. Must be more than a kilometre in total. Yes. That's probably it, one kilometre. I'm sure now, because it's almost a fifteen-minute walk, so that has to be about right. And then back home again, so all in all that's half an hour." She put on an expression as if she'd just solved a complicated algorithm.

I wiggled impatiently in my chair and cast a meaningful glance at my watch: I didn't have time for this jibber-jabber. But she completely missed the hint and reeled off a hundred woes.

"These days, a short stroll has gotten too much. I can no longer manage to go shopping by myself. It feels terrible you know." She looked at me again to make sure I was staying focused. "The realisation that you are unable to take care of yourself. Argh. How I dislike the feeling of dependence. I have a new cleaning lady who also does my shopping for me. But I don't trust her one bit." She leaned forward as if she were sharing a confidential piece of information. "I have a sneaking suspicion that she once pinched a tenner." She leaned back, raised her eyebrows and crossed her arms. "No way that lady is gonna lay her hands on my purse anymore. I'll just give her the cash she needs to pay for the groceries so that I'm sure she won't be snatching anything. Those foreigners, can't trust 'em."

I cringed. I knew it was an important part of my profession to offer a sympathetic ear to people, but I couldn't handle this nonsense. There were far worse things in the world. My gaze wandered outside, where dark clouds had gathered. Rain had been forecast for this afternoon and I was afraid I'd get soaked on my way home.

I looked at my patient again and cut to the chase. "Mrs van Brock. Please tell me why you came to see me. What's the matter?"

She looked at me, obviously offended. "In a hurry, are we? Calm down, doctor. I was just about to get to it." She shifted her weight. "So I was saying that ever since my husband died, walking has become increasingly difficult. It seems like …"

My thoughts wandered to the red lace knickers. I was sure they weren't mine, I didn't even like brightly coloured underwear. I had a hard time recollecting all the details Detective Armstrong had shared with me over the phone, as it all had gone so fast. I remembered him stating that nothing unusual had been encountered and no forensic traces were identified. Did this imply that they hadn't found any foreign fingerprints or objects there?

"… the left seems normal. But the right leg is leading a life of its …"

I had no alternative but to accept it. It was as if my world had come to a grinding halt while I'd been waiting for the results of the investigation into Oliver's death, as if none of this was real, and Oliver would one day walk back through our front door. But the detective had left no ambivalence in his statement – the case had been closed. Oliver would never return to this earth. And so I needed to focus all of my efforts on the future. I had little choice but to go on with my life.

"Hello, doctor. I asked you a question. Are you even listening?"

Mrs van Brock was staring at me with an expression of disparagement on her face.

I shook my head. "My apologies. Could you repeat the question?"

She sighed. "I asked: do you think my leg can get better? There shouldn't be such a difference between left and right, should there?"

Mrs van Brock was a classic case – after the death of a spouse you would see patients slowly go downhill. I saw them in my practice almost daily. "It's imperative that you carry on exercising every day, Mrs van Brock, to strengthen your muscles. You should get out for a stroll as much as possible. Try to go and do your groceries yourself again."

"That's the problem, you see. I really can't do it anymore. It's just too far," she countered.

"First start with a small stretch, then continue to work on increasing the distance you walk. Just a little further each day, until you make it all the way to and from the store."

"But it's only the right leg that's not working prop ..."

My telephone rang and interrupted Mrs van Brock.

"Hi, it's Tom," I heard. "Can I consult with you for a moment?" he asked in his New Zealand accent.

I rubbed my forehead and closed my eyes. "Go ahead."

"I have a patient with me who I believe is suffering from an appendicitis. He's showing all the classic symptoms. Can you come by to confirm my diagnosis?"

"Have you already performed the abdominal test?"

"What do you mean?"

I started to lose my temper. Was he not supposed to know this by now? "Press the belly and release abruptly," I blurted.

"I forgot about that," he faltered.

"First think for yourself Tom. Then call me," I retorted.

"Yes, right. How silly of me. Really sorry," he added quickly.

I sighed deeply. "Perform the test and if the result is positive, send your patient in for blood works, okay?"

"Will do, doc. Thanks a million."

I hung up and flung the phone back onto the desk a little more harshly than I should have. Mrs van Brock looked at me with her lips pressed tightly.

I narrowed my eyes. My head seemed to be a jumble of thoughts. "Sorry. Where were we again?"

She opened her mouth to start talking but I beat her to it. "Ah yes, I remember. It's important you stay active. Go out for a saunter every day, do some chores around the house. Alright, Mrs van Brock?" I asked, relieved that I hadn't forgotten the name of my patient.

"Doctor, you don't understand. That's not the point, I ..."

Out of the blue something snapped inside my head. My temples started to thump and there was an almost deafening ringing in my ears. I raised my voice. "There's not much more to it. Try to adopt a positive attitude and associate more with happy people. You'll notice life will start working for you, rather than against." I couldn't restrain myself anymore. It was as if a monster had been unleashed – I went on a verbal rampage. "You ought to stop yourself from complaining so much. Believe me, you could be far worse off."

Mrs van Brock turned as red as a tomato. She was continuously blinking, her eyes bulging, and looked distraught behind her glasses. She dabbed her forehead again with the paper tissue, which she squeezed tightly in her hand.

I finally came to my senses. What was I doing? I'd gone berserk. This was unheard of – I couldn't verbally abuse a patient like that. This had never happened to me before.

Suddenly I felt a heavy weariness settle over me. I rested my head in my hands for a moment. Subsequently I looked into my patient's eyes before backpedalling. "I'm truly sorry. I shouldn't have lost my composure like that," I said, shame burning on my cheeks.

The shocked lady rearranged her white blouse, under which the strap of her skin-coloured bra was visible. "No doctor has ever spoken to me like that," she said with an air of contempt. "When doctor Baker was still working back in the old days, things were much better around here." It was a reproach that had been hurled at me on more than one occasion during the first months after my instalment. It had initially led to a feeling of insecurity, but I'd become knowledgeable over the years and learned not to feel offended by it. I'd usually reply by saying: 'they don't make 'em like that anymore, do they?' This time, however, I knew my patient had a point.

I bit my lip. "My sincere apologies. It's not an excuse, but I've had a very difficult time lately."

She had a look in her eyes I couldn't quite read. "I'm sure you have." Mrs van Brock slowly rose and grabbed her handbag. "I'll be leaving now."

"No need to worry. If you keep exercising regularly, you'll see that progress will be made," I attempted to placate. "Don't hesitate to make an appointment again via our assistant if you have any other concerns."

I gave her a clammy hand and, after she'd left the room, lowered myself in my chair.

I interlaced my fingers and folded them around my neck. I couldn't believe how I'd ranted at that patient. I felt ashamed to the core. Sure, she was an old grump, but this was completely out of line. I could only cross my fingers and hope she wouldn't file a complaint against me.

It was obvious I'd totally lost a grip. No matter how difficult life was for me now, this was unacceptable.

I leaned forward and rested my forehead in my palms. And then I suddenly recalled something. She'd tried to convey the message, but I hadn't been listening properly. Only the right leg had the problem, the left was functioning normally. It wasn't until now that it hit me. This wasn't a normal age-related complaint – my patient might have had a stroke, which prevented her right leg from functioning properly.

I jumped up, swung the door open and searched the waiting room where a number of patients stared back at me expectantly. It was evident that my patient was no longer here and so I scurried outside. My eyes scanned the main street in opposite directions, where a hodgepodge of trams and cyclists impeded my search. Mrs van Brock was nowhere to be seen. I swore again.

I stood fretting on the pavement while I bit my nails, trying to figure out how to proceed. Should I hazard a guess that she'd turned right towards the tram stop and head off in that direction to find her? I couldn't afford to run late any more. The alternative of asking our assistant to find her meant I would have to confess to what had happened. Either option didn't seem particularly appealing.

Suddenly I felt a hand on my shoulder. "Are you all right?" I heard a voice from behind me.

The cool air only now seemed to penetrate my thin blouse. I looked like a complete idiot standing on the streets without wearing a jacket.

I swivelled and saw Simone look me up and down, buried deep in her woollen coat.

My thoughts were running wild. I bobbed my head absently and turned my back to her again. Why did she follow me out here? "Just leave me be, okay?"

"Clearly not in the best of tempers, are we?" she chirped, which pissed me off.

A scooter roared passed us, causing a swirl of air. The vibrations were spinning around in my eardrums and hurting my brain.

"There are three patients waiting for you inside," she continued with a nagging voice.

I felt my exasperation rise to boiling point. "I told you, just leave me alone for a moment. I'll be right there."

"No need to bite my head off. I'm just trying to help, you know." I heard her heels click on the pavement as she walked away from me.

I wrapped my arms around my body, trying to keep out the cold, or maybe it was to keep myself together. I couldn't handle this any longer. I felt like a loose cannon. Hans was probably right when he suggested I'd gone back to work too early. I was jumping out of my skin at the smallest of things.

I made a conscious decision and went back inside.

Ignoring the inquisitive looks in the waiting room, I entered my consulting room. I knocked on the connecting door to Hans's room and asked if I could have a word with him.

He said something to his patient after which he entered my room. As soon as he'd closed the door, I burst into tears.

"I can't do this any longer, I'm falling apart," I cried. I confided in him about what had just happened with Mrs van Brock. "Ever since Oliver died, I've had trouble keeping my head clear. I miss him so terribly," I said and started to weep, my shoulders heaving as each sob welled up.

Hans silently handed me a tissue.

I blew my nose and shook my head. "I'm sorry for being so unprofessional."

He dismissed my objection with a wave of his hand. "Nonsense. If anyone around here's unprofessional, it's me," he said, looking with self-mockery at his alternative clothing style.

I smiled through my tears and blew my nose again.

"You're going through a hard time, to put it mildly. Anyone would be struggling after all that happened. You've lost your husband, your best friend," he said tenderly.

I nodded and felt tears welling up again.

"Cut yourself some slack. These things take time. You can't just continue with your life and pretend that everything's still fine. Your body and mind have taken a blow," he said in a touchy-feely manner. "It's time to pause for reflection."

"That might be a bit overly dramatic," I responded. But I knew deep down he was right.

He ignored my comment. "Give yourself the grace to grieve over your loss. If you ask me, it would be wise to call in sick for the time being."

His message came as a shock, even though this suggestion had already crossed my mind. My work was my life, my buoy to which I held on for dear life. It was terrifying to let go of this crucial pillar. But I pulled myself together and decided to follow his suggestion. "I think you're right. What about Mrs van Brock?"

"Don't worry. I'll contact her and make amends." He smiled paternally and I could see how he'd handle his patients. "How about you stay home for the rest of the week? And next week," he added cautiously. "You know the saying," he said and put on a Texas drawl, "if Mama ain't happy, ain't nobody happy."

I laughed. "What about all of my patients?"

"I'll ask Simone to hand the urgent cases over to me. The less serious can wait for now. By the way, we can also give Tom some small chores." He gave me a wink. "Let's make the most of him."

I smiled and on the spur of the moment gave Hans a hug, something we never normally did, despite our good relationship. "Thanks Hans. You're the best colleague I could wish for."

He seemed to blush for a moment. "It's nothing. Just make sure you take a break and replenish your energy."

Not too long after our heart-to-heart I left the practice. It felt odd not to know how I'd spend the rest of my day, or rather the next two weeks. I decided to first cycle past the police station and pick up Oliver's belongings. When I arrived there after a short ride, I took the package from the receptionist and decided – with a rush of shame – to leave Tim at the day-care centre and go home by myself. If I wanted to address this period of reflection properly, I needed to take time for myself.

As I cycled into my street, I noticed a fire engine parked in front of one of the houses. An elderly lady was being strapped down onto a stretcher and was going to be lifted down to the street via a window on the second floor. When I'd first moved to Amsterdam, I'd been standing on the pavement watching a similar case, captivated by the process, as were a handful of passers-by. A mixture of medical fascination and shame had run through me while the geriatric person, unable to be carried down the narrow staircase of the ancient house, was evacuated.

As I clutched the package containing Oliver's items under my arm, I opened the front door to our – or rather, my – home. The authentic, brightly coloured tiles, which were now nearly a hundred years old, adorned the entrance. The door jammed, as it often did, but after a few thrusts with my shoulder I managed to open it.

A familiar figure suddenly appeared in front of me in the living room, with her back towards me. I was taken aback to find her working today, as I'd usually see patients at this hour.

"Alejandra," I said.

She uttered a shriek. "Holy crap," she cursed, then covered her mouth with her hand in disgrace. She'd been living here for years, but had never lost her strong Spanish accent.

I started laughing.

"Excuse me, Mrs Smits," she said formally, even though I'd told her countless times to call me Jennifer.

"It's okay," I said and gave her a smile to put her at ease. "I should be apologising for startling you like this."

She took a deep breath, then turned around and picked up her cleaning activities, motes of sun-dappled dust swirling around.

"How are you doing, Alejandra?" I asked kindly.

She paused in the act of dusting, turned around and looked at me. "I'm fine, thank you. How's Timmy?"

Even before I was able to answer her question, she put her hands on her hips and puffed out her chest. "He big boy now, huh?"

I gave a chuckle and confirmed that he'd grown.

While Alejandra took off to start cleaning upstairs, I decided to make myself a cup of tea and settled in the living room on our outrageously expensive couch, a gift from my in-laws. I opened the package that I'd picked up at the police station. Oliver's clothes were neatly sealed in plastic, as if they'd come from the dry cleaner. When I tore the wrapper however, Oliver's familiar smell was released, bringing back tender memories and filling my eyes with tears.

I hadn't had much time to myself since Oliver's passing, but now I was able to let go of my brave front. The vacuum cleaner bellowed down the landing and I allowed myself to release some of my sorrow.

After a few minutes I decided that enough was enough. I picked up a tissue from a box on the coffee table, blew my nose and dabbed my eyes. I took a sip of my tea and looked at Oliver's items one by one. The package mainly contained his clothes – his non-iron Eton shirt, brown chinos, black loafers and finally the *pièce-de-résistance*: the red knickers.

I carefully held them up at the edges, turned them around and looked at the cheap, velvet fabric. How utterly hideous. These certainly didn't belong to me. Despite my monumental collection of underwear, I was certain I'd have recognised them if they were mine.

Why would Oliver have worn something like that? I tried to remember if I'd ever noticed any strange sexual escapades or interests, but nothing came to mind. I could hardly imagine him purchasing this kind of underwear on his own accord. Hence I wondered, could the knickers have belonged to someone else?

I decided to divert my mind and took one of my Vogue magazines out of the reading basket. Lately, I'd barely been able to find time for myself. I flipped through the fashion items without reading a word. Outside, the voices of passers-by were dulled by the double-glazed windows to a buzzing murmur. The clock on the fireplace ticked regularly and above me I heard Alejandra moving back and forth. My head felt a messy mixture of dull over-tiredness and racing thoughts.

I threw the magazine back on the stack and tried to get the confusing story about the red knickers out of my head. There would never be answers to the questions and ambiguities surrounding Oliver's death. I decided to pick up Tim early. He'd be delighted if I told him we were heading to the playground.

An hour later I found myself at Tim's favourite place, just around the corner from our house, in the Vondelpark. The clouds had lifted somewhat and made way for dappled sunshine under a canopy of autumnal trees. Despite the fact that it was lunchtime on a regular Tuesday morning, the sandpit was full of people ranging from tourists to locals.

My telephone rang. 'Lindsey', I saw on the display of my mobile. I answered, but kept my eyes on Tim, who was frolicking in the sand with a German-speaking girl.

"How are you?" Lindsey asked.

"Fine," I replied. "How about you?"

"That doesn't sound too good," she reacted, knowing me better than anyone. "What's the matter? I'm all ears."

"Had a really bad day at work."

"Poor you," she responded sympathetically. "We all have those days. I'm sure, tomorrow will be better again."

I paused. Fragments of the conversation with Hans resurfaced. "I decided to call in sick for a while."

It remained silent for a moment on the other side. "Call in sick? Are you feeling under the weather?"

I explained what had happened this morning, including the degrading lash outs to various people and the red knickers, which Detective Armstrong had briefed me about.

She laughed out loud. "What a bizarre story. Do you have any idea what it's all about? I mean ..." Lindsey swallowed audibly. "Would Oliver really have donned such a thing?" she asked in all seriousness.

My attention turned back to Tim and the playground. All of a sudden he seemed to have disappeared. I anxiously scanned the children's heads scattered throughout the playground, until I spotted him on the swing with a girl, to my great relief. "I highly doubt it," I went on. "And I know for sure they weren't mine."

"Could the knickers perhaps have belonged to ..." Lindsey wavered for a moment. "... belonged to that woman?"

I'd told Lindsey about the encounter I recently had with Sandra, she however didn't approve of it and I'd therefore kept the details to myself. "To be honest, the thought had crossed my mind. But she told me they'd only seen each other about three times in total. It doesn't make sense that Oliver would have her underwear."

"Given her history, I'd take everything that woman says with a pinch of salt,"

Lindsey commented.

I'd taken a seat on a steel railing, but now the cold crept through my cloths and made me shiver. "You've got a point."

Tim pulled the girl he'd been playing with out of the playground by her ponytail, whereupon she roared. I rushed over to him. "Tim, stop that immediately!" I cried and jerked him by the arm. My reaction was too harsh, and I instantly regretted it. I saw the child's mother shoot a disapproving look at me. Easy enough to make judgments, I thought, she probably doesn't have sole responsibility for her child from early in the morning until late at night, without a man who can support her.

I mumbled an apology to Tim and directed him to a climbing frame.

Then I turned my attention to Lindsey again. "Maybe I should talk to her again. Confront her with it."

"Are you sure that's a good idea?"

I was on guard. "What do you mean?"

"I'm not sure about the whole thing. I mean, Oliver's gone. And he was wearing red knickers you've never seen before and they probably belonged to her."

"I don't understand what you're implying."

"There are a lot of crazy people out there. Just don't do anything reckless, you barely know the woman."

I reassured Lindsey, and then we hung up.

Tim and I entered the little cafe adjoining the playground where I treated him to a glass of lemonade and ordered myself a cup of tea.

I spotted an empty seat in a quiet corner of the quaint building, where I hoped no one could overhear me. I'd stored her number in my mobile and pressed the green button.

"Hello, it's Sandra," she said in a reserved manner.

"Hi, this is Jennifer."

As she hushed for a moment, I heard snippets of conversation in the background. I got to the point straight away. "I was wondering if we can meet again?"

She sighed audibly. "What's left to talk about? We've been over everything there is to discuss, haven't we?"

"There's one other pressing question I need to ask you."

"Why don't you ask me now, over the phone? I have a busy schedule," she declared, although I wasn't too sure about that.

I was reluctant to show my cards just yet as I wanted to see her face when I confronted her with the red knickers. "It doesn't have to take long," I insisted.

She caved in. "Alright. I have a spot this afternoon."

I was surprised to hear she was yet again available during the day, although it suited my current schedule.

"How about four o'clock? Same location?" she suggested.

"Fine. And thanks," I replied after which we disconnected.

A few hours later I'd left Tim with our neighbour upstairs so that I could meet Sandra alone. As I entered Coffee Cups I noticed that Sandra hadn't arrived yet. I'd have killed for a glass of wine, but I restrained myself – I didn't want to pick up Tim in an intoxicated state. I ventured a guess and ordered two lattes. Then I took a seat on a leather couch. The red knickers were kept tightly in my pocket, like a mistress hidden under a blanket.

Sandra entered the cafe, said hello and sat down in front of me. She'd just been to the gym judging by her outfit and the purple sports headband on her forehead. I questioningly shoved the latte in her direction, to which she nodded.

She gave a meaningful look at her watch. "I don't have much time. I'm having friends over for dinner tonight and I still need to shower and change," she declared and gestured to her clothes.

I got the message and wanted to get this over with quickly. But suddenly I sensed a tightness in my shoulders and the sweat in my palms. How should I approach this?

"The police returned Oliver's clothes, the ones he wore on the day he died."

A compassionate expression passed over her face. "That must have been hard." She looked at me calmly, probably wondering where this was going.

I yanked the knickers out of my pocket and threw them onto the table.

A look of shock crossed her face. "What are these?"

I snickered. "Look familiar, huh?"

Her jaw dropped. "They're mine! I was wondering where they'd gone." She snatched the knickers off the table, looked around in humiliation and clutched them in her fist. Her mouth repetitively opened and closed like a fish gasping for air. When she did finally speak, she practically spat the words out. "Where the hell did you find these?"

I wasn't impressed by her anger – I leaned back, folded my arms and raised my eyebrows. "Oliver was wearing them. On the day he died."

Her mouth remained open. "What?" she blurted. "Oliver wore them? How on earth is that possible?"

"I was hoping you'd be able to provide an explanation."

She shook her head in astonishment. "I have no idea. Honestly."

I stared intently at her before speaking again. "I got a call from the police saying Oliver died as a result of a fatal accident. He presumably lost his balance, fell down and his head hit a rock. When they undressed him, he was, as it turns out, wearing your underwear."

Confusion now seemed to have the upper hand. Or was she faking all of it?

Her left eyelid fluttered. "What are you saying?"

I leaned forward and set my palms down flat on the table. "You know exactly what I'm saying. Are you somehow involved in this? Were you with my husband when he died?"

"Of course not." She began to blink nervously. "Honestly, I wasn't. We've only seen each other three times. I told you that last time, remember?"

I started to lose my temper. Surely, she didn't think she could play me for a fool? "I'm not an idiot. I know what you told me," I said explicitly. "But how do I know you're being truthful at all? For all I know you might be spinning tales."

"I'm not messing with you. You have to believe me. I was totally unaware of the fact that your husband was away for a weekend, let alone know the whereabouts of the holiday park."

I needed a moment to process the information. "So how did he end up wearing your underwear?"

"I haven't the faintest clue." She paused and seemed to be musing on it. "He might've taken them with him after one of our encounters?"

"Huh," I snorted. "Why would he do that? As some kind of trophy?"

She shook her head. "No idea."

I didn't believe it for a second. "Surely you would have noticed if you'd suddenly lost your knickers?"

"I'd sometimes bring a clean set of underwear. For when we finished …" She turned red as she was searching for the right words. "For when I went home again."

I felt like throwing up.

She quickly continued speaking. "He may have snatched them from my bag. In any case, I've got nothing to do with it," she stated, with an increased amount of confidence.

She suddenly plucked the knickers with a sense of composure and determination and started to put them in her bag.

I grabbed her arm. "Give them back."

"What do you want them for? They're mine."

I squeezed harder. "Let go." I couldn't quite put my finger on why, but I had to keep them. It was the only tangible clue I had. A small form of proof that something didn't add up about Oliver's death.

She was pleading with me. "Stop. You're hurting me," she whimpered.

But I refused to loosen my grip and she finally relented and let go of the velvet fabric.

I released my hand and slid the knickers back in the pocket of my jacket.

She rubbed her arm with a face of agony. "My goodness, woman. What's wrong with you?"

Somehow her words snapped me back to reality. It was as if I saw myself from a distance, as it if wasn't me who had gone off the rails, once again.

I regained my senses and blew the air out of my lungs. "I'm really sorry," I said softly. Sandra must think I was a lunatic. What had gotten into me? I had no control over myself. I no longer knew who or what I should believe and felt utterly stupefied.

I drew in a long breath and took a mouthful of my coffee, which had turned cold, and tried to regain my composure.

We sat in silence for a while.

"Do you think something happened to Oliver?" Sandra asked. She shook her head. "Er … I mean, do you think it wasn't really just an accident?"

I dug my nails into my palms, trying to hold back the tears. "I don't know what to think anymore. There just seems to be more to it than meets the eye. I keep going over it. I have no simple explanation for the fact that he wasn't wearing his own underwear. Yet at the same time it doesn't necessarily imply foul play."

I rested my face in my hands. "I feel so tired. The grief of Oliver's death hadn't even fully sunk in when I heard of your existence, and now this. I can't seem to get my thoughts in order."

"I see," she said, empathically.

It was painful to have to acknowledge it, but perhaps she'd known other sides of Oliver's life than I had. "Do you know if something unusual had been going on before he died?"

Sandra strummed with painted nails on her lips. "The only thing that comes to mind is that odd phone call about that client Van Santen that I told you about last time. It was clearly a case that demanded a lot from him."

I too had seen in the months leading up to his death that Oliver's work at the firm had occupied him, but I hardly knew the details of what he'd been up to. "Can you recall anything else about that phone call?" I asked.

She swivelled the cup, which was empty by now, in her hands while thinking. "No, sorry. Nothing specific comes to mind."

"Your husband was one of the partners at Mason & McGant, right?"

Sandra nodded.

I hesitated for a moment before I asked. "Does your husband still not know about er … Oliver and you?"

She shook her head.

"Could you perhaps ask him about that case?" Oliver's fierce reaction, when Sandra had started talking about Van Santen, made me feel uneasy. I couldn't fully explain why, but I felt a strong desire to find out more about the last client for which he'd worked. "As the head of the office, your husband is surely in the loop on all cases."

Sandra didn't seem to care much for my suggestion. "I'm not too sure whether that's a good idea. My husband and I try to keep work and personal life separate."

"Come on," I beseeched. "It's not that much trouble, is it?"

She sighed and seemed to mull it over. "Fine. I'll ask him about it."

I gave her a nod. "Thank you. I'm sure it's nothing," I said trivialising, but in reality I doubted that.

I glanced at my watch and stood up. "I have to go and pick up my son."

Sandra slid her arms into her jacket. "I'll call you when I know more."

As I walked out, something came to my mind. Sandra had promised to quiz her husband, but there could be an alternative way to gather information.

I pulled my phone out of my pocket and looked up Oliver's former employer's number.

The receptionist answered my call, "Mason & McGant, how may I help you?"

"This is Jennifer Smits. Can you put me through to Benedict van Suyten from the mergers and acquisitions department?" Benedict had started working as a paralegal at Mason & McGant in the same year as Oliver and the two had become close colleagues.

"One moment please."

While the other end of the line fell silent, I put on my headphones, got on the bike and left in the direction of Tim's day-care.

"Benedict van Suyten," I heard, moments later.

"Hi Ben, this is Jennifer, Oliver Smits' wife."

His voice sounded friendly. "Hi Jennifer, great to hear from you." We hadn't spoken to each other since Oliver's funeral. His tone softened. "How are you doing?"

"I'm alright," I replied.

"How's the little man doing?"

I smiled. "Good. Tim's growing before my eyes."

Benedict laughed. "I'm sure he is. He takes after his father. How are you holding up without Oliver?" he asked, a sound of genuine concern in his voice.

"I don't know. Fine, I guess," I answered, not quite sure what to add. I clammed up as the traffic rushed past me. "How have you been?"

"Good, good … busy. Up to my neck in cases." He guffawed. "As always, the partners at Mason & McGant keep hurling cases at us." Nothing had changed at the firm, by the sound of it.

"Ben, I'd like to ask you something. I've received two e-mails from the secretary of Oliver's department saying there's a box with his belongings. I don't know what it contains, but I intend to come over and collect it soon. While I'm there, would you like to go for a coffee together?"

Benedict and I had always had plenty to talk about whenever we saw each other at one of Mason & McGant's drinks and he reacted as expected with enthusiasm. "Sounds like a good plan. How about early next week?"

"Perfect. Would you happen to know what's in the package?" I asked tentatively. Recent developments had made me curious about its contents. I was hoping the box would provide clues on the case that Oliver had been working on.

"No idea. But you know what? As luck would have it, I'm close to the secretary right now," Benedict replied. "I'll have a look for you."

I keenly accepted his offer. There were some voices in the background as I was cycling.

He returned to the phone. "It's Ben again." I heard a crackling sound. "There are some practical items in it, such as a writing pad and a few ballpoints, and a picture of the three of you. That's about it."

"I see," I said with a feeling of disappointment.

I knew Benedict was busy and didn't want to fritter away his time, but I had to bring it up. "Ben, I wanted to ask you one last thing. Oliver seemed to be swamped at the office in the last few months before his death. Do you know what he was working on?" Benedict was positioned in a different department to Oliver, but they'd regularly have lunch together, so perhaps he was up to date on what had been going on.

There was something distant in his voice. "Not really."

I contemplated how I could clarify myself. "I recently got the impression that there may have been something out of the ordinary going on at the firm."

"Might be. You know how things are around here. Never a dull moment," Benedict quipped and laughed, but there was something disingenuous and evasive about his manner.

He didn't seem to understand what I was getting at. "Would you have any idea what case he was assigned to? Could it be that he defended a master criminal, a client who was seeking to exploit the loopholes of the law?" I asked without holding back.

There was a short pause. When Benedict spoke again, kindness had disappeared from his voice. "What exactly do you want from me, Jennifer?"

I was shocked by his reaction. "It would be good if ..." I faltered. "I'd just like to know what case Oliver was working on. He was away from home so much and seemed to be worried about something, but I have no idea what was really going on."

"What's the point? You know that as lawyers we're sometimes forced to defend mega crooks and keep secrets to ourselves. It's part of our profession."

I felt uneasy. "You're probably right. I'm just asking because finding answers would help me gain some closure."

"You're well aware that as a lawyer, Oliver often had to deal with the big boys. There's no need to know any more than that. You're better off leaving the matter to rest."

He had a point. The traffic light turned green and I cycled on.

I tried to sound jaunty in an attempt to smooth over the hostile atmosphere that had so suddenly arisen. "Never mind. So, when will coffee suit you next week?" I had all the time in the world now that I'd taken a breather from work. "I'd love to hear how you, Melanie and the kids are all doing now," I tried to ingratiate myself to him, but in reality I had a glimmer of hope that he might confide in me if we saw each other in person.

Benedict coughed. "I just realised that I am completely full next week."

"What about the following week? Any time and day is fine for me," I chirped.

He rejected my proposal. "We're going on a ski trip with the family for a week, alas. I won't be able to make it any time soon I'm afraid."

"Right," I mumbled.

"I'll make sure the box of belongings will be couriered to you, to save you a trip to the office," Benedict said.

"Oh, that won't be necessary. I will come ..."

He cut straight across me. "I insist. I have to go now. I'll call you another time, okay?"

Before I was even able to utter another word the phone was disconnected.

12

Two days later, I was waiting for my cappuccino and slice of chocolate fudge cake in a coffee shop, when my phone screen lit up.

"I spoke to my husband," Sandra whispered.

I was barely able to make out what she saying over the buzz of conversation around me and covered my other ear with my hand.

"Roderick told me Oliver was involved up to his neck in an extortion case," Sandra continued. "Oliver represented some guy named Mark Van Santen, a well-known figure in the property business. You know, one of those guys operating on the edge of what is and isn't allowed. Notoriously difficult to get folks like that behind bars. They apparently have henchmen everywhere to protect them."

I sat on the edge of my seat. "Go on."

"He was already one …"

I interrupted her. "Can you speak up? I can barely hear you."

"Hold on," she whispered. I heard footsteps and a door close. Moments later she spoke, sounding jittery. "I'm in my bedroom."

I noticed that Sandra was home yet again on a weekday. She seemed to be the kind of woman who didn't have a paid job, but presided over all sorts of volunteer organisations and committees.

"I haven't much time," she rushed. "My husband is working from home today and I don't want him to eavesdrop on our conversation. I could tell his suspicion was raised when I was asking about the case and he was quite reluctant to share any information."

My order was delivered on a tray and I acknowledged the waitress with a nod. "So what explanation did you provide for asking him all these questions?"

"I spun a tale of how we happened to meet in the park and started talking. I kept rambling pathetically about how you'd love to know what Oliver had been up to in the last few months and what his life at work looked like just before his death. I sold him a line that it would give you peace, or whatever."

"What else did your husband let slip?"

"Oliver had been preparing the case for several months. The hearing was due to take place a week after his death," she reeled off.

I thoughtlessly stuck my fork into my pastry, but my appetite had disappeared. "Do you think Oliver was caught up in something shady? Do you reckon this Mark Van Santen had something to do with his death?"

"No idea, but we shouldn't rule anything out."

I was cautious of confiding in Sandra about the conversation I'd had with Benedict. After all, I hardly knew anything about this woman that Oliver had been attracted to. On the other hand, she'd stuck her neck out by quizzing her husband, so I decided to give her the benefit of the doubt. "I reached out to one of Oliver's former colleagues. They were pretty tight knit so if anyone at Mason & McGant were to know if something was wrong with Oliver, it would be him."

"Interesting. What did he have to say?"

I brought Sandra up to speed on the phone call during which Ben had initially responded heartily to my proposal for a cup of coffee, until I started talking about the case that Oliver had been slogging away at before his death.

"So his attitude only changed after you'd touched upon the subject?"

"That's right. He's usually as friendly as a puppy, but suddenly his schedule was fully booked." I also told Sandra that Benedict said I shouldn't poke my nose in the things Oliver had been working on.

She cleared her throat. "It almost seems as if something is going on at that firm, which people desperately want to keep behind closed doors. Maybe we should try to obtain more information in a different way."

I was surprised to hear her speak of "we" and had my doubts about her motives. "Why are you so obliging all of sudden?" I blurted out in a tone snappier than intended.

"I don't know," was her reply. She remained quiet for a moment. "Let's put it down to feeling a tad guilty. Besides, I'm starting to wonder what exactly is going on."

The answer wasn't fully gratifying, but I was curious to hear her ideas. It was obvious that Benedict wasn't going to be of much assistance and Sandra's husband didn't seem willing to share much about it either. "What exactly do you have in mind?"

"We could pay the office a visit and try to lay our hands on the file Oliver was working on," she suggested. I was somewhat shocked by her air of levity, as if we were dealing with a pick-up of an everyday package.

I didn't feel like spending any more time with Sandra than absolutely necessary. After all, she had been Oliver's mistress. I'd much rather have had Lindsey by my side, whom I could trust blindly, but I felt ashamed to confess to

Lindsey that I knew so little about what had been taking place in Oliver's life. I was well aware that I probably needed Sandra's helping hand if I were to find out more. She'd been one of the last people to play an important role in his life and she knew the drill when it concerned the world of law. Like it or not, she was basically my ally in all of this.

"We can't just walk into the office, can we?" I countered her suggestion, warming up to it, but feeling far from convinced. "A file like that is surely highly confidential and wouldn't be left out in the open for people to find." I remembered what Oliver had told me about how security had been heightened ever since the office had been hacked last year. A number of employees had responded to a fishing email and, as a result, quite a few heads had rolled within Mason & McGant.

"We have to choose a time when nobody will be present so that we can browse around quietly. Lawyers are apt to start working quite late and sometimes won't head home until around midnight." Sandra spoke in a tone that suggested she was planning an exciting treasure hunt through a forest, rather than trespassing in the office of a hugely powerful law firm. "What if we go very early in the morning?"

I felt terror-stricken at the thought of sneaking in and sniffing around in the dead of night, but I saw no other option. The circumstances surrounding Oliver's death seemed to be getting hazier and more mystifying by the minute and I wanted Tim to know the truth about what exactly had happened to his father.

"Alright," I said, hoping I was making the right decision. "How about five in the morning?"

"Okay."

A male voice suddenly sounded in the background. "Nothing," Sandra yelled. "I'm on the phone with my mother." She muted her voice again and turned back to me. "I have to go."

"Wait. How will we get in at that time?" I said, thinking of the security guards, which Oliver had once told me were present in the building twenty-four seven.

"Leave it up to me. I'll take my husband's key card. So long as I make sure to get back home before seven thirty in the morning, when he gets up. Otherwise he'd certainly get suspicious. I never start the day that early."

13

Intrusive, annoying shrieks sounded from far away and jolted me awake. It took a while before I realised it was my alarm clock. My bedroom was enveloped in darkness. I rolled over and pounded the aggravating device a few times until the noise silenced, swearing as I'd been needlessly awakened in the middle of the night. I fell back onto my pillow and closed my eyes.

Suddenly, I remembered. The alarm clock display confirmed that it was half past four. Instantly I was wide-awake. I threw off the duvet and jumped out of bed on a wave of adrenaline. As I hurried down the corridor towards the bathroom, I glanced at Tim's empty cot – he'd stayed with my parents last night. It was time for me to convert his bedroom into one suitable for a toddler and purchase a proper bed for him. It would be the first step in Tim's life that I'd take without Oliver, I thought with a feeling of sadness.

I took a quick shower, prepared a sandwich and threw on my coat. Outside it was cold and eerily quiet on the streets. A dense cloud shrouded the moon and the streetlights cast a ghostly glow on the pavement. I buried myself a little deeper into my woollen jacket and scurried towards my Volvo. Despite the fact that the firm was much more accessible by bike, I didn't want to expose myself to any unnecessary risks.

After five frantic attempts, the old beast finally started. The car was in dire need of a check-up at the garage. In the past, Oliver would have sorted that out for me, despite his busy schedule. I glanced at my watch, it was five to five. I stepped on the accelerator and sped off towards the financial heart of the city.

I decided to park a few blocks away from Mason & McGant and continue my way on foot in the direction of Amsterdam South train station. By doing so, I was hoping to draw the least attention to myself.

As it was a regular weekday, the place would soon be packed with commuters, but aside from an early bird on his way to the train station, the road was currently deserted, making me feel uneasy.

I jumped when my phone suddenly rang. I answered.

"Where are you?" Sandra hissed.

"I'm nearly there." I looked around with a feeling of apprehension, the icy air stinging my lungs. "Where are you?" I asked in exasperation.

"I'm standing at the bottom of the steps, near the bus station."

I didn't come here that often and needed a moment to orient myself. "Right, I'll see you soon," I replied and disconnected.

Not too long after, I spotted a figure in the distance, wearing a hoody and waving at me.

I ran towards her, feeling relieved not to be alone in the darkness anymore. When I arrived, I was unsure how to greet her and decided to simply raise my hand.

"I'm so on edge," she said with a jittery laugh. "This was a crazy idea."

It had been her suggestion for crying out loud. "You can't bottle out now," I exclaimed. I was determined to find out more about the case that Oliver had been assigned to.

She looked at me, clearly in two minds whether to push on.

"Let's just go. There's not much time," I insisted and nodded towards the Mason & McGant's building, standing tall and stately in front of us.

Sandra squared her shoulders. "Let's pray for the best."

We crossed the square and headed towards the entrance, walking alongside each other.

Out of nowhere an invisible hand pulled me aside by my sleeve. A nauseating stench enveloped me, making me feel dizzy and disoriented. Amidst the confusion I heard Sandra hollering behind me, "Let her go!" A row of yellow teeth snarled at me, just centimetres from my face.

"Ten euros," the homeless guy roared, surprising me with his unyielding grip around my wrists, his remarkably strong arms contrasting with his skinny build. The dreadlocks in his hair suggested that he hadn't washed for months and his clothes were way too thin for the wintery night. The fear I'd just experienced was replaced by a feeling of pity.

I took my purse from my handbag and to my relief found a twenty note. "Here. Take it."

The poor bloke probably hadn't expected to get that much. His face lit up as he snatched the money out of my hand and for a moment I realised that in another life he could have been just an ordinary guy with a job, married with children.

"If someone asks, you never saw us. Got that?" I barked, feeling like an actor in a second-rate Swedish crime series.

He nodded without expression, swivelled and staggered over to a cardboard box sheltered by a bench.

We scurried on towards the entrance of the building in which Mason & McGant had their offices. Sandra pulled a key card out of her bag, held it against the card reader and we watched the little light turn green.

We pushed the door open and entered the reception area, welcomed by the sudden warmth that hit us. The last time I'd been here, the lobby had been brightly lit and festively decorated for the Christmas party I'd attended as Oliver's 'plus one'. This time, the place was empty and dim.

"Damn it! There are security guards behind the reception desk," Sandra hissed and quickly took off her hoody. "Try to act as casual as possible."

I went out of my way to look like it was perfectly normal for us to come in here at five in the morning dressed in sportswear, of all things, but I could feel my heart pounding in my chest.

"Good morning, gentlemen," Sandra said with a charming smile to the two men in blue, seated only a few metres away from us, and for a moment I could see why Oliver had fallen for her.

One of them raised a hand at us without saying a word, while his gaze remained focused on his mobile phone. The other one was closely monitoring a series of security footage, his back towards us.

My palms were sweaty and my feet felt as heavy as lead as I restrained myself from breaking into a run.

Once having passed security, we bounded towards the corridor, where we jabbed the lift button. "Do you reckon they know everyone that works in this building by sight?" I asked, referring to the guards.

Sandra patted my arm. "I'm sure they don't. There must be at least ten different companies located in this building and probably hundreds of people working here. We'll be fine," she assured me, ostensibly the most cool-headed of the two of us now.

The lift shot up silently to the fifth floor, where we got out and turned right, passing the colossal painting depicting the two American founders after whom the office was named. Two spot-lights illuminated the canvas. As if you'd otherwise overlook it, I thought facetiously. One founder was seated in a brown leather arm chair behind an oak desk and the other one stood beside him with a fat cigar in hand.

We trod as lightly as we could towards the entrance to the office, where Sandra again used her key card to unlock the door, and we entered the grounds of Mason & McGant. Closing the door behind us, we looked at each other. "Well, now what?" I asked, wondering if I was really up for this.

"We start searching for the Van Santen file, of course," Sandra replied briskly.

I'd visited this part of the building on only a few occasions and had no idea where the firm kept all of their files. "Do you have any suggestions of where to look? Do they store the documents in a central location or would each lawyer keep them at his or her own desk?"

She scratched her head and shrugged. "Let's first check his former office. Where is it?" she asked, and I was glad she didn't know – I'd already been forced to share so much of Oliver with her.

I led Sandra to the end of the dimly lit corridor, where Oliver used to work. A strange feeling came over me as I strode the path that my beloved husband used to walk every day.

Very cautiously I pushed the door to his office open a crack, and I instantly recognised the two traditional wooden desks. Without wasting any further time, I turned right.

I immediately noticed that the spot on the desk where a picture of Tim and I used to be had been filled with a family snapshot of strangers. I took it in with a mixture of wistfulness and sadness.

"Oliver's desk is already occupied by someone else," I mumbled, even though I knew it was self-evident given that he hadn't been here for several months now.

Sandra looked at me, a frown puckering her forehead, and ignored my comment. She cast a nervous glance towards the door. "Let's start searching the drawers. Your husband's successor may have taken over his clients." It was somewhat gracious of her to describe Oliver as my husband instead of calling him familiarly by his name. Even though of course I knew they'd been intimate, I appreciated the gesture.

I opened the two drawers – with a sense of uneasiness since we had nothing to do with the current occupier – but to my disappointment, they were virtually empty with the exception of a few ballpoints, a calculator, business cards, and an unused writing pad.

"Right," Sandra mumbled. "You can't say those guys at Mason & McGant aren't tidy," she remarked dryly, evoking a nervous laugh on my part. The second desk in the office also contained no significant papers. The orderly drawers were in line with the very strict regime of confidentiality Oliver had repeatedly told me about.

We let our gaze wander around the rest of the office, but apart from two seemingly languished plants, which contrasted with the appearance of order in the rest of the room, it was immaculate and sparse.

"We won't find any files here," Sandra rightly concluded.

Suddenly my eye fell on a rack of DVDs in the corner of the room. I could hardly imagine lawyers having the time to watch a DVD during working hours, besides, it seemed rather old-fashioned and certainly not in line with the professional and cutting-edge image the firm was eager to uphold. So what where they doing here?

I walked over to the shelf. The DVDs were each labelled with a year on their spine. I randomly took one of them out and read the title out loud. "Paralegals of 2009" and then a list of names. I went back in time in my head. "Oliver was hired by Mason & McGant in 2006," I calculated and when I pulled out the right DVD from the shelf, I immediately saw his name on the front of it. I mulled it over for a while. What on earth could this DVD contain?

Suddenly we jumped up in panic from the rattling sound of a set of keys coming down the hallway.

I swore and hissed, "Someone's coming our way!" I scanned the virtually empty room, offering no cover whatsoever. "What should we do?" I squeaked.

I looked at Sandra, who seemed to be thinking feverishly, her cheeks flushed.

The sound was getting closer and closer and we could clearly make out two male voices. "They're almost here," I gibbered.

"C'mon," Sandra ordered and dragged me by the arm. "Get under the desk."

We got down on our hands and knees and crawled over the thick red carpet seeking cover from the robust desk. Right behind the drawers of the desk on the right was a little nook, which I prayed wouldn't be visible to someone standing in the doorway.

We had no other choice but to crawl up against each other, our arms wrapped around our knees. For a split second we gazed into each other's eyes, our faces a mere centimetres apart, and strangely enough, in that fleeting moment a bond was formed – it was us against them.

Sandra gave me a reassuring nod, but I could see in the tiny ray of light that fell on her face that her eyes were wide open with fear. I clasped my arms tighter around my knees, which were trembling uncontrollably.

I couldn't hear the voices anymore and for a moment I thought they'd already gone past our room, until all of a sudden, I heard a man nearby. "Hey, somebody's left the lights on in here."

The jolt of fear almost made me bump my head on the desk. I tried to breathe as quietly as possible, but it felt like I was choking. Two counts in, three counts out, I tried to calm myself down. I slowly turned my head and peered at Sandra, but she was looking straight ahead.

Two pairs of dark grey shoes and blue trousers were standing less than a metre away from us. "Lawyers. They think they're so smart, but they can't even find the light switch," one of the men sneered and laughed at his own joke.

Just as suddenly as they'd shown up, the feet turned around. The lights were switched off and the guards continued their way through the building.

I gasped for air. Sandra stayed silent and motionless under the desk and now that the room was covered in darkness, I could no longer examine her face in the moonless night. I tried to pull myself together, however quite some time passed before I finally managed to collect myself.

When I was absolutely sure I couldn't hear the guards' chatter in the distance anymore, I took my phone out of my pocket, turned on the torch and pointed it at Sandra.

She appeared to have regained her senses and shrieked, "Stop that. You're blinding me."

"Sorry," I said, directing the light away from her.

I crawled from under the desk, clapped the dust from my hands and straightened up. "That was a close call. So what now? We won't be able to find anything in here. This place is as empty as space," I said, struck by a sense of despondency. Perhaps we should just give up and go home before we get caught.

Sandra frowned. "On our way in, I kept a keen eye on the signs above our heads and noticed one of them indicating 'archive'. How about we go in there and have a snoop around?" she suggested, and I could hear the treasure hunt tone returning again.

I was dithering – we'd escaped detection by the skin of our teeth and the thought of bumping into a guard again filled me with terror, yet on the other hand I wasn't ready to throw in the towel just yet. I didn't want our visit, or rather break-in, to have been in vain and was committed to gleaning more information about Oliver's final case.

We were in doubt whether to walk out of the room openly, portraying an image of us belonging here, or to make a beeline for the archive room. We opted for the latter and darted across the corridor like the wind. Sandra held her pass against the key reader, which, to our relief, unlocked. We entered the room and closed the door behind us. It took a moment before my eyes adjusted to the darkness that enveloped us.

I used my phone as a torch again and we soon noticed rows of storage racks, each arranged by year. Each shelf could only be reached with a rotary wheel. I walked up to it and used all my strength to get to the row marked '2020' as quickly as possible, beads of sweat forming on my forehead.

After about a dozen of spins the row of interest appeared. I let go of the wheel and shone the torch over the files.

"They seem to be arranged in alphabetical order," Sandra concluded.

We frantically checked all the file names until we came across a thick folder with the name 'Van Santen' hand-written on it.

I couldn't believe our luck. "This must be it," I shouted.

Sandra put a finger to her lips. "Shhh!"

"What now?" I whispered, clutching the file to my chest, as if it were as precious as gold. "We can't just take this with us. They might notice it's missing."

Sandra took my hand and directed the light from my phone toward the entrance of the room. A copier.

"Perfect," I breathed, feeling glad I had her as my companion.

I picked up the folder, pulled out the haul of papers and laid it onto the copier. After pressing the button, the sheets were run through the machine at lightning speed making a tremendous noise and exasperating my nerves, but I knew it would be faster than taking pictures with my phone.

"Let's go, we've got what we came for," Sandra whispered and restored the folder to its original location.

She rested her head against the door to the hallway and listened. After a quick nod, Sandra slowly opened the door, stuck her head around it with the utmost caution and looked both ways.

"The coast is clear," she declared and slipped out, turning right towards the lifts.

I quickly followed her and tried to walk as relaxed as possible, although everything in my gait felt awkward and unnatural. Once downstairs, we passed the reception again, where there were now four security guards who seemed to be occupied with the handover from the night to day shift and thankfully didn't notice us.

Once we'd slunk out of the building, the square seemed worlds apart from our arrival earlier. Where there had been an abandoned, shady atmosphere before, now dawn had broken, bringing with it a vast number of commuters rushing to start their day at some of the most important firms and offices located here in the financial heart of Amsterdam.

I experienced a huge feeling of relief and leaped for joy. "Yeah, we did it," I exclaimed.

Sandra laid a hand on my arm. "Easy tiger. Someone might notice us."

Our comfortable outfits had been very suitable for the night, but now our hoodies stood out starkly among the business attire surrounding us. I felt foolish, suddenly fully aware of it. "You're right. We must be careful not to draw attention to ourselves." I gently pulled Sandra by her sleeve. "Come on. Let's go to my car, so we can talk for a bit."

We weaved our way through the crowd and not much later, Sandra was sitting next to me in my Volvo, pulling out the copies from her bag. We decided to divide the enormous stack of paper in two and each go through half at home.

I glanced at my watch and remembered what Sandra had told me. "Shouldn't you be leaving? Otherwise your husband might start asking questions."

She shrugged and seemed to have changed her mind. "I'll just say that I went for a run. It'll be fine, as long as I make it home before half past eight so I can slip the key card back in his briefcase. He's not really interested in my whereabouts these days," she said with a sad look in her eyes. "He's lost interest in me a long time ago. The only reason I'm staying with him is because of his money," she said coldly. "And the only reason for him to stay with me is to have a beautiful wife by his side, for him to show off at parties."

This personal note that came out of nowhere filled me with horror. I was gobsmacked there were people who could lead their lives like that. "I'm sure it can't be all that bad? You must have been together for this long for a good reason," I tried half-heartedly.

She emitted a cynical laugh and plucked her trousers, avoiding my gaze.

There was a painful silence as we looked out through the windscreen, where it had started drizzling. I was searching hard for the right words, feeling uncomfortable, but in the end decided to leave it at that.

"How about I phone you later today to go over the contents of the file," I suggested. A feeling of tiredness had washed over me and I was looking forward to snuggling up on the couch with a warm cup of coffee and a buttered croissant.

I seemed to have interrupted Sandra in her ponderings. "What?" she said blankly. "Oh right. Sure."

14

I opened the front door and saw the love of my life standing on my doorstep.

"Mummyyyyy," Tim yelled and threw himself into my arms. I lifted him up and swirled him around.

"Baby, I'm so glad you're back," I said, hugging him tightly. He wrapped his chubby arms around my neck and nuzzled me.

My mother watched us with a smile on her face, her grey hair tucked tightly into a bun.

I stepped aside and pulled her gently by the shoulder. "Come inside, Mum."

"Well, well, well, it took me ages to find a parking spot again," she muttered, though in a friendly manner. She wiped her shoes on the doormat before stepping in. "I can't understand how you manage to go through that every day. Not to mention how expensive parking rates are around here. I'm getting too old for this," she grumbled half-heartedly. It was part of a fixed ritual upon her arrival – my mother was unable to accept the inconveniences of a big city like Amsterdam.

"I know Mum, ridiculously expensive," I feigned agreement, although of course she never had to pay since we had a visitor's parking pass.

"How did the sleepover go?" I asked when she'd hung up her coat in the hallway and was sat at the dining table.

"It was lovely. We had so much fun together. Tim polished off the spaghetti your Dad made and slept in his cot from half past seven until seven this morning." She raised her eyebrows and looked at me smugly. "At our place he always sleeps like a baby."

"It takes a village to raise a child, mum," I responded with a crooked grin. My parents were of the opinion that their tough love approach would make Tim listen better. "I used to be as sweet as an angel whenever I went for a sleepover at my grandparents, remember?"

My mother dodged my comment and carried on summarising the events.

"Granddaddy got up with you this morning, didn't he, Timmy, so your grandmother could sleep in for a bit." She lifted him onto her lap and buried her nose in his neck. "We had a wonderful time together, didn't we darling?"

Tim nodded and my mother gave him a peck on the head.

He slid off her lap and trotted towards his toy kitchen. "Tim play."

"You go and play, sweetie," my mother responded. She leaned over to grab something out of a bag and then put a plastic box on the table. "I made you diner."

I lifted the blue lid at one end and peeked through the opening: macaroni with a pureed, red sauce. Although I couldn't shake off the impression that it was a subtle hint I ought to make a proper diner more often for Tim and me, I elected to thank my mother for the food.

"Cappuccino?" I asked.

"Sounds delicious."

I went to the open plan kitchen, placed a mug under the coffee machine and pressed the button. Then I poured milk into the frother and waited for it to foam. The sink was a mess and failed to do justice to the ultramodern and high-end kitchen that we'd had installed in the house last year. I had my back turned towards my mother and rubbed a hand across my tired eyes. After returning home from my nocturnal adventure with Sandra this morning, I'd been so exhausted that I'd gone back to bed, but each time I nodded off I instantly woke up again. The thoughts about our search at Mason & McGant had kept going in circles around my mind. I was also mystified about what could be on those DVDs that I'd chanced upon.

"I love what you've done with the living room," I heard my mother say.

I looked up and noticed how she was standing by the original marble mantelpiece, which adorned the living room, her hands clasped behind her back. On top was a photo of Oliver in a silver frame next to a flickering candle in a glass vase. My mother and Oliver had never been the best of friends – she felt our backgrounds differed too much – but over the years she'd had a change of heart as she watched our relationship cement and eventually came to appreciate his good characteristics.

I put down my mother's cup of coffee in front of her and we both sat down at the dining table.

"Thank you." She looked intently at me. "So what exactly were you up to last night?"

I turned my gaze and looked outside. The garden made a desolate impression in the winter. "Nothing," I tried, alarmed by the sudden maternal probing.

"Oh come on. You called us last minute to ask if Tim could come over and stay with us for the night," she said as if she minded, which we both knew wasn't true. "The least you can do is be honest about what's been going on," my mother put the squeeze on.

I buckled and told her about how I'd learnt that a complex case at the firm had demanded much from Oliver, and how Sandra and I had snuck into the firm last night and copied the Van Santen files. I didn't feel like sharing what role Sandra had played in Oliver's life, as it was all too raw and painful.

My mother touched my arm. There was a look of concern on her face as she spoke with a catch in her throat. "Darling, are you sure this is a good idea? Oliver worked for criminals," she stated, which was, technically speaking, correct. Nevertheless, it bothered me that even after his death she still seemed to frown upon his choice to defend potential criminals in order to earn a large salary. "I don't think it's wise to get mixed up in things like that," my mother continued.

I couldn't deny that she'd struck a chord and I sighed. I nodded at her cup. "Another refill?"

She smiled. "Yes please."

I stood up and while I made the coffee I reflected on her comments.

"You're right," I responded, after putting a second cup in front of her on the table.

Tim was still playing in his kitchen, happy, without a care in the world, and came up to me, bringing an imaginary ice cream. "Thank you, pumpkin." I licked it demonstratively and spoke in a cheerful voice. "It's delicious."

After he hobbled back to his toys I carried on. "But I really need to know what happened in his life in the last few months."

My mother frowned and looked concerned. I'd never shared our relationship dip with her, so she was probably surprised by my statement. "Why don't you come and live with us for a while?" she suggested.

"How would that help anything?" I blurted out, but I regretted it immediately after I saw the hurt expression on her face. "Sorry Mum, I didn't mean it like that. Surely, you must understand I can't just pick up my belongings and move? I've got everything here, my work, my home, my girlfriends. Tim goes to a day-care centre he really enjoys. I can't just throw it all out of the window."

My mother took a sip of her coffee. "It would only be temporary. You could drive to work from our place, right? Even at rush hour you'd make it within one hour. Besides, if you lived with us, Tim wouldn't have to go to day-care. We could take care of him," she said with a look of hopeful enthusiasm. I was an only child and my mother evidently liked to see me close to her. "If you'd like to grab a bite with your friends after work, you wouldn't have to worry about finding a babysitter." She gave a sigh of bliss. "Ah. It'd be wonderful for us to all live together again in our little village. You've never been a city girl at heart, darling. Wasn't that always Oliver's influence?"

I didn't quite grasp why, but I felt affronted. Perhaps it was childish and even a tad condescending, but I'd always considered myself as someone who had outgrown the countryside. Surely, the provinces were too dull for me, weren't they? I loved the liveliness and anonymity here in the city, particularly now that Oliver was no longer around. The thought of having to live in a small town community again, where everyone surely had an opinion about me, was quite stifling.

I patted her arm. "That's really kind of you to offer, Mum," I said, forcing a smile. "But we're managing just fine here."

She shrugged and gave me a wink. "You can't blame me for trying." My mother looked at her watch, drained her coffee and stood up. "Aunt Anne is coming over to have lunch with us." Since my parents had both retired early last year, they'd filled their lives with gardening, cycling and lunch appointments.

My mother said goodbye to Tim and walked to the corridor where she slid her arms into her winter coat. She frowned. "Will you promise to be careful, darling?"

I nodded, and she closed the front door behind her. With Tim on my hip, I waved at my mother through the window.

After lunch with Tim, I picked him up and went upstairs. As always, we gave 'Daddy a kiss' together. Then I tucked him into bed for his afternoon nap, turned on his musical bear and headed downstairs.

I resisted the urge to take a nap myself and took the copies of the Van Santen case out of my handbag. I felt jittery – would my nosing around ultimately bring skeletons out of the closet?

I went through the pile of papers one by one and stumbled upon detailed transcripts between various lawyers and their clients. Next to the client names, numbers were written in brackets. The lawyers were abbreviated with two letters. One was OS, which presumably referred to Oliver Smits. An RH and LT were also mentioned. I wondered to whom these belonged. I went over and over in my mind, trying to come up with names, but none of the colleagues Oliver used to mention corresponded with the abbreviations.

I then discovered a separate page on which a table was drawn by hand, containing a schematic overview of the various clients. The scribble looked familiar and I was pretty sure I recognised Oliver's handwriting. A list of clients was included with notes next to each name, categorised into two groups: forensic evidence and telephone data.

I looked up. My head was spinning as a result of all of this information. The table supposedly helped Oliver to create some sort of overview, to bring order to the chaos, but I couldn't make heads or tails out of the scrawled notes.

Furthermore, the name Van Santen didn't show up in the file at all, even though it had been on the cover, which diverged from common practice, as Oliver had once told me that files were named after their client's name. This file, however, gave the impression of simply being a summary and an overview of several cases.

I was curious to see whether Sandra had found any information about Van Santen in the stack of papers she'd taken home and decided to ring her.

It didn't take her long to answer my call.

I cut right to the chase. "Sandra, it's me. Is this a convenient time for you to talk?"

"I have to leave in ten minutes. I'm meeting my personal trainer. He is going to whip me into shape again," she added with a lascivious giggle.

I raised my eyebrows. She seemed to be preoccupied with many other things. "Have you gone through the papers yet?" I asked, somewhat irritated.

'Papers? Oh right, read them this morning. A lot of gobbledegook, if you ask me," she said rather ignorantly.

I informed her about what I'd found in my half. "It looks like Oliver was making an overview of a number of clients who in the past had been availed of legal counsel by the office. I find it strange that I didn't come across the name Van Santen anywhere, but apart from that there are few indications that he'd been involved in a shady case."

"I see what you're saying," Sandra responded. "On my end, I've nothing special to report either. I did some digging through those papers and swiftly put them aside again. Full of lawyer mumbo jumbo that I couldn't make any sense of." That seemed to be the end of the matter to her.

We weren't making much progress. "There must be something in those papers," I said in despair. I didn't want to let go yet, this was my final resort.

"Well I did notice the same two categories you mentioned," Sandra suddenly remarked. "Forensic evidence and telephone information," she summed up. "In the first category a reference was made to the Dutch Forensic Institute. Would you happen to know what that is?"

As a result of my profession I did have some knowledge of the forensics field. "It's an institution that conducts forensic investigations for the prosecution in cases like murder, rape and the like."

"What was that again, forensic investigation?" Sandra asked in a way that showed she didn't have the slightest idea.

I managed to suppress a sigh. "DNA testing of traces. Hair, sperm. Things like that," I put in a nutshell. Sometimes I wondered what in the world Oliver had seen in this woman. She certainly wasn't the sharpest tool in the box.

"Oh right, that's it," she responded. "There was also a name of a person written next to the entry for the Dutch Forensic Institute."

My eyebrows rose in surprise. "Do you reckon it was someone who works there?"

"Possibly," she said, and I heard her swallow something. "Sorry, I'm eating a banana. Need to quickly pump up my energy levels before I get started," she added. "The words 'senior scientist' were written in brackets by the name," she continued, articulating the words slowly.

That indeed sounded like someone who was employed at the institute. Why would Oliver have been interested in this person?

"Next to the telephone details there was a company name, TelExact Ltd," Sandra spoke again. "With various numbers and arrows scribbled on the page."

It was difficult for me to comprehend the full extent of the data that Sandra was summing up over the phone. "I think it's crucial that we assemble the documents and view them together," I said. "You seem to have access to a lot more information than I do. Let's meet up again."

There was a pause. "There's something very fishy about this case. I'd rather not get involved any further, Jennifer."

"But ..." I started.

She interrupted me. "Listen, I understand this is all very hard for you," she said without a trace of emotion in her voice. "But I believe I've contributed my fair share. I want to go on with my life and leave all of this behind me before we're in over our heads. What I can do for you though is scan the pages and put them on a shared drive in order for you to continue working on it by yourself. I'll send you the link with a password later."

I was surprised and, admittedly, rather impressed by this sudden decisive act, but managed to hold back an unfriendly remark. "Splendid, thank you." Something came to my mind. "There's one thing I haven't told you yet. When we were prowling Mason & McGant last night, I happened to notice a few DVDs in Oliver's old office. Just as I wanted to bring it up, we were startled by security."

Sandra chewed loudly before she spoke. "Alright, so you saw a bunch of old DVDs. So what?"

"They weren't movies or anything like that – I noticed ascending dates on the side. When I took the one marked '2006' off the shelf, I saw the title: 'paralegals' with a number of names, including Oliver's. In 2006 he started working for Mason & McGant." I remembered how happy he was when he heard he'd been hired to work at the largest illustrious law firm in Amsterdam. At that time we'd just moved in together in a tiny, one-bedroom flat in the south of the city.

I seemed to have caught Sandra's attention. "So what do you think these DVDs are about?"

"I really don't know. But the very fact that there's no simple and benign explanation for them makes me think that they contain something that's worth viewing. A clue that may help propel our search for answers."

"It's a possibility. So what are you suggesting? Do you want to go back to Mason & McGant?" Her decisive attitude from before had given way to a vibe of nervousness. "The last time we were lucky the security guards didn't find us. I'm not sure if I want to take the risk again."

I heard Tim starting to toss and turn in his bed, through the baby monitor. It wouldn't be long before he'd wake up and call out for me. I hated being dependent on this woman, who had turned my life upside down, but I swallowed my pride and pleaded with her. "I have to do this, Sandra. I need to find answers – I simply can't just let it rest. Would you please go with me one last time?"

She released her breath with a long, weary sigh. "Do you have any idea what you're asking of me? You know my husband is a partner at Mason & McGant. If you and I get caught, he'll find out all about it and my marriage will be on the line." Even though she'd been quite gloomy about the relationship with her husband up until now, she seemed adamant to save it and obviously cared for her spouse. Or perhaps, on reflection, the comfortable life she appeared to lead might depend too heavily on her marriage.

I was desperate and felt forced to play the trump card I'd kept in reserve for a time like this. "I understand what you're saying. Honestly." I winced. "But in all fairness, Sandra, you owe me."

It seemed to work. "Wow, that's really below the belt, Jennifer," she scoffed. She gave another sigh. "Fine, I'll help you out. Just know I'm really putting my neck on the line here – it's the final thing I can do for you. After this, you'll need to stop badgering me."

"Thank you. I genuinely appreciate it," I said, trying to placate her.

"I have a party at the Club tonight," Sandra said and I had no idea what she was talking about. "I'm available tomorrow night," she added.

"Let's meet earlier this time, four in the morning. Who knows we might just avoid the surveillance rounds," I said.

After we hung up, I intended to call my mother to ask her to take care of Tim for another night, but changed my mind. I knew I'd be able to make someone else tickled pink with a sleepover. I searched my contacts and pressed the green button.

"Bernadette Smits," my mother-in-law said formally, even though she could have seen my name flash up on her display.

"Hi, it's Jennifer. How are you doing?"

"Hello Jennifer. I'm alright, thank you. Just keeping myself occupied with playing golf, tennis and bridge, but the days sometimes seem endless." She paused for a moment. "In the evening I'm relieved I made it through another day and that I can go back to bed." I felt a stab in my heart when I thought about how I'd feel if I'd have lost my son. My husband had been taken away from me, but Bernadette had been bereaved of her oldest child, her only son, forever.

"I was wondering how you'd feel if Tim comes to sleep over at your place tomorrow evening? He'd really enjoy it," I tried to charm her.

Her voice softened. "You have no idea how delighted we would be. Darling," she called out, presumably to her husband. "Timothy is coming to stay with us tomorrow."

I agreed with Bernadette that I'd bring him over tomorrow afternoon and hung up.

15

This time I arrived at our destination earlier than Sandra. I looked around, a feeling of uneasiness and apprehension in my throat. In the distance I could make out a couple of vagrants lying curled up together in the moonless night. I clutched my handbag, containing my laptop, tightly under my arm. Snow had been forecast for tonight, but luckily as yet I'd failed to notice any precipitation.

I glanced at my watch – it was five past four. What was taking her so long? Surely, she wouldn't stand me up, would she? A shudder ran through my body. I was just about to ring her, until, to my great relief, I saw a familiar figure from afar running towards me.

Moments later Sandra stood next to me, catching her breath. "So sorry," she panted. "My husband woke up out of the blue. I had no alternative but to wait until he was fast asleep again."

"No problem." I said and frowned. "What if he'll wake again and notice you're not in bed anymore?"

A sad look appeared on her face. "He'll probably assume I've gone to the guest room. Happens more often than not."

I shrugged my shoulders. I had a hard time keeping up with the ups and downs of her marriage. "Quick, let's go."

We scurried towards the entrance of the stately building, held Sandra's key card against the reader and entered the lobby. After waving as casually as possible to security, we took the lift to Mason & McGant on the fifth floor.

We tiptoed down the corridor, which was only lit by a few night lamps, and entered Oliver's former office where we immediately closed the door behind us. I had no desire for another surprise visit from a security guard.

The rack with the DVDs was still located in the corner of the room. Sandra seemed to follow my gaze and spotted it. I felt sweat forming in my palms. Something was drawing me towards them, I had to watch those DVDs.

I opened my laptop, which was on standby, while Sandra pulled a DVD from the shelf. She held the disk, labelled '2006', questioningly up in the air and whispered. "This one first?"

I nodded and nerved myself to insert the disk into the reader. I felt sick with apprehension about what we were going to watch. I'd driven myself crazy the past few days trying to find a sensible explanation for what could be on those DVDs.

A menu appeared on the screen, displaying various names. We clicked on Oliver's and a film started playing.

A dark room with a cocktail bar was the first thing that was visible. Red leather benches were arranged in a U-shape on which scantily clad ladies draped themselves over a bunch of willing men, a look of lust glistening in their eyes. Deafening dance music boomed out of the speakers and drowned out the conversations. The cameraman was moving slowly through the room, but the image remained stable as he recorded everything meticulously. We had to be dealing with a professional here, not someone taking a random video with a mobile phone.

Men with unbuttoned smart shirts and loose ties casually hung over their shoulders staggered to their feet, swaying in and out of the footage, while the brightly coloured disco lights illuminated the sweaty faces of hollering party people on the dance floor. I recognised a number of Oliver's former lawyer colleagues.

"That's up here," Sandra muttered, a look of horror slowly spreading across her face. "It's Mason & McGant's private bar, on the top floor of this building."

I felt lost for words and merely nodded.

The cameraman suddenly swung to the right and then headed for the cocktail bar. He zoomed in on a young woman with a perfect figure lying on the bar, wearing nothing but purple lace knickers. She arched her back, making her artificial looking breasts stand proudly and daringly upright. The lawyers were whooping with arousal at the young woman.

I cursed. "What the hell is this?"

The cheers of the men intensified. "Do it, do it," they chanted with glasses of transparent liquor in their raised hands. The camera zoomed in on the girl's bosom. A line of white powder lay perfectly straight in between her two breasts, waiting to be snorted. And then, out of nowhere, a man appeared in view.

Something snapped in my head. I could hear my blood rhythmically whooshing in my ears and for a brief moment, it drowned out the noise of the film. Stupefied, I swayed slightly and for a moment I thought I was going to pass out.

A much younger Oliver turned his head and looked dazed at the camera. He held a straw up for the camera to see and shouted with drunken bravado, "This girl wakes a mighty tiger behind my fly."

He gesticulated wildly at the bunch of men to stimulate their clamour and placed the straw between the breasts of the girl, who was smiling sensually into the camera. Then he leaned over and snorted with all his might while the roars of the men rose to a crescendo and transitioned into a noisy applause. The man, who seemed like a stranger to me, staggered for a moment, but picked himself up again and started licking the young woman's breasts. Oliver moved his tongue over this unfamiliar, yet intimate area as if his life depended on it, while his colleagues hailed his triumph.

I couldn't stand to look at it for one more second and slammed the laptop shut, suddenly silencing the hubbub of laughter and shouting.

A sudden nausea took hold of me. I looked desperately around me for a bin or something that could pass for one. I already felt the first wave coming when I hurled myself toward one standing next to the desk. My stomach was emptying itself and pumping out acid so violently that I fell to my knees.

When it was all over, I was slumped over the waste bin, panting as if I'd just run a marathon.

Suddenly I felt Sandra's warm hand on my back. "Are you okay?"

I took a moment to catch my breath and then nodded.

I slowly rose to my feet, rifling through my handbag, looking for a handkerchief and wiped my mouth in embarrassment. Sandra offered me some chewing gum that I gratefully accepted. I found my hand was shaking when I brought the piece of gum to my mouth.

She looked apologetically at her watch. "We shouldn't linger. I think we need to examine the other recordings."

She was right. We had no time to waste. I was unable to make a copy with my laptop, nor could we smuggle them out as someone might notice them missing. We had to inspect them now, although I dreaded to imagine what other disturbing content we would come across.

As we played the 2006 recordings one by one, I recognised some of the men. They were all Oliver's former colleagues and each one of the videos was compromising to the paralegals involved, making my blood run cold. Various interactions with young, promiscuous ladies all with one common denominator – they should never be seen by anyone outside the firm.

I noticed the time on my phone. "We need to leave. It won't be long before one of the guards comes along." I thought back at how their appearance last time had made our teeth chatter, and shivered. The films we'd discovered had made me realise that the firm wanted to keep any anomaly a secret, at all costs.

Sandra nodded. "Let's put the DVDs back on the rack. We're no longer in need of them."

We made sure to position them in the exact same way as we'd found them and hurried down to the exit.

As we raced across the corridor, my head was a jungle. Why were recordings made of so many paralegals? Who was the person behind the camera and who had scrupulously preserved the imagery? Was there a simple explanation of a colleague with a twisted sense of humour, or was there more to it? I looked at Sandra, but she looked straight ahead.

After an uneventful exit past security we left the building, and I noticed that everyday life on the square of the financial district was beginning to unfold for another day.

"Let's have breakfast somewhere," Sandra proposed. "My husband is starting work a bit later today so there's no rush."

I nodded, although I had no appetite – my stomach was still in knots.

Sandra looked around and then pointed in the direction of a coffee shop across the square. "What about over there?"

I shook my head. I wanted to get out of this place as soon as possible. All I wanted now was to go home, although I had no desire to take Sandra with me nor, paradoxically, did I feel like being alone at the moment. "I know a nice place just around the corner from my house."

I had deliberately said 'my', instead of 'our' house. There was no more our or us – this much had just become apparent.

We decided to leave my car – I was in no condition to drive now – and take the tram.

We spent the tram ride in silence. My eyes strayed outside, to the cyclists racing through the streets, in lashing rain. I felt intensely sad.

When we reached my stop, I gestured to Sandra, who was sitting on the opposite side of the aisle, that we had to get off. There were hardly any tourists around, this early. I put up my hood for cover and without saying a word, I started walking over to the coffee shop. Slowly, here in my own, familiar environment, I could feel myself start to relax.

Sandra followed me inside and ordered some food for herself and two coffees, while I settled back in a seat next to a Japanese-looking businessman. I was freezing cold and cuddled up against the radiator.

"I don't know what to say," Sandra declared after she'd joined me.

I took a sip of my coffee and stared into the distance. "There's nothing to say. My marriage didn't mean a thing. It's safe to say it was a farce. A show in which all players apparently knew it was a performance, except for me."

Sandra touched my arm. "There, there. Don't jump to conclusions now."

I withdrew my arm and exploded. "Jump to conclusions?" I shot her a glare. "Do you not have eyes in your head? These videos leave little to the imagination."

The Japanese businessman looked up curiously from his phone. I gave him a defying look – bite me.

She frowned. "Calm down. I'm not the one who did this to you."

"That's quite a flippant response. Try to imagine seeing your husband in that footage," I said, but the sudden flurry of anger had already made way for a feeling of defeat. I wrapped my hands around the hot coffee mug, but still felt chilled to the bone.

Sandra stayed quiet, removed the wrapper from her cream cheese and started spreading it over her bagel.

I looked outside where dawn was breaking, resulting in a beautiful pallet of pink and blue hues. Who else would be in the know about the existence of those films, I wondered.

A queue had formed at the counter consisting of people in a rush to get breakfast to go, before their working day would start. I decided to apologise for my sudden outburst, which had become quite a common occurrence lately. "I'm sorry. It's very hard to watch your husband with someone else like that. I'm sure you can imagine."

She nodded and took a bite from her bagel.

I gave her a piercing look. "I never expected to dig up yet another surprise," I said with air quotes.

She lowered her brown eyes. "I understand."

"No, you don't. Not really," I responded and checked my tears. "You have no idea what it's like to discover your marriage was a complete sham. Finding out your husband was involved in all kinds of deceitful exploits behind your back and you had no idea what was going on inside his twisted head. The worst thing is that I'll never have the chance to confront him."

Sandra paused and seemed to think for a moment. "Fair enough. I don't know what it's like to see images like that and find out that your husband has been cheating on you," she admitted. "But I do know what it's like to be in a failing marriage."

"Is your relationship so rocky?" I asked, forcing myself to sound sympathetic.

All of a sudden Sandra looked dewy-eyed and regretful. Blinking rapidly, she looked away, her lips twitching. "Our marriage has been in dire straits for years, but lately it's tearing me up inside. Long story short – I've decided I'm leaving him. We won't be able to patch things up anymore."

I didn't know how to respond and wondered if the affair with Oliver had played a role in this. "Are you sure? Maybe you should stick it out for a bit longer? Give it one last chance."

She shook her head decisively. "No. I'm certain. You don't just decide these things overnight. I've been thinking about it for months. We've been together since we were sixteen – high school sweethearts." She snickered without mirth.

"Party's over," she concluded in an attempt to sound witty, but there was a profound look of sadness on her face.

She seemed to dither for a moment, but then carried on frankly. "Things went downhill between us when, after years of trying to conceive and going through cycles of IVF, we found out I'm infertile. We each dealt with this tragedy in our own way. My husband wanted to try and find a surrogate mother, but the prospect didn't appeal to me at all." She shook her head. "It would always feel like someone else's child."

I nodded and tried to think about what Oliver and I would have done if we'd been faced with this dilemma. Surely it would have taken its toll on us as well.

"I believe he's always harboured resentment over it, although he's never admitted it," Sandra continued and shrugged.

"Why don't you try going to therapy?" I asked. "I'm sure it could be helpful to address these open wounds with an outsider who has a fresh take on things." I thought about Frederique who had once confided in me during one of our drinks. "I have a friend who told me it saved her marriage."

"We tried that. My niece gave me the number of a counsellor who was apparently specialised in this area, but after three sessions, my husband threw in the towel. He thinks we should solve the matter just between the two of us, but that's never going to happen." She straightened her back. "It's okay. I've come to terms with it now. I'm ready for the next step in my life. Who knows what, or who, will cross my path," she said, arching her eyebrows with a salacious smile.

It made me think of the workouts with her personal trainer she'd told me about and I imagined how she'd do all kinds of exercises in a tight outfit. I laughed.

A surprised expression flashed across her face, and I dropped my smile to look serious once more. Sandra continued. "Ah well. Sometimes life throws you a curveball and things turn out to be different to what you expected."

The question was burning a hole in the back of my mind. "Would you have wanted to carry on your affair with Oliver?"

She looked at me in surprise. "Oliver? No," she guffawed and threw her head back. "No," she said again, this time with determination. "Oliver was a nice guy.

He made me realise in what an awful state my marriage was and I'm grateful for that. But it was nothing more than an innocent fling."

Perhaps for you it was, I thought cynically, but that so-called innocent fling had destroyed my marriage.

She looked me in the eye. "Also to Oliver it didn't mean anything. I'm sure of it. He may have had secrets and of course he's made mistakes, a lot of mistakes. I'm not denying that. But he did love you. He once told me that his family meant everything to him, I could tell he was being sincere."

I felt tears filling my eyes. Did he really say that to her? If this affair had really meant nothing to him, why would he have put everything at stake? I just wanted to punch him for being such a fool.

Something came to my mind. "I thought you weren't aware of Oliver being married?"

She took a bite from her bagel and chewed mechanically. "Let's talk about the films we found."

I considered interrogating her, but decided it didn't matter anymore. "What are your thoughts about them?"

"I find it very coincidental that those paralegals are all captured in these compromising images."

I nodded. "They've definitely taken a methodical approach. The videos weren't just filmed at random, the cameraman has ensured that all relevant events were captured razor-sharp. But why would he or she have done that? And who gave the order for this?"

Sandra was tapping the table with her nails. "I wonder if the footage was used to blackmail the lawyers."

The thought had occurred to me as well. "But why? And what exactly would they have wanted to blackmail those lawyers with? Perhaps it wasn't so much blackmail, but actually making sure they keep their mouths shut."

"Presumably, those DVDs were intentionally placed in their offices, as a permanent warning, to make sure no one would grass on the firm. As if to say 'We're watching you'. I wonder if there's somehow a connection with the Van Santen file."

I agreed with her reasoning, yet at the same time it seemed farfetched. "In the file, it looks like Oliver was trying to identify something that was going on internally and make an outline of it."

"Something that shouldn't be shared with the outside world, otherwise he wouldn't have used those codes to record the information. But what exactly?" Sandra asked.

I felt light-headed – I'd been up for hours and hadn't eaten anything.

My brain felt like it was wired with electricity and, as a result, my thoughts were racing a million miles an hour. "There were various client names and colleagues mentioned in the file. Perhaps he was drawing up an overview of all cases at Mason & McGant involving blackmail?"

She bit her thumb. "I think we might be on to something here."

"Oliver had uncovered evidence of illegal activity at the firm. Maybe he was planning to let the cat out of the bag?"

Sandra nodded. "Very possible. They couldn't allow that to happen at Mason & McGant, because there was too much at stake. They had to obliterate all liabilities," she added, which made sense although I didn't know who she meant by 'them'. "In all likelihood, there must have been a great deal of money involved."

I was suddenly aware of the people around us who were eating their breakfast, who might overhear. I leaned forward and started whispering. "Do you think they killed Oliver?" As soon as I'd spoken the words, I realised how ridiculous the suggestion sounded.

Sandra bit her lip. "Perhaps," she responded and I didn't know whether to be relieved that I wasn't losing my marbles or to be in utter shock.

I sat up straight. "Come on," I exclaimed. "Are you serious? Things like that," I said euphemistically, "happen in movies. Not in real life, not at a professional, honourable law firm."

I saw a nerve twitching in Sandra's right eye. "It's obvious that things are taking place at that law firm that are far from honourable. It seems to me that those images are proof of that." She shook her head. "We're treading on thin ice, Jennifer. We might be better off not sticking our nose in this anymore. I think it would be wise if you go to the police."

I could see where she was coming from, but there was a flaw in her reasoning. "We have no proof whatsoever to show them. We haven't taken or copied those recordings, remember?" It dawned on me that I should have taken a video with my phone while the DVDs were playing. I had been in such a state of shock that I hadn't thought of it.

"You could tell them about the videos and show them the copies of the file we made last time we went to Mason & McGant. Maybe they can make some sense out of it. Who knows, it might be enough to get a search warrant," she suggested.

I pictured the scene in my head: '*Mr Policeman, illegal practices are taking place at Mason & McGant*'. "I'll think about it," I said flatly, but it sounded like a worthless plan.

Sandra glanced at her watch and suddenly sounded rushed. "Shit. I have to go." She got up and started putting on her coat.

"So what now? What should our next move be?" I asked.

There was a determined look in her eyes. "There's no next move. I don't ever want to set foot in that firm again. We've opened a can of worms. As I said, you need to turn it over to the police. That's what those people are for. I'm washing my hands of this."

I understood her point of view, but surely she had to acknowledge that I'd never be able to solve this on my own. "I need your help, Sandra," I said reluctantly. "You can't leave it at this."

She gulped her coffee and slammed the cup on the tray. "Sorry, Jennifer. I'm drawing a line in the sand. I've got other issues at home that need taking care of."

I slowly released my breath. "I understand. Take care. Many thanks for your efforts."

16

"Good morning," I called out breezily to Simone as I walked into the practice. Simone looked up from her computer behind the reception desk and smiled. "Good morning."

I entered the small administration office, rubbing my hands together. It had unexpectedly frozen last night and I'd forgotten to wear gloves on my bike. My hands were red raw from the cold.

"Best wishes for the new year," I said, when Simone got up from her chair and gave me a hug.

"To you as well," she responded good-humouredly and sat down on her chair. "Ready to get back to work?"

"Yes, I'm right as rain again," I quipped. The past few weeks had done me good. I'd extended my time off by an extra week so that I didn't have to work over the Christmas holidays, which thankfully I'd survived and were now behind me. Hans didn't mind manning the practice at this time of year, and it was generally quieter than normal, making it a piece of cake for him.

"Wonderful," Simone responded, focusing on her work again.

I thought back to our last interaction a few weeks ago and was overcome by a feeling of shame. The poor girl had only started working here recently and had already been barked at by her boss. "Simone," I said in a muffled voice, as I didn't want any patients in the waiting room to overhear our conversation. "I'd like to offer an apology for the way I acted last time I was here. I shouldn't have spoken to you like that, it was very unkind and unprofessional."

She looked at me with a friendly expression that made me feel even more guilty. "Don't worry about it. You've got a lot on your plate right now. I can imagine sometimes it all becomes too much," she reasoned.

I solemnly pledged not to let it happen again.

We were interrupted by an elderly patient who came up to the counter. "Excuse me, how much longer do I need to wait? I have an appointment with

Doctor Nolten and have been waiting for nearly half an hour." Hans usually took on the early consultations and was apparently running late.

Simone glanced at her computer. "You had an appointment at ten to eight. That was only fifteen minutes ago, sir," she said. "You'll have to be patient with us, I'm afraid. Please have a seat. The doctor will be with you shortly." Her firm attitude pleased me.

I stealthily glanced at the waiting room, which was packed with people.

"I need to hurry up before we rile any more patients," I said and winked at Simone.

She gave me a thumbs up.

I entered my office, switched on the lights, turned on the radiator, and started up my computer. My schedule was fully booked with consultations for the next few hours, followed by three home visits in the area.

By the end of the morning, Hans and went out for lunch so that we could catch up, which deviated from our usual routine of eating at the practice. Hans was the kind of person who had never been at the forefront of my life, but nevertheless formed a stable pillar in my existence, something I was in dire need of at the moment.

"Are you feeling better?" Hans asked as he ambled beside me, towards a Turkish sandwich cafe nearby, where they had a large range of lunch options. The air had the humid expectation of a shower, but it wasn't raining for the time being.

"I guess so," I responded. I still didn't feel quite like myself, but certainly small steps had been made. Perhaps I'd never completely feel like the old Jennifer again, but that was okay.

"It's actually quite nice to get out," Hans said as we entered the cafe. "We should do this more often."

I ordered a sandwich and a bottle of still water, and then chose a spot by the window. We were surrounded by a mixture of business people out for lunch, and locals from the community.

The place was plainly furnished with plastic tables and chairs that resembled garden furniture, but the owner's friendliness was genuine and endless, and the sandwiches excellent.

"So how have you been doing?" Hans asked, looking up at me with his pale green eyes. I noticed his messy, black hair was showing streaks of grey at his temples. The well-worn blue cable jumper, which looked like it had been knitted by his mother years ago, was hanging loosely around his waist.

"I'm okay," I answered.

He quietly chewed his sandwich and looked at me expectantly.

I felt somewhat uncomfortable with the silence, which was probably a deliberate tactic on his part to make me speak. I caved. "It felt good to be working this morning. I have the impression that I can behave again," I tried to joke.

Hans smiled graciously. "Good. Have you been able to relax a bit and spend some quality time with Tim?"

I thought back on the two night-time visits to Mason & McGant and snooping through the Van Santen file, and wondered if in all honesty I could call this relaxing. "Mwah, just a tad," I said and suddenly found I couldn't look him in the eye.

He seemed to accept my answer, which left me with a feeling of guilt. We'd known each other for so long that it felt wrong I was keeping him at arm's length.

"Care for a refill?" he asked, holding the bottle of water over my cup, which was still half full.

I thanked him, after which he emptied the bottle into his own cup. It fell silent again, and I felt a knot forming in my stomach. The sandwich didn't sit too well. Suddenly I wished we'd opted for lunch in our own practice, where I could have been comforted by familiar surroundings.

"Jennifer, you don't have to confide in me," Hans interrupted my thoughts. "It's okay. Just know that I'll always be there for you if …"

"I do want to confide in you," I blurted. I inhaled deeply and let the air run out of my lungs with a lot of noise. I placed my sandwich on the recycled, brown cardboard plate in front of me. "I just don't know where to start," I said, suddenly feeling overwhelmed. Hans wasn't up to speed on anything yet. Oliver's affair, the red lace knickers found on his body, the puzzling suspicions regarding Mason & McGant. "I feel so confused."

He gave me an encouraging nod.

"My thoughts are mixed up all the time. There seems to be little improvement, even though it's been a few months now." I shook my head. "I'd expected to get some sort of structure back in my mind. Am I making any sense?"

Hans nodded and swallowed his chunk of bread. "Sure, but perhaps you're demanding too much of yourself, so soon after Oliver's death. I think it's quite normal for you to be completely lost in the first year when a loved one has died," he said compassionately. "The ground has been swept away from beneath your feet. All the more because his death was unexpected. The love of your life, the father of your child, is suddenly gone," Hans summed up aptly.

I looked past him, outside to where a tram trundled past and felt tears welling up.

"Sadness is a very strong emotion," came Hans' voice.

"It's not just sadness," I said softly. "If only it were. At least I'd know how to feel. But my feelings entail so much more. I'm angry and harbour resentment towards Oliver. I've been blatantly lied to."

Hans looked at me puzzled. "What are you talking about?"

I turned my head away. Entrusting my friends with the details about Sandra had been pretty easy as I'd always shared the ups and downs with them. Here in this work setting, however, it felt like failure to admit that my marriage wasn't what it had seemed to the outside world, even though I considered Hans a friend. I glanced around and lowered my voice, "I found out Oliver was having an affair just before his death."

Hans' expression didn't change, he just laid his hand on my arm and patted it. "How awful."

"The liaison allegedly wasn't a big deal. That is, according to his mistress. I met her." I made a silly face. "You must be thinking, why on earth did I go and find her?"

He said nothing but raised his eyebrows.

I continued my story without waiting for an answer and explained what Sandra had told me. Hans listened intently to everything I said.

"I wonder if our whole relationship was built on sand. It feels like the ultimate betrayal – seeing someone on the side and then sneaking off forever, leaving me stranded and without the ability to confront him," I said as if he'd run away instead of died. But it was the best way to describe how I was feeling.

Hans nodded.

I clenched my fists as I spoke. "It's only now that I realise how furious I am with him," I said in a raised voice. "He had no right to be messing around with another woman, while I'm left facing the reality of raising our son on my own."

My voice broke with emotion and I felt tears welling up. From the corner of my eye I noticed the people at the table next to us had paused their conversation for a moment and were gaping at me.

"Oh dear," Hans breathed with an air of awkwardness.

I was mortified and quickly wiped away the tears. "I'm okay. Really," I added, though I wasn't particularly convincing. "To be frank, times are tough – I feel like I'm spinning plates. I hardly have a moment's rest, now that I'm doing everything on my own. I don't sleep well and during the day there's either work or Tim to attend to. I've become a couch potato in the evening due to exhaustion. There's hardly any time left for me."

He nodded. "I don't want to justify Oliver's behaviour. He arguably made poor choices and what he did was wrong. But every relationship has its blips. From what I just heard, the affair didn't mean anything. There isn't a doubt in my mind, he would have eventually come to his senses and realised what he was doing was wrong, and would have ended the relationship. It's very unfortunate he didn't get the chance. I wouldn't draw any firm conclusions about your marriage as a whole."

I pressed my knuckles against my teeth trying to hold back the tears and only managed to mumble something incoherently.

"You might not expect it, but Nathalie and I also had a rough time in the past."

I was nonplussed – I couldn't ever picture Hans having an extramarital sweetheart. The thought of my colleague, with his sizeable belly and the silly outfits dating from a previous decade, chasing ladies, made me laugh out loud.

"What's so funny?" Hans asked in surprise.

I shook my head and looked down. I didn't want to give him the feeling that I was making fun of him, although a good laugh did help me to release some of the tension. I took a bite of my sandwich. "I just didn't see that coming. When?"

"Over eight years ago, before I knew you. We survived the hard days with Sofia and Marcus being young, but appeared to have lost each other somewhere in the process of changing nappies and nights of broken sleep. I was an absolute pest to live with at the time and we were this close to getting a divorce."

"Blimey, I had no idea," I said, but I could imagine. In our case, the many weeks of Tim's crying when he was a baby had left considerable scars on our marriage.

He took a sip of water. "It was a long time ago. These things are easily forgotten with time. My point is that if Oliver hadn't died, he'd have redeemed himself and your relationship would probably have survived. It would have been a mere stain on your marriage, which would have been smoothed over after a while."

I pondered his words for a moment. "But then I might never have found out about the whole affair," I said, outraged at the thought.

"Maybe he would have come clean. Maybe not." He shrugged. "And maybe it doesn't really matter that much. I didn't see Oliver often, but on the few occasions I did run into him, I saw a man who really cared about his wife and child," Hans said and smiled.

His comforting words helped. I wasn't sure whether it was true what Hans was claiming, but I wanted to believe it. This heartfelt one-on-one with my colleague made me realise that I'd missed the talks Oliver and I used to have at the end of the day. A partner, a friend who was always there for you to discuss anything. Would I ever be able to find that again?

I slid my arm across the table and gave Hans an amicable pat on the shoulder. "Thank you. Nathalie is lucky to have you."

"I know," he said without a trace of sarcasm.

I smiled and finished up my sandwich.

"Listen," Hans said suddenly. "In light of all of this, what would you think if you were to work one day less for the time being?"

His proposal caught me by surprise and before I could respond, Hans pressed on.

"Like you said, you hardly have any time for yourself. In the past you were able to do something fun over the weekend or in the evenings. Sports, or something," he said, as if it was an activity he'd never choose himself. "Or meet up with a friend."

"I've got my parents," I sputtered. "They help me out quite a lot."

"Happy to hear that, but if you were to have a full day each week to yourself, it'd give you a little room to breathe."

I scratched my face. "Maybe you're right. But how would we manage the practice?"

"Tom could probably pitch in. He's already starting to become a lot more independent. If you'd be flexible about which day you'd take off, then we can probably make a schedule that suits all three of us."

The thought of a weekly day off gave me a rush of energy. A wonderful feeling of lightness flowed through me as I began playing "what if" scenarios in my imagination. It'd be perfect to have a moment of no obligations and responsibilities. "Yes, of course, that shouldn't be a problem at all. I'll leave the arrangements at Tim's day-care as they are, so that I really have that day to myself," I said with a slight feeling of guilt, which I immediately shook off again. It was in Tim's best interest that I looked after myself. After all, I was everything he had now, and I had to ensure that I remained well equipped to take good care of him.

"Alright then, that's settled," Hans said firmly, leaving no room for second thoughts on my part.

He glanced at his watch. "We ought to go, Jennifer. Duty calls."

Was it that late again? I'd intended to inform Hans about the visits that Sandra and I'd paid to Mason & McGant and the findings we'd made, but there hadn't been any opportunity. Sandra didn't want anything to do with it anymore, that was clear, but I wasn't ready to call it quits. I'd hit a dead end and I was in two minds as to how to proceed. To my regret, there was no time left to discuss the matter with Hans – the patients would be undoubtedly waiting for us back at the practice.

That evening, I curled up on the couch with a cup of tea and turned on one of my favourite Netflix series. I'd already finished the last season with Oliver, but had started watching it from scratch again. This time, however, I was struggling to stay focused. I'd tried to find closure with regards to Oliver's sudden death and focus on the future, but I had such a strong suspicion that Oliver's death was linked to some illicit practices at Mason & McGant, that I found it increasingly hard to let it go.

My stomach started growling. A glance at my watch told me that I'd normally have dinner around this time. Tim was staying with my parents tonight and so I had the house to myself. I paused the series and headed for the kitchen. I opened the fridge and had a look inside, but to my disappointment, there was little left at my disposal for a nutritious meal. I decided I'd order a pizza later on.

I grabbed my phone from the coffee table. Sandra had been crystal clear about no longer wanting to do me a good turn, yet I still wanted to make one final attempt to persuade her otherwise. She was the only one who, like me, believed that something shady was going on, moreover, she had something I needed.

An unfamiliar man answered my call, sounding deflated. "Hello."

I was befuddled. Had I called the wrong number? "Er … It's Jennifer," I stammered. "Jennifer Smits. Who's this? I was looking for Sandra."

"You're speaking to Sandra's husband."

"Right," I said, feeling relieved. "Can I speak to her?"

I'd expected him to say something along the lines of 'sure, just one sec' or 'she'll be right there'. Instead he replied, "Sandra has passed away."

I felt the wind knocked out of me. The nausea that had been bothering me so often lately, was suddenly present again, ever so fiercely.

I sank down on the sofa. "Passed away?" I croaked.

"She was involved in an accident three days ago on her bike." He spoke without a trace of emotion. "She was hit by a tram."

I gasped. This was unbelievable. Everybody living in Amsterdam knew you had to be careful with trams. Sandra didn't seem like the type to be reckless. "What happened?" I whispered.

"The precise circumstances are still unknown. An investigation has been launched," he stated, as if he was a police officer, but I knew that wasn't the case and presumed his formal speech was due to a state of shock.

I started pacing up and down the living room. "Where did the accident take place?"

"In the Baarsjes neighbourhood, she was smashed by tram twelve." The man named the exact street, which I knew to be a long and busy road, winding through the city. "It's all so surreal," he added, his voice sounding raspy.

"So surreal," I repeated softly. What was Sandra doing in that less affluent neighbourhood? I'm sure she would have considered it to be 'the wrong side of the track'. Although I wasn't aware of her exact address, I knew that the location of the accident was a considerable distance from her own neighbourhood and even though the Baarsjes was now considered an up and coming area, I had the impression that Sandra preferred to remain in the more exclusive parts of the city.

'I'm really sorry. I need to go," the man apologised. "There's so much that needs taking care of."

"Of course," I responded, feeling somewhat appalled at my own lack of sensitivity. I was bombarding that poor man with all these questions, while I of all people knew how much he had on his plate. "I'm truly sorry for your loss," I added solemnly.

"Thank you."

Something suddenly came to my mind. "Hold on. When is the memorial service going to be held?

"Tomorrow at eleven o'clock." He gave the name of the crematorium. "I can't quite comprehend that she's never coming back," he whispered.

"I know how you must feel. It's gut-wrenching," I said, and for a moment the devastated feeling of the first week after Oliver's death washed over me again.

He didn't seem to have heard me, or perhaps he didn't want to go into it. "You're more than welcome to attend. The more of Sandra's friends and acquaintances show up, the better. How did you know my wife, by the way?"

It seemed out of the question to give an honest answer. There was no point in hurting that man any more than necessary. I knew exactly what it felt like to discover secrets after your spouse's death – the intense feeling of loss and sorrow suddenly clouded by a mixture of anger and confusion. "I was a friend of Sandra's," I answered.

"I see." He seemed satisfied with my answer. "Right then, I hope I'll meet you tomorrow."

I mumbled something in agreement, wished him all the best, and ended the conversation.

I leaned back and stared outside, where the slanting light of dusk came pouring through the windows. It was unfathomable – Sandra had been killed in an accident. How was this possible? I considered ringing up her husband again and offering my help as I knew he could certainly use it right now, but then decided it would be odd considering the situation. He presumably had plenty of friends and family to assist him.

I walked to the kitchen to pour myself a glass of Pinot Grigio. Lately, I appeared to have regained control of my drinking habits as I managed to spend the weekdays without any alcohol, but now I desperately needed a drop to calm my nerves.

I took a sip of the cool liquid and felt it burn in my empty stomach, sending a rush of heat through my body. I suddenly came to the realisation that without the access card from Sandra, I wouldn't be able to gain entry to Mason & McGant and continue my search for answers. I immediately felt ashamed by my selfish thinking.

The sound of my phone ringing disrupted my thoughts.

I answered the call and returned to the living room.

"Hi Lindsey," I said and heard how flat I sounded.

She knew me all too well. "What's the matter? I thought you were enjoying a relaxed evening without Tim."

I took another sip of the wine and lowered myself onto the soft cushions of the couch. "I just received some rather disturbing news," I responded. "Remember I recently went to Mason & McGant with that Sandra woman?"

How could she have forgotten? I'd shared it with her during our appointment on Boxing Day and she'd made no secrets of her concerns. "Of course I remember you trespassing. Twice, actually," she said pointedly.

I ignored her reproach and told her what I'd just heard.

The sound of her voice changed. "Oh dear. What a horrible accident," she said. "Hit by a tram you said? She's had terrible luck, to put it harshly."

"You can say that again," I responded, gulping down more wine. "I still can't believe it." I wanted to share with Lindsey that I found it all very disturbing – first Oliver had died as a result of an accident and now Sandra. But I knew Lindsey's opinion was that I should leave all this behind me and I therefore decided to keep my mouth shut.

"I hadn't known her that long and the circumstances in which we met were far from ideal, that goes without saying, but she wasn't that bad," I said truthfully, feeling the wine slowly relax me.

"It's awful," Lindsey said, then changed the subject. "I thought you'd decided to let the matter rest. Why did you ring her up again?"

I swallowed audibly. "I wanted to ask if I could borrow her husband's key card," I reluctantly admitted. I was willing to go all out to gain access to Mason & McGant so that I could record the images on the DVDs with my phone and share them with the police.

She let out a loud sigh that turned into a grunt. "Jen, what in heaven's name is going on? You really have to stop this quest. You ought to focus your attention on yourself, make a fresh start. I told you before that I think you're reading too much into it, but if you really want to undertake anything, you should go directly to the police. Those people are trained for these things."

"Yeah sure," I responded, biting my tongue, but I didn't feel much for her plan. Arguably she was right, but I wanted to leave no stone unturned to make sure I'd have sufficient, concrete evidence to convince the detectives. I got up and walked to the kitchen to pour myself a refill.

Lindsey carried on remonstrating. "This is starting to sound like a wild-goose chase, if you ask me. Of all things, you definitely shouldn't break into Mason & McGant again. Imagine someone catches you this time. It would all blow up in your face."

I uttered a yelp and cursed loudly. I looked at the bottom of my foot, and discovered a Duplo block attached to it. I removed it and angrily tossed it into the box it should have been stored in.

"What happened?" Lindsey asked, now sounding worried.

"Nothing," I grumbled and yanked open the fridge. I still hadn't taken the effort to find someone to fix the stiff door. I emptied the bottle of wine into my glass and saw that it was my last. Maybe it was for the best.

"Can you please promise me you you'll let it go and try to move on?" Lindsey pressed on.

I winced and held the phone away from my ear.

"Do something fun and relaxing for yourself. Something positive. Something constructive," I heard Lindsey babbling from a distance.

This sounded like a slogan coming straight from the advertising agency where Lindsey was a project manager, I thought, and frowned.

"Try to get it out of your system. Why don't you go on one of those yoga retreats on Ibiza or whatever and ask your parents to watch Timmy?"

A sigh escaped my lips.

"Well?" she insisted.

I didn't want to make any false promises, but there was something I had in mind. "Alright. I'll plan something fun." I told her about the agreement I'd made with Hans and that I'd have a full day off every week for the time being. "Maybe we can have lunch together?" I suggested, something I normally wouldn't manage on workdays, since my practice was located too far from Lindsey's office.

"I have a much better idea," she chirped. "Why don't we go out for drinks tonight? Let's go out the old-fashioned way, go clubbing. We could head to Paradiso or better still, Jimmy Woo."

I moaned internally at the thought of a night on the town and leaned my head back against the fridge door. I felt like taking a rain check, but acknowledged it would be good for me to get out, instead of being cooped up in the house in front of the television with a tub of chocolate ice cream, my mind wandering off again.

I opened my eyes. "Maybe it's not such a bad idea," I said, perking up.

"It's settled then," Lindsey responded, before I could change my mind. "I'll pick you up around nine."

17

"Ow," I groaned with a mouth as dry as dust. My tongue stuck to my palate like a piece of leather, my lips were cracked and chapped. I was in desperate need of a glass of water. I couldn't recall the last time I'd had such a throbbing headache. My feet felt swollen and stiff as a result of a night spent teetering on high heels.

I gingerly opened one eye. A stabbing pain in my forehead made me promptly close it again. The sun was shining unhampered into the bedroom as I'd evidently forgotten to close the curtains last night.

As I turned onto my right side, the room starting spinning around me. A wave of nausea surged over me – I solemnly pledged never to drink this much again.

Although I felt miserable, I had a smile on my lips – it had been a wonderful evening. Our clubbing night had accomplished something that I hadn't been able to do for ages, sleep for hours straight without tossing and turning. I picked up my phone from the nightstand and saw that I'd received a photo from my mother, in which she was finger-painting with Tim. I smiled in the knowledge that I didn't have to get up or take care of anyone for a while and dozed off.

Not much later, the parched feeling became so prevalent that I had to drag myself out of bed. After I chugged two glasses of water and inspected myself in the bathroom mirror, I took a long, hot shower.

As I gorged on a double sandwich with fried bacon and egg, I skimmed through the newspaper, with a cup of coffee, while sat on one of the kitchen stools. It was wonderful to take the time for myself without worrying about Tim.

I read through the funeral announcements, scanning the names of the deceased, but they didn't include a Sandra. I only now realised that I had no idea what her last name was.

I tapped my foot on the metal frame of the stool and glanced at my watch. The memorial service was due to start in half an hour. Sandra's husband had said he'd like me to attend it. It somehow felt intrusive to go there, but surely it would be the decent thing to do, to pay my respects?

I dashed upstairs to my bedroom, pulled open the drawer of the wardrobe and found my smart black trousers, freshly washed and ironed by Alejandra. I combined them with a light grey blouse, scurried downstairs again, grabbed my coat from the rack and got on my bike. I looked up the location in my phone and concluded that I should be able to arrive within twenty minutes.

Battling on my bike against the gusts of wind, I made it by the skin of my teeth, the back of my shirt all wet from sweating as I strode past the hearse that was parked at the entrance of the crematorium. As I quietly closed the glass door behind me, I noticed the large turnout to the memorial service. The church had been packed at Oliver's funeral as well and I remembered how much comfort and warmth it had brought me. I quietly joined some people standing behind the last row of chairs, not wanting to draw attention to myself. Cautiously I looked around me, but didn't recognise anyone.

At the front of the aisle stood a closed, oak coffin with a framed photo on top. It was hard to grasp that Sandra was really in there. The vivid memories of Oliver's farewell service seemed to grab hold of me and left me with a sharp ache in my heart.

I started blinking rapidly. Don't think about that now, I tried to soothe myself.

A man seated in the front got up from his chair and went to stand behind the lectern, the deep lines in his face and dark circles under his eyes visible even from where I was standing. He squared his shoulders and then introduced himself as Sandra's brother. The broken man held an emotional eulogy on how he and Sandra used to be inseparable when they were growing up. Behind him, photos of a young Sandra were displayed in a slide show on a screen. Around me I heard snivelling and sobbing.

Amidst the large crowd, I noticed a man with brown hair in the front row, a spasm of pain contorted his face. Although I couldn't entirely see him, I estimated that he was of a comparable age to Sandra and made the assumption he was her husband. Next to him was an older couple, their heads bent forward, hunched and with rounded shoulders, presumably Sandra's parents. The old lady sobbed inconsolably while the man I conjectured to be Sandra's husband slid an arm around her.

The brother continued his narrative about what Sandra had been like as a teenager. I turned my head away and closed my eyes. I couldn't bear the sadness that was hanging almost tangibly in the air. The scab of my own wound was too fresh and vulnerable. I felt a wave of nausea washing over me.

I decided to leave. A few more people had arrived after I did and I had no choice but to shuffle past them in order to exit the building, stammering my apologies. When I'd finally managed to get myself outside, I took a deep breath of fresh air. Birds were chirping cheerfully from up high in the stately row of oak trees flanking the long driveway and I felt myself slowly relax.

I got on my bike and took a detour to clear my mind, before heading for the city centre where I was going to meet Lindsey for lunch.

When I opened the door of our favourite lunch spot, which was just around the corner from Lindsey's work, the pleasant warmth greeted me. It was a few minutes shy of noon and there was still plenty of space. After choosing a comfortable couch in the corner, I looked outside and saw tram number fourteen draw to a stop for a red light. When it pulled off again and trundled on, I saw Lindsey popping up behind it.

She held her woollen, pink pea coat closed with one hand, glanced left and right, and then scurried across the street in my direction. After entering the establishment, she kissed me once on the cheek, and I caught a hint of her floral perfume. Her gaze remained on me. "My goodness Jen, you're as pale as a sheet."

I made a silly face. "How many drinks did we get through yesterday? I knew we shouldn't have left you in charge of the kitty," I said laughing.

She looked at me with concern. "We didn't even drink that much. I don't feel a thing. Is everything okay?"

"Sure," I answered, dismissing her worry with a wave of my hand. "I'm probably coming down with a cold," I said, playing it down, and started sniffing demonstratively. "That must be it."

Lindsey let the subject rest, peeled off her coat and draped it over a chair. She was wearing a tight, leather, burgundy coloured skirt, combined with a green blouse. Her pumps in a matching colour completed the outfit. Even on this workday she looked arresting.

She took a seat opposite me. "I need to finish an important report this afternoon, otherwise my boss will have my guts for garters, so I can't stay terribly long."

"No problem," I said. "I'm happy you could free up your schedule for me."

"Are you off today?" Lindsey asked, glancing at the menu, although she'd probably order the baguette with tuna salad, knowing her.

"I won't have to work until later. I've got the evening shift at the out-of-hours clinic," I said, and, as usual, felt a tad apprehensive about it. Those kind of shifts always had a sense of unpredictability and volatility in them. An average Friday evening usually meant tourists out of their minds on drugs or teenagers who had had one drink too many. "Tim's staying with my parents for another night."

Lindsey smiled. "You've lucked out to have such parents. If I had a child, I'd probably get no help whatsoever," she said matter-of-factly, but a double-edged pain resounded in her statement. She didn't have a child and had a strained relationship with her parents. She never confided in me about a possible desire for children and I didn't dare ask about it either. I touched her arm and squeezed it gently.

The waitress came to take our orders.

Lindsey frowned. "Didn't you attend the funeral, this morning? For er …?"

I nodded. "Sandra, yes I did." I wrinkled my nose.

Lindsey ran a hand through her shiny, blond hair that was beautifully styled as usual. "How was the service?"

"Nice," I answered automatically. "Or actually, terrible. Someone that young shouldn't die, especially not in such a horrific way." I shook my head. "I didn't take it well and left early."

Lindsey reached out her hand, grabbed mine and squeezed it tightly. "Oh poor you."

I smiled briefly, patted her hand resolutely in response, and pulled away. I wanted to keep the atmosphere light, even though the funeral still weighed on my mind. "Let's talk about something else," I said jauntily. "How's work going?"

Lindsey brought me up to speed on her most recent advertising project. She'd been awarded an assignment for one of their most important clients and was happy with the promotion.

In the meantime, the waitress brought the sandwiches and tea.

I pecked at the bread, but it didn't go down well. I laid my hand on my stomach and chewed slowly.

Lindsey looked up from her tuna sandwich. "Are you okay?"

I pressed my fist to my mouth and looked anxiously towards the bathroom. I jumped up, causing a wave of tea from my tea to spill over the table. Thankfully the nausea subsided just as suddenly as it had come up. I lowered myself slowly.

Lindsey lifted her head and propped her chin in her palm. "Gosh, Jen. Something's not right. Have you been experiencing this a lot lately?"

I wiped up the puddle of tea with my napkin and pondered it for a while. "Come to think of it, I have been feeling nauseous more often lately. But isn't that to be expected with everything that's been going on in my life?" And with all the alcohol I've recently been consuming, I added in silence.

She shrugged and looked confused. "I guess."

"My stomach has always played up in times of stress or hardship. It seems to be some kind of personal weakness."

Lindsey suddenly sat up, her eyes bulging. "Oh my god, Jen. You're pregnant!" she exclaimed.

I laid a hand on my stomach as I spoke with a mock solemn expression on my face. "Yes, I am expecting."

She slammed her hands on the table, her long hair flying around. "No way," she shrieked.

"I'm kidding. Me, pregnant? You're cracking me up," I said and started laughing at the ridiculous suggestion. "From whom for heaven's sake?"

She raised her eyebrows suggestively. "You probably know the answer to this better than I do. Since Oliver died, have you not had …?" Her voice trailed off.

I wasn't sure whether to be shocked or offended by her suggestion. "Of course not," I cried. "What do you take me for?"

She wrapped her hands around her cup of tea. "These things happen. The grieving process is different for everyone, sometimes you just have to act on how you feel," she stated, as if she were reading advice from a women's magazine. "Can't the baby be Oliver's?"

"There is no baby!" I exclaimed and rolled my eyes. My dear friend seemed to have lost sight of the laws of nature. "Oliver passed away more than three months ago – you do the maths," I said, feeling positive of my case. I emitted a mocking noise. "Seems to me I'd have noticed by now."

She held onto the subject. "I didn't want to say anything to you before, but er … you look as if you've filled out a bit lately." She blew in her tea and prudently took a sip.

This was getting better by the minute. "Thanks a lot Lin," I said, raising my eyebrows. Then I thought of something. "I've got an explanation for it. It's because of my affair with Ben. We're together every night on the couch," I quipped.

Lindsey practically choked on her tea. "Ben?"

"Ben & Jerry's," I said with a cheeky grin and threw my head back.

"Ha, ha, ha," Lindsey said sarcastically and started smiling. "Well, I guess I'm wrong then."

"I guess so too," I said kindly but firmly and took another nibble of my sandwich. "Give me a good night's sleep and I'll be back on my feet."

An hour later I had returned home and stood by the mantelpiece in the living room. I ran my thumb over the photo of Oliver, which I'd put into a silver frame after he died. Lindsey's words earlier had refuelled a deeply cherished desire. More than half a year ago, Oliver and I had decided to try for a second child.

Even though I'd had misgivings about whether it was wise in view of our relationship struggles, emotion had won over reason and we'd agreed to try. Since Oliver's death there'd only been room for sorrow and confusion, but now suddenly that strong longing for another child had resurfaced, just as ardently and fiercely as it had been when Oliver was still alive. The agony over dissipated possibilities almost took my breath away.

I gave myself a stern talking to – I should consider myself lucky to have Tim. "I love you, darling," I said to Oliver's photo and headed for the hallway to turn on the washing machine on the first floor before leaving the house to work the evening shift. I noticed that, despite Alejandra's weekly help, I kept falling behind regarding household matters. I considered asking her to up her hours, although I was reluctant to increase my spending. It wasn't clear to me yet what the financial consequences of Oliver's death exactly were, and – although I obviously wasn't living on the breadline – as long as that was the case, I preferred to stay frugal.

As I opened the door to the hallway, I noticed there was a stack of mail lying on the doormat that I had overlooked when I'd arrived home from lunch. I bent down to pick up the envelopes and was tempted to toss them unopened under the coat rack, onto the heap that had been growing over recent weeks, when my eye fell on a loose A4 paper that slipped out of the pile and was floating down to the ground.

The colourful letters in a decorative font danced over the page. *'Don't stick your nose into other people's affairs.'*

My heart was racing.

What in heaven's sake was this?

I reached out to pick up the piece of paper that was entirely blank except for those alarming words. It seemed to be a threat addressed to me. Was this serious and if so, who had sent it? Or was this just a sick joke and I shouldn't read too much into it?

I tried to calm myself down and took a few deep breaths, the note shaking with my trembling fingers.

I straightened my back and lifted my chin. Whatever it was, I had no intention of letting this message defeat me. I stormed back into the living room, crumpled the paper and chucked it in the bin.

18

"Tim, get off that at once! Mummy said no climbing on the frame," I yelled, but he wasn't listening to me, as usual. I'd had little energy to discipline him over recent months. I wasn't sure whether he was acting out because he missed his father, which made it harder to be firm with him.

Ever since Sandra's funeral, I'd promised myself not to brood about the circumstances regarding Oliver's death anymore. Dwelling on it wouldn't get me anywhere – Oliver was no longer here and sadly would never return to this earth. I'd resolved to start a new chapter. I tried to blank out the note I'd received so unexpectedly through the post and instead, focused on Tim and my work. So far this approach was working out quite well.

I walked towards Tim in a don't-mess-with-mummy way and directed him back to the blue, plastic sandpit, which contained enough toys to keep him entertained for a while. To my relief, he accepted my authority, which made me resolve to be strict more often. I walked back to the sun-drenched bench where I had a good view of Tim, and sat down. The first crocuses were poking through the ground, which was still cold and hard from winter, suggesting spring had started earlier than usual this year.

A man of a similar age to me on the adjacent bench gave a friendly smile. "Children," he said knowingly.

I shrugged my shoulders in a gesture common to all parents and mustered up a faint smile in return. Then I leaned back and tilted my head towards the sun, closing my eyes and feeling the delightful rays warm up my face – I could do with a bit more colour on my cheeks after the long winter, I thought to myself.

"What's your son's name?" the man asked, eager to strike up a conversation.

I opened my eyes and replied curtly. "Tim." I had little interest in small talk.

He nodded. "I've got a three-year old," he carried on. "A girl. Toddlers are wonderful, but they have a mind of their own," he chuckled.

I made a half-hearted attempt to see which child in the playground he was referring to, but then decided that I wasn't bothered and merely nodded.

He didn't take the hint. "She's not here, actually. Bella goes to her mother from Tuesday to Saturday afternoon. We're divorced," he added, shrugging apologetically.

I stared at him in astonishment. Why was he sharing all of this with me? I glanced at Tim who was building a sandcastle with a bucket and a spade.

The man continued his story. "We split up just six months ago. It's hard, you know. Really tough. You think it'll last forever, but it transpired that I was the only one who'd made that assumption."

I moaned internally and muttered something incomprehensible. What did this guy want from me?

He needed little encouragement to carry on expressing his melancholy. "I'm only off work on Wednesday afternoons, so I hardly have time to come to the playground. That's why I sometimes sit here at the weekends, just by myself, and reminisce about the times when all three of us came here together."

Holy cow – was this man for real? He wouldn't stop blabbering on about his life. "Right," I responded politely, and then immediately closed my eyes, hoping he would end his lengthy monologue. As far as I was concerned, this conversation was over.

The man wasn't in the slightest bit thrown off though. "You must think I'm being pathetic." He leaned forward and rested his forearms on his muscular thighs, hands clasped together, and grinned. To my annoyance, it was an attractive, boyish smile. "Alright, I admit, I can be a sentimental fool," he said disarmingly.

I rolled my eyes when he wasn't looking. "Oh no, not at all," I said, gritting my teeth. Why couldn't this man just leave me alone? I considered taking Tim home early, but the fear of a tantrum made me decide otherwise.

"So what about you? Happily married, I presume?"

The ball was in my court now. I raised my chin. "Not quite. I'm a widow." Perversely enough, it felt satisfying to be able to take advantage of my unusual status. Surely that would silence the man. He was visibly shocked. "How … How awful. I'm truly sorry for your loss." My message had obviously taken him by surprise, as it always did when I informed people. "I had no idea that …" His voice trailed off. Just when I thought he was going to remain quiet, he asked me an unexpected question. "Do you mind if I sit next to you?"

He didn't even have the courtesy to wait for an answer but stood up and lowered himself next to me, whereupon I jumped up and moved to the far end of the bench. This wasn't part of my plan, I thought, while my heart started pounding wildly.

As he chatted about how sorry he was for me, I noticed the wrinkles surrounding his intense brown eyes, that revealed themselves every time he smiled. A five-o'clock shadow gave him an edgy, dishevelled flair that enhanced his strong features. His gaze was attentive and formed a refreshing contrast to the way most people looked at me with pity when they heard my sorrowful life event.

He somehow seemed familiar and I remembered reading somewhere that if you feel like you've met someone before it means that you find them attractive. To my dismay, a fierce wave of desire passed through me and I felt completely overwhelmed by it.

"Was it sudden, or had he been sick for some time?" came the man's voice.

I tried to focus my attention on his question. "He died as a result of a tragic accident. So it was all very sudden," I said, gazing ahead. I considered giving more details as I knew my brief summary of events would presumably raise questions, but then decided to refrain. "He just had terrible luck."

He ran a hand through his shiny, curly hair. "Blimey, that's awful. When did this all happen?"

A cloud slid across the sun, sending a chill through me. I pulled my hands inside the sleeves of my jacket. "He died last year." Something caught my attention and I jumped up. "Tim. Stop that! Don't throw the sand." I waited to see if he carried on, but my resolute response from earlier must have made an impact and shouting directions from a distance was sufficient to correct him. I sat down again.

"At work there was also a guy who died at a young age, leaving his wife and child behind. I guess I shouldn't be complaining then, at least Bella still has her mother."

A shiver went down my spine. "Where do you work?"

He directed his gaze towards me. "You probably wouldn't know it. It's an American law firm called Mason & McGant."

I could feel the blood rushing to my head, making my temples throb. Had I just heard right? "You're kidding," I mumbled. "My husband worked there."

It took a moment for him to comprehend what I'd said, but then I saw the bafflement in his eyes. "Was your husband Oliver? Oliver Smits?"

Was this a joke? Coincidences like this made me very nervous and suspicious. "That's him," I whispered and felt my mouth drop. "I can't believe it."

A look appeared in his eyes that I couldn't quite read. "I met Oliver a few times during meetings." The man was wearing fashionable heavy-framed glasses and pressed them onto his nose. "I didn't know him well though. He worked in a different department to mine and started out as a paralegal, right? I joined Mason & McGant later than him, but directly as a lawyer. I did my years of paralegal work at a different firm."

Suddenly the letters written with a black marker on the DVD appeared in front of my eyes again. Would this man also have been recorded on camera or did he beat the rap because he entered the firm with experience, rather than being a paralegal?

I shook my head, struggling to repress the image. "You look familiar to me – I must have seen you before at one of the firm's parties."

"Might well have." He leaned back and rested an arm on top of the bench, opening out his chest towards me, and raised his eyebrows. "Although I highly doubt I would forget an attractive woman like you."

To my horror, I started blushing as a result of his cheesy remark and averted my eyes. Jennifer, get a grip for crying out loud, I said to myself. I looked like a bloody schoolgirl.

I ignored his flirty comment. "Do you live nearby?"

He mentioned a neighbourhood where Oliver and I had once viewed several sought-after houses, but Oliver ultimately wanted to move to an area with more grandeur. "It's about five minutes from the Vondelpark."

"Nice neighbourhood," I responded.

"Where do you and your son live?"

The sun reappeared from behind the clouds. "In the Valeriusstraat. It's very close, in the Museum Quarter."

He drew his breath in with a whistle. "Not bad."

I smiled graciously.

Tim came up to me with a cup filled with sand and wanted me to have a bite of his pretend pastry. He spilled half of it over my trousers, but I was glad he was playing more appropriately now, so I kept quiet and played along with him.

He wobbled back to the sandpit with a bright smile on his face as I brushed the sand off my legs.

The man, who I now allowed myself to call attractive, held out his hand. "I'm Dan Bernstein, by the way."

I enclosed his fingers with mine. "Jennifer. Jennifer Smits."

He held on to my hand a second too long with an intense look in his eyes. "It's a pleasure to meet you." The man's deep voice stirred a wave of heat inside me. I lowered my eyes.

Dan let go of my hand, stood up and zipped his jacket. He handed me a business card with the all too familiar logo printed on it.

Daniel Bernstein, Lawyer.

"You seem a lovely woman, Jennifer. Give me a call if you ever feel like meeting up in the future."

I looked up at him for a moment, while he was waiting for my response, my hand shielding my eyes from the sun. Was this the way people over thirty flirted? No beating about the bush, just say it like it is? It had been such a long time since I'd been single, I felt like an alien trying to adapt to a completely unfamiliar habitat.

"I'll think about it," was my diplomatic answer.

But I wouldn't dream of it. My head was nowhere near dating.

19

"Cheers!" Frederique said.

We raised our glasses of Chardonnay over the wooden table and clinked. Lindsey and I were seated on a bench on one side of the table, our two other friends sat opposite us.

"To what shall we make a toast?" Lindsey asked and looked around.

I dithered for a moment. "To new love?"

Lindsey wavered before responding and I wondered if she was thinking of the stranded relationship with Paul, although 'affair' might be a better word to describe it. She'd just confided in me that after a few months of dating she'd discovered the bastard turned out to be married. According to him, the divorce was just a formality, but it was enough for Lindsey to kick him to the curb. "To new love," she responded firmly, taking a sip, and I could tell she'd already bounced back.

"It's wonderful we're all together again tonight," Lindsey continued, her blond hair looking silkier than ever. She'd taken the rough break-up with Paul as the perfect opportunity for an appointment with her hairdresser.

"Without men," Karen chimed in eagerly, and then looked at me with a guilty expression.

I waved my hand to indicate I didn't take offense.

"Without children," Frederique added with a sigh and sipped her wine, savouring every drop. Her three children were at home with the nanny tonight. "Mmm … Delicious," she declared with the air of a *connoisseur*.

Not much later, the cheese platter arrived, which we gratefully began devouring. It was the first time since the winter that we were able to sit outside on the terrace again. The heater was certainly necessary – nevertheless it was a long awaited sign of the warmer months that lay ahead.

Today's pleasant weather had moved the topic of conversation to holiday plans and Frederique informed us breezily about the trip to the Maldives that she was going to take this summer with her family of five.

As Frederique and Karen chatted excitedly about their holiday plans, Lindsey and I were having a heart-to-heart.

"So … to new love … what was that all about?" she whispered and looked at me curiously.

I should have known she'd pick up on it. I smiled and bit my lip. "What are you talking about?"

She threw her head back and laughed. "Don't act all innocent with me, gal." Lindsey jabbed her finger into my arm. "You know I'll find out if something's going on, Jennifer Smits."

I laughed and raised my right hand. "I confess, your honour. There may be something."

Lindsey swung a leg over the bench so that her body was now facing me. "Seriously, Jen?" She wasn't able to play it cool anymore and grabbed my arm. "Tell me or I'll have to kill you."

I described how I'd met Dan Bernstein at the playground in the Vondelpark. I had intended to blank out the encounter, but the attractive stranger just kept popping up in my mind.

"He somehow managed to crawl under my skin," I ended my story. "Isn't that ridiculous? Oh, I feel terribly guilty towards Oliver." I thoughtlessly ran my fingers over the plastic tablecloth that was draped over the table.

She shrugged and frowned. "Why would it be ridiculous? There's no need to feel guilty."

In the past, if someone had immediately started dating again after a break-up, I would have been strongly opinionated about it, but being in that position myself now, I slowly came to the realisation that things were sometimes out of your hands. "Don't you think it's too soon to be attracted to someone else? Oliver died less than six months ago."

She laid her hand on mine. "You can't put a time stamp on it. It's completely normal for someone to make you feel butterflies in your stomach again. You're still young, right?" She laughed and gave a me a wink. "Every woman has her needs."

I gave her a warning look. Behind me I heard a boat sliding through the ancient canal a mere metres away from the terrace, making the water splash against the quay, and it gave a me a comforting feeling of being home.

"But what about Tim?"

Lindsey shrugged. "Don't get ahead of yourself. We're not talking about nuptials, are we? It's just the first time since Oliver that someone makes your heart skip a beat. Now you know you're still alive." She held up the platter.

"Cheese?"

"Thanks," I said as I cut off a piece and put it in my mouth. Lindsey was right. "The silly thing was that he was actually annoying me terribly." I chuckled while munching on the Camembert. "He seems the type to wear his heart on his sleeve as he wasn't at all afraid to show his emotions. Very different from Oliver, that's for sure."

Lindsey held up the bottle of wine to offer a refill and I slid my glass towards her. "That's how things go sometimes," she said shortly and to the point, emptying the bottle into my glass.

I cut off another piece of cheese. "Coincidence has it that he was a former colleague of Oliver's."

Shock crossed Lindsey's face. "What?!"

"Well, a distant colleague. He only knew Oliver by sight."

Lindsey's expression had turned from jolly to austere. "I don't want to rain on your parade, but you'll have to agree that this is too weird. Surely, this can't be a coincidence?"

A shudder went through me. I swallowed the Camembert and remained silent.

"First, out of the blue, Oliver stumbles and crashes down a slope, fatally hitting his head on a rock. Then that Sandra woman, with whom you sneaked into Mason & McGant, suddenly dies, and now some guy randomly approaches you in the park, who works at that same firm. I find it all very remarkable."

I felt sick. I shouldn't have eaten so much of the Camembert. "You've got a point." When she put it like that, it did seem suspicious.

There was a frown on her forehead. "How exactly did Sandra die?"

"She had a collision with a tram, somewhere in the Baarsjes neighbourhood. That's all I know." I pushed the glass of wine away from me. "You're scaring me, Lindsey," I said, although I didn't know exactly what she was suggesting and neither, it seemed, did she.

She laid her hands on both of my thighs. "I'm sorry. I didn't mean to worry you. It just suddenly dawned on me that there's a lot at stake for Mason & McGant. They can't afford for someone to expose them and jeopardise their reputation."

I nodded. Sandra and I had already formulated this hypothesis not long ago, but I'd later dismissed it for being vague and for lack of evidence. Lindsey had actually been the one saying I was chasing phantoms and that I should try to blank it all out, but now her reaction made me question the whole thing all again. "Do you think Sandra's accident might have been foul play?"

"It's unlikely, though not impossible," she answered after a brief pause. "For argument's sake, let's presume that it is the case. I wonder then how they could have found out that Sandra had been nosing around in Mason & McGant. You two didn't get caught, right?"

I shook my head and reflected on it for a while until it suddenly hit me. "Sandra must have been identified on Mason & McGant's security footage," I exclaimed. My heart started pounding wildly when I realised what the inherent implication was. "There's a good chance they've recognised me as well."

Lindsey stiffened up.

I felt a burning sensation in my chest and tried to swallow the acidic taste in my mouth. Frederique asked us if we wanted to order another bottle of wine, but my mind had gone to mush and I just waved no with my hand.

I mulled recent events over. Subconsciously, I'd found it odd that a man would hang around in a playground without a child. Also, that threatening note I'd received made me jittery. It could very well mean nothing – youngsters pulling a prank, or an oddball in the neighbourhood who was upset about something. But no matter how hard I tried to rationalise it, I couldn't quite shake off a feeling of apprehension.

"Do you think they've sent this Dan guy after me to follow me around?" I mused. "Maybe it's his job to find out how much I know."

Lindsey looked at me ruminatively. "I don't know. It sounds absurd, but we can't rule anything out. In any case, this is starting to become a whole different ball game and you may have been right that something's going on. I think you should seriously consider contacting the police, as soon as possible," she urged with a look of genuine concern.

20

I sat on the couch in the living room and looked over at Tim. He was playing quietly on the rug with his toy cars, making vroom vroom sounds and crashing noises. I rubbed my eyes, feeling drained. The last two nights I'd had a tough time sleeping, as I kept brooding over my conversation with Lindsey. Just when I finally thought I could leave everything regarding the deaths of Oliver and Sandra to rest, this mess suddenly dominated my whole life again. Even though I knew deep down that Oliver's accident had a strange and inexplicable edge to it, I had more or less come to grips with it. But now, to my horror, it was beginning to resurface.

I opened one of the garden doors and walked onto the flagstones. It was windy and drizzling, which didn't benefit my state of mind, but nevertheless it was nice to have a breath of fresh air.

I took my phone out of the back pocket of a brand new pair of jeans that I'd recently ordered online, looked up the number of the police station in Amsterdam and asked to be connected to Detective Armstrong. It wasn't long before he answered his phone.

"Armstrong," the man barked.

"Good morning, this is Jennifer Smits speaking. I'm Oliver's wife, the man who died in a holiday park after a fall a few months ago."

There was a pause. "Right. I remember. What can I do for you, Mrs Smits?"

I launched into my story. "Some strange things have happened since my husband's death." I explained how Sandra had suddenly died as a result of a tram accident. "She was a friend of ours," I said, obviously being cryptic for good reasons.

"I'm sorry to hear that. It must have been tough losing two people close to you in such a short space of time," the detective responded. "But I don't quite understand what this woman's death has to do with your husband's accident."

I scratched my eyebrow. There was such chaos in my head that I had to strain to convey the story in a coherent fashion. "Sandra's husband works at the same law firm that my husband worked at. She and I recently discovered that Oliver was conducting a secretive, internal investigation. I omitted the details of how we had learned about this information, as it arguably wouldn't contribute to my credibility if I added that we had misappropriated documents from Mason & McGant. "All information suggests that my husband was slowly unravelling secret activities that were taking place at his firm. I find it quite remarkable, to put it mildly, that both he and Sandra died under suspicious circumstances. I believe there is enough circumstantial evidence to reopen the investigation," I ended my plea.

The detective sounded weary. "Mrs Smits, I informed you some time ago that there was nothing suspicious about your husband's death. We've done various investigations and tests. Your husband died as a result of a nasty fall."

"What about Sandra?" I protested. "Doesn't it strike you as odd that she got hit by a tram in broad daylight? It doesn't make any sense. Shouldn't there be a more detailed inquiry to determine the precise circumstances of her death?"

"I've heard of this accident," the detective responded. "My colleague was in charge of the case. I can assure you that he's laboriously examined everything and gleaned information from various sources, but nothing suspicious came out of it. With this in mind, I'm confident to say we can rule out any criminal wrongdoing."

I felt the conversation slipping through my fingers, but I wanted to do everything in my power to persuade him to start another investigation. "What about the red knickers my husband wore when he was found? You have to admit there's something not right about that."

"Well," he said, laughing. "Wearing a pair of ladies knickers certainly wouldn't float my boat, but who am I to judge? You're not suggesting your husband was killed over some ladies knickers, are you?"

I shook my head. He didn't understand me and I started wondering if the police had botched the investigation. Wasn't there such a thing as tunnel vision, where they'd cross off theories too early?

I pressed my face against the window to check up on Tim who was still inside. Then I turned around and rested my back against the cool glass. "Who was the detective on Sandra's case?"

"Unfortunately, I can't reveal that kind of information," the detective replied.

I was considering informing the man about the threatening note I'd received at home, but I knew it would be pointless. I'd failed to hold on to it, something I now deeply regretted.

I bowed my head, as if admitting defeat. There was nothing more I could think of to say. "Thank you for your time."

"I wish I could help you more in this hour of need. You take care, Mrs Smits."

I hung up and kicked a pebble that landed against the shed with a sharp tap.

I lowered myself onto one of the garden chairs that I'd recently taken out of the shed, all excited over the sudden arrival of spring, but jumped up swearing when I realised that my trousers had become soaked.

I wrapped my arms around myself as I stood outside, musing over the phone call. On second thought, maybe the detective was right and I was establishing imaginary links. Admittedly, I'd recently concluded myself that there was no substantial evidence whatsoever linking Oliver's death to Mason & McGant. Undoubtably, if the police were to dig around the place, something would come to light that could be frowned upon, but a firm committing murders and sending lawyers after people was an utterly ludicrous suggestion.

I wiped my feet on the mat and went back inside.

"Mummy," Tim yelled, running towards me. I sank down on my knees as he threw himself into my arms. I held him tightly and forgot about all the worries in my life for a brief moment.

He wriggled himself loose. "I want a biscuit."

"Can I have a biscuit?" I corrected him.

He repeated my words, after which I praised him. "C'mon." I lifted him up and planted him onto one of the kitchen stools, something he hadn't been allowed to do before.

Excitement started spreading across his face.

"Can you sit by yourself?" I asked and cautiously let go of him.

He nodded and beamed with pride, his legs wiggling with delight. I grabbed my phone to take a picture of him to send to Oliver, until I realised that it was no longer possible. And then out of the blue, I was overwhelmed with a feeling of grief, as raw and fierce as it had been months ago.

Before I could hold them back, tears were rolling down my cheeks.

"Mummy ouch?"

I explained to Tim that I missed his father and asked him tentatively if he ever thought about Daddy. I wanted so desperately for him to keep vivid memories of Oliver, but I knew he was too young.

He looked at me with eyes wide open and nodded yes. I didn't often break down in his presence, but this time I couldn't help it.

I pulled myself together, smiled, and gave Tim a pat on his head, after which I handed him the promised biscuit and filled up the kettle.

Tim nibbled on his biscuit, his little legs sticking horizontally over the edge of the stool while I waited for the water to boil, my thoughts straying to Sandra's death. Her husband had told me over the phone that she'd been hit by tram twelve. But had it really been an accident or was there foul play involved? Detective Armstrong hadn't been the one assigned to the case and wasn't willing to share with me which colleague it was. I was prepared to pull out all the stops to uncover the truth about Sandra's collision, in order to determine whether I was in danger or not. But if I didn't know which investigator was on the case, how could I find out more?

Once the kettle had boiled, I made a cup of tea for myself and Tim. I added some cold water in Tim's cup and then put it in front of him.

Suddenly I had an idea.

I took my phone from my pocket and called Sandra's mobile. Her husband had presumably heard more about the circumstances in which she died.

But to my great disappointment, I heard an unknown voice say the number no longer existed. Sandra's husband evidently must have ended her phone contract.

I sat down on a stool opposite Tim and took a sip. "Isn't this nice, the two of us sitting together?" I asked rhetorically. "You're getting so big, baby. Daddy would have been as proud as peacock," I said and to my surprise, found myself not feeling sad or gloomy.

My thoughts wandered off again and I realised that I didn't know anything about Sandra's life that could provide a lead to work with – her husband's surname, her address, the gym she was a member of or an employer.

Tim rolled around onto his belly and let himself slide down the stool. "I want to play."

I was about to say 'sure' when on the spur of the moment an idea came to me. I was grasping at straws, but there'd be no harm in giving it a try.

"Tim? Mummy has a surprise for you." There was something I knew he enjoyed, but we only did once in a blue moon. "Would you like to take a ride on the tram with Mummy?"

He threw his chubby, little arms in the air. "Yeah," he yelled and started running in circles around the room in sheer excitement.

I smiled. "Come on, sweetheart, let's put on your coat."

After pulling on my jacket too, I opened the front door and Tim stepped outside, his tiny legs moving cautiously over the doorstep. Then I realised that I didn't have a snack with me to keep him quiet if he needed distraction. "Wait here. I'll be right back, baby," I said, and turned towards the kitchen.

Moments later I returned to the front door only to find out Tim was no longer where I'd left him.

I looked left and right, calling out his name, but he was nowhere to be seen. It wasn't a busy street that we lived on, but it made me feel uneasy. Tim was far too young to be out by himself.

I scurried about a hundred metres to the left, where I got to an intersection. "Tim, where are you?" I yelled. The air was cold and crisp and the sun was shining in the bright, blue sky – little white clouds of vapour were rising from my mouth each time I called out his name. With my hand above my eyes, I peered down both ends of the side street, but with the exception of a single walker, I didn't see a soul. I felt like an idiot, I couldn't believe I'd let him out of my sight.

I turned around and rushed back over the pavement, passing my house, and continued my way to the next side street. I checked both directions, but this part of the neighbourhood was filled with little shops and coffee bars with their trendy chalkboards full of cheerful messages blocking my view of the pavement. After moments of dithering, I decided to return home and devise a plan from there, my heart skittering in my chest.

As I ran into my street again, I noticed my upstairs neighbour step out of her front door. She had presumably seen me running around the neighbourhood. "What's wrong, Jennifer?" she asked kindly.

I clung on to her, feeling distraught and bewildered. "Timmy's gone. He ran off." I barely managed to check my tears.

She wrapped a woollen scarf around her neck and closed the door behind her. "I'm sure he won't be far. I'll help you look for him."

"Thank you," I whispered.

She pointed into the direction of the Vondelpark. "I'll go that way. Maybe you can check the playground," she suggested. "He may have gone there."

I felt stupid for not thinking of that myself. "I will."

I rushed across the road and headed for his favourite playground.

It was probably less than a minute later when something happened behind me. I can't recall what I heard first – it's quite possible that it took place simultaneously – the piercing shriek of my neighbour that vibrated through my heart or the sound of a car coming to a screeching halt.

I turned abruptly. "Tim!" I screamed at the top of my lungs. As fast as my legs could carry me, I ran in the direction of the sound, my legs nearly buckling under me.

As I turned the corner, I saw a car halted in the middle of the road. A red pushbike was lying on its side in front of the car, a dent clearly visible in the bumper. My neighbour stood over the bike with a look of concern on her face.

I came to a stop, brought my hands to my cheeks and froze. "Oh God, no," I whispered. "This can't be happening."

I could see the car driver getting out of his car, looking as pale as a ghost, covering his mouth with his hand.

Somehow, I was able to move again and managed to sprint towards the scene of the accident. When I almost got there, I saw a child lying on his back in the road, in front of the car. The boy with the blond curls slowly clambered to his feet and started crying. My dear neighbour wrapped her arms around him and held him gently.

Despite the short distance, I was out of breath when I arrived.

"He had a narrow escape," the neighbour said softly and passed Tim to me. "That car missed him by a hair's breadth."

Tim wrapped his arms around me and started balling his eyes out. I gently stroked his back, whispering words of comfort into his ear.

The driver came up to us, a disconcerted look still written across his face. "I'm terribly sorry," he muttered. "The boy hurtled across the road out of nowhere."

I looked at the man. "It's my fault." I wiped away tears from my face. "I should have kept a closer eye on him."

I noticed the neighbour exchanging a look of understanding with the motorist. "Perhaps he's a bit too young to be playing outside alone."

"Of course he is," I responded defensively. "I never let him out by himself. We were about to leave the house and then I forgot to bring something with me and then …" I broke off and shook my head, trying to collect myself. "Never mind."

I put Tim down as he'd stopped crying by now, and inspected him. To my relief, he seemed to be unharmed.

The man spoke again. "Well if he's alright, I'll be leaving now." He gave Tim a pat on the back of his head. "No more cycling on the road for you, young fellow."

Tim nodded, his face all red and swollen from weeping.

"I'm so sorry for all this fuss," I said.

The driver raised his hand, got into his car and continued on his way.

I put Tim on his pushbike, thanked my neighbour extensively and hurried home, my hand on Tim's back. I noticed my armpits were soaked when I spoke to him firmly. "Promise me, you'll never take off without mummy again."

He didn't react to my reprimand. "Mister had cookies."

I frowned. "What's that?"

"Mister had cookies. For Tim."

My heart started pounding and I felt sick.

I stopped the pushbike, squatted next to him and looked him in the eye. "Did a man tell you he had cookies for you?"

Tim nodded.

"Was it the man from the car?"

He shook his head. "Man with the hat. Tim had to come."

It felt as if my heart was going to burst out of my chest.

"Did a man with a hat tell you to come with him, and that you would get cookies from him?"

Tim lowered his eyes and slowly nodded. "Tim naughty?" He'd probably noticed the anguished expression on my face.

"Oh no, baby," I responded and pulled him into my arms. "No … Don't you worry, alright?" Then I let go of him and looked at him, my eyes piercing into his, innocent and trusting. "But please promise Mummy, you'll never – and I mean never, ever – talk to a stranger again. Alright?"

Once we arrived at our front door, I decided to exchange the pushbike for the buggy. As expected, Tim objected by stiffening up like a board and squealing like a pig, and it was only after I offered him a lollipop I managed to fix the straps and started walking towards the tram stop. Although the Baarsjes was a considerable distance away in the south of the city, I was lucky that the number twelve tram stopped less than a ten-minute's walk from our house.

It had started drizzling and I unfolded the hood of the buggy, so that Tim wouldn't get soaked, flipped the hood of my winter coat over my head and upped my pace. On the way to the tram stop I passed the numerous restaurants and coffee bars that Oliver and I had found so charming when we bought the house and where we'd spent many an hour with friends or just the two of us. I thought about the implication of Tim's remarks – it seemed there had been someone who had tried to lure him or even abduct him. Should I interpret this event as a warning directed at me or did it have nothing to do with my search? Was it in any way related to the threatening letter that I'd recently received at home?

There was, of course, the possibility that Tim's imagination had gotten the better of him, but in any case, it made me feel unsafe and jittery.

We arrived at the Museumplein stop, where the atmosphere changed from residential to tourist. Around me I heard people chatting in foreign languages, taking pictures of the points of interest surrounding us. I was glad my hood was partly shielding my face and hoped it would prevent visitors from asking me directions.

Tim jumped up in his seat at every tram that arrived at the stop. "This one?" he'd exclaim, and I smiled and told him "not yet".

After I'd seen tram twelve pop up in the distance, we got on and I prudently walked towards the front of the tram, pushing the buggy ahead of me, and braced myself as the vehicle started to move.

Due to the dreary weather, there were fortunately few tourists in the tram, and I managed to put the buggy away from the aisle on its brakes.

The tram driver's head was about half a metre away from me, his hair thinning considerably and exposing the white of his scalp here and there, and I felt the tension in my stomach rising. I glanced at Tim, who seemed to be enjoying himself, feasting his eyes on the scenery that flashed past the windows, and decided to approach the man casually.

"Sir, may I ask you something?"

"Yes, miss," the driver answered, his gaze still on the track.

I pretended to be unfamiliar in the city and asked him if the tram would make a stop on the street where Sandra had been involved in the accident.

"It goes quite a long way over it. Where exactly do you need to be?" he asked.

Off the top of my head I tried to come up with something that was nearby and gave the name of a hardware store.

The man, who looked like he was in his fifties, turned his head towards me and gave me an inquisitive gaze. Then he turned his eyes back to the track again. "In that case you'll need to get off at the third stop," he replied, his face flashing with pride, presumably from knowing the map of Amsterdam by heart.

"Thank you, sir," I said, raising my thumb.

The tram drew to a halt at the next stop where a large number of passengers exited.

"Nice weather all of a sudden, isn't it," I said with a mock serious face, lingering at the front of the tram and trying to strike up a conversation.

The driver pressed a button to close the doors, checked his mirrors and gently accelerated. "Tell me about it. It's been chucking it down nonstop for the past hour," he responded. "Oh well, I'm locked up in this beast anyway." The driver, who must have weighed over a hundred kilograms, gave a deep-throated laugh, his belly shaking under his blue uniform.

Tim started fussing in his buggy. "Hush darling," I said as I rummaged in my bag, relieved to find a second lollipop. It was against my principles to keep him quiet with unhealthy food, but lately I found myself throwing these good intentions out of the window.

"I heard about that accident with the cyclist and a tram the other day through the grapevine. Wasn't it just awful?" I gave a gasp and covered my mouth with my hand like a second-rate actress in an am-dram trying to simulate shock.

"Yes, someone told me about it during my lunch break." The man shook his head. "How awful."

"Awful," I echoed his words flatly.

He looked at me for a moment. "It affects us all, you know. A horrific accident like that is a tram driver's worst nightmare."

"I'm sure it is."

The tram driver pressed his intercom and informed the passengers that we were almost arriving at the Vondelpark. He needed little encouragement to carry on speaking, feeding my need to find out more about the circumstances in which Sandra had died. "It happened in a flash, so I heard. I just don't understand people, they rush across the street in a hurry without looking and don't seem to realise what a giant a tram like that really is. If you get underneath it, you'll be smashed beyond recognition or repair, there'll be nothing left of you."

I closed my eyes, shook my head and tried to wipe the image of Sandra under the tram from my mind.

The doors opened again and a couple of people entered, whereupon the tram driver said "good morning". I moved over to let the passengers filter past.

My heart was beating faster as I worried the driver would start asking questions about me poking around, but I did my utmost to make my voice sound calm. "By the way, didn't that accident happen on this line? Number twelve?"

"You're right. Yes, my colleague Archie was on duty that day. Decent chap. We've known each other for years. Riding the tram was his life and soul, but now he's become a shell of a man. Spends his days at home now. From what I've heard, he can't get the accident out of his mind, poor sod."

It wasn't just horrible for Sandra and her family, but it had obviously taken a large toll on the driver, as he was presumably traumatised by the collision. "Oh gosh, that's dreadful," I coaxed, hoping for more details. I glanced at Tim, who had almost finished his lollipop. I was getting closer, but I needed to hurry up.

The driver shook his head. "The irony is, that it all happened just around the corner from that poor guy's house. So each time he goes out, even if it's just for a walk from his flat to the deli, he's reminded of the accident."

My ears pricked up at this point. "Is that so?" I mentioned the name of the street where the accident had supposedly taken place to the tram driver.

"He lives just around the corner from there, opposite that Turkish greengrocer who was recently mugged. Archie and his wife have a flat on the third floor. The children left the house years ago."

"Isn't that something," I whispered, imprinting this valuable piece of information to memory.

There was a pause as we were each caught up in our own thoughts, until Tim started whining and I turned my attention to him.

Even though I had achieved my goal, I didn't get off the tram until we arrived at the stop the driver had mentioned, in order not to raise suspicion.

I waved to the driver and pretended to walk away from the tram stop.

Once the tram was out of sight, I crossed the track to get to the other side of the road. "Tim, Mummy has surprise for you again," I chirped. "We're going to take another ride."

While I was waiting for the tram heading back home, I entered a number of search terms on my phone. It didn't take me long to find a local newspaper's item with a mention of a Turkish greengrocer recently robbed in broad daylight, not too far from where I was right now. On my digital map I saw that it was a side street from tram twelve's route and that there was a deli just around the corner. "Bingo," I exclaimed.

21

It was two days before I had the opportunity to take further action after discovering Archie's address. It had felt like a long wait as I was keen to pick the tram driver's brain, but then again, the delay had given me the chance to think about a sound approach.

As I turned the final corner before his house, I saw crates of fresh produce from the Turkish greengrocer on the pavement. I parked my bike on the opposite side of the road against a lamppost and inspected the various buildings, looking for nameplates, which unfortunately turned out to be absent. The first building – a large, family house – was ruled out immediately as I had been told Archie lived in a flat. The second building housed a company, but the third consisted of three flats.

I said a little prayer and rang the upper doorbell.

"Yes," a female voice barked through the intercom.

I could feel my tongue sticking to the roof of my mouth as I started to speak. "Good morning, my name is Doctor Van Dijk. I'm the company doctor at your husband's work. I've come to see how he's doing."

There was a silence on the other side.

I knew I took an immense risk – anything could go wrong. Perhaps an occupational health physician had already come by, or Archie would start asking questions and smell trouble. Worst-case scenario, I could end up losing my license. But as I thought it would be best to stay close to my own expertise as a health professional, I opted for this approach.

The woman pressed the buzzer without saying another word. I heard a click and subsequently pushed open the door.

I climbed the staircase to the third floor where a woman, who looked around fifty years old, with bouffant blond hair and copious amounts of makeup, was awaiting me in the doorway. She was wearing an old-fashioned beige blouse with prominent shoulder pads, covering an enormous bosom.

I reached out my hand to introduce myself and recalled my fake name just in

140

time.

"Maria van Daal," the woman responded.

She took my coat and hung it on a rack in the narrow hallway.

"Please follow me," she continued in a distinctive Amsterdam accent. "My husband is inside."

I followed her into the living room, where plain linoleum lined the floor, adorned by a tiger skin rug in the seating area. On one side of the room stood an antiquated oak dining table and four chairs, with a checked tablecloth. On the other side was a cream-coloured couch on which an older man was seated, his shoulders drooping and his eyes straying outside, through the net curtains.

My gaze lingered on a display cabinet containing various medals.

The woman appeared to have noticed. "He's an official darts champion. Every spare moment he has, he goes out for a game."

She looked with compassion at the broken man, who was still gazing without any expression on his face at the streets where life was a constant hustle. "Or rather, he used to play darts. Ever since the accident, he won't go out anymore. Doesn't feel like doing anything but sit on the couch – all day long."

The grief was almost tangible in the room and seemed to pass into my body, smothering me.

Her gaze returned to me. "Coffee?"

I gave a sigh. "That'd be lovely. With milk please."

She gestured to have a seat on the couch. "Archie," she said loudly and deliberately, as if he were deaf. "The doctor is here to see you."

The poor man turned his head into my direction and only now seemed to realise there was a visitor for him. "What? Oh, right."

I reached out my hand to introduce myself, but his gaze had already turned outside again. I retracted my hand and decided to sit down on the two-seater diagonally across from the man. The heating was presumably turned to its max, as it was almost tropically hot and stuffy in the room, and I felt little beads of sweat forming on my forehead.

I heard the antique clock ticking in the background while I was desperately searching for the right words to enter into dialogue, but as I was about to come up with something, the woman entered the room again, holding a tray in her hands containing two cups and saucers, a milk jug and a sugar bowl, all from the same floral china set. I wondered if she'd arranged this off the cuff, or whether it had been ready on the counter top, in the event of an unexpected guest showing up unannounced on their doorstep.

It was as if she'd read my mind. "It's not every day we welcome important visitors."

I gave her a smile.

She leaned over to place the tray on the glass coffee table and the brown fabric of her skirt stretched tight. She poured a cup for me and her husband. "I'll be in the kitchen if you need me."

I gave her a nod as a thank you, then poured a dash of milk in my coffee and stirred it with the polished silver spoon, while the man was still staring outside mutely, his cup of coffee untouched.

I took a sip of the hot beverage that tasted bitter, and cleared my throat. "Mr van Daal, how are you doing?"

He turned his head and looked into my eyes. "I'm all right, thank you doctor," he replied, but you didn't have to have a medical degree to see this was anything but the truth.

I nodded and thought of the most common complaint after a trauma. "How have you been sleeping?"

The man leaned over to pick up his coffee – it was the first time since I'd arrived that I'd seen him move. "Since the doctor prescribed me some pills, it's been better."

He took a sip of his coffee, placed the cup back on the colourful saucer on the coffee table, and looked away again. The miserable tram driver seemed to have little need for visitors, so I decided to get to the point. "Would you mind if I asked you a few questions about the accident?"

The man jolted his head towards me, his green eyes suddenly alert. "Are you from the police?"

I laid my hand on my chest. 'Me? Oh no," I stammered. "I'm a doctor."

The sudden level of vigilance had subsided and the man seemed to be lost in thought again. "I'm sure you are, love," he mumbled.

"Could you describe for me how the day of the accident exactly …"

He interrupted me, a fierce look in his eyes. "Why have you come here?" There was a hint of irritation in his voice. "The police already asked me these questions."

So the police had been here with him? They most likely performed a routine investigation, I concluded. "What kind of questions did they ask you?"

He shrugged and then spoke surly and cantankerously. "Things like whether I was paying attention at the time of the accident, what my speed was and if I obeyed the traffic rules." It dawned on me that the tram driver seemed to be afraid I wanted to put the blame on him.

I tried to reassure him. "Don't you worry, Archie. I've been informed that there is no blame attached to you," I mouthed in breathy, soothing tones, trying to bring a confident expression to my face. "I'd simply like to hear how you experienced the day. If we go over it together, it might trigger new memories. It's important for you to talk about the event with the people around you and with professionals so that you can work through this traumatic experience." I felt ashamed of this superficial jibber-jabber solely for my own benefit, although it did contain a grain of truth.

He shrugged indifferently.

I interpreted the gesture as an agreement to carry on. "Can you describe what your day looked like on the day that Sandra …" I corrected myself. "I mean, the cyclist, got hit by the tram?

He sighed deeply and then blew out the air ever so slowly before starting his narrative. "I was working the evening shift, which means you start at four in the afternoon and work until the last tram. Everyone knows these are the crappy shifts. You take the full evening rush hour, crowded trams with people tired from a day in the office, who are getting in each other's way. Just when things are getting quieter, around nine o'clock the scum come in. Cheeky bastards who intimidate each other, young kids who wanna ride the tram without paying the fare. Little blighters who should have been in bed long before, so they can go to school rested the next day. They've got weapons, knives, clubs, everything." He looked at me with an intense expression of exasperation. "A colleague of mine even had a gun to his head once."

I puffed out my cheeks and bulged my eyes to show I was both impressed and shocked.

The man looked away again and shook his head in cynicism. "A lot has changed in the thirty-eight years I've been a tram driver. The people these days just have no respect or manners."

He stirred his coffee absentmindedly. "Did you know I've been doing this work for so long?"

I shook my head as I took a sip of my coffee.

"I was twenty-one when I started. Was the youngest tram driver in the company," he boasted, puffing out his chest. "I was nearing forty years of loyal service. But that's all out of the window," he said, spitting out the words. "I'm never setting foot on one of those rotten trams ever again.

I felt a lump in my throat. "So you started your shift at four o'clock. What happened thereafter?"

"I was stationed on the number twelve, which starts its route at the train station. Rush hour came by as usual, lots of those overly-inflated-self-important desk jockeys leaving their offices by tram, heading to the station to take the train home, out of the city. Around half past seven it started to die down. All in all, everything was business as usual."

I felt my heartbeat accelerate. "Then what?"

Archie mentioned the name of the street on which I knew Sandra had been hit by the tram. "We were riding on this street, which is long and winding. We turned the corner – it's a rather dangerous part of the route as you can't see far ahead at this particular point. And right there …"

He broke off, stiffening before my eyes. The poor man needed a moment to compose himself.

"A woman on a green bicycle suddenly darted across the track," he said, rocking his body back and forth as if to console himself. "Just like that. It all happened in the briefest of moments. I hit the brakes hard – I kept pumping them with all my might." He looked at me pleadingly. "Believe me, I was doing everything I could to slow that beast down."

I gave a reassuring nod, my eyes fixated on the man, seated on the edge of the couch.

The tram driver shook his head violently. "But there was no stopping. She was so incredibly close and I simply had too much speed, too much momentum – I went straight for her. Before I knew it, my cabin had smashed into that poor, wretched woman. The look in her bulging eyes," he began, but the words died on his lips, as he brought his hands to his mouth. "It was utter, deathly fear. I'll never be able to erase that image from my mind."

I nodded, completely lost for words upon hearing this vivid description of Sandra's final moments.

"And the noise of the crash … it was beyond imagination. That thumping sound at the moment of impact mixed with the screeching of the brakes that were scraping the wheels. Every night that clash haunts me in my sleep." He squeezed his eyes shut and pressed his fist to his forehead as if to drive the gruesome sound out of his memory. "Immediately after, it felt like we were going over a bump. Poor lassie. That must have been …" Tears welled up in his eyes. "It must have been her body."

My head felt woozy and a wave of nausea washed over me. I turned my face away, struggling to draw in air. My voice sounded hoarse when I spoke. "You said she was riding a bicycle. Can you describe what happened? Did she intend to cross the track and simply made an error of judgement? Or perhaps the bicycle tire got stuck in the rails?" I asked, trying to keep my hands from shaking. "What happened?"

"I've gone over and over the order of events in my mind, but I haven't worked it out. I know for sure that the bicycle tyre didn't get stuck in the rails. She came out of nowhere from the right and scooted onto the track. Just like that, she was in my way," he muttered with anguish on his face and in his voice.

I wiped my forehead with the back of my hand. The heat in the room had become nearly unbearable. "Did you notice anything else?"

He chewed on the inside of his cheek. "It all went so fast." He pondered the question for a while before speaking again. "There's one thing that stayed with me. That poor woman's back was arched in an odd way, her body just seemed contorted."

I presumed that was a result of the impact of the vehicle. "You mean after the tram slammed into her?"

He shook his head. "See, that's the weird thing. This happened just before she hurtled across the track. She was unexpectedly accelerating, causing her upper body to bend backwards, as if at the very last moment she was pedalling with extra force. Or rather, as if someone else had given her an extra push."

The room started spinning violently, I could feel the blood rushing through my veins. The dizziness made me grab the couch and hold onto it tightly.

"Ah well … What's the point in going over all of this again?" a voice from far away sounded. "We won't ever be able to change anything."

I slowly came to my senses. "Thank you," I stammered. "You explained everything very well."

I couldn't endure the suffocating heat in here for one more minute. "I need to leave. All the best to you, Archie," I said and quickly rose to my feet.

"But wait," the man yelled. "What about my sick report and all that?" he asked.

I could have kicked myself when I realised I had completely broken character. "Right. Don't you worry about that for the time being," I said and managed to muster up a reassuring smile. "My colleague will contact you in due time about a reintegration plan," I added, praying to god I wasn't too far off.

I once again wished the man all the best and then left the living room.

In the hallway, I said goodbye to the woman who seemed to be preparing lunch in the kitchen and pulled my coat off the rack.

I dashed down the stairs until I reached the pavement where I halted, took a deep breath of fresh air and slowly began to calm down.

As the traffic rushed by, I let my mind go over what the tram driver had just shared with me – Sandra had been arching her back in a strange way just before the moment of impact. Was it possible that someone might have intentionally pushed Sandra onto the track as the tram advanced around the corner?

Maybe I was becoming delusional and this was just an unfortunate, fatal accident after all. I had to entertain the possibility that Sandra herself had been pedalling extra hard as she saw the tram approach her, in a final and failed attempt to go past it. It seemed pretty unlikely for someone who lived in the city and had a great deal of experience with trams, but I couldn't rule out this benign explanation.

I remembered the words Lindsey had said during our drinks with the girls. If Sandra had indeed been bumped off by the firm for what she'd discovered, then I could very well be in danger too. The letter I'd received might after all have been an intentional warning directed at me. And what about Tim, who claimed to have been lured by a man with cookies – was there a direct connection to all of this or was that just a figment of a toddler's imagination? Finally, the man in the playground, who so eagerly engaged in a conversation with me, was this stranger dispatched to keep an eye on me or was it just an ordinary flirt? All these events could be dismissed with an innocent explanation, but I felt increasingly nervous about the whole situation.

I reached into my pocket and found the card with the well-known logo that the man had handed me. I hadn't ever intended to reach out to him, but perhaps I should give him a call, if only to confirm that his intentions were harmless and genuine, so I could rule out any foul play. Besides, as he worked for Mason & McGant, he might be able to be of assistance and provide me with more leads.

I grabbed my phone and entered the digits.

He answered in a brisk, business-like tone. "Daniel Bernstein."

"Er …" I stammered. "Hi. This is Jennifer Smits."

There was a pause and I started pondering how many women this guy dished out his card to. "We recently met in the playground?"

The tone in his voice changed. "Right, of course. I remember now. So sorry. How nice of you to give me a call, Jennifer."

"I was wondering how you'd feel about having a cup of coffee together?"

"Sounds marvellous. I'm not available during the day though, I'm swamped at the firm. How about we grab a bite together instead? My treat."

I was surprised by his thorough approach. "Oh … okay then, sure."

"How about tomorrow evening?"

I wasn't sure if I felt comfortable bringing Tim to my parents again – he'd been on more sleepovers in the last few months than over the previous two years combined, although both he and my parents seemed to take pleasure in it. Perhaps Oliver's death had indirectly made space for a deepening of other relationships Tim had with the people around him.

"Sounds great."

"How would eight o'clock at 'Home' suit you? It's a restaurant in the city centre."

"That works for me. I'll see you then."

As we hung up, I felt the fluttering of butterflies in my stomach and a surge of adrenaline racing through my body. For the first time since my relationship with Oliver I was going on a date again. I let out a whoop of excitement and watched a passer-by look at me in wonderment.

I called myself to order – it was imperative I stayed focused and vigilant.

22

The doorbell rang. I put the dishcloth on the counter, walked towards the hallway and opened the door.

"Hello Mum," I said with a smile and stepped aside to make room.

My mother entered the hallway, rubbing her hands. "Hello darling," she said, gave me a peck on the cheek and slid her arms out of her grey woollen coat. Just when everyone thought we wouldn't have a proper winter this year, a cold front had suddenly crossed the country. Her eyes widened. "You look absolutely beautiful."

My father, who followed in her wake, mumbled something similar.

I smoothed the black silk dress that I'd immediately ordered after the phone call with Dan yesterday. "Thank you," I responded and closed the door.

We entered the warm living room, where Tim sat, eyes fixed on the television screen.

"How wonderful you're going on a date," my mother said and squeezed my arm.

I smiled and walked around the kitchen island to the sink where I'd just cleaned up the remains of the diner I'd prepared for Tim. My mother followed me and sat down on a kitchen chair.

"So tell me. How long have you known this man for?"

I wiped down the luxuriously thick granite countertop with a dishcloth. I'd have liked a more industrial look using concrete, but Oliver preferred the classic look and I'd acquiesced. I popped a tablet in the dispenser of the dishwasher and turned it on. "I only just met him," I said casually, but as I uttered the words, I realised what the implications were. Was I making a huge mistake meeting up with this Dan, because, in all fairness – what did I really know about the guy?

"We recently met in the playground," I continued and omitted on purpose where he worked.

My father had taken a seat next to Tim on the couch and seemed to have developed a sudden interest in children's programmes.

"Lovely," my mother responded, oblivious to my sudden disquietude about the whole thing. "Who would have thought you could meet someone there. I suppose he also has a child then?"

"Yes. He's divorced and has a daughter." I held up the kettle, trying to steer the exchange onto an easier subject. "Tea?"

"No, thank you darling. We won't be staying long, otherwise it will become too late for Timmy," she said and I smiled at her concern.

My father had apparently overheard more of the conversation than I was aware of, given the alarmed look he shot at me from the other side of the room. "Will you be careful, love? There are so many crazy people nowadays. Just look out for yourself and stay alert."

Under normal circumstances I'd have given an inaudible sigh, smiled and uttered, 'Yes, dad,' but the threatening events of the past few weeks suddenly made me nervous.

I bit my lip. "Will you keep an eagle eye on Tim while he's at your place?"

My mother looked up completely nonplussed. "Yes of course. We always do, you know that, right darling?"

I nodded, but still wasn't feeling reassured. "Just please don't let him out of your sight, okay?"

My mother opened her mouth to respond, but at the same moment, Tim roared as my father turned off the television, which distracted her. I got up and corrected Tim, telling him to say hello to his grandparents.

Tim's face lit up as he threw himself into my mother's arms. "Nana," he yelled.

My father watched the scene, visibly moved. "Are you coming to stay with us again tonight, you big boy?"

His proposal went down well with Tim, as he scampered like an overgrown puppy.

I headed to the hallway and handed Tim's suitcase, which I'd already packed, to my mother. I gave Tim a warm hug and then passed him onto to my father, who carried Tim out on his arm.

After they'd left, I walked up to the mirror in the bathroom and stared at my reflection. I squared my shoulders and felt a rush of strength and confidence run through me. If they thought they could intimidate me, they had another think coming.

I touched up my makeup, checked my outfit and set off.

A little while later I parked my bike by a tree flanking the canal. I felt a slight tickle in my stomach as I tottered over the cobblestones towards the entrance of the restaurant where I was meeting Dan.

As fate would have it, seconds before arriving at the entrance, one of my stiletto heels got caught between the little stones. I slammed forward and smacked my upper body against the glass door. I managed to regain my balance and straightened my back, rubbing my sore shoulder, and swiftly opened the door, feverishly hoping no one had noticed my undignified arrival.

At the counter I asked for Daniel Bernstein and a blonde waitress told me to follow her.

As we were heading towards the back of the restaurant, I saw Dan seated at one of the tables, wearing a green shirt with a well-ironed collar, his hair styled with the intent to look dishevelled. A mixture of nerves and excitement ran through me as Dan's gaze locked onto me as I approached. How could I not have noticed when we first met that he was so incredibly attractive?

As I arrived at the table, Dan stood up and I saw that despite my high heels, he was quite a bit taller. "Hello Jennifer," he said and kissed me on the cheek. His freshly shaven, pronounced jaw ever so lightly brushed against my face, a waft of Hugo Boss drifting into my nostrils, and a warm feeling passed through my belly.

Dan stealthily ran his eyes over me. "You look amazing."

I fluttered my eyelashes and smiled, taking a seat opposite him, while the waitress asked what we'd like to drink.

I cast an inquiring glance at Dan, who apparently hadn't ordered yet.

"How about we start the evening with a glass of champagne?" he suggested.

Although it probably wasn't wise considering my empty stomach, I couldn't resist. "Sounds great," I replied.

Dan turned his attention to the waitress. "Two glasses please. And some bread with garlic butter."

The blonde girl noted our order and left.

Dan casually ran a hand through his shiny wavy hair, his almond-shaped brown eyes locking onto mine, and straightened his shirt with a smile on his face. I thought about the suggestion that he was sent by Mason & McGant to follow me to determine how much I knew. Was he assigned with the task of assessing whether I could be a potential threat to the office? Now that Dan was sitting before me, his face open and friendly, it seemed like a preposterous idea.

"How was your day?" I started the conversation lightly.

He puffed his cheeks. "Bu-sy. The firm just keeps on stacking files onto my desk," he said, rolling his eyes and then giving me a wink.

I thought of Oliver and raised my eyebrows. "I know all about that."

He didn't respond to my comment and waved his hand. "Anyway. All of that doesn't matter now that I'm here with you." He laid his forearms on the table and leaned forward with a huge grin on his face. "Tell me something about yourself, Jennifer. I'm curious to learn more. What kind of work do you do?"

The waitress returned with our order, together with two menus, and then retreated.

We clinked our glasses. "To a wonderful evening," Dan said, gazing into my eyes.

I recalled my mission and smiled sensually before sipping my champagne with a delicate motion, letting it flow smoothly. "Mmm, delicious," I said. I resolved not to drink too hastily and put the glass down in front of me.

"I'm a doctor," I answered his earlier question. "I've had my own practice in Amsterdam-West for a number of years now, together with a colleague." I made a funny face. "The bad part of town." Being a doctor in a poorer, disadvantaged neighbourhood usually intrigued people when I mentioned it, and I made a guess that he'd fall for it too.

He raised his chin and squinted. "General practitioner. I can see you in that kind of role. You seem like a socially-engaged type."

"Oh really? Is that so?" I purred. I took a sip of champagne and licked my lips while I continued to look intently at him. "Perhaps I am."

I repressed the urge to keep touching my hair to make sure it was still in proper shape and went on. "While everyone around me was doubting what they wanted to do with their lives, I actually knew from the age of fourteen I was going to study medicine. It gets into your blood after a while."

He seemed fascinated. "Is this part of a long family tradition?"

I thought of my parents and laughed. "No, not at all," I replied and decided to leave it at that for now. "A few years ago I was given the opportunity to become co-owner of the practice and I absolutely love it. You can really make a difference, particularly in a deprived neighbourhood," I added, although that term was actually no longer fully applicable to the now up-and-coming area where my practice was located.

He nodded. "That makes sense. I'm sure your profession must be very rewarding."

"Absolutely," I said truthfully. I talked more about how I'd had a hard time at work in recent months, but that I'd found a renewed sense of motivation – all the while the champagne was going down rather quickly. I'd had a firm intention not to drink too hastily, but the tension over the date caused me to fail miserably.

The waitress came to take our order. While Dan requested a tournedos and a glass of Merlot, I glanced at the menu and decided to opt for the salmon with a glass of the same wine.

"How about we share a bottle?" Dan proposed.

A bottle was really too much for me, but I didn't want to be a bad sport and so I replied it was fine.

The waitress scrawled everything onto the paper and left us again.

Dan began to talk about the fact that he'd recently attended a wine tasting course and how he'd learned to appreciate all the differences in flavours there were. As he kept chatting, I noticed how I was gracefully slanting my head, supporting it with one hand, while every now and then daintily flipping my hair over my shoulder, keeping my eyes fixated on his. I smiled at myself – it had been years since I'd been flirting like this, going to great lengths to charm him. It was as if these rusty gestures had been stowed away safely all this time, to be finally taken down from the attic and polished up again.

"Don't you think?" I suddenly heard Dan ask, his index finger slowly circling the rim of his wine glass.

I snapped to attention. "Er …" I stammered and considered the option of answering in the affirmative. "I'm sorry, I got distracted for a moment," I confessed, my cheeks flushing.

He laughed. "Am I that boring?"

"Quite the opposite," I assured him. I laid my hand on his bare arm, where the sleeves of his shirt were rolled up. It was an intimate gesture that evoked both a sense of guilt towards Oliver and a sensual desire deep down, leaving me feeling confused.

"I was just dreaming away," I said, with an expression on my face that was supposed to reflect both charm and shyness. His hair tickled my fingertips, which seemed more sensitive than usual, sending a rush of heat through me.

He laughed again, louder this time. "It's okay. It's probably not that fascinating, this obsession of mine with wine." The corner of his mouth rose mischievously. "You're quite the dreamy type, aren't you? Considering your arrival here tonight."

I stared at him in horror. Did he perhaps …?

He grinned. "I saw you stumble your way in here earlier," he explained. "And smack against the window," he added, giving the final blow.

I almost spat out my wine. "Oh my goodness, you saw that?" I lowered my head into my hands, feeling a wave of red creep up my neck until my cheeks flamed. Then I looked at him warily. "How utterly mortifying."

"Don't worry about it." He peeled my hands off my face and held them in his, which felt soft. "You're very cute when you're embarrassed, do you know that?"

The soft brush of his hands on my skin made me feel floaty and warm and alive. Only now did I realise how much I'd missed being touched by someone.

I came to my senses. "Okay stop now," I insisted, shaking my head and smiling. "Different topic," I persevered in an attempt to steer the conversation towards safer ground. "Tell me how a tease like you ended up in the legal profession?"

He released my hands and I pulled them back, smoothing my dress. "My father was a construction worker, something he always enjoyed," he said, now serious again, and I noticed a sense of pride in his attitude. "At the age of forty-two he was involved in an industrial accident, which left him permanently incapacitated and unable to work."

"How awful."

Dan nodded. "The company he worked for tried to put the blame on him so that they wouldn't have to cough up the compensation money. He was lucky to meet a good pro bono lawyer who felt a real passion for his work – he helped get justice for my dad and a respectable pay-out. Without that man things would have turned out very differently."

The waitress brought the bottle of Merlot to our table. Dan peered at me questioningly, but I rejected his offer to test the wine, knowing that he'd probably be a better judge of it.

He seemed satisfied with the bottle and after our glasses were filled, we toasted to a wonderful evening. Dan glanced at me with an intense look as he took a sip, smacking his lips.

He continued his story. "I witnessed that lawyer making his argument in court. He went the whole nine yards to get the most out of it for my father – that's when I knew I wanted to be able to do what he did."

"Wow, that's an impressive and inspiring story," I said and took a sip of my wine. "So how did you go from wanting to be a world-enhancing pro bono lawyer to ending up at a pocket-filling firm like Mason & McGant?" I teased.

Dan laughed. "*Touché*." He lifted his shoulder in a half shrug. "Well, somewhere over the last twenty years, that memory has faded, I guess. I've been seduced by the real money," he admitted, and gave a wink before changing the topic. "Do you have a babysitter at home watching Tim tonight?"

The glass of champagne on my empty stomach had loosened my tongue. "He's staying with my parents tonight," I replied, gauging his reaction, until I was hit by a hint of shame. Surely I couldn't be flirting with someone this soon after Oliver's death, let alone with one of his erstwhile colleagues?

He raised his eyebrows and I noticed a little scar running across one of them. "I see."

I couldn't put a stop to another wave of desire moving through my body –

this man was unbelievably irresistible.

"What about Bella?"

"Bella?" His sultry mood instantly seemed to vanish. "Er … No, she's with her mother."

I nodded and quickly chatted on to dispel the uncomfortable feeling that lurked among us, wondering if I'd said something to upset him. "My parents have been an enormous support ever since Oliver died. I don't know what I'd do without them, and without my upstairs neighbour," I added laughing. "Tim frequently visits her for an hour or so."

"It must be wonderful to be surrounded by people like that. You're very fortunate." The friendly tone from before had returned.

He slowly leaned forward and my breath quickened. "And I'm fortunate to have a date with a beautiful woman like you." He was quite the smooth operator. "I'm glad you called me. It's been wonderful so far getting to know you better."

I looked at him with a grin on my face as I finished my glass of Merlot. "Same here."

We fell quiet for a moment. The wine seemed to be clouding my thought process and the man opposite me was making my head spin, distracting me from my goal, but suddenly I remembered why I was here.

My palms were feeling sweaty and my heart started to pound. I had to bring it up.

I cleared my throat. "You seem like a really great guy, Dan. But that's not the sole reason I reached out to you."

A wrinkle formed between his large, black brows.

"I was wondering …" It felt so ridiculous to bring this up that I didn't dare. I waved my hand. "Ah, never mind."

"No, go on," he insisted. His uncertain smile was veiled by a friendly tone in his voice. "What did you want to ask me?"

I scratched my forehead and then decided to jump right in. "Dan, have you been sent to me by Mason & McGant?"

He tilted his head, a look of bafflement spreading across his face. "Are you asking if I came here straight from the firm? No, I went home first to freshen up."

I shook my head. "No, that's not what I meant." I folded my arms and rested them on the table, looking him straight in the eyes. "Did the firm send you after me to find out how much I know?" I tried to read every emotion in his face, while the question was sinking in.

He now laughed, but seemed on guard. "Why would they have sent me after you? I don't think anyone there even knows about our date." His expression suddenly changed. "Oh wait. Now I know what you're getting at. You mean because you were Oliver's wife?"

He took the bottle of wine from the caddy and held it up questioningly.

I shook my head and he only refilled his own glass. I decided to remain quiet to see where this was going.

Dan leaned back, holding his glass of Merlot loosely in his hand and looked up in the air as he spoke again. "I actually hadn't thought about it like that." He turned his gaze towards me. "Do you reckon they'd find it inappropriate for me to date the wife of a deceased colleague?" He seemed to ponder it for a moment and then shook his head. "Anyway," he said lightly. "Ultimately, it seems a matter for you and me to decide on. Nobody else has any say in it, don't you think?"

I closely examined the man opposite of me – he didn't seem to understand at all what I was getting at. Or was he just bluffing, pretending not to know what I was insinuating?

Dan seemed to have left the subject behind and declared in a matter-of-fact tone that he was hungry.

I was driving myself crazy, I concluded. This man knew nothing about any treacherous actions – it was a closed case. Dan seemed to be genuinely interested in me. It was obvious I had become paranoid as a result of all the snooping around at Mason & McGant.

I rested my hand back on his forearm, gently patted it, while I leaned over and smiled. "You're right. It's nobody's business whether we're dating or not," I said in a whisper. I floundered in a sea of shame and guilt towards Oliver, yet at the same time it felt fantastic to be admired again by someone after months of being only a mother and a widow. I decided I was going to enjoy it while it lasted.

He looked ardently at me for some seconds longer, slowly bringing his face closer to mine, releasing a handful of happy butterflies fluttering through my stomach. I could feel the warmth of his breath as his mouth came closer and closer, his lips almost brushing mine, when I bowed my head. However much I revelled in Dan's company, he was moving too fast.

Suddenly I heard a little cough behind me and I looked up.

"Your order." The blonde waitress stood at the table carrying two plates in her hands.

Over the following hours we enjoyed delicious food and wine and talked endlessly, discovering we had so many things in common. Dan paid the bill, after a somewhat feeble and fruitless objection on my part.

Once outside, I noticed it had cooled down considerably and I shivered, rueing my decision to wear a summer coat.

Dan leaned in towards to me. He gently rubbed my upper arms with his hands. His brown eyes seemed to sparkle as he spoke. "Would you like to have a drink at my place?"

I heard my father's words echo in my head.

'Will you be careful, love? There are so many crazy people nowadays.'

I gazed into Dan's eyes and found myself inching towards him – somehow I felt he could be trusted. "All right." I raised my index finger. "One drink."

I walked towards my bike and fished the key out of my handbag. The canal was awfully close and I wasn't sure whether it was the anticipation of going home with Dan or the alcohol that made my fingers tremble. I planted my feet on the cobblestones as firmly as possible considering my high heels and ignored the little voice in the back of my mind that said 'this is all going too fast'.

We cycled together towards his neighbourhood and after arriving, we ascended the nearly hundred-year-old stone stairs to his flat, with beautiful double-hung sash windows in the typical Amsterdam Art Deco style. After stepping inside, Dan took my coat and we entered the living room.

Three walls were painted in a light grey shade, the wall opposite was decorated with mirrored tiles, creating the illusion of more space than there actually was. I noticed the flat contained many authentic details, forming a pleasant contrast to the sleek, light-coloured Scandinavian furniture. There was a white three-seater sofa, two upholstered seats and an ultramodern plastic armchair in the shape of a sphere. "Fancy a glass of port?" I heard behind me.

I swivelled. "Make it a small one."

While Dan popped into the kitchen, I ambled through the room, letting my eyes wander. The walls were bare, with the exception of a neoclassical painting that adorned the restored, original mantelpiece. The house was different to what I'd imagined – something seemed to be missing, but I couldn't quite put my finger on it.

Dan returned with two glasses of port and handed me the smaller one.

We clinked our glasses and took a sip.

"Nice flat," I said, and then I suddenly realised what it was. "Where are Bella's pictures?"

He looked at me with a blank expression for a brief moment. "Pictures? Oh, right. I haven't hung them up yet. I only moved in a couple of months ago, you know. After the divorce I rented something temporarily before looking to buy something."

I raised an eyebrow. It didn't look like Dan had just taken up residence in this place. Even the finest details such as candles on the dresser were attended to. "It's actually looking absolutely perfect."

He looked at me mysteriously. "Shall I tell you a secret?"

A sickening feeling crept into my stomach and the hairs on the back of my neck bristled with tingly trepidation – I had uncovered enough secrets lately.

"I didn't do this myself," he said smilingly and let his eyes wander through the living room. "I hired an interior designer to decorate the place, an old friend of mine. The first thing I did when I got the keys to this house was ring her up." A laugh broke from his chest – he was completely oblivious to the apprehension I'd felt to his words. "I'm a complete mess when it comes to home decoration. I couldn't even match a sofa with curtains. My ex-wife did all of that."

I gave a nervous titter with relief.

He raised his shoulders. "Ah well. I'm not ashamed of hiring someone else to furnish the place for me. You have to acknowledge your weaknesses, right?" he said, showing that gorgeous smile of his. "Besides, I think she's done a brilliant job."

I nodded.

He drew closer to me and gave me a mischievous grin. "Since we're talking about the flat – would you like to see upstairs?"

I felt the smile stiffen on my face and turned away, panic welling up inside me. How on earth was I supposed to handle this?

He flinched away, presumably having noticed my hesitations. "I'm sorry. Am I going too fast?"

I coughed, feeling flustered.

He regained his composure and laughed charmingly. "I sometimes misread the signs when I like someone."

"No … No! It's not you," I hurried to say.

He leaned against the cupboard, crossed his legs at the ankle, hands in his pockets, and waited for me to resume speaking.

I scratched my neck, desperately searching for the right words to describe how I felt. "Oliver died just six months ago …" My voice trailed off, I'd lost my thread.

He filled in the blanks. "You shouldn't be afraid of what other people think. Nobody can tell you when it's the right moment for you to er …" he said. "Do you find it too fast yourself?"

"No, I guess not," I replied.

But perhaps I did. I let out a sigh. If I wanted to give this relationship a real chance to work, I should be honest with Dan. "I don't know. It's hard." The many glasses of alcohol I'd consumed over the evening caused a fog in my brain. I shook my head and then looked at him. It had been a long time since I'd put myself out there. I felt terrified and ever so vulnerable, but I decided to not beat around the bush any longer. "I like you, Dan. I really do."

He stepped forward, gently wrapped his arms around my waist and tenderly pulled me closer towards him. "You're not so bad yourself, Jennifer," he said with a flirtatious smile and brushed a strand of hair back from my face.

I felt warm and fuzzy. There was still a bit of uneasiness as to whether I was doing the right thing, but it felt absolutely wonderful to be cherished by someone again.

"I understand you're in a delicate position. We're both single, but your situation is so different from mine. My ex and I, we were no longer an option – I was relieved when we separated. Of course, I still love her as the mother of my child, but there's nothing more than that. But your marriage was suddenly ripped apart, without you wanting it to be."

I considered telling him about the little blips during the last few months of Oliver's life, and the doubts about our marriage that were fuelled by everything I'd discovered recently. But it was too much for now and so I just nodded.

"It's all quite overwhelming. This," I added, pointing my index finger at him and back at me a few times. "I really enjoyed our diner tonight, and yet all kinds of feelings of guilt are overwhelming me. I'm not sure I feel ready yet to become a laid-back, happy single. I'm sorry."

Dan let his hands slide off my waist, retreated and turned away from me. He seemed lost in thought and ran a hand through his hair, leaving it to stick up in peaks and making me laugh.

He looked at me in surprise. "What's so funny?"

"Nothing. Sorry," I said and quickly dropped my smile to look serious again.

"If you want it to end here, I completely understand. The whole situation is making it all very complicated. I'm making it all very complicated," I corrected myself. I scooped up my handbag from the couch where I left it. "Do you want me to leave?"

He shook his head. "No … No. Give me a minute. I have to take it in," he said, stepping back a little. He absent-mindedly took a sip of port, walked over to the couch and flopped down, knocking a few cushions to the floor.

I started tugging a loose piece of skin on my finger as Dan kept staring into the distance. Outside I heard a noisy group of people clearly having a good time, making quite a racket. Inside there was absolute stillness.

I took a few steps in his direction. "Dan?" I whispered.

Only now did he seem to become aware of my presence again. "What?" he said blankly, but then the stern expression on his face softened. "Oh. I'm sorry."

He stood up from the white leather couch, leaving a small indent, and advanced towards me and looked deep into my eyes. "I get that it must be very hard for you. It is all a bit complicated and, admittedly, after my turbulent time with the divorce and everything, I was feeling more like a simple, carefree date."

I swallowed and looked away. I could empathise with him, but his remark had struck a nerve. "I understand," I whispered.

Dan took my hands, which I left hanging lifelessly in his, and gave them a gentle tug to make me look at him. "But then again – who am I kidding?" he asked rhetorically. "We both have a child and have been married before – things will never be uncomplicated anyway." He let go of one hand, lifted his and let it gently move down my cheek, sending bolts of electricity through me.

I couldn't speak and merely nodded.

He whispered, his lips just a breath away from mine. "You're a fascinating woman, Jennifer, and I'd love to get to know you better. Let's just take the time to see where this leads. I have an extra room with a spare bed in it," he said and smiled. "We're in no rush."

I felt my shoulders relax. Dan was right – we could just take our time and see what would happen.

Dan's fingers stroked my cheek, sliding down to cup my chin as he shifted towards me. I shivered briefly at his touch, hearing his breathing suspend as he brushed his mouth against mine in a gentle, lingering kiss. I closed my eyes while his wonderful, strong hands were caressing my back like feathers, forgot about everything and relished his warm lips on mine.

23

An unfamiliar noise roused me from a deep sleep – I slowly opened my eyes to see rays of sunlight filtering through two red curtains, forming a rainbow pattern against a bright white wall.

I suddenly realised I was in Dan's guest room and felt a smugness wash over me at the bold move of sleeping over at a strange man's place. Last night Dan and I had shared a wonderful evening of kissing, talking, me lying in his arms and kissing again. It was hard to resist taking things further – that man was irresistible – but I didn't want to rush it. If this all worked out between us, there'd plenty of time for that.

I flung off the yellow-and-white checked duvet and swung my legs over the side of the bed. I noticed the white shirt I was wearing, belonging to Dan, and a grin spread across my face. I checked my phone and saw that I'd received a message from my mother, saying Tim was doing well.

I moved along the corridor with a spring in my step and heard all kinds of unfamiliar sounds coming from the kitchen. I gently eased down the creaking wooden stairs, varnished with a high-gloss white as the smell of freshly brewed coffee filled the air. Somewhat discomfited, I tugged at the shirt when I entered the gallery kitchen – I'd never managed to shake off the last few pregnancy kilos after Tim's arrival.

"Good morning, sunshine," Dan said. His hair was tousled and a dark stubble was visible on his lower jaw – he was just as attractive as last night. He was only wearing boxer shorts and a white shirt. I tried to avert my eyes from the beautifully toned contours of his body.

Dan leaned forward to give me a kiss, making me feel special yet somewhat uneasy at the same time. "How did you sleep?" he asked, while putting a few rolls into the oven and turning it on.

"Like a rose," I replied, as I self-consciously lowered myself onto one of the two grey stools that slotted under the small, high table, barely fitting in the narrow kitchen. "Quite a decent sofa bed," I added, although to be fair, the copious amounts of alcohol from last night probably contributed to my deep sleep.

"I'm glad to hear that," Dan said, while he turned on the tap and filled a saucepan with water. "Fancy a boiled egg?"

It had been ages since someone had prepared breakfast for me – I felt blissfully coveted. "Sounds delicious," I replied with a smile.

We talked a bit about how spring was just around the corner, while Dan filled a tray with all the necessities for a proper breakfast. Then we walked into the sun-drenched living room, to an already set, wooden dining table.

"Do you have any plans for the weekend?" I asked Dan, while I slathered a croissant with strawberry jam.

"I have to work from home for a few hours after which Bella will come here. We often do something fun together, go for a walk through the Vondelpark or eat an ice cream somewhere." His eyes lit up when he spoke about his daughter, which made me smile.

"Do you always work on weekends?" I asked tentatively. I was wary of engaging in a relationship with someone who had the same work ethic as Oliver once had.

Dan seemed to pick up on my feelings and waved his hand. "Don't worry. I occasionally work from home, but I'm certainly not a workaholic. I believe it's important to spend enough time with Bella – one day a week I take parental leave to see her," he said with a proud expression on his face.

"You deserve a medal," I bantered.

He gave me a loving tap on the cheek.

I took a swig of my coffee. "I didn't know they approved of working part-time, at Mason & McGant," I said now with a serious tone. Oliver had once told me his manager had laughed out loud when a colleague had raised the question of taking parental leave.

Dan shrugged. "It probably won't make me a partner of the firm, working less than fulltime, but I think it's essential to have a good work-life balance.

Satisfied with his answer, I chewed on my croissant while the sun warmed my face. I closed my eyes for a moment – wasn't life wonderful?

All of a sudden I remembered why I'd agreed to this date in the first place and my eyes flew open. I wanted to make sure that Mason & McGant hadn't sent Dan to find out how much I knew. Last night I'd allowed myself to believe that his intentions were sincere, but now, in hindsight, I wondered whether this conclusion was too premature.

The relaxed, blissful feeling of moments earlier vanished like vapour. I had completely let myself go last night – I'd recklessly spent the night with an unknown and potentially dangerous man, and had become side-tracked from my original motive to meet him. Just because we'd shared a wonderful evening and he'd attentively prepared a nice breakfast for me didn't mean I should precipitously exclude him from playing a role in Oliver's death. He had an ostensibly casual attitude towards the firm, but perhaps this was all part of his cover up.

Dan stood up and popped into the kitchen to get another cup of coffee while my mind was racing. If my suspicions were legitimate and Dan was indeed part of a widely branched scheme, why did he make me feel on cloud nine? Surely I would have noticed something was off, or not? Perhaps I was mistaken – for all I knew he could be completely oblivious to all fraudulent practices at the law firm – he too could well have been, without having any knowledge of it, recorded drinking and snorting drugs on camera.

My palms suddenly felt cold and sweaty and my heart was pounding. I had to put Dan to the test once more, I couldn't escape it. I decided this time to take a different angle – I needed to determine which way the wind was blowing.

Dan walked back into the room with a pot of coffee. "Would you like another cup?"

I shook my head.

He put the coffee pot on a coaster on the table and sat down in front of me, unsuspecting of the turmoil in my head.

I took another bite of the croissant, but it didn't taste as good anymore. I coughed nervously and decided to come straight to the point. "Did you know that Mason & McGant has stored DVDs of its paralegals?"

Dan sprinkled some salt on his egg before taking a bite. "Hmm, what's that?"

I laid down my croissant, looked at him, and waited for him to give me his full attention. "Mason & McGant produces compromising footage of all their new paralegals, on which they're seen cavorting with young, promiscuous ladies," I mouthed slowly and deliberately. "To use them as a means of blackmailing them," I added, and although the latter was just an assumption, it had been the most plausible scenario Sandra and I could come up with.

Dan looked at me in bewilderment. "What in heaven's name are you talking about?"

I leaned back in my chair, folded my arms and looked at him with an intense expression, trying to read his face. A nerve twitching, a dark glare, eyes that couldn't look into mine – any sign that informed me that this man knew more. But he didn't flinch one bit – I saw nothing but an open face that looked at me with a sincere and baffled expression.

I increased the pressure. "Don't play dumb. I think you know exactly what

I'm talking about."

He scratched his forehead. "I'm sorry, but I haven't the faintest idea. We were just having breakfast together, but now all of a sudden you seem angry and start saying all of these crazy things about the firm I work for." There was a hint of irritation in his voice. "What's going on?"

I let out a big sigh before I started talking about the red underwear that was discovered on Oliver's body. How it had formed the first sign that his death wasn't simply the result of a terrible accident. How I then stumbled upon hours and hours of footage of my husband and many of his colleagues, performing all kinds of unsavoury acts under the influence of drugs.

Once I'd finished speaking, Dan was gazing outside into the street, his mouth dropped slightly open, and the air in the room froze in suspense. He stayed painfully quiet as he ran a hand through his hair, which stuck up in peaks like yesterday – this time though, I didn't dare laugh.

After a long silence, Dan stood up, started pacing up and down the room, and then turned his attention to me. "So, let me get this straight: you're claiming that Mason & McGant deliberately puts their paralegals in a compromising position, records this all on camera, in order to ultimately be able to blackmail them?"

I nodded, following his movements with my eyes.

"And where do you think this all would have taken place?"

"In Mason & McGants' house bar, on the top floor."

"You've seen this footage with your own eyes?"

I lifted my index finger and nodded. "Yep."

"Where's the footage right now?"

"It's still at Mason & McGant, in Oliver's former office," I reluctantly admitted. "I didn't want to take the risk of removing them," I clarified, but the argument sounded weak.

Dan shook his head in pity – I felt foolish under his gaze and bowed my head. "I'm sorry Jennifer," he said, darkness crossing his eyes. "This story you're telling doesn't add up. I've never heard of such a bizarre thing. It seems impossible to me that I could have worked at Mason & McGant for several years without anyone ever mentioning this. And if you're wondering whether they've also subjected me to this kind of initiation, the answer is no."

Where his eyes had been friendly a while ago, a clear look of annoyance and wariness had now spread across his face. "But as I told you before, I did my training as a paralegal at another firm. So in that regard it fits exactly into your theory that they only do this to paralegals, doesn't it?"

I cringed at his sarcastic tone and started doubting myself again. The confident attitude I'd adopted before had completely withered as my eye

twitched in dismay. Was Dan truly unfamiliar with the dark side of Mason &
McGant? If that were the case, then I'd shattered my chances of having a
relationship with a wonderful man. On the other hand, if he did know about what
was going on, he might be deliberately attempting to dismiss my suspicions as
nonsense to throw me off the scent.

"Last night I was full of understanding for your mixed feelings towards
dating, considering your husband's recent death. I was happy to give you all the
time to deal with that. But this here …" A groan accompanied the roll of his
eyes, ripping whatever was left of my confidence to shreds.

He didn't finish his sentence, but gave a big sigh as he shifted towards me
and looked at me like I was some kind of maniac. "I'm sorry, but you're
imagining things. Obviously losing your husband has taken a really heavy toll on
you. I'm sure it must be very hard, but I can't help you with this."

He straightened his back and folded his arms, a harsh look spreading across
his face. "Let's just say we had a very pleasant evening and keep it at that." He
lifted the corners of his mouth, but the result was more a bitter grimace than a
smile.

Wait a second. Was he being serious? I glared at him, my cheeks flushing.
"Are you kicking me out?" I hissed.

His lips formed a straight line and his jaw thrust forward. "I think it's best
that we leave it at this."

I found his condescending tone infuriating. There was a roaring in my ears
and a red mist appeared before my eyes. This guy had some nerve.

I ferociously pushed back my chair and jumped up. "That's just charming," I
said coolly, my face a mere centimetres away from his, but inside I practically
exploded. "Thanks for the nice breakfast. I wish you all the best." At that
preposterous, shady firm of yours, I added in silence.

Even before he could utter another word, I stamped upstairs, blind with rage,
slipped out of his shirt and tossed it onto the bed. I flung on the clothes that I'd
draped over a chair last night and snatched my handbag off the floor.

I ran downstairs again, opened the front door without saying a word, and
slammed it shut behind me.

I stomped down the stone stairs to where I'd secured my bicycle to a
lamppost. I jerked the wretched bicycle lock, which wouldn't budge. When I
finally succeeded in opening it, I jumped onto my bike without looking back.

The ten-minute ride home, leading me through the Vondelpark, which was
already filled with a substantial number of people on this surprisingly sunny
Saturday morning, did me good. The fresh air and the peaceful atmosphere in the

park made the anger over the confrontation with Dan slowly subside. I thought about his reaction to my statements and came to the realisation that I should have seen it coming that he wouldn't just buy my story. The leads I'd shared with him about Mason & McGant were far from water tight and convincing. The man had only just met me, so it was a no-brainer that he thought I was loopy.

When I arrived home, I saw on my phone that I'd received a message from Lindsey asking if I wanted to go for a bite with her and the girls the following evening. I shuffled into the living room while replying I'd join them only for drinks around eight and plopped down on the couch with a loud sigh.

24

"Speak of the devil!" Karen shouted as I entered the restaurant the following evening. "Our happy single," she added with a grin as I arrived at the table to greet my friends. Before my encounter with Dan I'd sent a message to Lindsey saying I was going on a date, and included the name of the restaurant. I didn't want to reveal to her who it was – she'd left no doubt as to how she felt about the situation when we last saw each other – but it felt like the responsible thing to do to inform someone about my whereabouts that evening.

Frederique poked Karen in the ribs. "K, it's a tad too soon for statements like that."

Karen seemed unaware of any wrongdoing. "Why?" She looked at me. "You're dating again right? Or was I misinformed?"

I gave Frederique a reassuring pat on the arm and said to Karen, "Yes, I am." Karen's remark confronted me with the fact that going on a date half a year after Oliver's death was moving awfully fast, but I pushed the self-conscious feeling quickly aside.

My girlfriends had finished their diner and were having a cheese platter for desert. I gave them all a peck on the cheek, peeled off my coat and draped it over a chair before sitting down at the massive wooden table. Under the table I noticed that Karen was yet again wearing her particularly charming walking shoes – very comfortable as claimed by her. Lindsey, on the other hand, was looking fabulous as always – her blonde hair was styled perfectly and she was wearing an elegant green blouse with tight white trousers, accentuating her long slender legs, and matching green stilettos.

"Now that we're all here, I can share the good news," Karen said, looking thrilled. "I've been offered a new position as an orthopaedic surgeon."

"How wonderful for you," I exclaimed. "Congratulations.'

"Thank you," Karen said, before sharing the nuts and bolts of the post she was taking up next month.

"I'm so impressed by how you do that, being in the operating theatre every day. Working as a surgeon must be such a demanding job," Frederique sighed, with a strained expression on her face. "I wouldn't be up for it, bearing the responsibility for another life, dealing with the stress when something goes wrong. I'm glad I have so much freedom working as a freelancer."

Karen rolled her eyes at me without Frederique noticing. I knew she didn't regard Frederique's web shop for home-made jewellery as work – rather as a hobby – but sometimes it seemed as if she was jealous of Frederique, who had a loving husband with a high salary. The man thought it was all very well so long as his wife managed the household and was content. Luckily, Frederique was as blind as a bat to Karen's mocking.

Lindsey took up the praise. "Add taking care of two children to that, which may be even harder," she said, smiling faintly. There was a hint of sadness in her eyes and I wondered if that smile was masking a hidden longing.

Karen grinned. "Thank god for au pairs."

Frederique raised her eyebrows. She wasn't the type to judge someone openly, but it was obvious what her opinion was on Karen's children not spending much time with their parents.

A waitress came to ask if we wanted something to drink. I looked around and saw that my friends had just finished a cup of tea. "Darlings, I didn't come here to have tea with you," I said jokingly. "How about we share a bottle of wine?" I felt like celebrating the first time I was out with my best friends again without me acting like a wet blanket.

Frederique waved her hand. "Sorry, I'll pass. I need to drive back home. I'd like one last tea, please," she said to the girl, who looked like a student with a side job.

Lindsey and Karen were up for a bit of indulging and agreed.

"Chardonnay?" Lindsey suggested.

"Sounds great to me."

After telling us more about her new job, Karen decided to direct the attention to me. "Enough of this boring work stuff. Jennifer, don't think we've forgotten about you," she said with a wink. "How was your date yesterday? We want all the juicy details."

I saw Lindsey looking at me with interest. I'd told her earlier in a message that I'd spent the night at his place, but that had been all.

I pressed my teeth into my lower lip and tilted my head. "Absolutely wonderful … And at the same time, awful."

Frederique frowned. "I don't follow."

"Thank goodness, here come the drinks at last," Karen said.

I waited for the waitress to distribute the order, toasted and took a sip, feeling a warm glow of relaxation move through my body. I realised that only Lindsey was up to date on everything that had happened lately – my suspicions regarding Mason & McGant, the file with the confusing notes that Oliver made before he died and the sudden death of Sandra due to an unusual tram accident.

It was too much to put into words and I decided to not go into detail right now. "We went out to dinner last night at a very nice place. It was great fun," I said, grinning at the memory. "We talked so easily, time just run away from us, as if we've known each other for ages. It was the first time since Oliver died that I was laughing and enjoying myself, feeling so carefree again."

Frederique looked at me with a warm smile. "Oh darling, I'm so happy for you. You truly deserve it."

Karen chimed in with similar words of consent.

"Actually, you're touching upon a delicate subject," I said doubtfully. "Sometimes I wonder if I do really deserve a new chance of happiness. It's only been six months since Oliver passed away and so much has happened since then that I feel I haven't been able to put things to rest," I said, being deliberately vague.

"You mean Oliver's *faux pas*?" Karen asked, clearly expressing her judgment of him.

That mistake had set a chain of events in motion, but it was too much to elucidate it all now. I felt overwhelmed and nodded. "Yes, mostly that. I don't know how to perceive our relationship anymore – was it simply a colossal mistake on Oliver's part, and would we have been able to reconcile and move forward together? In that case, we could have been happily married for the rest of our lives, if he hadn't had that accident." I paused. "Or was he in fact leading a double life and actually a completely different person to the man I thought he was?" I rubbed my eyes. "I feel so muddled all the time."

"I understand," Frederique said softly. "It's complicated." She laid her hand on my arm. "If only Oliver were still here – things would have been different. You could have talked it all through with him and found out the truth about his affair and his feelings for you."

I lowered my eyes and bit my lip, feeling tears welling up. I didn't want to cry again – not here. I pulled my arm away from under Frederique's hand. "It's okay." I attempted a reassuring smile. "Let's talk about it another time," I said and drank a mouthful of wine.

"Sure, darling. Whatever you want," Lindsey said.

Karen had shared little with us about her love life ever since her divorce two years ago. "How about you Karen, what kind of person would you like to date?" I asked, eager to deflect attention from me. "Your guess is as good as mine." She chuckled. "Someone with a heartbeat?"

I laughed.

"You always know how to create diversions, don't you, Jen," Lindsey said and laughed. "Surely, you're not expecting us to let you off the hook that easily, are you? Tell us everything there is to know about your date! Does this guy live in Amsterdam?"

"Yes, he does," I replied and took another gulp of wine. "He actually lives quite close to my place."

"Oh really, how convenient," Frederique said and blew on her tea. "Does anyone want my biscuit?"

Karen took advantage of her offer and gobbled it up. How she was able to put that away together with the Chardonnay was beyond me.

I recounted the dinner I'd shared with Dan in broad terms.

"How exciting," Frederique exclaimed.

Karen raised her eyebrows teasingly. "Yeah, yeah, we get the picture. Nice food, chatting the evening away … Ho-hum. So what happened *after* dinner?"

"He gave me a tour of his new house," I responded dryly.

"Anyone else care for a refill?" Lindsey asked, holding the bottle of wine over my glass, which was nearly empty.

"Fill her up," I answered.

"All right, now we're getting somewhere," Frederique said, sitting on the edge of her seat. "Tell us straight up, did you spend the night there?"

I nodded.

Karen threw back her head and howled like a wolf.

Frederique raised her eyebrows. "Seriously? You cheeky minx." She looked into the far distance with a dreamy look in her eyes. "Oh, I'd kill for a night like that – living without a care in the world. Just have a good sleep without interruptions – no children crying because of a bad dream or a lost dummy." She pulled away from her musings and looked at me. "Although you probably didn't get much sleep at all, or did you?"

I cackled. "I take great offense at your suggestion," I said, mimicking the expression of a demure girl in boarding school. "I managed to restrain myself and slept in the guest room."

"Sure you did. And you expect us to believe that?" Lindsey said with big round eyes.

Frederique put her cup of tea on the table and leaned back as if she were getting ready for a chick flick in the cinema. "Guys, this is really ear-candy for me. Nothing ever happens in my life anymore. You've made my day, Jennifer."

I grinned. For almost fifteen years I hadn't experienced anything particularly exciting either, but in the last six months I'd become involved in more drama than I cared for.

"Go on, you," Lindsey urged. "Did you have breakfast together in the morning?"

I nodded. Memories of the date that went down in flames came flooding back. "Yes," I said curtly and took another swig of wine. "But enough about me. Girls, how are you all doing?"

Frederique ignored my attempt to deflect and started firing questions at me. "Wait a minute. Not so fast. How did it end? Did he say he'd call you again? Would you want him to? Or was it just a one-night fling?"

"I don't know," I said evasively. I was starting to become ever so slightly irritated by their interrogation.

"Did something happen between the two of you?" Lindsey asked.

I replayed the moment where I'd fled his flat, tail between my legs, and wrinkled my nose. "It didn't end that well."

Karen shook her head. "Why not?"

I sighed. Perhaps it was the right moment to confide in my friends, for after all, they'd always supported me in the past. I knew for sure they'd be understanding this time as well.

And so I commenced talking, describing how Sandra had informed me about the case that Oliver had been working on in secret in the lead-up to his death and how his former colleague Benedict hastily backed away on our plan to meet for coffee when I'd queried him about the case. I also told them about the nightly visits to Mason & McGant and the incriminating DVDs we uncovered, and finally about how Dan had responded to all this information.

When I finished, three pairs of eyes were gazing at me. The silence at the table was fraught with unspoken questions. Karen took a swig of wine, fiddling with the frayed seams of the chair she was seated on. Frederique averted her gaze when I tried to look her in the eye.

I picked up the bottle of wine, topped up my glass and noticed that Lindsey's was still nearly full.

Why didn't anyone respond? I'd finally gathered enough courage to confide in them, and now they were all goggling at me with eyes of abject and unspoken condemnation.

"So … I've finally spilled the beans, is anyone going to say anything?" I broke the silence.

Frederique exchanged a clandestine look with Karen, who made a face like I'm-not-saying-anything.

Frederique coughed. "Darling, it's such an ordeal you've had to go through," she began, choosing her words with care. "First the death of Oliver and then finding out that he'd had an affair," she summarised, as if I could have forgotten about it. "A situation like that would mess with anybody's head."

"What are you saying? I need to see a shrink?" I snickered and immediately regretted it. Surely she had good intentions, right?

Frederique carried on talking as if she hadn't heard me. "I can only imagine how it must have knocked the ground from under your feet. Your whole world has been turned upside down," Frederique went on.

The waitress came to ask if we'd like to order another drink.

"No," I replied with a scowl on my face. She raised her eyebrows and retreated.

"Is it perhaps possible that all the sadness and turmoil may have had a bearing on your …" Her voice trailed off. "… on your judgment? You're just not thinking straight right now."

I threw Frederique a glare, my cheeks flushing. "What's your point?"

She bit her lip and continued, avoiding eye contact. "It must be hard to accept everything that has happened to you. I once read in a psychology magazine that if you're a victim of a traumatic event, the mind will come up with all kinds of explanations to deal with it – as some kind of survival mechanism. Does this make any sense?" she asked gingerly.

I had to bite my tongue to restrain myself. She had quite the nerve comparing the situation I was in to something she'd read in some lame magazine. As if those people had any idea what they were talking about. They simply had to meet a deadline and wrote whatever rubbish they could think of. "I'm not imagining anything. Surely you can all see how the signs add up to something sinister?"

I saw Frederique exchange looks with Lindsey, whom I expected to take sides for me, but to my horror she jumped in for Frederique. "Come on Jen. You have to admit, how likely is it that Oliver didn't have an accident but was actually …" She looked around before lowering her voice. "… killed by someone? And that a similar fate befell Sandra, with a large law firm trying to cover it up with a tram accident."

My fists clenched underneath the table. My supposed friends looked at me as if they'd just explained that the earth was round and not flat and I was too ignorant to understand.

I chugged the last bit of wine in my glass before I spoke. "It's a long shot. But it's not impossible. I have little evidence, but I just know, I just feel that something is wrong," I said, trying to convince them. But I could tell by the look on their faces they took me even less seriously because I was making such an emotional plea.

Frederique took over 'the intervention' again. "This is nothing like you, you're always the sensible one, Jennifer. Really, you're starting to see things that aren't there. Please believe us. That's probably why your date reacted that way."

She befuddled me for a moment. The vast amounts of wine had gone to my head, clouding my thought process. I rubbed my eyes.

"Darling. Don't take this the wrong way," Frederique said and gently rested her hand on my arm. "I believe I'm speaking on behalf of all of us when I say we're just a little concerned about you." Her brown eyes were full of compassion.

But Frederique's remark only added fuel to the flames. "I don't need your concern."

Without making an announcement, I pushed my chair back, jumped up and for a moment the world started spinning around me. I swayed a little and had to grab the table to stave off falling backwards into my seat. I finally managed to continue speaking. "This is a real kick in the teeth. So much for trust and friendship, huh! I'd never imagined you all to be fair-weather friends. I had expected a wee bit of help – or at the very least some support and trust in me," I exclaimed, giving the nosy onlookers the cold shoulder. I shot a glare of contempt and infuriation at Lindsey. "Particularly from you."

She looked down with a contrite expression.

I grabbed a tenner from my purse and hurled it on the table. "I'm out of here."

I left the restaurant reeling, trying my best not to bump into any of the tables and flung open the door. Once outside in the cold night, it took me a while to locate my bike. I tried to put my key in the lock, but my hands were trembling terribly.

Suddenly I heard a voice behind me. "Please don't leave. Not like this, Jennifer."

I swung around and saw Lindsey standing there, pulling her cardigan tightly around her. "Why not?" I responded. "If even my friends are impugning my judgment and believe I've gone bonkers, then I don't feel like staying anymore."

She rolled her eyes. "Don't act all hysterical. We don't think you're loopy at all. You're going through a difficult time, that's all. All we want for you is to get back on your feet again."

I folded my arms and averted her eyes, feeling an imaginary wall rising up between us. "Don't worry about it. I'm sure I will."

She took a step in my direction. "I told you before that you and I were seeing eye-to-eye that this was all very suspicious. I advised you to stop searching yourself and go to the police. But you ignored my advice and started contacting that guy."

I gave an insouciant shrug. "Yes, I did. So what? I don't have to answer for what I do or don't do," I said, even though I was well aware I'd been lying to her through omission.

Lindsey looked at me in astonishment. "You went on a date with that Dan and spent the night there," she exclaimed. "Who knows what could have happened. At the very least, you could have given me a heads up."

I bit my lip. Now that she said it like that, it sounded like a very rash and risky action.

"To be honest, I feel ever so faintly put-out." She looked away, clearly hurt. "You fooled me, Jennifer. You pretended that the date was with someone else."

"What nonsense," I said, done with her haranguing me. "I don't owe you an explanation about who I'm seeing." I knew I was rubbing salt in the wound, but I wasn't bothered.

Lindsey didn't seem to have heard me. "What was that?"

I repeated what I'd said with renewed efforts, trying my best to articulate clearly, but my lips seemed unwilling to cooperate.

She narrowed her eyes. "You're slurring your words. How much have you been drinking lately?"

Her question caught me off guard. "Not much," I answered automatically. But is that really true, a voice in my head asked. "I just didn't eat that much tonight. The wine probably didn't go down well."

She stared at me with a look that I couldn't quite grasp. Suddenly it hit me. "Oh my god, you really think I'm delusional, don't you?"

"No, I don't. Cut me some slack, will you! I'm just worried that …"

I interrupted her. "Save your breath. And by the way, what's it to you? I'll decide myself how much I drink. I'm not causing any harm by it," I scoffed. But I thought of Tim, who I'd probably have to entertain with the tablet again tomorrow morning, until the throbbing headache would subside.

I knew Lindsey didn't hold with me drinking too much and that I was spoiling for a fight, but I somehow just didn't care.

Lindsey crossed her arms. "Hey, there's no need to talk to me like that."

Now I'd made her angry too, which felt good. It seemed I was on a mission to burn some bridges tonight.

I shrugged and looked down the street to where a tram announced its departure and pulled away from the stop. A group of men who'd just gotten off, loudly sang a song with obscene lyrics – probably another raucous stag party.

I put my foot on the pedal. "I'm going home."

Her face softened. "Please, Jennifer. At least give me a hug," she said, spreading her arms.

I answered her conciliatory gesture with a limp arm around her and then disengaged myself from her embrace.

"I'll talk to you later, okay?" I said.

I didn't wait for her answer, but turned on my heel and cycled off.

25

Something wet on my face jolted me awake. I wiped away the sticky substance with my hand and rolled over, away from the source. The world was spinning for a brief moment before coming to a halt again. Sunlight trickled through the curtains and moved in dizzy patterns across my face, causing a fierce stab in the back of my head. I closed my eyes and dozed off.

A hand pulled at my shoulder. "Mummy."

I moaned.

"Mummy," it sounded louder this time. "Wake up. Tim get up."

I rolled over and held my son in my arms, my eyes still shut. His familiar, lovely scent softened the thumping in my head. I gently stroked his beautiful soft little curls. It came back to me how he'd been crying during the night and didn't want to go back to his cot anymore, so he ended up in the bed with me.

Tim had enough of the hugging sooner than I did and wanted to go downstairs. With a lot of moans and groans I managed to drag myself out of bed. After the head-to-head with Lindsey last night I'd felt worked up when I got home and taken a nightcap, but now I regretted it.

As I stood up, I felt a wave of nausea washing over me. Gently and slowly, I shuffled to the bathroom where the cold floor under my feet provided some relief. I opened the medicine cabinet and took the last two paracetamol tablets from the box. I made a mental note to pick up some more today. I cupped my hand, filled it with water and knocked back the pills.

I heard Tim on the landing fumble at the stair safety gate. "Mummy, c'mon." I'd promised myself not to ever let him bear the brunt of any sadness on my part, but today I was flunking big time.

"I'll be right there, baby," I yelled back as I slid my arms into my dressing gown, which was gathering a number of smudgy stains. I bent down to pick up Tim's slippers, walked to the landing and slid them onto his feet, while he protested. "Your feet will get cold, dear," I said wearily, noticing they'd become too small for him.

I unlocked the safety gate, trundled down the stairs in front of him and reminded him to hold the bannister properly as he shuffled down step by step. In the living room on the coffee table stood the remnants of my night cap – a glass of Baileys spreading a sickeningly sweet smell throughout the room. I was glad that I'd blocked off the first two consulting hours at the practice, but the notion of talking to patients later on didn't exactly fill me with enthusiasm.

Tim tugged at the belt of my robe. "Tim wants a bottle." Obviously, he was getting too old for that, but I replied it was fine and suggested he play with his toy cars while I headed to the kitchen.

I opened the fridge and noticed there was only half a pack of milk left. When Oliver was still with us, he always took care of the weekly groceries and we never fell short. Since his death, I hadn't succeeded in getting into a new routine and consequently I'd regularly stumble upon a half-empty refrigerator. To my shame, I'd developed the habit of serving Tim ready-made baby food, something he'd long grown out of. But at least he'd be eating something, I told myself.

I made myself a cup of coffee and put a bottle of milk in the microwave for Tim. With my hands wrapped around the hot mug, my eyes gazed out through the patio doors into the garden, which was looking untended and glum. Now that spring had started, it was time to rid the flagged stones of the green algae that emerged without fail every winter and plant some pansies and marigolds here and there, but I couldn't bring myself to do it – I unfortunately hadn't inherited my mother's green fingers.

Despite neglecting some of the household duties, the last few weeks I'd finally been feeling a bit better. Even though the date with Dan had ended in disaster and it was obviously out of the question to make amends, it had sparked a flicker of hope for a brighter future. But after the falling out with my friends last night, a feeling of loneliness left a heavy mark on me.

I screwed the cap onto the bottle, trudged back to the living room and handed it to Tim. He eagerly took it with both hands and started drinking. I pulled him onto my lap, wrapped my arms tightly around his warm little body, and closed my eyes for a moment.

After he'd finished his milk I noticed the coffee had done its job and I started to feel better. We'd played together for a while and had breakfast, then I put Tim in front of the television, took a short cold shower, and decided to sit in the garden with a cup of tea.

My thoughts returned to last night – I'd never imagined my friends giving up on me. Their reaction, however, made me doubt myself again. Were they right – was I seeing things that weren't there? Lindsey had suggested going to the police, but I'd already tried that and it was clear that I couldn't expect any assistance on that side. Perhaps it was wise after all to just leave it be, I couldn't get Oliver back and it was taking its toll on me. I took a sip of my tea, tilted my face towards the sun, and closed my eyes.

But if there had been some form of foul play, did I not owe it to Oliver to get to the bottom of things? The thought that something or someone had ended his life with impunity and turned mine upside down was unacceptable. I opened my eyes and leaped up. No matter how hard I tried, it was impossible for me to let the matter rest.

I rushed inside, where Tim was still watching television, to get the copies of the Van Santen file, that Sandra and I had made that night at Mason & McGant. I sat down on the couch and flipped through the pages until I reached the page where Oliver had made notes in his all too familiar sloppy handwriting. It presented an overview of the different types of evidence, as Oliver had once clarified to me, grouped by four different cases. The name Van Santen was nowhere to be found … Out of the blue I had a hunch that this might not have been a real person after all. Could Oliver perhaps have adopted it as a code name, to avoid attracting the attention of his colleagues or partners?

It dawned on me that something must have been out of the ordinary regarding the evidence of those four cases. Something that had caught Oliver's attention in such a compelling way that he created a file for it as some sort of cover up, like a shroud of mist covering his crusade. Sandra had said there was more information in the pages she'd taken home, with regards to the different types of evidence, even mentioning names of people and companies. I suddenly remembered that she'd promised to put the documents on a shared drive shortly before her death, but I couldn't recall whether I had in fact ever received an email from her about it.

Tim suddenly started to cry loudly, which made me jump. He seemed to have fallen from the couch. "Oh, pumpkin," I said after picking him up, and gave him a gentle kiss on his forehead, where a small bump had become visible. "Did you have a fall? It's all right, baby," I soothed.

While he was still sobbing, I placed him back firmly on the couch and turned on another film for him. He was apt to get tired of watching television after half an hour, so I had to hurry up.

I logged into my laptop, opened my mailbox and searched for the name Sandra – there were no results. Perhaps the e-mail had been sent from the server where the shared drive was placed, so I searched all messages received in the week when I'd last talked to her on the phone, but nothing popped up.

I bit my nails and pondered about it. Perhaps her promise had slipped her mind? Or maybe she simply hadn't got around to scanning the papers and sending them to me before she died.

Feeling somewhat dejected, I glanced across all my email folders lined up on the left side of the screen, and realised with a jolt of hope, that I hadn't yet checked my junk mail folder. I clicked on the icon and instantly my eyes fell upon a message from WeShare.

"Sandra is inviting you to view her files."

I opened the message and clicked on the link. I was redirected to a secure website that, to my bitter disappointment, asked for a login and password. Would Sandra have forgotten to share it with me?

I returned to my mailbox and to my relief found a second message from WeShare containing the login and password. After copy pasting them into the right tabs and hitting enter, I got access to a folder with three documents, each one appeared to consist of twenty-five scanned pages of the Van Santen File. "Yes!" I exclaimed.

I glanced at Tim – he was still watching television. I laboriously scrolled through all the pages until I came across the chapter that Sandra had pointed out. There were two consecutive pages titled: 'forensic evidence and phone records'. I also saw the same four clients receiving legal counsel from Mason & McGant, which I'd come across in my set of papers. But then I stumbled upon something that set my heart racing. Extortionate sums of money had been scrawled next to each of the four cases – we were dealing with six-figure numbers here. To my bewilderment, arrows had been drawn, running from the four cases to the DFI, with the words 'paid to DFI'. The DFI was a government agency that supposedly acted as an independent party to carry out forensic analyses for criminal lawsuits brought by the government – why would they have been paid by Mason & McGant?

I knew instinctively that I'd chanced upon something important. These documents reeked of potential forgery and bribery.

I glanced at my phone. It wouldn't be long before my first patient of the day would be waiting for me. I now had actual clues on paper that should provide sufficient grounds for the police to reopen the investigation into Oliver's death, and that notion filled me with hope. If I had an opening at work today, I'd call Detective Armstrong immediately.

"Tim, baby," I said in a high voice. "We're going to day-care. Mummy has to go to work."

Half an hour later I'd reached the practice and parked my bike close to the entrance. "Good morning," I trilled to Simone, who was on the phone and raised her hand in acknowledgement as I walked towards my consulting room. The first thing I felt when I swung open the door was the unexpected gust of wind that punched me in the face. I instinctively knew something was terribly wrong.

My hand flew up to my mouth which had dropped open in shock. I didn't know where to look – the room was scattered with what seemed like a million tiny pieces of shattered glass. The white blinds in the window frame were fluttering before an enormous, gaping hole where the windowpane should have been, the rays of sunlight dazzling off the broken shards of glass.

Stupefied, I cautiously edged closer towards the window, but froze when I felt the glass crack underneath my shoes.

"Hans," I shrieked. "Hans!" My voice sounded eerily loud, like I was hearing it ricochet back through an amplifier.

Hans must have heard the distress in my voice, because despite the fact that he had a patient in his consulting room, he dashed out within seconds. "What's the matter?"

"Someone …" I began, but the words died on my lips – I merely indicated the room with my hand, which felt heavy and incapacitated.

Hans swore out loud, which was unusual for him, as he assessed the appalling scene. "What the hell happened in here?"

My eyes fell on a foreign object lying underneath my desk. I stepped as cautiously and lightly as I could between the fragments of broken glass and stooped down to pick up a grey pavement tile. My gaze moved to Hans. "They must have used this."

It wasn't until I held the tile up to Hans I noticed a note had been affixed with duct tape to the bottom of it.

"Are you really listening?" I muttered and swallowed the acidic taste that had suddenly washed into my mouth.

"Sorry, of course I am," Hans responded, not realising that I wasn't talking to him, but rather reading the message from the perpetrator. "You said someone used that tile to break the window," Hans added.

I shook my head. "No, look!" I exclaimed, my voice sounding shaky. I turned the heavy object with the message attached to it towards Hans. He read aloud the colourful letters in the decorative font, which looked identical to the threat I'd received at home not long ago. "Are you really listening?"

We gazed at each other for a moment, lost for words. I was the first to look away and took in my impaired consulting room. It was one broken, chaotic mess, which sadly formed a striking metaphor for what my life resembled at the moment.

"I'm calling the police," Hans stated grimly and dashed out of the room.

I was still nailed to the spot, with the pavement tile in my hands, when I suddenly felt Simone touch my shoulders. "Why don't you come to my room –

I'll make you a cup of tea," she said softly.

I just nodded and turned around. I conscientiously laid the tile back on the floor – it had been foolish of me to pick it up. I might have compromised the only piece of evidence there was.

Not too long after, I was sitting at our lunch table, staring ahead of me and absent-mindedly dipping a tea bag into the mug with hot water that Simone had brought me.

Hans swung open the door and barged into the room – a breath of cold, fresh air wafted over my face and I shivered. "Nothing seems to have been taken from your room. You didn't have any personal items in there, such as a phone or purse, did you?"

I shook my head. "I'd only just started my day at the practice, I'd planned the first few hours off for today," I answered in a small voice, although my colleagues had undoubtedly been aware of my absence this morning. I suddenly noticed that my tea had become way too strong and jerked the bag out of the water.

My face probably reflected how I was feeling, since Hans walked over to me and laid his warm, big hand on my shoulder. "Try not to worry, Jennifer."

I looked up and smiled reassuringly at him, but inside I felt jittery and full of dread – someone was targeting me.

Simone entered the room. "I've rescheduled all of your patients due in the next hour for later in the week and explained to them the circumstances."

"Thank you, Simone," I said and lifted my mug to take a swig of the tea, but my hands were trembling so terribly that it spilled over the edge onto the table, forming a small puddle.

Simone looked at me with concern and then grabbed a cloth to wipe it up.

I heard the sound of the front door opening and immediately afterwards an unknown voice calling out, "Amsterdam-West police, good afternoon."

Hans walked towards the corridor. "We're in here. Please, come in."

I didn't know what exactly I was expecting – perhaps an entire team dressed in white suits, ready to crawl over the crime scene. Instead, merely a single police agent in uniform stepped into the room, introducing himself as Peter, with a smile on his face and a distinctive Amsterdam accent.

After the officer had examined my consultation room, established that a pavement tile had been hurled through the window from outside – as if we hadn't come to that conclusion already – and had read the note, he started entering all the information into his laptop. Simone brought him a cup of coffee with a biscuit. She seemed to find it all immensely fascinating and I imagined how she'd delight in recounting every last detail to her friends tonight.

The agent looked alternately at Hans and Simone, as I'd told him that I'd only just arrived at the practice. "Did you hear anything out of the ordinary, or see anyone suspicious in the last few hours?" Hans and Simone looked at each other and shook their heads. "No, nothing at all," Simone answered, looking like a deer in headlights.

"We both haven't been in my colleague's consultation room today," Hans added. "Is it possible that it happened during the night?"

The agent made a face suggesting it was anyone's-guess and kept typing in silence, the table vibrating each time he hit his keyboard.

I took a sip of my tea, this time succeeding without spilling it, hoping the warm liquid would calm down my nerves, although it felt like I'd need something stronger to do the job.

Hans leaned back against the door, his eyes fixated on the agent, who was still taking notes, and rubbed his chin. "Do you have any clue who might be behind all of this?"

The agent calmly finished his report and then pushed the laptop aside. He leaned back, crossed his arms and looked at Hans. "Look. We can never tell for sure with incidents like these. But given the message on the note and the fact that nothing was stolen, I'd venture a guess that this might be the work of a disgruntled patient." The agent's gaze turned to me. "Have you had any altercations with a patient recently, or has any complaint been filed against the practice?"

Simone glanced at me, then quickly lowered her eyes again.

I thought back to how I'd been ranting at Mrs van Brock a while ago and felt a wave of red creep up my neck until my cheeks flamed. She hadn't been the only patient I'd riled recently.

Hans responded like a diplomat addressing a problem in the Middle East. "Disgruntled patients are not uncommon here. It's a rather dynamic neighbourhood that we're serving," he declared, which was obviously a euphemism. He smiled at me, making me feel supported. "Wouldn't you agree, Jennifer?"

I nodded, feeling in a fog, as if the world around me was moving too fast.

The agent looked searchingly at me. "Dr Smits, has anything like this happened to you before? Has anyone ever threatened you in any way in the past?"

My mind went back to the note on my doormat, which nobody knew about. When I'd stumbled upon this second note just now, I was absolutely positive that it was written in the same spirit, but now I started to have my doubts. Why in the world had I been such an idiot to toss that first message out? Now I had nothing tangible to compare this second note with.

Before I could answer, Hans responded. "On one occasion, there was a patient who wasn't too pleased with how she was treated by Dr Smits. My colleague has had a rough time lately and we're all only human after all. However, we had a sit-down to clear it up and reconciled with the lady in question, so I don't subscribe to this incident having anything to do with her."

I nodded, feeling rattled and flustered about the whole situation.

The agent tapped his knuckles on the table for a moment and then pushed himself out of the chair. "Right. I've entered everything into the system. You'll receive a letter shortly with an overview of everything that happened." He grabbed something from his bag and handed it to me. "In this flyer you'll find tips from the police to prevent burglaries in the future."

I smiled dutifully and said "thank you", although there was obviously little use locking the barn door after the horse has bolted.

"I'll be heading off now." He winked at Simone. "Thanks for the coffee, love."

Simone started fiddling with her hair and smiled at the man with the broad shoulders.

Surely he couldn't be finished already? "Shouldn't you be doing something, take photos of the room, collect trace evidence or secure fingerprints? Things like that," I asked in a panicky voice.

He grinned and answered me, his Amsterdam accent even more pronounced, "No offense, Doc, but I think you may have watched too much CSI. If we start doing that for each minor case like this, we'll be powdering ourselves into a corner and never catch any real crooks."

Simone tried to stifle a giggle and I gave her a glare of contempt.

"Secure the place with one of those yellow tapes?" I tried.

There was an ever so slightly dismissive look of on his face as he shook his head. "This whole mess can just be cleaned up now."

"Well, this is a fine kettle of fish," Hans responded, apparently disappointed in the minimal approach as well. Then he turned his attention to Simone. "Can you go and get the dustpan and brush please?"

Simone left the room with a face like a smacked bum.

"I'll see myself out," Peter said, raising his hand, and strode out towards the hallway.

I had a bad feeling about this. I jumped up and followed the agent with brisk steps. "But how are you planning to find the perpetrator without any evidence?"

The agent swivelled, his bright blue eyes looking kindly at me. "Doc, people are being burgled twenty-four-seven. During the time we've been talking here, three other places have already been broken into. You're lucky nothing has been taken. I'm sorry to break it to you, but the chances of nabbing these fellas is slim to zero. Even if we were to collar the culprits, we're probably dealing with obnoxious, little punks who'll be released again after three days of litter picking."

I folded my arms in front of my chest and remained silent with a furrowed brow.

The agent shook hands with Hans and me. "Take care, Dr Smits," he said.

Hans closed the door behind the man and turned to me. "Oh dear."

My legs felt as if they were about to buckle from underneath me. "Surely, they can't get away with it that easily?"

26

I hit the pedals of my bike, feeling beads of sweat forming on my back. Yesterday I'd been so upset by the devastation in my consultation room that I had to devote all of my energy to carry out my work properly – there had been no opportunity to phone Detective Armstrong. But I felt increasingly edgy and knew there was no time to lose. I wanted to get hold of the detective as soon as possible and share my latest revelations and suspicions of forgery and bribery concerning Mason & McGant, so I decided to ring him before my first consultation of the day. While I waited for the traffic light to turn green, I fished my phone out of my pocket and scrolled through the contacts until I arrived at the right number.

He answered my call. "Detective Armstrong."

"Good morning, this is Jennifer Smits speaking," I began in a friendly tone. "It's been a while since we last spoke. I'm Oliver's wife, the man who died half a year ago at a holiday park.

"Yes, yes, I know who you are. You called me not too long ago," he grunted.

I resumed, feeling slightly pressured. "You may also remember I told you before about the secret file my husband had been working on at the law firm. As it turns out, I recently …"

"Yes I do remember, Mrs Smits," he interrupted me, his voice raised. "And I explained to you we cannot do anything for you. The outcome of the investigation was irrefutable – there's no indication whatsoever to assume that your husband's death had a non-natural cause."

I clutched the phone between my ear and my shoulder as the lights turned green and swiftly cycled off. "Hold your horses. Last time you said that I couldn't provide evidence for all my hypotheses. This has now changed – I have evidence."

There was a pause. "And what kind of evidence might that be, ma'am?" he asked, without a trace of interest in his voice.

"It's too complicated to clarify over the phone. Would you have an opening for me to stop by?"

"Ma'am, I have other pressing engagements," he said resolutely. "There are a ton of files piled up on my desk. You have no idea what kind of workload I'm under – after last year's round of budget cuts, our department has shrunk by forty percent while the big shots above us expect the same output," he complained.

I was thinking about how I could win him over when a black SUV suddenly emerged from my right. With all my might I squeezed the brakes of the bike, skidding over the asphalt. After what seemed like an eternity – but in fact was most likely less than a second – my bike screeched to a halt. The nose of the front wheel was only a few centimetres away from the bumper of the car. I'd escaped getting run over by the skin of my teeth.

"You idiot!" I yelled at the motorist, who was gawking at me in astonishment. "You almost hit me."

"Excuse me?" I heard the detective ask.

I was standing still on the bike path, my heart beating wildly in my chest. Didn't that moron have eyes?

"Mrs Smits, are you still there?"

The man in the car seemed to come back to his senses and lowered his window. "Are you trying to get yourself killed? Didn't you see, I was coming from the right!" he yelled.

I realised that he indeed had priority and needed a moment to catch my breath. "Yes I'm here. Sorry about that," I spoke into the phone.

Detective Armstrong gave a sigh. "Mrs Smits, I really need to go."

I ignored the driver, who was still cursing and hollering at me, put on my headphones and cycled away.

This was my last chance. "Ten minutes of your time is all I ask, no more. I will stop badgering you after that. I promise."

There was another sigh. "Alright then."

We agreed that I'd stop by during the lunch break. The detective gave me an address that, to my relief, was less than five minutes from my work by bike. I'd be able to duck out for the meeting without too much trouble – I didn't feel like informing my colleagues about my plans.

"See you later," I said, feeling elated and cycled along the last few streets towards my work.

After a hectic morning in the practice, I was knee-deep in administration when I noticed it was almost time to meet with Detective Armstrong.

Hans stuck his head around the corner of my room. "Lunch?"

"I'm not eating in today," I said, stowing my phone in my handbag, avoiding his eyes.

"Oh, that's a shame. Not hungry?" Hans asked kindly.

My cheeks were turning red. "I er ..." I faltered. "I have to pick up something at a friend's house." I felt sick as soon as the lie had passed my lips, but I told myself it was for a greater cause.

"Right. I see. Just make sure you have something to eat while you're on the go," he said lightly, but there was slight sound of concern in his voice, which I found completely unwarranted – there was nothing wrong with me. "Sure, I'll grab something on the hoof," I assured him. I demonstratively pinched a piece of belly fat. "I need to keep that muffin top in shape, right?"

He seemed reassured and laughed. "Exactly."

I slid my arms into my coat. "See you later," I yelled over my shoulder and dashed out.

Outside I decided to ignore my growling stomach and cycled straight to the police station – I didn't want to give Detective Armstrong any reason to cancel our appointment.

A while later I saw an imposing, modern edifice fronted with glass panels rise up in the distance. This police station was nothing like the concrete, dilapidated building that I'd been taken to by the police months ago when Oliver had just died. Memories of that horrible day came rushing back, but somehow the intensity of the grief seemed to have abated with time.

I ascended the black, stone steps to the entrance and saw a counter inside where, according to Detective Armstrong, I had to register. I walked over to it and gave my name through the protective glass shield. "I have an appointment with Detective Armstrong."

"One moment please," the lady in the blue police uniform said.

She asked for my identity card, the number of which she noted down and made a phone call.

Then she turned to me again. "This is a visitor's pass that will provide access to the building. If you hold the pass against the scanner, it will get you through the gates." She pointed towards something in the far distance. "Then take the lift to the third floor and Detective Armstrong will be waiting for you upstairs."

I thanked her and followed the instructions. As the lift doors opened on the third floor, I was greeted by a man of about sixty years old, with a grey moustache masking his upper lip. His pink scalp was visible through the thin gauze of his wispy white hair and he was towering about ten centimetres above me. The amiable-looking man extended his hand and introduced himself.

I answered his firm handshake. "Jennifer Smits."

"Impeccable timing," he remarked and gave me a nod. "Let's head to my office."

We walked silently over the blue carpet towards the end of the corridor, where he held the door open for me. The large window in the room offered a panoramic view over the flanking canal.

"Take a seat," he said, indicating a hard wooden chair. He walked to the other side of the table and lowered himself onto a chair which squeaked under his weight. He pulled a blue lunchbox from his backpack, secured with an elastic band. "Mind if I eat while we talk?" Four neatly cut sandwiches and some fruit filled the box. "I have another meeting with my team at one o'clock."

I said that it was no problem and felt my heart pounding in my chest. This was the moment to run my ideas by the detective and convince him to reopen the investigation. If this didn't work out, I'd have no other options at my disposal to resolve the mystery surrounding Oliver's death.

The detective got straight to the point. "You wanted to discuss something with me? Fire away."

I rifled through my handbag and pulled out both my pack of papers and Sandra's, which I had printed out late last night, and began talking. "I told you before that my husband was secretly working on a file entitled Van Santen, right?"

The detective chewed noisily on his sandwich and mumbled something in consent.

"I gained access to this document after his death," I said, being purposely vague about the way we had appropriated it. "Based on this, I reached the conclusion that there was actually no such client named Van Santen. This was the first point that deviated from the usual procedure at Mason & McGant."

"Who were Mason & McGant again?" asked the detective.

His remark made me feel disheartened – he apparently didn't recall anything about Oliver's case.

He gobbled up a chunk of bread, immediately grabbed a new sandwich from his box and admired it. "Can't beat a good old cheese sarnie," he said and eagerly sunk his teeth into it.

I rolled my eyes and dug my nails into my palms, trying to stay calm. "Mason & McGant is the law firm my husband used to work for, remember?"

He nodded his head vigorously. "Oh yes, now I remember. Go on."

"We've been scrutinising the documents and raked over every detail. It transpires my husband was investigating a number of suspicious cases within his office and organised the results in a file with a pseudonym, 'Van Santen'."

The detective took a grape from his lunchbox, tossed it in the air and moved his head so he could catch it in his mouth. He missed and the grape bounced off the table, vanishing somewhere underneath his desk. His obvious and almost offensive lack of attention made me question whether he was taking any of this seriously.

I waved the pile of papers in the air in a desperate attempt to redirect his focus before speaking again. "My husband drafted a chart containing the evidence gathered for the four cases and categorised them into two different types." I placed the chart on the table and turned it a quarter so that we could both read it. "I'm not an expert in this legal jargon as I'm a doctor by profession, but it transpires that something unusual was going on with regards to the evidence of those cases. Something that was so significant and illicit that he felt the need to give this document a pseudonym. He didn't even mention it to me, his own wife." I deliberately left out the fact it wasn't the only thing Oliver had been hiding from me.

"Hmm," he muttered wearily and snatched his last sandwich out of the box. He glanced at his watch. "I have a few minutes left."

I felt like a noose had been forced around my neck – I hadn't gotten to all those other suspicious things yet, I could feel my glimmer of hope in a good outcome fizzle out.

"Do you remember the compromising DVDs we found, showing all the lawyers who received their training at Mason & McGant?"

This piece of information seemed to have jogged his memory. "Oh right," he said, a chunk of bread crammed in his left, bulging cheek. "Now it's all coming back. That is where it got ugly. Wasn't your husband captured in that footage?" he asked, but I could tell by the look on his face he knew the answer to his rather indelicate question.

My cheeks flushed with disconcertment. "My theory is that the paralegals are deliberately recorded on tape during their first year," I said, evading his question. "So that they can be silenced later on during their careers whenever they witness things at the firm that are illegal or otherwise in breach of the law. Or even worse, used to put the squeeze on them to actively participate in criminal activity." I paused a moment letting the detective take it all in, before I concluded my story. "I have a strong suspicion that the Dutch Forensics Institute is playing a major role in this as well."

He attentively wrapped the elastic band back around the lunchbox and slid it into his backpack. Then, to my astonishment, he pulled out one of those boxes of milk children take to school with them. "I see where you're going," he said, puncturing the aluminium foil with the straw and taking a sip. "By the way, who are we?"

I looked at him, puzzled. "I don't follow."

He narrowed his eyes. "You said: *we* went through the documents."

I had to admit, he was sharper than I'd perceived him to be. Perhaps I'd been underestimating him so far. "Sandra and I," I wavered.

"And who is Sandra?"

A wave of crimson crept up my neck. "Sandra was my husband's mistress," I confessed, immediately regretting it. I should have said she was a friend of mine.

I quickly continued. "After we found these documents, she died under suspicious circumstances, not far from here, as a result of a collision with a tram."

"Oh yes, I remember," he cut me off. "There was nothing suspicious about it, Mrs Smits. It was just a terrible accident."

"Wait a minute," I said. "I'll get to that in a moment."

The detective was adamant. "Mrs Smits, one of the best detectives was assigned to that case. With a team full of professionals, he investigated everything at the scene of the accident. There was absolutely nothing suspicious about this poor woman's death."

"How can you know for sure?" I muttered. "I spoke with the tr …"

He broke me off. "Yes, yes, you told me all that over the phone last time."

"But," I tried, but stopped when he raised his hand and closed his eyes.

He looked at me. "Listen, Mrs Smits," he began. There was that look of pity again, which I'd seen in people's eyes so often lately and couldn't stand anymore.

I turned my head away and stared out of the large window, where I noticed it had started drizzling.

"You've been through a lot lately. Your husband was snatched from this world before his time and you didn't even get the chance to say goodbye to him. Suddenly you're all alone, left behind with a toddler. You apparently discover that your husband has been, er …"

I looked at him, lifting my chin and squaring my shoulders, daring him to say it out loud, but this time he was the one who averted his eyes in discomfiture.

"Anyway. This lady suddenly dies as a result of a fatal bicycle accident with a tram. It must have been an incredibly traumatic time for you. There are people who'd lose their marbles over less."

I felt anger welling up. "Are you suggesting I'm losing my mind?" "Oh no. Of course not," he hushed. "I'm merely trying to say it must be overwhelming." He folded his hands together like a priest presiding over his congregation. "After your husband's death, I spoke extensively with my colleagues in the south. They've done an excellent job over there and meticulously examined all traces," he said proudly. "After you and I spoke on the phone a while ago, I went back over the report and I reiterate – I one hundred percent agree with their findings."

I wielded the piece of paper with the chart presenting the evidence that Oliver had prepared so scrupulously, and shook it in his face. "But this here is new information," I sputtered, but I knew I'd lost the battle, any objection would fall on deaf ears.

He raised his voice. "This isn't proof of murder. It's not even a starting point. Neither of us know what your husband's intentions were when he drafted this document. Maybe his supervisor had requested him to make an overview of some cases. It's anyone's guess basically."

He glanced at his watch again. "I'm sorry, I have to go."

I gave a little whimper of protest. "Please," I said, trying not to burst into tears. "I am desperate. You are my last resort. I received a threatening note at home the other day and yesterday a tile was thrown into …"

He released his breath with a long, impatient sigh. "Look. If it would ease your mind, I'll promise to go over it later." He grabbed the stack of papers and tossed them to the corner of his desk, on top of a tall, disorderly pile.

The detective was merely humouring me – we both knew he wouldn't seriously examine that evidence. Best-case scenario, he'd skim through the document and toss it in the bin. More likely, it would lay on his desk for months, collecting dust, only to be fed to the shredder during a clean-up.

I was overwhelmed with defeat – I'd been unsuccessful in trying to win him over.

I stood up and gathered up my belongings, acknowledged my loss and shook his outstretched hand. "Thank you for your time."

He nodded and smiled. "All the best to you, Mrs Smits."

It was still drizzling when I left the police station. I pulled up the hood of my jacket and swiftly unlocked my bike. As I made to cycle off, I noticed a young man on a scooter, shielding his face with his hoodie. I waited for him to go first, but he kept lingering, his head slightly bowed and hidden from my view. I shrugged and started pedalling towards the practice.

Along the way my thoughts turned to the past few days, in which everyone around me seemed to have been doubting me and questioning my sanity. I'd ruined the date with Dan – he'd clearly concluded I was a lunatic, my girlfriends thought that I wasn't thinking straight and Detective Armstrong had made it abundantly clear my suspicions were completely unfounded as far as he was concerned.

Perhaps the grounds for Oliver working on the Van Santen file were entirely different after all. It was clear that the document didn't belong to a client and so the name was indeed a pseudonym, however, there were countless innocent explanations for this, as the detective already pointed out.

Perhaps my mind was playing tricks on me and I was barking up the wrong tree. Admittedly, I hadn't felt like myself in the past six months, I was suffering from a perpetual lack of sleep and the alcohol was flowing a little too profusely.

I stopped at a traffic light and pressed the button a few times as the rain intensified, swooped by the wind across the road. I managed to fish my phone out of my pocket and noticed I had only ten minutes left until my next consultation. I would have to ask Simone to get me a sandwich.

Sliding my phone back into my pocket, I was alarmed by a rumbling sound coming from directly behind me As I looked back, I saw a figure on a white scooter wearing a blue, utterly soaked top, just a few metres away, looking familiar. Wasn't that the same guy I just saw as I left the police station? The rain was beating down on my face, obscuring my vision, and I was unable to make out the face that was hiding underneath the hood. I abruptly turned my head forward again and felt my heart skittering erratically in my chest. There was something unnerving about this guy and the way that he'd been loitering outside the police station, but had now caught up with me.

The light turned green and I cycled on hurriedly, my hand over my eyes trying to hinder the plump drops of rain. The scooter didn't overtake me as I would have expected it to, and my fears began to grow. After a few minutes of hearing a continuous hum of the engine behind me, I plucked up the courage to ever so carefully look over my shoulder. For a brief moment I caught a glimpse of the hard gaze in his dark eyes boring straight into me, but the man immediately bowed his head again.

He was following me! I pedalled as fast as I could, even though he could obviously catch up with me at any moment if he wanted to. The pounding rain felt like a thousand tiny pins stabbing my face. I veered right, towards the practice and when I cautiously looked back over my shoulder again moments later, he'd disappeared.

I halted by the side of the road and took a moment to catch my breath, my head spinning. Why was that guy following me? Was there someone out there that wanted to keep an eye on me? Did it have something to do with the two threatening notes I'd received or the man Tim had spoken about?

I tried to calm myself down. "Get a grip, Jennifer," I said out loud. There was probably a simple explanation for all of this.

When I entered the practice minutes later, my trousers were sticking to my legs and my shoes squelched loudly as I walked. I only had a few minutes to smarten up.

"Oh gosh, you're drenched!" Simone said, looking at me from head to toe. "Take your time. Your patient hasn't arrived yet," she added and handed me a towel.

"Thanks," I responded, hanging my soaked coat to dry on the coat rack. I swept the wet strands of bedraggled hair away from my face and made a few attempts to dab myself dry with a towel. I glanced at myself in the mirror – I'd had better days, but this would do.

My eyes fell on the small window in Simone's room, offering a wide view of the busy main road on which our practice was located. "Simone, have you by any chance ever seen a young fellow in a blue hoodie on a white scooter passing by?"

Simone spun around on her office chair and looked at me in surprise. "I see so many people from here, it's one of the busiest roads in this part of Amsterdam. I'm sure there would have been someone who fits that description."

I stared into the distance. "You're probably right," I mumbled.

There was a short pause. "Are you all right?"

My gaze turned to Simone. "Yes, yes, I'm fine," I responded with a faint smile and fled to my consultation office.

As I put my phone on mute I noticed I'd received a message from Lindsey.

'Jen, I hope you're not cross with us anymore. We love you and only have your best interests at heart. How about we go for drinks soon?'

I tossed my phone back into my bag and decided to respond later. I plopped onto my desk chair and watched sheets of rain stream relentlessly down the windows. It wasn't until then did I realise how tired, cold and hungry I was.

I opened our administration programme and saw that Mrs Peters had already registered into the practice. I leaped up, walked to the counter and asked in hushed tones. "Simone, could you get me a sandwich?"

She stared at me in astonishment. Behind her I saw Hans, who was making a fresh pot of coffee, look up with eyebrows that had risen several centimetres. "It's almost two. Haven't you had any lunch yet?" Simone queried.

I threw out an excuse. "I was running late. Just make it a cheese or ham sandwich." I laid a note on her desk to cover the costs. "Thank you."

Before either of them could comment, I dashed into the waiting room. "Mrs Peters, you're next."

27

I'd curled up on the couch with a cup of herbal tea and switched on the eight o'clock news. I tried to listen while Tim hummed through the baby monitor, but it was hard to keep my mind focused. After my appointment with the detective, I'd promised myself to let go of everything related to Mason & McGant, however, this morning I'd remembered that in the email I'd received from Sandra via the Shared drive, there had been a telephone number listed with the Amsterdam area code. It could have been her landline and thus formed a means to get in touch with her husband. Didn't I owe it to Oliver to put that man to the test? After all, he worked at the same firm and I had to therefore consider the possibility he knew more about what was going on at Mason & McGant. The universe seemed to have thwarted my every move so far, but had now thrown me this last buoy – surely I couldn't leave this opportunity untouched?

I grabbed the remote control and turned off the television, ignoring the little voice in the back of my head that told me to let the matter rest, opened my laptop where I soon found the number.

I keyed in the numbers on my phone and after ringing three times, the call was answered. "Roderick DelaHaye," came an unfamiliar voice.

"Good evening, Roderick," I said in the most polite manner I could muster. "This is Jennifer speaking." There was an anticipated pause. "Jennifer Smits? Sandra's friend," I clarified as if we'd been BFFs, having weekly get-togethers over wine and olives.

"Oh right. Hello Jennifer," the man said, but it was evident he didn't recognise my name, which was probably for the best given my plan.

"How have you been doing?" I said in the pitiful, compassionate tone that people had so often used with me since Oliver died.

He gave a big sigh and sounded worn out when he spoke. "Oh well, I'm okay."

I laid out the next steps of my plan. "Of course you and I never met when Sandra was alive, but I'd love to perhaps visit you, Roderick. We'd become like two peas in a pod, San and I," I said and winced at this lie. "Maybe I could pop by for a cup of coffee? I'd really like to reminisce about that wonderful lady with someone who shared my fondness for her," I wheedled and prayed that I wasn't pushing my luck.

I heard him dither. "Oh right. Perhaps that might be a good idea. Come to think about it, I believe Sandra did speak about you."

I frowned. Was he just being polite, or could Sandra have mentioned my name to her husband just before she died?

"Wonderful," I exclaimed in feigned delight.

"Would you like to come over to our place for tea, tomorrow afternoon around three?" he proposed. "I only work mornings at the moment, I can't concentrate for any longer than that," he said with an air of gloom.

"I understand, it must be hard," I responded empathically, but inside, I was rejoicing. "Three o'clock sounds perfect."

"What's the address?"

It remained silent for a moment. "I thought the pair of you were so tight-knit, weren't you?"

I squeezed my leg hard, while thinking on my feet. "Oh, without a doubt," I confirmed, lying through my teeth. "We just never met at home."

He seemed to buy it and gave me an address, just south of the financial heart of Amsterdam.

"See you tomorrow," I said brightly and hung up.

When I cycled into the street that Roderick had directed me to the following day, I saw a number of immense, ultra-modern residential towers rising up in front of me, with all kinds of café bars, boutiques and eateries at the base. I'd never travelled to this part of Amsterdam before, although it was fairly close to Mason & McGant. One of the towering buildings turned out to contain the number I was looking for and I walked up to the intercom. The glass walls of the building were tinted, concealing the inside, giving the impression of being an extravagant, high-end property. To my surprise, there wasn't a doorbell per flat, but only one general entrance button for me to press.

The buzzer sounded and a posh voice asked me which resident I required. "Mr DelaHaye," I answered.

Access was granted after which I heard the door unlock, and automatically and slowly open itself. I entered the building and found myself in an enormous, empty lobby, where a man in a blue uniform seated behind a counter was watching me with piercing eyes.

I walked towards the counter and told him I had an appointment with Mr

DelaHaye at number 220.

With a surly and somewhat presumptuous expression on his face, he shoved a list towards me. "Please enter the name and house number you're visiting, madam."

This is a lot of palaver just to visit Roderick, I thought to myself. I managed to hold back a cutting response and did what the man had requested and then walked across the shiny, marble floor towards the lift. The metal sign flanking it indicated that number 220 was located on the 23rd floor – the top of the building.

The glass lift whooshed upwards ultra-fast, hardly making a sound, and offered stunning views over the city. When the doors opened, I saw there were two penthouses residing at this highest level.

I rang the bell for 220 and almost instantly the massive, wooden, double front doors swung open.

An older lady in a work uniform stood in the doorway with a straight back. Her thick head of grey hair was tied up with a silver pin.

"Mrs Smits?" she asked. "Mr DelaHaye is expecting you." The housekeeper gracefully stepped aside to let me in.

The walls of the hall were covered with dark, wooden panels, giving the impression of a hotel. The marble floor was spotless with the appearance of having been polished recently, and a small side table with a framed photo of Sandra on top was the only object in the room that gave a hint of this being a home.

The lady delicately took my coat and hung it in a separate cloakroom. She led me into a room without windows, containing an immaculate, brown leather couch and a glass coffee table adorned with a selection of carefully positioned magazines, which were – judging by their covers – all business related.

"May I offer you something to drink?" she asked.

"I'm fine, thanks."

"Mr DelaHaye will be with you in a minute," she declared and retreated with an almost invisible bow. I walked a few steps and let my eyes wander through this odd, immaculate room and noticed a painting on the wall in van Gogh style. I got the impression that Roderick received clients or colleagues here in his home.

It wasn't long before the other door in the room swung open.

"Jennifer," I heard someone call out behind me as if he'd known me for years. I spun around and took a brief moment to observe him – Sandra had told me her husband was of a similar age to her, but he looked at least ten years older. The top two buttons of his blue-and-white striped shirt, which was wrinkled where I'd imagine it would have usually been perfectly laundered, were left undone, exposing a few wisps of chest hair. The dark circles under his eyes were probably the culprit for my misjudgement of his age.

I dithered about whether to shake his hand or if it would seem too formal, but before I was able to decide, he moved up to me with wide open arms and drew me into an embrace. A whiff of his eau de cologne assailed my nostrils, but was hardly able to mask the musty, unpleasant and overwhelming scent enveloping him. I held my breath until he finally let go, only to hold me tightly by the shoulders. There was something defiant in his voice when he spoke. "It is an absolute delight to meet you, Jennifer."

I made my eyes sparkle with enthusiasm, trying to pull the wool over his eyes. "Roderick, how lovely to finally meet Sandra's beloved husband."

He nodded, a big grin on his face. "Sandra told me a lot about you," he said, looking deep into my eyes. But this time I knew it was a lie.

I flashed him a smile.

He laid a hand on my back and gently ushered me towards the door. "Let's head to the drawing room."

We walked into the next room, which, in contrast to the one I'd been waiting in, was bright and airy with white walls flooded with light coming from the full length windows. The space was sleekly decorated in a mixture of white and black furniture with various glass side tables – clearly the work of an interior designer – and must have cost an arm and a leg. I surveyed the collection of modern art on the wall and pulled an expression to feign appreciation. "Those are some fine pieces of art."

"That's entirely Sandra's merit. She managed to lay her hands on a lot of these works at a snip," Roderick said and waved his hand in a grandiose gesture. "She took immense pleasure in scouting out young artists with a great talent and helping them move forward in their development – you know, making sure they'd be noticed. My wife always seemed to, one way or another, come up with a dilly of an idea to get their careers off the ground." Roderick's eyes were glowing as he spoke. "Well, I don't have to tell you all that, of course you already know this."

I nodded vehemently. "Sandra had many talents."

I walked up towards the windows, which offered a magnificent view over the entire city, unequalled by anything I'd seen before, and in the distance I thought I recognised the Rembrandt Tower.

"What a fantastic panorama," I said, while my gaze remained fixed outside. "Sandra never told me you have such a phenomenal place."

"Ah, she was modest," I heard Roderick say from behind me.

I swivelled and saw Roderick walk up to a pristine, glass table with a number of carafes on it. "Care for a glass?" he asked, indicating something that looked like vodka.

"Sounds good," I lied, assuming an expression of rapt interest.

He poured the transparent liquid into a hand-crafted, heavy crystal glass and handed it to me.

We made a toast. "To Sandra," I declared. I took a sip and tried to ignore the burning sensation in my throat.

"Good stuff," I managed to utter as casually as possible, venturing a guess that this wasn't a cheap bottle from a random off-licence store.

It worked like a charm. "You're a woman with fine taste, I notice." Roderick held his glass up in the air and looked at it with a sense of pride. "I had my assistant import it from Poland. Made with hand-picked bison grass, with a dash of almond and vanilla," he crowed.

Demonstratively, I took another sip and nodded, suppressing a grimace.

"Why don't we sit outside?" Roderick walked up to the windows and with just one click opened them along the entire width of the room, folding them like a harmonica.

Holding the crystal glass in my hand, I followed Roderick out onto the tiled roof terrace, the size of which was at least double that of my garden. The wind was howling like a wounded dog at this height and I pulled my jumper tightly around me with one hand. Aside from a lounge set in one corner, the terrace was sparsely decorated with only a few perfectly trimmed bonsai trees in ceramic pots. The whole space was enclosed by a glass fence about a metre high. Imagine one would lean too far over it, I thought, and shuddered.

"Shall we sit over there?" I asked and pointed towards the couch.

Roderick nodded and led the way.

I took a seat next to him and looked him in the eye. "So how have you been, Roderick?"

His gaze strayed as he ran a hand over his chin. "I'm all right."

His eyes were so profoundly sad that I suddenly experienced this almost irresistible urge to hold him, comfort him and tell him I knew exactly how he felt. The emptiness during the day, the loneliness at night. The grief that hits you in the face early in the morning, when you wake up from a long and restless night. But I stifled my empathy – it was too early to acquit him. "You are a strong man. I can tell," I said.

He jerked his head towards me. "How did you meet Sandra?"

His question caught me off guard and I felt nervous, in spite of the vodka. Fragments of the one-on-ones Sandra and I'd had flashed through my mind. "We got chatting in the gym and it turned out we had the same personal trainer," I made up. "We really clicked and since then we saw each other several times a week." I wondered where, for heaven's sake, with my demanding work at the practice and Tim, that I would find the time for this indulgence and hoped he wouldn't start asking questions.

He stared into the distance again. "Oh yes, that personal trainer," he echoed in a heartbroken way that made me wonder if Sandra had ever had an affair with that man. She'd made it seem as if her husband cared little for her, but I began to question how much of it had actually been true.

I gave a sad smile. "I miss her terribly," I said and was immediately ashamed of this lie. But I saw no other option – I had to find out if this guy, this grieving husband sitting next to me, knew anything.

Roderick shook his head. "The loss is unbearable. We were so close, Sandra and I, in spite of me working ridiculous hours. I know she had a problem with it and I couldn't blame her." His thoughts seemed to jump around all over the place, something I recognised from myself in the weeks after Oliver's death. "Maybe I shouldn't have been so focused on my work and instead spent more time at home. We'd just planned a weekend getaway to Tuscany, to rekindle our love. She was really looking forward to that."

I was puzzled. The last time I'd spoken to Sandra, she told me she intended to leave her husband – it had seemed like a *fait accompli*. On the other hand, she sometimes appeared to have a somewhat volatile and impulsive personality. I couldn't rule out that she'd changed her mind after our conversation.

"She never complained, but suggested to spend more time with each other," Roderick continued. "If only I'd listened to her more. Maybe she would still ..." His words trailed off in the wind.

I laid my hand on his arm. It felt too intimate and rather unnatural, like a rehearsed gesture. "You mustn't say that. Sandra was the victim of an accident. You played no part in that."

I carried on sipping my glass in a demonstrative way, but made sure to swallow only modest amounts. I couldn't afford a slip.

He looked me in the eye. "You're right. She was in the wrong place at the wrong time." He shook his head again in despair. "And yet, if only I'd put a bit more effort in, listened to her requests for date nights every now and then, treated her more like my darling wife. Instead, I made the choice to be working like a Trojan all the time, which seems so incredibly futile now." He looked at me. "Do you know I'm a partner at a large law firm called Mason & Mc Gant?"

I nodded. "I believe Sandra once told me."

"I practically lived at the firm. What have I been doing there all this time?" Roderick whimpered. "I should have tried to find a better balance between work and home."

I patted his arm amicably. "Don't be too hard on yourself. We would all make other choices in life with twenty-twenty hindsight."

I swallowed before making my next move. This was the clincher. I thought for a moment about the precise formulation of words to use. "You've had tons of things on your mind. I understood from Sandra there'd been some challenging cases at Mason & McGant lately," I said ever so carefully.

He looked at me mystified. "Challenging cases?"

"Well, of course I'm not familiar with all the ins and outs," I said, waving my hand casually, but inside I felt my heart beating so violently I was afraid Roderick would hear it. "I believe I remember Sandra mention something about a file with a pseudonym. A minor problem that needed to be investigated internally, all rather hush-hush." I was taking a huge risk by revealing this detail, but I knew I needed to give him a proper prod to find out if he knew something.

Roderick looked me directly in the eye. "I think you're mistaken. I did share with Sandra how hectic things were at work lately – she may have just misunderstood me. You know what she was like." His gaze softened and he gave me a wink. "Legal matters weren't exactly her cup of tea. In any case, there are no secretive investigations or issues at Mason & McGant, fortunately." He laughed. "I'm in no state to deal with any drama at the firm right now."

I took a moment to let it sink in and smiled. "You're right. It must have been a misunderstanding on my part."

I relaxed my shoulders, stretched my legs and took a swig of my drink. Roderick clearly knew nothing about the Van Santen file or any criminal wrongdoing going on within Mason & McGant. The man here beside me on the couch was a grieving husband – everything in his demeanour evoked a sense of recognition and understanding in me. How could I have questioned that?

I decided to open up to him. "By the way, there's something I didn't share with you yet," I said as lightly as possible.

He raised his eyebrows. "Something about Sandra?"

"Oh, no," I hurried to say. "It's about my husband. He was suddenly ripped from my life too – he died half a year ago as a result of a terrible fall. So I think I know exactly how you feel."

He gently touched my shoulder. "I'm so sorry to hear that."

"Thank you." I lowered my gaze. "It gets better with time, really," I said, but to be fair I sometimes had doubts about that.

We chatted for a while until I glanced at my watch. "I'm afraid I need to leave." I placed my glass, which was half full, on the table. I leaped up and spread my arms. "Roderick."

He stood up and held me tightly, only this time I'd lowered my guard and felt the warmth of his embrace. The fact that we'd endured a similar tragedy forged a bond between us.

He released me and said with heartfelt compassion, "You're a kind woman, Jennifer."

I nodded. "It was wonderful to meet you, Roderick." I swung my handbag over my shoulder. "I'll see myself out."

With firm steps I walked over the windy terrace, into the reception room towards the corridor where the housekeeper was awaiting me with my coat, which seemed to have been brushed clean.

"That's very kind of you to brush my coat," I said, sliding my arms through the sleeves.

The woman looked at me with an expression I couldn't quite interpret. "Mr DelaHaye requested it."

I froze and peered quizzically at her. This was odd.

The woman remained silent and folded her hands in front of her.

With an indefinable feeling I said goodbye, opened the door and left the penthouse.

28

"Good morning, you little monkey," I said gleefully, lifting Tim out of his bed. He wrapped his arms tightly around me.

"Did you sleep well?" I asked.

He nodded.

"You slept through the night," I gushed and poked my finger in his chest. "Timmy deserves another sticker on his sheet, don't you sweetie?"

With Tim on my arm, I opened the curtains and looked out onto our street where life was slowly resuming for another day. The sun was peeking over the four-storey, hundred-year-old houses across from us, shining into my face and providing a lavish warmth. Directly opposite was a building screened by scaffolding, the decorative ornaments and patterned brickwork of the gables restored to their full glory by craftsmen. Down the street at my favourite cafe, the first cups of coffee were being served to early-bird commuters.

Tim had enough of my reverie – he wriggled out of my arms, jumped nimbly to the ground and starting scampering off in the direction of his wardrobe. Together we selected an outfit for the day – a blue and white polo over a pair of jeans. Oliver would have been pleased to see his son dressed so smartly, I thought to myself. After sliding into my favourite jeans and a clean shirt with the scent of lavender, I headed downstairs with a spring in my step. I let Tim watch some television while I prepared breakfast. I slotted two slices of bread into the toaster and turned it on, set the table and made myself a cup of coffee. I'd resolved that, no matter how incredibly sad it was that Oliver was gone, I had to go on with my life.

I suddenly realised that I hadn't yet responded to Lindsey's message from the other day, so I grabbed my phone.

'Thx for your message, sweetie. Really sorry for my outburst. I was just a bit overwhelmed with everything the other day,' I typed generously. *'Feeling much better now. Sounds perfect to go for drinks. Xxx,'* I ended my message.

About an hour later I parked my bike in front of the practice and after a brief chat with Simone and Hans, entered my consultation room. My phone buzzed with a text message from Lindsey.

'So happy to hear from you, Jen. I'll see you soon! X.'

I smiled and slid my phone into my handbag.

The morning went by in the blink of an eye and when I entered our lunchroom at midday, I noticed a brown paper bag on the table – Simone had apparently already picked up our order. I peeked inside the bag and took out my tuna sandwich with a bottle of sparkling water, while Hans and Simone joined me.

Hans sat down opposite me. "Hey Jennifer, did you enjoy your day off yesterday?" he asked, while Simone absent-mindedly scrolled through her phone.

My mind went back to my visit to Roderick and I smiled. "I met up with someone who recently became a widower," I answered and took a bite of my crusty, French baguette, causing crumbs to fall on the floor.

Hans looked awfully serious. "Did you join a support group?"

I laughed. "I wouldn't exactly call it that. It was more or less a coincidence that I bumped into him," I said, immediately realising it was yet another lie, though this time an innocent one.

"That's great," Hans continued kindly. "I hope it helped?"

"Very much," I said sincerely. "It has brought me more than I could have imagined."

Hans had a puzzled expression on his face, but before he could ask any questions, my phone rang.

I picked it up and stared at the display in incredulity.

"I have to take this one," I mumbled, leaping up, and dashed out towards my consultation room.

Never in a million years had I expected to hear from this man again. Memories of our last encounter flooded back into my mind, crushing my sunny mood.

I closed the door behind me, locked it and answered the call. "Jennifer Smits."

"It's Dan. Daniel Bernstein."

"Dan," I echoed coolly. Surely he wasn't going to act like it was all water under the bridge now? He'd kicked me to the curb like I was some kind of dirty hook-up. I may have behaved rather oddly, but that didn't give him a free pass to treat me like that.

There was a hint of diffidence in his voice. "Do you remember who I am?"

"Of course I do," I retorted. "I don't make a habit of hooking up with strangers and staying over at their place. Do you?"

He ignored my question. "You were right," he said.

I felt the blood drain out of my face. "What are you talking about?"

"After our chat that morning, I started having doubts about what you'd shared with me. I told myself it was inconceivable, but I somehow couldn't shake it off. Later that night, I sneaked into your husband's former office, found those DVDs and watched them all at home one by one. On each labelled disk, I recognised all the paralegals who were hired at Mason & McGant in that particular year – exactly as you'd described."

I was in shock. Just when I thought I had put this ordeal behind me, Daniel popped up in my life and turned it upside down again. I stumbled to my chair and collapsed into it.

Dan's voice sounded far away. "Since the footages corroborated your story, I decided to run a search for the Van Santen file in our system at Mason & McGant," he continued. "It was blocked and only accessible via an additional security password, which is highly unusual."

I recovered from the blow, leaped up and began pacing up and down the room, hanging off his every word.

"The next day I tried to access the file on my computer again only to find it had suddenly been deleted. There was nothing left of it in the system. Vanished. Totally disappeared into thin air," Dan said, sounding worked up.

"I just can't believe it," I stammered.

"I don't know what the hell is going on, but it's crystal clear that something's up."

I clenched my fists. "So I wasn't going loopy then," I couldn't refrain from saying, although perhaps this was directed to me rather than to Dan. "I knew all along something was wrong."

Dan sounded remorseful as he spoke. "You were right. I should have listened to you."

I felt like bursting into tears with relief at the knowledge there was finally someone out there who believed me.

"I need your help, Jennifer. If we work together, we may be able to find some answers."

I chewed on my finger. "I don't know, Dan. I had just convinced myself I needed to let it go. Everyone around me claimed I was imagining things, my girlfriends, the police, you. Yesterday I went to visit Sandra's husband ..."

Dan interrupted me. "They're all wrong," he blurted. And then with a tad more uncertainty, "At least, I think so. I've racked my brain over it, but there's no plausible explanation for those DVDs and the file that was first blocked and then covertly erased. As a firm, we are required by law to store all documentation related to our cases for at least seven years."

I thought of how Hans moved all the data in our practice to the archive disk once in a while, whenever the system started to fill up. "Couldn't the file have been archived?" I suggested.

"We keep everything both digitally and as a hard copy, but there's nothing to be found about Van Santen in the archive," he responded.

I leaned my back against the poster of the human skeleton, bearing the Latin names for each bone, which I'd received as a gift from my parents when I finished my medical studies. "That's odd. Sandra and I discovered the papers in that archive room no too long ago."

"Exactly."

I stared out of the window through the blinds and thought back to the nightly visits that Sandra and I had made to Mason & McGant – it felt like an eternity ago. I had finally found peace and now everything was being raked up again. Every part of me was screaming, *I don't want this*. I'd had enough of the tension and the restlessness – I wanted to get on and just live my life.

Dan interrupted my thoughts. "You told me that morning that you'd copied the file. Can you tell me again what exactly it contained?"

I told Dan how, after our date, I'd reviewed the papers Sandra had shared with me and that they revealed more details about the evidence of the four cases.

"So there were four case file numbers listed?" Dan asked.

I took my handbag and started rummaging through it until I realised I'd of course left the papers with Detective Armstrong. I did have a copy safely stored at home – it had felt too definite to dispose of them. "I believe the numbers all started with a year, followed by a five-digit code," I added hesitantly.

"That does sound like our file number structure. It's not much Oliver left us to work with, but it should give us a good starting point," Dan said, sounding excited. "I think it would make sense for us to meet up and comb through those documents together. These types of files are right up my alley so I can probably extract more information from them."

I dropped onto my chair again and rested my head on my hands – I was afraid of getting dragged in, feeling again like I was out of my depth, but there wasn't really another option. I sat up and gave in. "All right, then."

He made a proposal. "How about we meet at Mason & McGant and look for those four case numbers in the system? I'm hoping we may uncover details in them that will throw light on the notes in the Van Santen file."

"Ohhhh," I moaned. "I'm not exactly keen on sneaking back in there for a third time."

"This time we'll do things by the book. I'll register you in our system to have an official visitor's pass created for you. We'll just act like it's a business meeting."

I gave it a thought and concluded it ought to be safe.

"When would be a convenient moment for you to come over?" Dan asked.

I took a seat behind my PC and searched my schedule for a gap. "How about four o'clock tomorrow afternoon?"

"Okay, see you tomorrow," I said and hung up.

I checked the time and concluded that my lunch break was nearly over. I unlocked the door, dashed out and almost ran straight into Hans. "Hello stranger, do you still work here? Must have been an important call to miss lunch – again," he said jokingly, but his voice told me he was a bit upset. "I came to see if you were still alive," he added, which made me realise I wasn't the only one who'd been rattled by the incident with the tile.

"Sorry, Hans. It was my Mum – some problem at her volunteer job. Ever since my parents retired, it seems like they have a different sense of time," I said and rolled my eyes excessively, but I could feel my hands trembling.

He accepted my apology and together we walked to our lunchroom where Simone, wearing ear buds, was listening to music on her phone. "It looks like I wasn't the only one who was being antisocial," I whispered to Hans and gave him a wink.

He smiled. "Don't forget to eat," he said, indicating my sandwich.

I nodded and quickly took a bite when something came to my mind. I tapped Simone gently on the shoulder – she removed an ear bud and looked questioningly at me.

"Can you keep my schedule empty after half past three tomorrow afternoon?"

She shrugged. "Sure."

Hans looked at me with a scrutinising look on his face. "Other plans?"

"Appointment at the dentist," I lied. "Completely forgot about it."

He narrowed his eyes and turned up the heat. "Check-up or cavity?"

"The first," I croaked, feeling sweat collect in my armpits. I'd had my fill of lying and scheming and longed for all this secrecy to be over.

I nodded at the clock that hung above the lunch table. "Time to get back to work."

29

I was running late for my appointment with Dan and decided to park my bike south of the train station, which was at the heart of the financial district. I looked around a few times to make sure no one was following me before crossing through the station *en route* to Mason & McGant.

My phone beeped – it was a message from Dan.

'Five minutes late. Wait for me at the entrance.'

I slowed down my pace and ambled along on this Friday afternoon, weaving through the shifting sea of people rushing to get out of the city and eager to start their weekend. Once through the station, I walked across the square flanked by lofty glass buildings reflecting the glorious afternoon sun. Here and there folks were seated and chatting on stone benches with a glass of wine in their hands, sheltered under the fragrant blossoming hawthorns. I passed several bars where the atmosphere was relaxed and jovial ahead of the weekend – men with unbuttoned shirts and loosened ties, women untying their buns and shaking their hair free. The well-known TGIF drink formed an essential part of the lawyer's scene, where paralegals in particular, after a week of going above and beyond, bunked off early and relieved some of the stress with Mojito's and Heinekens. The buzzing pre-weekend vibe made me crave a drink as well, but that had to wait for now.

I felt a hand gently touch my shoulder and turned around – Dan's dapper appearance immediately instilled a flash of desire in me, knocking the air from my lungs.

He seemed oblivious to my internal reaction and just said, "Hi Jennifer."

I waved my hand awkwardly and then tucked it into the pocket of my coat. The other one rested on my handbag containing the file, which I guarded as if I were a money courier, about to top up a cash machine.

Dan was dressed in a three-piece suit, his hair tightly combed back in a side parting, using substantial amounts of hair gel to keep his natural curl under control. "Sorry I'm a tad late. I just came back from court."

"No problem." My eyes shifted nervously towards the Mason & McGant building. "Shall we?"

We walked silently towards the entrance and passed through the revolving doors. I followed Dan to the reception and thought back to the previous two times when I'd been eager to get in as quickly as possible. On the outside I was calm, but inside my heart was racing.

After receiving my visitor pass we took the lift – the tension was almost tangible in the air. From the corner of my eye I noticed Dan secretly glancing at me. I felt a powerful barrage of emotions surge through me.

"My room is across the hallway," Dan said as we stepped out of the lift. He opened the glass door, which gave access to his spacious office. In the left corner was an oval, wooden meeting table with matching leather seats; his desk was up against the window overlooking the square.

Dan closed the door behind me, wheeled one of the leather chairs over and somewhat uncomfortably, we both took a seat behind his desk.

I plucked the papers out of my bag and handed them to him. "These are the documents."

Dan flicked through them. "Perfect. These should give us a good starting point," he said perkily and handed them back to me.

As Dan operated the mouse on his computer, his arm gently brushed against mine and I could feel the electricity from his touch shooting up and down my back. I flinched away, keeping my arms tightly in my lap, and kept my eyes fixated on the computer screen, while we waited for the system to start up.

Dan turned his head to me and spoke softly. "I'm truly sorry for not believing you that morning Jennifer."

I lowered my eyes.

Dan carried on speaking. "Those allegations against our firm all sounded so implausible that I just couldn't wrap my head around it. I've been working here for many years now and have never even so much as heard a rumour. I recognise this is not by any means an excuse for my behaviour, but …" He didn't finish his sentence.

I nodded, still avoiding eye contact.

"Can you please give me another chance?"

I looked up at those big brown eyes of his full of remorse, and responded in a soft voice. "Sure, it's okay." Our faces were so close I could feel his warm breath on my lips. "I understand. You barely knew me and here I am sharing these strange and twisted accusations with you. No wonder you thought I was crazy."

"But I shouldn't have shoved you out of the door like that," he said.

I gave a crooked smile. "Not your finest hour."

He laughed, which made him even more irresistible and I felt a rush of heat run through me. I gave myself a stern talking to, *stay focused Jennifer*. "I'm just happy we're on the same page now. Let's get started, okay?"

He nodded and then turned to his PC. "The programme has started. Do you have a case number for me?"

I thumbed through the papers to get to the overview that Oliver had made and began to read aloud the digits from the first file.

Dan entered the numbers in the tab – a unique match with the title 'Van Brandt' came up, which had a classified status and a report attached to it.

Dan bit the inside of his cheek as he kept the cursor hovering over the file.

"What is it?" I asked.

He looked up and rubbed his chin. "Since the Data Protection Act has been implemented, Mason & McGant keeps a record of everyone who opens a document in our system."

"Are you saying that if we open the report, they can trace back who viewed it?"

Dan nodded. "This isn't a client of mine so I have no legitimate reason to browse the file."

I thought for a moment. "We have no choice but to take the risk. We need to get more information."

Dan nodded and clicked on the file, after which a report opened, showing a synopsis of the case.

I waited with bated breath, while Dan's eyes flew across the legal document. "Do you see anything unusual?" I asked.

He summed up the case while still reading. "I don't see anything out of the ordinary. A man named Van Brandt received legal counselling by our firm when he was accused of rape. The only thing that strikes me is that initially, there seemed to be a match between DNA traces found on the victim and the DNA of the suspect. After further analysis, however, the forensic sample turned out to be of such a poor quality that it couldn't be used in the case. That means, it was impossible to narrow down the suspect to near hundred percent certainty. The man was acquitted of the rape charge."

"Is that unusual?"

"It doesn't happen often. But it's possible."

"Hi Dan," someone shouted behind us.

Dan clicked the document away in a flurry. I jerked my head around and tried to block the view of the computer screen with my body.

A young man in his early twenties lolled in the doorway and looked familiar to me. "We're heading off for drinks at 'Fiesta'. Are you joining us?" Behind him there was the sound of a group of people, presumably waiting in the hallway to leave the office, their voices excited and cheerful.

"I'm still working on something," Dan mumbled matter-of-factly, but I noticed his cheeks were flushing. "I might join you guys later."

"Don't stay too long, we've been cooped up all week." Suddenly the young man's eyes grew large. He pointed his finger at me. "Aren't you Oliver's wife, Oliver Smits? What a coincidence. What brings you here?"

Then it suddenly came back to me – he was one of the paralegals Oliver had been supervising.

My heart was pounding in my chest. "I, er …" I stammered, as I felt my face turn deep red.

Dan laid a hand on my arm. "Jennifer and I used to go to high school together. I'm doing her a favour by defending her at the small claims court," he said quickly. "Some jerk scraped her car and drove off."

"I see." He suddenly seemed to recollect Oliver's fate as a look of compassion spread across his face. "How are you doing now?"

"I'm all right, thanks," I responded.

"Good thing you wrote down his license plate number, right?" Dan said.

"What?" I mumbled blankly. "Oh right, yes."

One of the colleagues in the hallway tugged the man's sleeve.

"I have to go," he shouted, now jolly, and raised his hand. "Later."

When he'd loped out the room, I breathed a sigh of relief. "This is killing me. We need to be careful, Dan."

He nodded. "Let's swiftly look up all four files, print them out and go somewhere quiet to examine them."

We typed in the numbers one by one, after which Dan sent them to his printer.

"All right, this should be enough for now," he finally said, sliding the papers into his brown, leather briefcase. Dan rose from his chair and slid his arms into his jacket. "C'mon. Let's vamoose." He glanced at his watch. "It's half past five. How about we sift through the files over dinner at some restaurant?"

I wanted nothing more than to say yes, but I knew Tim would be anxiously waiting for me. "I need to pick up my son from day-care."

Dan nodded. "Of course."

I thought for a moment – it was imperative we got through these files as soon as possible. "You could come over to my place tonight when Tim is in bed?" It felt rather intimate to invite Dan into my house, but there weren't many alternatives and I didn't want to postpone discussing the contents of these papers.

"I can't arrange a babysitter for him at the last minute," I clarified and dipped my head, too embarrassed to maintain eye contact. I didn't want him to think I had another agenda after our humiliating date.

"Fair enough," he said, and I believed I noticed a stifled grin on his face.

He wrote down my address and we agreed he'd be at my place around eight.

30

The bell rang. I slipped my feet into my high heels while nervously smoothing the fabric of the dress I'd changed into, checked my make-up in the mirror and rushed to the door. I'd spruced myself up as I wanted to make sure Dan knew what a catch he'd passed up on.

I opened the door and the light from the hallway spilled out into the dark night, illuminating Dan's face with a warm glow. His coat was casually open, and he'd exchanged the three-piece suit he was wearing this afternoon for tight jeans and a green polo. His gaze dropped as he took in my appearance. "You look stunning."

I whispered. "Quickly, come inside." Before I closed the door, I glanced in both directions down the street – I had this ever-present uncanny feeling that I was being watched – but saw nothing or no one out of the ordinary. I put a finger to my lips and pointed upstairs towards Tim's bedroom. He got the hint and quietly took off his coat, then followed me into the living room. "Nice place you have here."

"Thank you," I said, smiling, and indicated at the dining table. "Have a seat."

Dan lowered himself onto one of the fabric chairs, while I walked towards the kitchen.

'What can I get you? Coffee, tea?"

"How about a glass of wine?" Dan suggested.

I'd resolved not to drink any alcohol tonight – I couldn't trust myself around that man – but I didn't want to spoil the mood. "Sure, does white sound okay?"

Dan smiled. 'Sounds perfect." He gently slid the crystal vase containing flowers to one side and spread out the four reports that we'd printed out this afternoon over the table.

I took a wine bottle from the built-in wine fridge with a tinted glass door, which Oliver had insisted on buying when we'd had our new kitchen installed. I took two wine glasses from the cupboard and checked if the baby monitor was turned on. My eyes fell on the neighbour, nosily peering into my living room from a third floor window in the house behind mine, instigating a feeling of uneasiness. Other than the city lights, it was now pitch black outside and I decided to close the curtains.

"Here you are," I said, and slid the glass of Pinot Grigio, which Oliver's mother had brought back from France last year, towards Dan. I pulled out the seat opposite Dan, but before I could sit down he suggested, "I think it would be better if you sit here. Otherwise it's difficult for us both to read the papers."

I smiled and walked calmly to the other side of the table, although inside I felt flustered – whenever I got too close to that man my toes would clench and my chest would start to tighten.

As I plopped down onto the chair next to him, a faint whiff of his familiar scent reached my nostrils, bringing back memories of the lingering kiss we'd shared. I pressed the back of my hand to my nose, trying hard to concentrate.

"Since we ..." Dan started, until he noticed me guzzle half of the wine in my glass, in an attempt to control my nerves. " Is everything all right?" he inquired, looking surprised.

I nodded my head and gave him a reassuring smile, my hand waving in the air. "Sure, I'm fine."

Dan shook his head ever so slightly, the puzzled look still on his face, and then continued. "So, since we left the office I've buried myself in these files. I'm slowly getting an idea of what's been going on. In all four cases your husband documented, the suspects were acquitted. On all other aspects of these cases, however, there are substantial variations." Dan laid his hand on a stack of papers in front of me and tapped it. "This case is about a batch of cocaine that was found in a hangar in 2017, for which a guy name Santos was charged. The next case involved a robbery-homicide on a jeweller in 2018, in which a man named Casimir was a suspect. Later that year there was another case identified as De Mees, involving a dismantled drugs lab. And lastly, we have the rape story from last year, which we discussed earlier this afternoon." Dan drank a mouthful of his wine, ruffling his hair with his hand to remove it from his face. "At first I didn't see the shared characteristic between all of these cases – we're dealing with various types of offenses and suspects, spread over several years, and the crime scene locations were different. But I knew from Oliver's overview that there had to be something wrong with the evidence – there had to be a common denominator I was overlooking."

My heart thumped in my throat. "What was it?"

"Hold on. I'll get to that," Dan said as cool as a cucumber. "It's quite a lot of information we're dealing with, so I'm trying to go through it step by step."

"Sure, sure," I said feeling jumpy and took another gulp.

"With regard to the evidence, Oliver first looked at the forensic traces that were available, such as DNA. Then he analysed the phone records and came to the mind-puzzling conclusion that it always concerned the same people."

I looked at him, feeling dazed. "What do you mean by 'the same people'?"

Dan browsed through the pack of papers until he came to Oliver's overview. "Let's start with the forensic evidence: it was always analysed in the lab by the Dutch Forensic Institute, the DFI. Interestingly enough, in all four cases, the DNA that was found at the crime scene was handled by the same person at the DFI."

I looked at the overview and indeed noticed the name 'Joe de Smet, senior scientist,' written down, something Sandra had already pointed out over the phone weeks ago.

Dan took the last sip of his wine. I refilled both of our glasses and placed the bottle back in the silver wine cooler.

"What's so peculiar about the same scientist analysing the DNA?" I asked. "Maybe there's simply one person assigned per law firm or per region, or whatever."

Dan looked into my eyes. "It's possible, but because the name had been underscored by Oliver and thus apparently caught his attention, I went through the four internal reports with a fine tooth comb. It transpires that in all four cases, at first, a match had been established between the DNA trace they'd found at the crime scene and the DNA of the suspect. However, Mason & McGant impugned the results and requested a re-analysis of the evidence by Joe de Smet – in all four cases the DNA turned out to only be a partial match on the second test."

I couldn't follow. "What does that mean legally?"

"It means that based on the first test results, the suspect would have almost certainly been convicted. Only after a second analysis was carried out did the forensic evidence prove too weak to bring the case to a close and all four suspects were exonerated."

I shoved the wine glass away, leaned back and interlaced my fingers behind my head, while reflecting on this information. "Is it a regular occurrence, to impugn forensic results and request a reanalysis?"

Dan shrugged. "It can happen, but it's extremely rare. As a general rule, it's done when there's reason to question the method of analysis or if mistakes have been made in the lab. But in that case, the test has usually already been re-conducted before the results are even released to us by the DFI."

"So just to recap: four cases with re-analysis of DNA, all performed by the same senior scientist at the DFI? And as a result of this, all four suspects were acquitted of their charges, allowing them to walk free?"

Dan grimaced. "Exactly."

I felt a flush of excitement – this was actually going somewhere. "So this Joe de Smet chap at the DFI was supposedly bribed by Mason & McGant to tamper with the evidence?"

"It's a possibility we have to consider," Dan said, drumming his fingers on the table. "Look, we cannot yet rule out that this scientist made a few screw-ups and that we're simply dealing with a man not fit for his job – a square peg in a round hole, if you like. But it's improbable and …" There was a brief pause. "To find out more, we may be forced pay him a visit."

My eyebrows rose in shock. "Dan, stop. We have no idea what we're getting ourselves into if we open Pandora's box. You just listed a string of mega crooks. Those are all heavy hitters, if I understood you correctly. It feels like we're standing on the edge of a very slippery slope."

Something came to my mind. I rifled through the papers Sandra and I had copied at Mason & McGant, until I reached the overview of figures and the arrow pointing to the DFI, which had earlier raised my suspicions of bribery and forgery. I tapped the overview with my finger, looked at Dan and lifted my chin.

"I knew it," Dan exclaimed and smacked his hands on the table. "My mind has been going in circles trying to figure out the exact role Mason & McGant played in all of this. But what if … suppose those clients pay extortionate rates to Mason & McGant, who in turn ensure the forensic evidence is falsified by the DFI?

I nodded and complemented his words. "The younger lawyers, those who do the donkey work, are kept under the thumb by compromising footage to prohibit them from spilling the beans. All the while the partners are lining their pockets, without getting their hands dirty."

Our eyes locked and for a moment there was a click – we make a good team.

I was afraid that those piercing, big brown eyes of his would make my head start spinning again and so I looked away. "Do you think all lawyers at Mason & McGant are in the know?"

Dan shook his head. "I doubt it. If you ask me, I think they made the incriminating images of those paralegals as a means of pressure, to wield an influence only in case a lawyer smells trouble and starts asking questions. Otherwise, I'd have received word of it long ago."

"This whole situation makes my flesh crawl," I whispered. But there was a somewhat comforting aspect in all of this too – perhaps Oliver hadn't been hiding this secret from me for all these years and had only recently found out about it. "Do you think someone may have caught wind of Oliver's plans to expose the abuses?"

Dan nodded. "I imagine Oliver was intending to build the case fully before taking the evidence to the police, but the more he probed, the deeper he became caught up in a web of deceit and corruption. Someone must have found out what he was doing. We still can't exclude the possibility that Oliver died as a result of an accident, but it seems increasingly unlikely." Dan spoke softly. "Oliver knew too much and the stakes were too high for Mason & McGant. In all likelihood, he perished while searching for answers and uncovering the truth."

I stared into the distance. "So he probably was murdered after all," I mumbled. I needed a moment to process this bitter conclusion.

Dan gently caressed my face. "Are you alright?"

I was startled by this unforeseen, intimate gesture and flinched away. "I'm not sure. It's a lot to take in."

Dan retracted his hand. "I understand," he said and remained silent for a moment, running his fingers up and down the stem of his wine glass.

I pulled myself together and looked at Dan. "So what now?"

"We don't have the full picture yet. Since Oliver also recorded the name of a telephone company, they must also play a role in this, but I haven't worked out what that could be."

I pointed to the file on the right side of the table and opened my mouth to speak and at that very moment, Dan reached out for his wineglass, causing our hands to collide in the air. He took hold of my hand and gently enclosed it with both of his, turning me towards him and sending a rush of passion through me. His gaze shifted to meet mine, and we shared a look so intense I felt like it was boring deep into my soul. I swallowed audibly and felt the heat of a deep blush on my cheeks.

"You have the most beautiful blue eyes," Dan whispered and I felt my legs weaken. He gently pulled my hand towards him, his face now a mere centimetres away from mine, and brushed a lock of hair back from my face. "Dan," I breathed, but his lips swallowed up my words. I wrapped my arms around his broad shoulders and felt our bodies fold against each other as I leaned into his warm embrace, closing my eyes. The sound of the soft music in the background slowly faded away. He kissed me on the neck, his teeth nipping gently on my skin, subsiding the whirling flood of thoughts in my mind.

Suddenly I heard Tim coughing through the baby monitor and I instantly came to my senses.

I abruptly pulled away from Dan. "I'm sorry," I said, avoiding his eyes, and ran a hand through my ruffled hair to smooth it back into shape. "I can't do this. Not now. Not after our first date and with everything going on here. It's all too complicated," I said, indicating the chaos of papers on the dining table.

'It's all right. I get it," he said softly and gave me an uplifting smile. "We're not in any rush," he added, and my heart leaped.

I stifled a grin and tried to focus my attention on the documents in front of us. "Maybe we should call it a day. I'd like to let it all sink in."

"Sounds good," Dan said, knocking back the remainder of his wine in one go. "Do you mind if I take all of these papers with me?"

"No, go ahead. So where are we going from here?"

"I want to dig into the role of the telephone company over the weekend. Bella will return from her mother's tomorrow afternoon, so until then I'll have ample opportunity to do so."

"What about the DFI?"

"How would you feel about paying them a visit?" he asked, gauging my reaction. "They may recognise me since I've been in contact with DFI staff in the past – it would put us at risk."

I inhaled sharply and let the air escape from my lungs with puckered lips. "How exactly do you see that working?"

Dan thought for a while. "What if you were to pose as a lawyer working at Mason & McGant, requesting a re-analysis?"

"I can't, Dan," I countered, feeling blind sighted. "That's insane!" I cried.

"I concede it would be unusual," he said.

I stood up and placed the wine glass on the counter, letting my thoughts go over his suggestion. Then I walked back to Dan and responded to his proposal. "I'm going to sleep on it, okay?"

He narrowed his eyes and seemed to sense it was best to refrain from pushing me on the matter. "Of course." Dan collected all the papers and slid them into his briefcase. Then he brought his hand to my upper arm and stroked it tenderly. "Look after yourself. I'll call you after the weekend."

I nodded and followed him down the hall.

He slid his arms into the sleeves of his jacket, said goodbye and walked briskly towards his bike.

I peered quickly down the deserted street, shut the door behind him, and locked it with the deadbolt. Then I swivelled, rested my back against the steel frame and felt the coldness creep over my body. I brought my hands to my head and felt this bizarre sensation of excitement rush through me. "Oh my God, what's happening to me?" I said out loud.

31

"Hi, sweetie," Lindsey said, wrapping her arms around me.

I hugged her tightly and realised how terribly I'd missed her lately. I was relieved that we'd buried the hatchet.

She crouched down next to Tim and placed her hands on his cheeks. "Hello munchkin." Her eyes sparkled as she looked up at me. "Tim is starting to look more and more like his father."

I looked at my son and felt a warm feeling growing inside. "I know, he's almost the spitting image of him, right? It feels ever so good to keep a little piece of Oliver with me this way. Tim, will you give Lindsey a hug?" I asked him, and he flung himself into her arms.

She rose and squeezed my arm. "You look good, Jen."

"Thanks," I responded, feeling grateful we were starting with a clean slate.

Tim was pulling at my sleeve. "Yes darling. We're going to the playground."

Lindsay tucked her arm through mine as we wound our way towards the playground in the middle of the Vondelpark, surrounded by the excited chatter from birds roosting in the flowering trees, while Tim sped ahead of us on his push-bike. I made sure to keep him within my sight at all times. Ever since Dan had called me saying that he also suspected something illicit was going on at Mason & McGant, I'd been on guard. Upon arrival at the sandpit, Tim jumped off his vehicle, flung it aside and immediately picked up one of the spades. "Gentle with that bike, Tim," I said admonishingly. "We don't want to break it now do we?"

Lindsey and I sat down on the stone verge enclosing the sandpit, which was filled with young children messing about. She yawned loudly.

"Late one last night?" I asked kindly as I draped Tim's and my summer coat over a railing.

"Not exactly," Lindsey answered. "Some idiot in my street felt the need to start drilling through the walls at ten in the morning on a Saturday," she said with an utterly serious face.

I flashed her a scornful look.

She got the message. "Oh, right. I forgot. You think ten o'clock is late," she said and started laughing.

I laughed too and then changed the subject. "I truly appreciate you wanting to meet up with us in a playground." I rolled my eyes. "These weekends with Tim by myself are loooong."

"I'm sure they are," she said, her eyes fixed on something in the distance and for a moment I thought I saw a sad look flash across her face. I realised I'd been preoccupied with myself for the last few weeks. "So how have you been doing? Have you had any interesting dates lately?" I asked, clasping my hands in excitement.

Lindsey's eyes strayed to the sandpit, where Tim had started building a sandcastle with another child. A cool breeze blew in, pushing a string of clouds across the sun and it suddenly felt five degrees cooler.

"I'm back with Paul again."

It took me moment to process the information. "But, er ..." I struggled for words. "Wasn't Paul the guy who turned out to be married?" I blurted out with a snort, but instantly regretted it. "Sorry, that was inconsiderate of me," I backpedalled. But I was naturally wondering what had made Lindsey decide to get back involved with him.

"He's left his wife. So now we're seeing each other again," she said curtly and shrugged, avoiding my gaze.

Surely Lindsey didn't fall for this nonsense? They all left their wives, only to fall back into their warm, forgiving arms again after a few weeks. This was completely out of character – Lindsey was the impersonation of a self-confident not-to-be-messed-with woman. "Is he really going to divorce his wife?" I asked, with a hint of misgivings in my voice.

Lindsey shrugged. "They're on a break," she said, sidestepping the question. "He needs time to figure out what he wants." She loosened her hair and her long tresses fell in a wave, over her shoulder.

"I see," I said. As an awkward silence fell I closed my eyes, practising self-restraint and biting my tongue. I was grappling with a feeling of ambivalence – to support my friend on the one hand whilst knowing exactly how it feels to be 'that other person', the betrayed wife.

"Do you really think it's a good idea?" I asked, breaking the silence with trepidation.

She shrugged again. "A good idea, a good idea," she repeated crabbily. "I don't know. Maybe I just don't want to think about it that much. Being with him feels good for now and that suffices." She smoothed her hair over her shoulder with one hand.

"But, sweetie," I said, turning to her and laying a hand on her thigh. "You deserve someone who isn't playing around and messing with your feelings."

She shook her head and kept her gaze averted. "He's not playing around."

"I mean a guy who is really committed to you. Not a guy who cheats on his wife and embarks on an affair while on a break from her. You deserve someone who puts you on a pedestal and wants to be involved in a relationship devoid of mistrust and self-interest, an honest man who is eager to spend his life with you and ..." I paused for a moment and then tentatively added, "maybe start a family together."

"Who says I want all that?" Lindsey said disgruntled, now looking me in the eye. "Are you sure you're not projecting, Jennifer? And by the way, you just said it's really tough to take care of a child over the weekend, remember?"

I turned away and drew in a sharp breath.

"You've heard about the research that shows people are less satisfied with their lives after having children, right?" Lindsey added with a hint of scorn in her voice.

I ignored her rhetorical question and raised my eyebrows. "Maybe I am projecting."

Tim brought me a cake made of sand and I took an imaginary bite. "Yummy ... Don't go too far, pumpkin," I warned as he trotted back.

It remained silent for a moment before Lindsey spoke again. "Not everyone finds a responsible guy like Oliver who wants to settle down and live the quiet life while raising a family. Besides, who knows ... maybe *I'm* not the girl for the whole white-picket-fence life. Perhaps I'm the type longing for a different kind of relationship," she said, pulling her long, finely woven cardigan tightly around her. "I'm freezing. I'll go get us something to drink. What can I get you?"

I was trying to make out how to respond to her musings, but decided to let the subject rest. "How about we have glass of wine? I heard the Pinot Grigio is really good here." Some alcohol might ease the tense atmosphere, I thought to myself. "It's five o'clock somewhere in the world," I quipped.

Lindsey frowned. "Not for me, thank you. I just finished breakfast."

I tried to laugh away her disapproval. "Make it a cappuccino then."

Lindsey nodded towards the sandpit. "Apple juice for Tim?"

"Thanks," I replied, watching her as she strolled off towards the entrance of the restaurant, her high heels clattering on the cobblestone path and her long coat billowing in the wind.

While she was gone, I thought about how I could address the delicate matter of her deserving someone better than this Paul guy, but ultimately decided to refrain – I was afraid it would lead to another argument.

Lindsey came back carrying the drinks on a tray and didn't appear to be sulking anymore. She placed the cappuccino on a little step next to me, took her coat off and walked up to Tim with the apple juice. She let him take a few sips through the straw and then returned to sit with me on the verge of the sand pit.

She linked her arm through mine, pulling me closer. "I'm so happy we're back in contact again. It was hard on us seeing you in such bad shape," she said, referring to the other night with Frederique and Karen.

"Was it?" I responded and took a sip of my cappuccino, then stretched my legs in the sand and closed my eyes.

Lindsey pressed on. "Don't take this the wrong way, but you didn't appear to be thinking straight. You were imagining things that weren't really there, with that law firm and everything. I'm so relieved you've finally managed to let go of this conspiracy theory thing."

My eyes sprang open. Since that phone call from Dan the day before yesterday, my life had been turned upside down yet again.

Lindsey seemed to have noticed my lack of response and flashed me a look with a mixture of desperation and disapproval. "Argh, please tell me you *did* let go, Jennifer." There was a sharpness in her voice. "You do realise Oliver's death was an accident? I don't think I can take this nonsense for much longer."

I turned away. "No. Well, yes, but …" I began but didn't finish my sentence – I seemed unable to find the right words.

Lindsey frowned. "But what?"

"I received an unexpected phone call from Dan a few days ago," I said, now looking Lindsey in the eye.

"What?" she asked. "Dan was the guy from that date with the sour ending!"

I nodded weakly, smoothing down the hem of my skirt.

She rolled her eyes. "Okay, so he wanted to see you again?"

I bit my nails, keeping my eyes on Tim. "Do you remember I told you about the DVDs I found on which I saw Oliver with er …?" I halted.

Lindsey took a swig of her cappuccino. "Of course. You were devastated."

"Well, Dan told me he found the CDs and viewed them too. And it doesn't stop there – similar recordings were made of all paralegals who started working at the firm over the last couple of years. Nude dancers, prostitutes, alcohol, drugs – the whole shebang."

Lindsey ran a hand through her long, blond satin hair. Her eyes were fixed on something in the distance. "Jen, I don't know what to say." She sounded deflated, as if I was a lost cause.

Tim came scampering up to us. "I want juice," he declared, extending his sand-covered hands impatiently to the bottle.

I didn't have the energy to correct him. "Let Mummy help you." I put the straw in his mouth at a slightly tilted angle and he started sucking vigorously. "We'll save the rest for later," I said after a few moments, pulling the straw out of his mouth again. He licked his lips with his tongue, wiped his mouth with the sleeve of his jumper and tottered back to his sandcastle.

I took another sip of my cappuccino, which had cooled off considerably – as had the atmosphere – and launched into my story. I told Lindsey about everything that Dan and I had concluded from the documents. How the suspects in the four cases, which initially appeared to be open-and-shut, were unexpectedly exculpated, and that both Mason & McGant and the DFI appeared to be involved in some form of bribery.

Lindsey had a pensive look as she let it all sink in. "Hun, you need to back out of this," she whispered. "I have a bad feeling about it."

"You still don't believe me?" I asked, slightly affronted. I'd presumed these recent developments would have removed her scepticism.

"I really don't know who or what to believe anymore," she responded evasively.

I ignored her comment, but it did hurt. "You don't actually think Dan would bring all of this up and reach out to me if he wasn't convinced something was wrong? He's jeopardising his job, perhaps even his entire career." I couldn't quite grasp how she didn't appreciate the significance of all this new information.

She shrugged her shoulders. "Be that as it may, you barely know the guy – why do you blindly trust him? He's a lawyer at Mason & McGant – how do you know for sure he's not involved in this bribery thing? It's anyone's guess what secrets he may be harbouring. You need to be careful Jennifer, you could be getting yourself into seriously hot water here."

Lindsey's words triggered my doubts in Dan all over again – there was obviously some truth in what she said. Maybe he was trying to frame me and this was all part of a bigger plan to prevent me from going public with incriminating information regarding Mason & McGant. But if that were true, why would he have suggested to comb through those case reports with me? Memories of his soft, inviting lips on mine came flooding back, making me feel sick.

"You really have to abandon this search, Jennifer. To be honest, I'm growing tired of this charade. You must hear how absurd this all sounds?" She stared at me with a mixture of vexation and pity and, although perhaps unbeknown to Lindsey, I felt we were reaching a crossroads – a point in our lives which would either bring us closer or forever force us apart. "An international, renowned law firm maintaining a clandestine relationship with mega crooks, and a government organisation – the DFI – wilfully cooperating. Come on, these things happen in films, not in real life.”

The feathery clouds had lifted, bringing out the sun again and making the air feel pleasantly warm. “I know, it’s inconceivable,” I agreed. “And yet all the evidence is pointing towards this.”

Lindsey folded her arms. “I said it before and I’ll say it again – you need to go to the police with this. It’s the only sensible thing to do.”

Her arguments were undeniably sound and valid. In my mind I went back to the conversation I’d had with Detective Armstrong. With a great deal of pain and effort, he’d been prepared to lend an ear to my argument and had even taken the documents from me. But he’d made no bones about the fact that he’d never reopen the case.

“I recently paid the Amsterdam Investigation Department a visit, but they didn’t believe me.”

Lindsey flashed me a look of scepticism. “Well, Jennifer. Maybe you should have faith in their judgment – assessing whether there is foul play involved in an accident is what these people do on a day-to-day basis. They inspect all the clues, the forensic evidence and then make an informed decision,” she stated as if I was utterly clueless. “If you will, you can compare it to a situation where you as a doctor determine that a little wound I have isn’t inflamed and will heal by itself over time, while I, someone who’s never studied medicine, claim I need antibiotics,” she said with an air of smugness.

“That’s a ridiculous comparison,” I retorted, but to my exasperation the analogy was quite striking.

“Whatever you say, Jennifer,” she said resolutely, and finished her cappuccino with a gulp. “I am so done with this. I’ve said my piece, it’s up to you. If you intend to continue this nonsense, fine by me, but don’t expect me to stick around while you rip your whole life to pieces.” Lindsey leaped up, tying her pink coat tightly round her slim waist.

My mouth slackened. “Where are you going?”

“I’m heading off,” she announced, her jaw set. “I have a raft of things to do over the weekend.” But we both knew it was just an excuse.

I jumped up, a feeling of dread welling up in the pit of my stomach. “Lin, please don’t leave like this,” I pleaded, gently laying my hand on her arm, but I felt deep down that something had changed, the little invisible thread that connected us had snapped.

She brushed my hand away. “I love you, Jennifer – you know that,” she declared, her emerald green eyes gazing at me in an indefinable fashion. “But

I'm not going to sit around and watch you putting your life at risk." She gestured towards Tim who was blithely playing with a digger. "Why can't you just enjoy your beautiful son, your top job, your gorgeous house – you have the whole world at your feet." Lindsey narrowed her eyes. "We're not all as fortunate as you are, you know. And as for the things in life you can't explain, try to take them on the chin."

I had to restrain myself from clinging to Lindsey in desperation, seeking her approval. "I have no choice but to do this, Lin, I simply must. Not knowing what happened to Oliver that day is eating me up inside. Can't you understand that?"

"Oliver had an accident," she said, mouthing the words slowly and deliberately. "A terrible accident, Jennifer. You need to let it go."

I grabbed her hand and begged, "Please," but she was relentless and pulled away.

"Tim!" Lindsey called out and blew him a kiss. "Bye, pumpkin."

Tim looked up in surprise and then carried on digging unperturbed in the sand.

Lindsey put on her sunglasses. "I'll see you, okay?" She didn't wait for an answer, but turned on her heel and strode out of the playground, her stilettos clicking on the cobbles. She didn't look back.

I tried to stifle the tears that sprung up in my eyes, resulting in a lump in my throat. Suddenly I felt Tim's warm hand touching my arm. "Mummy, Lindsey gone?"

"Yes, baby," I replied, quickly wiping my eyes with the back of my hand. "But that's okay. How about if Mummy helps you with some digging?"

He gave a whoop of delight and started pulling me towards the sandpit by my hand.

When we arrived back home about an hour later, my eyes immediately fell on an item on the doormat.

Every muscle in my body went rigid as I drew in a sharp breath. I heard Tim babbling something to me as he carelessly trod over the note, but my ears were ringing and his words whooshed past me.

The letters dancing over the paper were of such a large font that I was able to read the message without bending down and picking it up.

'I SAID: Don't stick your nose into other people's affairs.'

Every nerve in my body was tingling as I stormed into the living room, jerked open the chest of drawers and starting flinging out all the papers. Seconds later I found the note I'd safely stowed away since it was 'delivered' not long ago at the practice. I held it up in the air with trembling hands, angling it so that the light fell on the words. The colourful, decorative font was a dead ringer for the one used in today's note.

When I'd received the first message at home I'd dismissed it and tried to convince myself it wasn't intended for me or that it was a stupid prank from some kid in the neighbourhood. As for the shattered window in the practice – that could have been the work of a disgruntled patient.

But this time I knew without a trace of doubt that all these threats had been sent intentionally to me. Someone out there was watching my every move and warned me to stop digging.

32

The next Monday morning I was back in work, staring at my PC in the practice, trying to finalise the administration of the morning consultations. I'd had a rough time getting through the weekend. The quarrel with Lindsey and the threatening message I'd received had really gotten under my skin. On Sunday my mother had invited us for lunch – an offer I'd solicitously accepted. Even though I felt I shouldn't be chased out of my own home, I was grateful for the safety and security that my childhood home offered. When my mother had inquired if everything was okay, I'd merely nodded. She'd filled in the blanks by saying the process of grieving for Oliver has its ups and downs and I was relieved that she'd come to her own conclusions and didn't probe any further.

I turned off my computer, grabbed my jacket and handbag, and glanced at the printed home visit schedule for the day.

I strode through the hallway towards the door, my eyes running over the paper in my hand, when Simone called after me. "Wait Jennifer, what would you like to have for lunch today? We're ordering from Little Buddha."

I was a huge fan of Indian food, but the last few days I'd had little appetite. "Er … Make it the tikka masala with rice, please," I answered.

"Great, I'll make sure it gets here for when you return."

As I left the practice, I noticed the wispy clouds of the morning had turned into a heavy rain shower and was glad I'd decided to come to work by car. Holding my doctor's bag over my head, I dashed towards my car, parked a little further down the road, opened the door and jumped in.

I was about to read the details of the first patient, the drenched sleeves of my coat sticking to my blouse, when I heard a message coming through my phone – it was from Dan.

'Bad news here. Can I call you during your lunch break?'

I felt a tightness in my chest. My gaze strayed into the distance, thoughts going around in circles in my mind, while the rain kept hammering the windscreen.

After putting the key in the ignition, I opened the window for some fresh air. I just typed *'Okay'* back to Dan and entered the first address into the navigation – I had to focus on my patients right now. I started the engine, wiped the inside of the windscreen with my sleeve to remove the built up condensation and stepped on the accelerator.

I forgot about Dan during the next hour while I was tending to the patients that were too sick to get to the practice by themselves. After my last patient had been transferred into an ambulance and taken to hospital, I realised it was nearly lunchtime and remembered Dan, who would be calling me any time now.

I arrived back at the practice and after hanging up my coat to dry on the rack since it was still soaked from earlier, I walked into the lunch room where the food had already arrived, judging by the distinct smell. I didn't see Hans yet – he was presumably still working on his last home consultation – and to dodge any questions or strange looks, I thanked Simone for the food, gave a swift excuse about overdue administration and slipped into my consultation room. Just as I was about to unwrap the aluminium foil from the takeaway box, my phone rang and my heart did a quick two-step.

I answered the call. "Hi, this is Jennifer."

"Dan here. Listen up, I don't have much time," he said in a jittery voice. "The shit hit the fan. This morning when I came to work, I was summoned at once by one of the partners at Mason & McGant and got an earful."

Beads of sweat formed in my palms and I felt a stinking headache coming on. "Why?" I exclaimed.

"I told you about the new Data Protection Act, right?"

I sank into my chair. "Yes."

"Turns out they found out I went through those files in our internal system last Friday without authorisation."

"Shit," I cried. "So what now?"

"They've put me on administration leave for the time being."

"On leave," I repeated flatly. I couldn't believe it. I jumped up and marched to the window, which had been repaired over the weekend, opened the blinds slightly with one hand and peered out onto the streets, checking for anyone skulking around. "Is it general policy for them to be so strict with these things?" I queried, recalling a local hospital that had been the centre of a shocking exposé in the media a while ago after employees had been prying in the medical file of a VIP – in that instance they had come off with a warning.

"I've never heard of it before, but this law was only recently implemented. Maybe they want to make an example out of me." There was a pause. "To be honest, I think they have an inkling that I'm onto something. There was an undercurrent of tension and veiled warnings in the way the partner addressed me. He said something along the lines of, you shouldn't stick your nose into things that aren't any of your business."

The colourful letters started dancing in front of my eyes again, making me feel sick. The second hand of the clock in my consultation room was ticking loudly, the sound ringing in my ears and rattling my nerves.

Dan's voice sounded from far away. "Jennifer? Hello? Are you still there?"

"Yes, sorry," I managed to say.

I brought Dan up to speed with regards to the three threats I'd received so far, as well as the man with the cookies Tim had spoken of and the young chap on the scooter who had followed me for a while. I felt foolish for not sharing these things with him before.

"The messages you received are virtually identical to the words the partner spoke to me," Dan whispered in a shaky voice.

"I know. Are you saying you believe the threatening notes came from Mason & McGant?" I asked.

"Let's just say there's a very strong possibility. It's certainly within the character of the kind of things they might do to try and intimidate someone. But whoever was behind it, there's no way that these events are simply innocent coincidences," Dan concluded, pausing for a moment. "Having said that though, I can't and won't leave it at this. Something rotten is happening at Mason & McGant and the world needs to know about it."

I started pacing up and down the room, my brain moving into fifth gear. "Dan, you must be careful. They don't have any footage of you at hand to blackmail you with. So as soon as they even have the slightest hint that you know more than they care for, you pose a huge risk to them. Who knows what lengths they'll go to in order to keep you quiet. I don't have to remind you of what happened to Oliver and Sandra."

There was sharp knock on the door, startling me.

Hans stuck his head around the door, making a gesture of 'Are we having lunch'?

"Hospital," I mouthed, pretending I was consulting a specialist about a patient.

Hans raised his hand and closed the door behind him, and I gave a sigh.

"You're right," came Dan's voice. "I can't take any risks and I need to think of Bella. I will ask my ex if Bella can stay with her for a while. Given the circumstances, I've decided to go into hiding somewhere in a hotel so that I can safely and quietly press on digging through all the evidence," he said in a matter-of-fact tone as if he was booking a quiet retreat somewhere instead of seeking shelter.

"When were you planning to pay a visit to the DFI?" Dan asked.

It felt like the screws were being tightened by the way he posed the question, as if the matter had already been settled. I thought of Tim and didn't know if I could and wanted to be as heroic as Dan seemed to be.

"If you do decide to go along with this plan, it should be on your own accord," Dan added, as if he'd read my mind.

"I'm not sure how I feel about it yet," I answered evasively. "I have a day off tomorrow, I might be able to make an attempt then." I remembered what Lindsey had suggested last Saturday. "But wouldn't it be better to contact the police instead? If we present them with the information we've accumulated in the last few days, they might see an opportunity to reopen the case."

"I very much doubt it. Given that Detective Armstrong was reluctant to take any action on the pieces you handed to him recently, I think we'll need a damn good story before they restart the investigation. We're just going to have to piece together a bit more evidence ourselves first."

Dan had a good point, but there was something that made me feel uneasy about this next bold step, as if I were crossing a treacherous line. "What about those threatening letters, I haven't told them about those yet."

"You said you threw away the first one, right? And the police agent that inspected the practice concluded the smashed window was likely an act of an angry patient. All in all, it seems to me that what we have right now is just too flimsy."

"Maybe you're right," I muttered, but I was increasingly feeling that I may have bitten off more than I could chew.

Dan was forging ahead with the next steps of the plan. "Last weekend I had some ideas about the role of the phone company in these four cases. Over the next few hours, I will try to work these out and see if I can persuade any work contacts to help me elbow my way into this place." He suddenly seemed to be in a hurry. "But listen, we shouldn't talk for too long, they may be tracing my calls."

I wondered what was making Dan think his phone might be tapped, but before I could ask, he spoke again. "I'm going to switch off this mobile after we hang up and will try to purchase a burner – I'll contact you afterwards as soon as possible. Are you going to try to get more info from the DFI in the meantime?"

Coming this far already, there was no other option but perseverance in order to get justice for Oliver and so I agreed to continue our quest. "Alright, I will," I said in a quivering voice.

"Don't worry. I've got your back," Dan said, although I wasn't quite sure what he meant by that.

"Promise me you'll watch out for yourself, okay?"

"Sure," Dan responded, trying to sound light-hearted, but it felt like an empty promise – we both knew the stakes were incredibly high right now and not in our favour.

After we'd hung up, I stumbled to my desk and plopped down onto the chair, my heart still racing. My life seemed to have become a succession of volatile emotions, rattling exchanges and perilous encounters ⁻ it was becoming a bit too much to bear. The thoughts in my head were racing at a million miles an hour and I no longer knew who I could trust.

My eyes fell on the forgotten lunch – I reached over and started absent-mindedly unwrapping the aluminium foil and removed the plastic cutlery from the bag. The meal had turned cold with little puddles of grease floating on the orange sauce, and while I usually relished Indian food I barely managed to get anything down. After pecking at the rice for some time, I wrapped the remainder of the meal in the plastic bag, tied it up in a knot and I tossed it into the bin. I opened the window of my consulting room to dispel the thick smell of spicy food in the air and noticed I had a few minutes left on my break.

I grabbed my phone and sent a message to my mother asking if Tim could stay with them for two nights on the grounds of unexpectedly taking over the evening shifts from a colleague. Although I didn't like the feeling of being at someone else's mercy, and I refused to abandon my home, I did feel adamant to safeguard my son against any harm.

Then I logged onto my PC, opened the internet browser and found out that the DFI was located in The Hague, directly alongside the A4 highway. I grabbed the key card used for my shifts at the out-of-hours clinic from my handbag and slid the paper from out the plastic cover. I made a search for the Mason & McGant logo on the internet, copied the picture and combined it with a picture of myself. After giving myself a fake name, I printed the homemade identity card on a piece of thick paper and carefully slipped it back into the plastic holder.

I held the card up in the air with a content smile. *"Et voila,"* I said to myself. It actually looked much more professional than I'd imagined. I now had one foot in the door.

33

After hours of tossing and turning, I finally fell asleep at two in the morning and woke up again at half past six. I didn't manage to doze after that and so I dragged myself out of bed, threw a splash of water on my face and staggered downstairs to consume a double dose of caffeine before feeling slightly human again. After breakfast, I pieced together an outfit from my closet that could pass for that of a lawyer. I tried hard not to think of what I was about to embark on, for fear of getting cold feet and backing out.

I slid my arms into my smartest coat, hung my key card stating I was a lawyer around my neck, strode out to my car and entered the address of the DFI into the navigation system. While driving, I kept checking my rear view mirror to make sure I wasn't being followed. Traffic was light at this time of the day so I arrived at the destination in just under an hour. The building turned out to be located in a suburb of The Hague and was situated on a spacious site. I slowly brought the car to a halt in the visitor parking area.

My feet felt as heavy as lead. I was fully aware I was in a make-or-break situation as I walked towards the entrance of the imposing, rectangular building that had four floors and was surrounded by greenery. After I entered the lobby through the revolving door, I saw the reception on my right. I walked towards it with a straight back, hoping I looked convincing.

A lady in a green and white uniform addressed me. "Good morning, how may I help you?"

"Good morning," I said, flashing a friendly, self-assured smile. "I'm looking for Joe de Smet."

"Which department?"

I pretended to rack my brain for a few moments. "Sorry, it just slipped my mind. He's a senior scientist and involved in DNA analysis," I said and fervently hoped this would do.

She typed a few words into her computer, her long nails clicking on the keyboard. "Found him," she said, then picked up the phone. "Do you have an appointment with him?" she inquired, keeping the phone wedged between her ear and shoulder while her fingers darted over the keyboard.

I apologised and flashed my homemade ID card at her. "I'm Jennifer van Doorn from the Mason & McGant law firm in Amsterdam. My colleagues have regular meetings with Joe," I bluffed. "I'm pretty sure he'll be able to free up some time for me," I added with an air of self-confidence, but inside I was shaking like a leaf.

The woman inspected my company card for a moment, her eyes squinting, and then entered the details into her system without further questions. "Mr de Smet. I have someone from the Mason & McGant law firm who would like to see you, Jennifer van Doorn," she said into the phone.

She hung up and looked at me. "He'll be with you soon. Have a seat, please," she requested and pointed towards the waiting area.

I walked towards the table and lowered myself into one of the comfortable armchairs. There was a stack of magazines in front of me. I took one entitled 'Science', leafed thoughtlessly through the published medical studies and then laid it back again. I stifled the urge to bite my nails and sat upright, a forced calm but friendly smile on my lips as I practised my lines.

A man who looked about forty years old approached me with the easy gait of an athlete, his brown hair showing streaks of grey at the temples. A feeling of dread overwhelmed me, urging me to scuttle off, but I knew I had to bite the bullet and face this head on.

The man, wearing a green, checked shirt and corduroy trousers, held out his hand to me. I jumped up and returned his handshake in a business-like manner, his skin warm and dry brushing against mine. "Jennifer van Doorn, lawyer at Mason & McGant," I stated, trying to curb the vibration in my voice.

"Joe de Smet, senior scientist. I'm curious to learn to what I owe this visit," he said graciously, then gave a short nod. "But let's head upstairs, where we can sit quietly."

I followed him up the steel spiral staircase, all the while telling myself I have a duty to do this to find Oliver's killer, however uncomfortable I felt. To my relief, the man didn't make an effort to engage in small talk.

Upon reaching the second floor, he announced, "We're turning left here."

We walked down a long, white-walled corridor, my heels clicking on the pristine epoxy floor, all the way to the far end of the building, passing by a string of laboratories that were well visible through the large windows. Joe noticed my gaze. "This is the lab where we perform DNA analyses."

I nodded. "Interesting," I said, feeling my tongue stick to the roof of my mouth.

We arrived at a conference room, where Joe halted and stooped to take a peek through the window. "This one's available," he concluded, opening the door to a windowless room, where posters illustrating what I presumed were scientific advances made by the DFI, decorated the otherwise blank walls. "Have a seat," he said with a gesture.

I sank down onto one of the wooden chairs, the waistband of the sheer, glossy tights I wasn't used to wearing underneath my skirt was cutting into my belly.

"Can I get you anything to drink?

"Water please," I replied, hoping it would fix my dry mouth.

While Joe left the room to fetch us drinks I kept rehearsing the lines I'd carefully plotted out in my mind until I suddenly had an idea. I fished my phone out of my handbag and scrolled through the various functions, realising I wouldn't have a sufficient amount of space left on my phone. I quickly opened data storage and, with a stab in my heart, removed a number of long films I'd taken of Tim. It's for the greater good, I told myself. Knowing Joe could return at any moment, I pressed the red button and the counter started running. I placed my phone on the table and strategically covered it with a stack of papers, hoping with all my heart that the conversation would be audible.

I wiped the drops of sweat that beaded along my forehead, and right at that moment Joe reappeared, holding two plastic cups of water in his hands. He closed the door behind him and took a seat on my right side with a notepad and pen ready to use. "So, Jennifer. What can I do for you?"

I gave a nervous cough, straightened my back and forced myself to look confident. "Thank you for allowing me some time," I began. "I'm sure you must be busy," I offered in an attempt to flatter him, although I really had no notion of what people in his position were doing all day long.

"No problem at all. We always make time for our colleagues at Mason & McGant, history has proven it's worth it," he said with a look in his eyes I couldn't quite read.

"I see our reputation precedes me," I responded, smiling warmly.

"If you don't mind, I'll need to pop into the lab later on. One of the new lab technicians in my team is working on a complex analysis, for which she'll need my help."

"Of course. No problem."

"You're welcome to join me in the lab ‾ it might be interesting to get an impression of how things work here."

"I'd love to," I replied, taking a swig of my water, and decided to get to the point. "So Joe," I began, laying my arms on either side of the paper stack covering the phone on the table. "I recently took over a defence case from one of my colleagues, who has been ill for quite some time. It's been a rather complex lawsuit, involving a suspect who has received legal assistance from our office on several occasions prior to this. We have a …" I made a pompous gesture. "How shall I describe it – a fairly close relationship with this man. We want to do everything in our power to avert a new prison sentence for him."

Joe folded his arms with an expression on his face that I found difficult to interpret. "Isn't that your job as a lawyer?" he queried.

I smiled tactfully. "Of course. We have all taken the oath admitted to the bar," I countered, pretending to be slightly affronted by his discourtesy. "But let me say that with some clients we have a somewhat stronger connection." I couldn't, by any stretch of the imagination, be considered a great actress, but so far Joe seemed to be going along with my performance.

There was a knock on the door – a young woman of about twenty-five in a white coat poked her head in. "Joe, I have reached step eleven of the analysis. Do you have time to come help me with this?"

Joe frowned at her. "Kelly, whenever you leave the lab, always make sure to take off your lab coat, remember?" he said admonishingly. "Even if you're only out for a few minutes."

Indignity flooded her, turning her face as red as a beetroot. "Oh right, I forgot. I'm sorry."

Joe smiled weakly at me, whereupon I shrugged, relieved that the attention had been diverted from me for a moment.

"Well, there's no point crying over spilt milk. Just make sure to remember it in future. Will you come along with us?" Joe asked me as he pushed back his chair, his tall, sprightly figure leaping up.

"Yes, of course," I tried to say with enthusiasm, but needless to say I was displeased by this interruption. While Joe was discussing something with the girl, I ever so cautiously slid my hand under the pile of papers and pressed the red button on my phone to save the much-needed memory.

I followed Joe and Kelly into the corridor and tried to take this moment to relax, while catching fragments of their conversation which was filled with jargon, making it hard to follow. After passing a few doors we arrived at the laboratory, which I'd already laid eyes on earlier. Joe held his card against the reader and a click of the door sounded. He held it open for me, allowing me to enter the room, where we were met with a long line of white coats hanging on a coat rack. Joe took what seemed to be his personal one off the hook and slipped into it, before his gaze went stealthily up and down my body, making me feel uncomfortable. "This will probably fit you," he concluded, grabbing another protective coat and holding it up for me.

Feeling a tad awkward I slid my arms into the coat, a whiff of an unfamiliar rose-scented perfume flooding my nostrils, and buttoned up.

Joe's voice rose over the hubbub in this vast, white-painted space filled with complex devices, pumping hoses and humming machines on the various work tops lined up in rows across the room. A dozen people or so all dressed in protective clothing and some wearing safety glasses were scurrying about, completely focused on their work. At the far end of the room, the large windows offered a view of a series of skyscrapers in the distance – presumably the city centre of The Hague.

I conscientiously stepped into the room in Joe's wake – laboratories were never really my cup of tea – making sure my greasy, mucky paws didn't touch anything. Kelly removed a pair of plastic, white gloves from a cardboard box and slid her hands into them, while continuously babbling to her boss.

Joe suddenly swivelled, his eyes sparkling with enthusiasm while he addressed me. "Kelly is conducting a DNA investigation on a forensic trace found at a crime scene. A so-called STR analysis is performed during this study, involving the determination of how often a certain DNA structure is repeated, as this is unique per individual."

"Interesting," I mumbled, shifting from one leg to the other.

"The DNA fragments are multiplied by an enzyme in a test tube in order to visualise them," he continued, but I had a hard time keeping up with him as I felt nervous and jittery. "The profile of the DNA material found can then be run through the database, in the hope of finding a match," he finalised.

"Righty-ho," I responded, hoping he would hurry up with helping the young lab technician. I couldn't wait for us to carry on our conversation in private again and leave the DFI behind me as quickly as possible.

After some moments Joe had shown the girl what to do next, and we headed back to the exit of the lab. Relieved, I took off the highly-perfumed lab coat and hung it on the rack.

We walked back into the conference room where I surreptitiously slid my hand into the stack of papers, unlocked my phone and pressed the red button.

Joe didn't seem to have noticed anything and tapped his ballpoint against his teeth. "Right, where were we?"

"I was telling you about the lawsuit I took over from my colleague," I began, trying to control the nerves surging through my body. "Over the last few days I've studied all the collected evidence and unfortunately things aren't looking particularly promising for my client."

"I'm sorry to hear that," Joe said, entangling his fingers in front of his chest.

"But I'm not sure what I can add at this point."

I tilted my head. "I was quite impressed just now in the lab by you and your skilful team of technicians," I ingratiated, flashing him my most enchanting smile.

But Joe wasn't impressed and responded to my charm offensive by pulling his lips into a thin line.

"I wouldn't be able to pull it off," I said truthfully. "Running a complicated analysis like that – phew – I'm sure lots of things could go wrong. Are there ever any mistakes made?" I tentatively queried, lowering my eyes so that I was looking from underneath my brows.

He shrugged, leaned back in his chair and folded his arms. "On rare occasions, but there is usually ample DNA left to run the analysis again," Joe replied without a trace of emotion in his voice.

I felt in the thick of this pivotal moment – if I gave up too much and Dan and I had been completely wrong about Joe's role, it would surely raise suspicions and lead to collateral damage.

I smiled. "We all have our bad days, don't we? I can imagine those new lab techs, eager to learn as they may be, can make a few technical glitches here and there," I suggested, choosing my words carefully.

"Sure. Anything's possible," Joe replied with a hint of irritation in his voice. "Like I just said, it's rare. And if it does happen, we'll repeat the analysis even before releasing the results. So seems to me, it's nothing you need to be concerned about."

I nodded fiercely. "Sure, sure. I understand," I soothed, feeling sweat dripping down my back.

I was racking my brain trying to figure out what I could say to get Joe to open up. That man had to be in the know, he just had to.

I suddenly had an idea. "By the way, before it slips my mind, how will I be able to leave the car park on my way out? The barriers were raised when I arrived – I'd like to avoid getting stuck here with my old banger," I said, laughing and waving my hand airily. "A 2004 Fiat Panda," I lied. "Still drives like nothing else though. Do you have a car of age as well, or do you prefer the kind of nought-to-hundred-in-five-seconds type of machine?" I queried.

He coughed, looking somewhat uncomfortable. "I drive a Tesla model Y. And I can arrange an exit ticket for you later," he added promptly.

I had to suppress the urge to gloat. An old friend from college was a scientist at a pharmaceutical company – she always complained about the low wages she made. There was no way on earth a man in his position could afford an extravagant car like that without receiving the odd backhander.

"Right, a Tesla. Not bad," I said casually before taking a mouthful of water. "Like I said, our firm entertains a warm relationship with this particular client. He claims to be innocent of the charge and we have every reason to presume this to be true. We're doing everything in our power – and I mean pulling out all the stops …" I said, taking a pause for the message to sink in, "… to defend him. We obviously wouldn't ever want for an innocent man to disappear behind bars," I said in my most syrupy tones.

There was a change in expression on Joe's face, albeit barely visible, but I knew I was on the right track.

I took a chance. "One of my partners at Mason & McGant advised me that it's within the realm of possibility to request a re-analysis of a DNA sample. He assured me that you are the very best in your profession and are always willing to lend a helping hand."

Joe visibly stiffened on the other end of the table, a scrutinising look in his eyes. There was no doubt I had his full attention now. "I do my best to be of service," he responded tentatively, as he bit the inside of his cheek.

I nodded bashfully, but inside my heart was singing – I got a bite.

Dan and I suspected there was a close liaison between Joe and the firm but the exact shape or form of this was still to be discovered, so I silently looked across at him, hoping it would encourage him to continue speaking now that it had become self-evident what the purpose of my visit was.

The scientist leaped up from his chair, advanced a few steps to the internal windows, which offered a view of the corridor and cast a furtive glance to, I presumed, rule out potential eavesdroppers.

He turned around and leaned back against the door. "There are colleagues who sometimes cut corners while performing their work, and anchoring errors will ensue. If this is the case I'm willing to offer my full cooperation to have the DNA sample re-analysed in my lab, if the party in question would so desire."

I gritted my teeth – Joe had moved too far away from my phone. If the most crucial information wasn't audible on the tape, this whole plan would go up in smoke. I slowly and as unobtrusively as possible slid the stack of papers in his direction while I kept talking with a smile glued to my face. "We would naturally be very grateful."

"How grateful exactly?" Joe asked circuitously.

I narrowed my eyes a bit. "I'd like to show our appreciation in the usual way," and hoped wholeheartedly this wouldn't put any strange ideas in his head.

Joe stared into the distance, tapping his fingers on his lips, before speaking again. "Did I mention my wife recently had an accident on the A13? Her treasured set of wheels was wrecked," he said and turned his face. "She was lucky to make it out alive."

"Oh dear. What a shame," I responded to his suggestion. "We'll take care of that. I'll personally make sure that your wife receives a car that matches yours," I said with satisfaction.

He cracked a smile, popped back into his chair and clicked down his ballpoint pen. "If you give me the file number, I'll arrange for the re-analysis to be performed by one of my lab technicians before the end of the week."

I felt an eyelid twitch as I forced myself not to gasp for air. "I'm afraid I don't have it with me. I'll email it to you later."

He frowned and pursed his lips, fixing his eyes firmly on mine and for a moment I was afraid he was onto me. But then he spoke in a casual tone. "Sure."

I was gathering the pile of papers, slowly removing my phone from underneath when Joe got up from his chair, advanced a few steps towards me before towering over me. "Jennifer, do you have your card for me?"

I bowed my head, hoping he wouldn't notice the sudden redness on my cheeks and started rummaging excessively through my handbag. "Oh how silly of me. I left my cards at the office," I uttered, trying to be the chaotic-yet-charming businesswoman, but I could hear my voice quivering.

I looked up, offering my best smile as my heart was pounding in my chest, while Joe's eyes scrutinised my face. I knew I'd taken a huge risk – it would take no effort for him at all to give Mason & McGant a call and check my name. I slid back my chair, increasing the distance between us and stood up. "Thank you very much for your time," I said, taking control of the situation again. I held out my hand. "I'll be in touch with that file number."

He dithered for the slightest moment before shaking my hand.

"I'll see myself out," I managed to produce, before scuttling down the corridor towards the exit. I forced myself to give the receptionist a friendly nod and a thank you for handing me an exit pass before pushing through the revolving doors.

Once outside, I came to a halt, breathed in the cool air and closed my eyes – an immense burden fell off my shoulders. I couldn't believe what I'd just pulled off. A huge sense of euphoria surged through me and I had to restrain myself from shrieking.

I strode forward and stepped into my car, leaned my head back against the support, thoughts whirling through my mind. The hypothesis that Dan and I had formulated appeared to be true – Mason & McGant had been systematically bribing this Joe guy in exchange for tampering evidence to their advantage.

I took my phone from my handbag and listened to the final part of the sound recording, which I surmised to be pivotal. The voices sounded muffled, but the dialogue was clearly audible. No doubt, this would be sufficient for the police to reinstate the investigation.

In my call history I searched for Dan's number only to remember that he'd turned off his phone and planned to purchase a burner. There was nothing else to do but wait for him to call me. The ball was now in his court.

34

After my visit to the DFI, I had the rest of the afternoon to myself, but I was feeling on tenterhooks. Ever since I'd received the third threatening note, I was apprehensive at home and so I spent the rest of the day roaming around the city.

Late in the evening I had little choice but to go home, but I still had not heard from Dan and was in an agitated state of suspense. Shouldn't he have called by now? He'd told me he was going to dive into the nitty-gritty of the role played by the phone company that had appeared in the overview drafted by Oliver. I was getting increasingly worried that Dan's snooping had been detected and he was starting to pose too great a risk to Mason & McGant. The thought that something could have happened to him was unbearable.

I closed all the curtains in the house and grabbed the remote control to distract myself with some brainless TV programme. After just a few moments, I jumped up and went to the kitchen to get myself a glass of wine. I grabbed the half-full bottle of Merlot from the counter, poured out the wine, the aroma wafting into my nostrils, momentarily pausing the anxious thoughts that had been consuming me. I'd rather have waited for more information on Dan's end in order for us to come up with a convincing case, but perhaps it was wise not to dither any longer and to reach out to the police first thing in the morning, informing them of the recent developments at the DFI. Today's voice recording would surely provide enough evidence to reopen the investigation?

The sound of my phone startled me. I rushed back to the living room and looked at the display – it was an anonymous caller.

"This is Jennifer Smits," I said vigilantly.

"Jennifer, it's me. Dan."

My heart jumped. "Oh my god, I'm so relieved it's you. I was starting to worry," I said, which was an understatement. "Where are you?"

"Perhaps best not to tell you." He sounded nervous and for the first time I realised he might be just as distressed as I was. "But don't worry. I'm in a safe place," Dan declared with an air of abstruseness.

"I have a lot to bring to the table," he went on, sounding upbeat now. "I'm sure there's material here that will take our case forward," he said, giving me a wonderful feeling of hope.

"I do too," I said, eager to impart my findings from the DFI. "But you go first." I sank down on the sofa, knocked back a mouthful of wine, and waited for him to provide a detailed account of how his investigation had progressed.

"I found out what role the phone company TelExact plays in this setup, I'll explain it in a bit. First I need to delineate how evidence in a court case is built up by a prosecutor," Dan said.

"Okay."

"For the prosecution to be able to prove in court that a suspect was present at the location at the time of the crime, phone records are often used. So far I'm telling you nothing new, I reckon," Dan was rambling so quickly that the words practically blended together. "What you may not know is that it's actually quite challenging to do this accurately. Showing that a person was in the vicinity of an area is a piece of cake, pinpointing the exact location is a whole different ball game."

I took another swig of wine and muttered something inaudible, dying to find out more.

"This TelExact company is apparently specialised in this field. They use three information sources to determine someone's whereabouts – the first is a Wi-Fi network to which a suspect might have been connected at the time. In addition, they use cell tower data from the general mobile phone network, albeit less accurate. Finally, they use GPS satellites as a radio navigation system. These three parameters combined will ultimately give you the location of the phone and therefore the suspect, up to a precision of several metres."

I finished my wine with a gulp and set the glass on the table, letting Dan's disclosures sink in. "It's quite a technical story, Dan. But I kind of get the picture."

"I know. It baffled me at first too, until I spoke to this guy at TelExact who really knows his stuff. He explained to me they use an in-house developed algorithm to combine the information from the three sources in order to arrive at an accurate fix of the suspect's location."

"That's all well and good," I said, slightly deflated, "but there is nothing conspicuous about this, is there?"

"Hold on, I'll get to that," Dan countered. "The four reports we found based on Oliver's overview all showed that the prosecution had initially proven the suspect was at the scene of the crime at the right time. Mason & McGant subsequently rebutted the results and requested a second opinion with another company …"

I leaped up from the sofa, interjecting. "TelExact," I said, slowly grasping the concept.

"Exactly. This TelExact company performed a second assessment of the accused's location showing he was indeed in the area, but not exactly at the location of the crime."

I bit on my thumb, thinking about the implications. "So, this piece of important evidence on the exact whereabouts of the defendant was shattered by TelExact?"

"Damn right it was. It made the case for the prosecution very weak. Add this to the DNA traces not being a conclusive match ..."

"And the accused gets acquitted." I finished the sentence for Dan, fitting the pieces together. "Free like a bird. So how exactly does TelExact go about this?" I asked.

"They're purposely being vague about it, hiding behind an allegedly complicated piece of software licensed and developed over in the States."

I had my concerns. "Could it not all have been a coincidence, a bizarre twist of fate, if you will, that this took place for all four cases?"

There was silence on the other end. "You're right, we cannot rule out this option yet. To be fair, what we have in our hands is still rather flimsy. I need to compare the details of the cases one by one, but it would be very coincidental if the four prosecutors on the case made an error regarding the location of the suspect and at the same time, the DFI blundered analysing the DNA traces."

Dan was right. This was highly unlikely and virtually impossible.

"I have my suspicions that there's someone at TelExact who is paid for his or her services."

"Similar to the DFI?" I asked, thinking of the *tête-à-tête* with Joe I'd had earlier.

"Yes, similar to the DFI, if we are able to get the evidence to prove that ..."

"Well, I think I can help with that," I said, chuffed to bits. "I went there this morning."

"No way. Tell me."

I summarised how my visit to the DFI had been, while pacing up and down the room.

"What a brilliant idea of yours to record your conversation with that guy," Dan responded, sounding impressed.

"Thanks. There's still a level of ambiguity to it though – after all, he didn't actually declare that Mason & McGant has paid him in the past, but I do think it should be enough for the police to review the case. In the end, bribery can only truly be demonstrated if suspicions of financial malpractice are confirmed in the form of transactions – and that's well out of our league." I plopped down on the sofa, my fingers mindlessly stroking the armrest. "What do you think if I ring Detective Armstrong tomorrow?"

"Hmm," Dan said. "I think it would be wise if I first finalise the allegations against TelExact. If we combine both our findings from the DFI and TelExact it would surely increase the chances of turning the criminal investigation department onto our side."

I felt caught between a rock and a hard place. On the one hand, I wanted to be able to put an end to this ordeal as soon as possible – on the other hand, I understood Dan's reasoning and had to grant him that. "I just want this chaos to finally be over," I said, breaking down. "My life has been turned upside down – my girlfriends no longer want to see me and my colleagues think I've gone haywire. I feel unsafe in my own house, can barely get any sleep – I'm constantly on edge and anxious. I'm at the end of my tether," I said, tears piercing my eyes.

"I understand," Dan said gently. "Why don't you stay with your parents for a while?"

"That thought did occur to me, but it just doesn't feel right. I don't want to drag them into this mess, and at the same time I'm reluctant to leave my house. I know it sounds strange, but it feels like I would be abandoning Oliver if I leave," I said, wiping my cheeks with the back of my hand.

"I see. Don't worry too much, okay? I'll probably just need one or two more days before we can hand things over to the police. We'll be able to present them with concrete evidence of a legal violation, and then they can take over, using their expertise and manpower to nail Mason & McGant." His voice suddenly changed and I pictured him showing that cheeky crooked smile of his. "After this is over, I'll take you out to dinner at the finest restaurant in Amsterdam."

I couldn't help but laugh, the unsettled feeling giving way to a warm glow inside. "I'll hold you to that."

"Listen," said Dan, adopting a brisk, unwavering tone again. "I'm going to give you my temporary number. Please save this under a different name in your phone, okay?"

I typed the digits and saved it under the name Mia, after my deceased grandmother.

"I'll be switching off this burner, but I will occasionally check it for any messages."

I bit the inside of my cheek, "Be careful. Please promise me, Dan."

"I will," he whispered. "Hang in there, this will soon all be over."

We disconnected and I gazed at the number he'd given, memorising it, just in case.

I closed my eyes and summoned a deep breath, holding it in. I was getting increasingly anxious that this situation was about to blow up in my face.

35

It was half past ten when the last patient of the morning consultation left my room. I gave a big yawn – after talking to Dan on the phone last night, I'd had trouble falling asleep. I trudged out of my room towards Simone to inquire about the home visits planned for today. At that moment the front door of the practice swung open and two police officers stepped inside.

"We are looking for Jennifer Smits," the female with a short and rotund figure barked at me.

I came to a halt and uttered, bewildered, "That's me."

Yesterday, Dan had been very clear that he wished not to contact the police until his plan had come to fruition. Would he really have changed his mind so soon after our call?

"We kindly request you to come with us to the station," the other officer said, an unmistakeably grave expression on his face. "We have a warrant for your arrest. You are being detained on suspicion of involvement in the death of Sandra delaHaye."

Stumbling towards the wall for support, I felt the blood draining from my face and my legs buckling underneath me.

From the corner of my eye I noticed Hans dash out of his consulting room, total shock etched in his eyes. He straightened his back and began speaking in a hostile voice, "Can someone tell me what on earth is going on here?"

I was unable to string words into a sentence. "I er … I er …" I kept repeating.

"Sir, can you please stay out of this," the male officer said brusquely and authoritatively to Hans, his hand up in the air while brushing past him.

"You can't just barge in here. This is my practice," Hans said, his eyes flaming, jabbing a finger into his chest. "And for the record, my colleague's name is *Doctor* Smits." There was an air to him that I'd never witnessed before.

The officer yielded, muttering something of an apology, and then turned his attention back to me. "Doctor Smits, can you please come with us? You will be interrogated at the station by one of our detectives."

I was clinging onto the bannister, trying to remain upright and thinking, this can't be happening. "There must be a mistake," I croaked. "You've got the wrong person ..."

The male officer interrupted me. "You can explain it all at the station. If you give your full cooperation now, we won't need to cuff you." There was something menacing in his demeanour that made me surrender.

I advanced a few steps and the two officers sandwiched me by the shoulders as the male one began intoning his lines. "You do not have to say anything. But, it may harm your defence if you do not mention when questioned something which you later rely on in court. Anything you do say may be ..."

His words whizzed past me as Simone dashed out of my consultation room, holding my handbag in her hands. "Here, take this with you," she said, a look of concern on her face.

I clutched my belongings to my chest. "Thank you," I whispered. My hands were trembling as I turned to Hans. "Can you please call my mother and ask if Tim can stay another night with them?" Although I could hardly imagine that I wouldn't be able to rectify this ridiculous accusation in the blink of an eye, I wanted to make sure that Tim was in good hands in case it took longer than anticipated.

"Of course. I'll relay the message." Hans held me by the shoulders, ignoring the on-looking officers. "Hang in there. This is all clearly a big misunderstanding," he attempted to reassure me, but I could see a flash of doubt in his eyes.

I limped alongside the female officer, who held a hand firmly on my back, as if I were a high-risk felon about to make a run for it. I turned my head and looked back, and saw Simone and Hans gawking at me with slumped shoulders and dangling arms.

During the drive to the police station, which only took a few minutes, my thoughts were racing in circles. My life had completely spiralled out of control – how on earth was it possible for them to believe that I had anything to do with Sandra's death? The more I thought about it, the more I began to wonder whether I'd misunderstood them. Perhaps they just wanted to interrogate me to get more information on the case? Surely they would soon realise I was not the one at fault when they heard the sound recording on my phone. I drew a sharp breath and slowly released the air out of my lungs, leaned back and stretched my legs, feeling more confident of a good outcome.

After the male police officer parked the car in front of the station – a place I'd visited not long ago – his female colleague opened the door for me and gave a nod, indicating I should exit the vehicle. I unbuckled my seatbelt and slid across the back seat to the opened door, glad to leave the musty smelling interior. Both officers were awaiting me on the pavement with stern looks. Meekly I trudged in between them to the entrance of the building, where I'd recently met with Detective Armstrong under entirely different circumstances. I shook my head – this was clearly all due to a misapprehension on their part. I was confident that as soon as Detective Armstrong saw me, he'd recognise there had been a mix-up.

We strode past the reception area, where a handful of lingering tourists dressed in brightly coloured shirts were gawking at me, and I bowed my head in humiliation. We advanced to the stairwell, where I was summoned to descend. Once we reached the basement floor, we turned right entering a long and narrow corridor, faintly illuminated by fluorescent tubes and I sensed a claustrophobic feeling welling up inside me. For a moment I was afraid that I'd have another hyperventilation attack, just as I'd had in the first few weeks after Oliver's death. I admonished myself and kept on setting one foot in front of the other.

At the end of the passage, the male officer pulled a key ring from his belt and unlocked the door. "Take a seat over there," he said, gesturing towards the other end of the room.

I inched into the white room, which lacked any form of natural light, and smelled damp and stuffy.

"Do you want some water?" the female officer asked, a look of pity flitting across her face.

My mouth felt dry as I opened it to speak for the first time. "Yes please."

The door closed behind the two officers with a loud, metallic click, leaving me alone in this confined space, wondering what I'd soon be faced with. There was this gnawing fear in the pit of my stomach that I was overlooking something.

After a few minutes the female officer returned with a plastic cup of water. I brought the cup to my mouth using both hands, but I was shaking so violently I spilled water on my shirt, sending a chill all over my body – it was freezing cold in here.

"The detective will be with you any minute," the officer declared and left again, the clang of the metal door slamming shut reverberating around the room, and in my head.

I let my gaze wander around the small space – the room was no bigger than a few square metres. Apart from an air vent high against the outside wall, there was nothing but four white walls, a steel door, and a table with two plain, wooden chairs. My phone had been confiscated before I'd stepped into the police car and as there was no clock I lost all sense of time, while the feeling of apprehension continued to grow.

After what seemed to have been an eternity, the door suddenly swung open and there was the familiar face of Detective Armstrong. I was about to jump up in relief – as soon as he set eyes on me he would surely realise there had been a massive error – until I noticed the precarious expression on his face. Something was seriously wrong.

"Doctor Smits," he said formally and shook my hand as I slowly rose. "I am sorry to see you again under these circumstances."

I tried to clear my throat and respond in a light-hearted fashion, as if we were old acquaintances crossing paths, catching up and exchanging pleasantries, but the words seemed unable to leave my lips.

The detective lowered himself onto one of the hard chairs and gestured that I should follow his example.

I sank down on the edge of my chair, gnawing my lower lip, the tip of my shoe uncontrollably tapping the floor under the table.

"Try to relax, Mrs Smits," he said, his voice carrying loudly in the small room.

I shifted back a bit in my seat.

He placed a tape recorder on the table, pressed a red button and verbalised the names of the attendees, the date and the time.

Then the detective directed his attention to me. "As you have been informed by my colleagues, you are being held under suspicion of involvement in the murder of Sandra delaHaye." "Detective Armstrong," I exclaimed nonplussed, jumping to the edge of my seat again. "This must be a mistake, I don't know …"

He closed his eyes and swiftly raised his hand, causing me to trail off and slowly sink back into my chair.

I tried to pull myself together – you must stay calm Jennifer, I tried to soothe myself.

"So why don't you tell me: where were you on Monday morning, the third of January, the day that Mrs Sandra delaHaye ended up under a tram?"

My thoughts went back to that time when I wasn't in a good place. After I'd made a few blunders at the practice, I'd taken two weeks off on the advice of Hans. During that time Sandra and I sneaked into Mason & McGant twice in the middle of the night.

"I was at home," I answered ruminatively. "Alone." During the day Tim had continued to attend his day-care as usual and I immediately recognised my solitude wouldn't work to my advantage.

The detective's impenetrable eyes and inscrutable countenance gave little away. "You're a general practitioner, right Mrs Smits? Can you tell me what a doctor does at home by herself on a Monday morning?"

My brain jumped into the highest gear while I considered all options – was it wise to get it all off my chest, or would it work against me and would I be better off making up a story?

"I'd been struggling with a few difficult situations at the practice, so my colleague suggested I take a few weeks off."

The detective's eyebrows raised a few centimetres as he spoke with a jeer in his tone. "You were put on leave?"

"No, I wasn't," I said, rejecting his suggestion indignantly. "I just wasn't feeling like myself," I elaborated, making light of the dire straits I'd been in. I took a deep breath and then decided to lay my cards on the table. "After my husband's death, I found out he'd cheated on me – it devastated me. Added to that, I'd returned to work way too soon after he died. But I didn't recognise any of that until I started falling apart," I said, gazing down at my feet. "I have a very considerate colleague who made me realise that a little breather would do me good." The thought of the always-supportive Hans almost reduced me to tears.

"I see," the detective said, his head tilted upwards, smoothing his moustache with his fingers, but I could tell from his face that he didn't fully believe me. This man here before me was nothing like the indifferent detective I'd spoken to before – I'd underestimated him.

He leaned over the table and slowly and deliberately repeated the question. "What exactly did you do on that Monday?"

I shifted in my chair, feeling unsettled as I racked my brain, but it was as if the information was shrouded in mist. "I barely recall the details of those two weeks that I was off – it's all rather hazy."

The detective rolled his eyes in exasperation. "You just said you were at home."

I rubbed my palms together vigorously, stifling a whimper. "Yes I know. It's very well possible, but maybe I was …"

He leaped up and cut in on me in a loud harsh voice that echoed in the hollow space, causing me to cringe. "Maybe you were what?"

I started to stutter. "I'm not sure, I may have run an errand, or taken a stroll around the block. My son attended his day-care centre so I spent my days pottering about the house by myself – it's all become a big blur."

"So let me recap: Your career was on the skids and you found yourself in a real predicament when you discovered your errant husband was fooling around with another woman." He stood behind the table, towering over me, and rocked on the balls of his feet for a while, his eyes locked onto mine.

Then the detective broke the silence. "Maybe I need to refresh your memory on your whereabouts on the day the victim died? You were in the Baarsjes district that morning."

"The Baarsjes?" I echoed. That was the neighbourhood where Sandra's accident had taken place. I shook my head, a feeling of anxiety growing in the pit of my stomach. "No, no, I certainly was not there."

He narrowed his eyes, his thumb and index finger holding his chin. "You just claimed you weren't sure."

"I hardly ever go there, I surely would have remembered," I said, but a little seed of doubt had been planted in my brain. Perhaps I had gone for a little errand – hadn't I been to a hardware store that day? I'd used the two-week break to catch up on a few odd jobs at home.

Detective Armstrong started pacing up and down the room, silence reigning for a moment, arms clasped behind his back. I followed his movements, my eyelids fluttering, while the train of thoughts in my head continued unabated.

The detective suddenly came to a halt, swivelled and advanced towards me. He placed his hands on the table and slowly leaned forward, without so much as a flicker of emotion in his icy eyes, until he was so close the smell of coffee on his breath made me queasy.

He spoke ever so softly that it was almost a whisper. "We have your telephone information. At the time of the accident you were less than ten metres from Sandra delaHaye."

I shook my head in total disbelief with bulging eyes, my voice sounding shaky and weepy. "That's impossible, there must be a mistake."

He retreated and seated himself in the chair, pinning me with a stare.

I was desperately trying to think if I was overlooking something. Was it possible, that by chance, I had been in the area that morning when Sandra died? It seemed too great a coincidence. I floundered – my mind just went blank.

The detective folded his arms over his chest. "Did you know we spoke to the driver of the tram that slammed into Sandra?"

I snapped to attention: Archie – the man in the flat on the third floor. The tormented expression on his face was etched in my memory. "That man, that poor man, I have seen …"

He cut straight across me. "Yes," he said with a drawl. "You paid him a visit, didn't you?"

"I wanted to learn more …" I muttered, but again the detective didn't let me finish and continued his monologue.

"That tram driver stated straight after the accident that it was an atypical event. Sandra came from the right and suddenly shot across the tram track, in broad daylight, while her body was leaning back. For the longest time, we had no explanation for it other than pure bad luck, until we recently spoke to him again – Archie suggested there was someone present, giving her an extra push, so that she wouldn't stand a chance."

"Yes, I know!" I yelled, taking exception to his concealed accusation. "He told me this too, but that person wasn't me."

My objection seemed to fall on deaf ears. "You posed as an occupational health physician," the detective went on. "What were you doing in that man's flat?"

I felt my cheeks glow. "I wanted to know what had happened to Sandra," I managed to utter. "I got the impression that something was wrong – that it wasn't simply a freak accident."

The detective stared past me and mused as if I weren't there. "We often see this – perpetrators of a felony obsessing over it and returning to the crime scene in the aftermath."

I dug my fingers into my thighs. "No, it wasn't like that. Not in the slightest."

"Witnesses have stated that you sneaked into Sandra's memorial service keeping a low profile at the back of the auditorium and scuttled off after just a few minutes. It all ties in with the same obsessive pattern," he said in a contemplative tone, as if he were a philosopher trying to work out a new theory on human behaviour.

I opened my mouth to clarify why I'd decided to pay my last respects back then, but it seemed that everything I said was being misinterpreted, so I kept silent.

The detective stood up and started strutting around the tight chamber again while formulating a hypothesis. "If you ask me, it all happened on a whim. You hadn't planned it, it was a spontaneous action."

I shook my head, muted as the consuming fear grappled at my throat.

"Perhaps you arranged to meet her there that day? Go for a girls-only shopping-trip, or enjoy an early-afternoon cocktail. You'd wormed your way into her life, had even become rather chummy by then, or were you feigning it all?"

I shook my head again, but the detective hardly seemed interested in my response and continued pacing around, unravelling the layers of his conspiracy theory.

"She came to your appointment on her bike, you may have gone there by tram." He waved his hand airily. "We still have to fill in the blanks, but in all frankness – they're trivial. She was waiting to cross the track, until tram twelve, with poor Archie behind the controls, had passed. Maybe you and Sandra had just had an altercation, or perhaps she had a suspicion, an inkling of what you were up to. Or maybe you were just fed up with her, because let's be honest here

– after screwing around with your husband, she just had it coming, didn't she?"

"No!" I screamed like a wild hyena, my eyes on fire, hurling my words at the pale stony face. "No, it's not true. I didn't do it."

The detective failed to respond to my denial, but strode back to his chair, lingering. Then, in what seemed like slow motion, he laid his hands out on the table in front of me, inching closer with piercing eyes, before whispering the final blow. "We found a piece of DNA on the luggage carrier of the bike. Alas, the sample didn't match with anyone in the National DNA database of convicted criminals, and seemed unusable ..." the detective was so close I could see his Adam's apple move as he swallowed, "... until we ran the sample through the DNA kinship database. Turns out your father was being a good citizen years ago when he heeded the call to find a rapist." The detective bared his teeth in a grimace. "He probably never anticipated playing a pivotal role in indicting his daughter for murder."

There was the sound of a pop in my head. Suddenly I heard a loud beep in my right ear. I blinked a few times and gasped for air. The room started spinning around me and I grabbed hold of the table.

"I want a lawyer," I breathed.

He pressed his lips in a tight line. "Sure, we'll get to that in a minute. One last thing." He leaned his elbows on the table and interlaced his fingers, resting his chin on them. "You have a son, right? A sweet little boy, does he look like you?"

"Like his father," I mumbled, feeling an unprecedented fear welling up deep inside.

"Sad to think a toddler will have to grow up without his mother *and* his father. Perhaps he has nice grandparents who'd be willing to raise him?"

I jumped up as an uncontrollable frenzy steamed within me. "I demand a lawyer. Now!"

The detective waved his hands. "Calm down, ma'am. You'll be allowed to make that phone call in a minute. You've had a flawless past – only one mammoth misstep. It'll be hard to convince the judge it was murder in the first degree, but manslaughter should be well within reach." He folded his arms and leaned back. "Four years, that's my offer. If you choose to decline, you'll take the risk of being incarcerated for the maximum of fifteen years in prison. By the time you get out of jail, your dear son is already going to college." He pushed himself out of the chair, advanced a few steps towards the door before swivelling around. "However, if you confess, you'll be reunited with your little munchkin before he starts reading, provided you show good behaviour. Take your time and reflect on my proposal with your lawyer."

He opened the door to the corridor, letting a gust of wind and much-needed oxygen flow into the room. "One of our officers will bring a phone to you shortly," he barked, then slammed the door shut.

After a few minutes in which the world seemed to have come screeching to a halt, an officer entered the room, carrying a mobile phone. "You have three minutes," he said and laid the device, serving as a symbol for my connection to the outside world, on the table, before leaving me alone again.

I typed in the ten digits with trembling fingers, feeling incredibly relieved I'd memorised them.

"Hello," said the familiar voice, prompting me to break down and burst into tears.

"Dan," I sobbed with heaving shoulders. "I've been arrested by the police. They think I'm responsible for Sandra's death."

"What?" Dan exclaimed. There was a short pause. "But how is that even possible?"

I wiped my nose on my sleeve and pulled my arms tightly across my chest, my eyes burning with tears. "They seem to have a pile of evidence against me. I'm at my wits' end. You have to help me, please. Do you think you could defend me, now that you've been put on hold by the firm?"

Dan seemed to be contemplating it for a moment. "Yes. Yes, I believe I can. The bar hasn't suspended my licence, so I'm allowed to continue representing clients as an independent lawyer. But honestly – it's not my area of expertise."

"I don't care. You're a top lawyer at an international firm, you're good at what you do, but more importantly – I trust you. Please help me, Dan," I implored.

"All right, I will."

My hands were shaking so violently, my pearl teardrop earrings clanged against the phone. "How long will it take you to get here?"

"Should be doable within an hour."

Something came to my mind. "Can you call my parents? I asked my colleague to ring them up to keep Tim one more night, but they must be worried out of their minds."

"No problem," Dan responded, then asked tentatively, "What shall I tell them?"

I dithered. "Please tell them that it was just an interview with the police, and that I now have to work an unforeseen extra night shift."

"Okay, I'll pass on the message," Dan said briskly.

I gave him my parents' landline number, which, as luck would have it, I'd always remembered, and the location of the police station where I was being detained.

The door swung open again and the officer spoke with a blank face. "Time's up."

I managed a slight bob of my head to the policeman and raised my index finger. "I have to go," I said to Dan, jacked up. "See you soon, okay?"

"Of course, don't you worry. We are going to rectify this," he assured me cool-headedly, as if were dealing with a wrongful traffic fine, and it gave me a glimmer of hope.

We hung up and I handed the phone back to the agent, who gave me a nod as a sign that I had to stand up. "I'll take you to your cell where you can wait for your lawyer."

I rose to my feet, fidgeting with my hands, trying to keep my sanity.

He pulled a set of handcuffs from his pocket and commanded, "Hands behind your back."

"But, wait …" I stammered. "That wasn't necessary when they brought me in. I promise you that I won't …"

He interrupted my plea and shrugged. "Sorry, it's standard procedure."

I yielded and turned around, bringing my hands to my back, trying to quell the panic rising in my chest as he secured the ring of hard metal around my wrists.

The officer steered me along the hall and up three flights of stairs, his gaze ahead and his hand in my back as if propelling me forward. As I was listening to the echo of my shoes on the concrete floor, I suddenly caught a glimpse of my reflection in a mirror on the wall and stifled a shriek. My face was smeared with streaks of mascara meandering down my cheeks, my eyes looked hollow and forlorn and my jumper was hanging loosely around my body – I was a shell of myself. The hand on my back steered me sideways turning us to the right, into another hallway where we stopped at the third green metal door. As I glanced at the viewing hatch, positioned at eye level on the door, a wave of dread washed over me - I was about to be locked up in a police cell. The man used one of the keys on his chain to open the door, gave a quick nod, and I shuffled into the small cell, containing merely a plain bed, a toilet and a sink, where he unshackled my wrists. "Food will be brought in half an hour," the officer barked.

But I had lost all appetite.

36

I was sitting on the hard bed, staring out of the narrow window where life outside just seemed to carry on as normal. I couldn't wrap my head around what was going on. Suddenly there was a grinding of the key in the lock and I looked up. The door swung open – there stood Dan in the doorway.

I'd never been this exhilarated to see someone in my life and I jumped up. Without any reservations I threw myself into his arms, resting my head against his chest. The clean detergent scent of his crisp linen shirt as well as the spicy fragrance of his aftershave reached my nostrils, causing a paradoxical feeling of comfort and shame over my own crumpled appearance. I let go of Dan, withdrew and muttered, "I'm so sorry." Feeling mortified over the mess I was in, I averted my gaze as we talked. "You have no idea how relieved I am that you're here."

He leaned in, closing the distance between us and tenderly brushed a strand of hair back from my face, bringing tears to my eyes, spilling onto my shirt. I quickly wiped them with the back of my hand.

"Come on," Dan said gently with a nod, his dark eyes full of compassion behind the elegant set of spectacles I hadn't seen him wear since the day we met. "Let's sit down."

We lowered ourselves onto the creaking bed next to one another, our knees almost touching, elbows brushing against each other.

I held my head in my hands, struggling to find words. "I don't know where to start. That detective's been taunting and grilling me, I seem to be directly in their crosshairs. How did I end up in this nightmare?" I asked, although I didn't expect a plausible answer from Dan.

Dan kept silent for a moment and stroked my back, as I gave a sob of despair, my hands still covering my face.

After a while, I pulled myself together, straightened my shoulders and ran a hand through my hair, before mustering up the courage to look into Dan's caring eyes. "Did you get a hold of my parents?"

"They are more than happy to take care of Tim for as long as it takes." His gaze moved to the tray, which had been delivered earlier, sitting untouched on the floor in the corner of the room. "Did you eat anything at all?"

I shook my head resolutely. "I can't get anything down right now."

Dan rose to his feet, advanced a few steps to the food and leaned over to pick up the plate. "Come on, just have a few bites," he insisted, holding out the cheese sandwich. "You need to keep your strength up."

I reluctantly took the sandwich from Dan, not feeling like arguing with him over it and with the utmost effort managed a few bites, just to please him.

Dan stood up and filled the plastic cup in the sink with water. "Here, drink up."

I washed down a piece of bread with the water, while bringing him up to speed about the harsh interrogation and the collection of evidence they'd garnered against me. As we sat back down on the bed, I ended my account of events with the proposal of four years incarceration that the detective had offered.

Dan raised his thick, brown eyebrows as he listened, observing me in silence.

"Do you think I should take it?" I asked, feeling a sense of surrealism as I uttered the words. "Accept the offer of four years in prison?" A voice in my head was telling me to maintain my innocence, but the thought of being sentenced for an even longer period made me wonder if it might be wise to settle.

Dan shook his head. "Absolutely not. The detective is using the carrot-and-stick approach to coerce you. We mustn't make any rash decisions." His tone was unwavering. And yet there was a look in his eyes I couldn't quite read.

"Dan, it sounded like they have pretty conclusive evidence to lock me up for years," I said, shifting on the thin mattress, coils poking into my thighs. "The phone details, my DNA on Sandra's bike, the tram driver's statement – it's almost a watertight case. To make matters worse, I've been unable to provide a good explanation for any of the allegations. With four years and good behaviour, I'll be home in no time," I tried to encourage myself.

"Don't you see it?" Dan said, a resoluteness in his voice. "The evidence is not real, it's fake. It has somehow been fabricated. Just like they did with all those previous cases at Mason & McGant." He paused for a moment, presumably for his words to sink in, but I hadn't the faintest clue what the connection between the two was. "This is how they work, Jennifer. It's their *modus operandi*, their means of operation."

I kept shaking my head, my mouth dropping open slightly.

Dan laid his hands on my shoulders and held them tightly. "Someone in high places at Mason & McGant wants to frame you for Sandra's murder. Remember, how they tampered with DNA samples and phone records to keep those clients from going inside?"

I nodded.

Dan continued with a grim look in his eyes. "In a similar way, they've managed to falsify the evidence to get you wrongfully arrested."

And then there was a click in my brain and the disturbing truth struck me – these people had, by hook or by crook, made it evident to the detective that the DNA found on Sandra's bike belonged to me and had localised my phone at the crime scene at the time of the murder.

My eyes strayed past Dan's shoulder, towards the blank wall opposite me – I felt gobsmacked by the ingenuity of it all. This methodical approach, involving infiltration of the highest levels of the criminal investigation department, was beyond imagination, but Dan had to be right. After all, I was certain I hadn't been in the vicinity of the tram accident on that day, and it was impossible for my DNA to end up on Sandra's bike. I felt foolish and feeble for buckling under the detective's coercion and starting to question myself.

I slowly rose to my feet, clasping my hands at my head as I muttered in astonishment. "It is all slotting into place. How does that rotten law firm manage to bend the world to its will, time and time again? It's as if it has monstrous tentacles wrapped around every aspect of the constitutional state, locking it into place."

I looked at Dan, who was ruminatively rubbing his chin. "They're clearly not lacking in guile. But I just can't wrap my head around how they got a hold of your DNA at the DFI. They would only be able to find a match if they have a sample of your genetic material at their disposal." He shook his head. "It'll have to wait. I'm working out a legal strategy in my head. We need to be able to provide as much evidence as possible to the criminal investigation department in order for them to cross you off as a suspect, so that they can turn their full focus of attention to Mason & McGant. Where did you save that audio recording taken during your visit to the DFI?"

"It's on my phone," I answered. "They confiscated it."

"I'll have to reclaim it to extract the recording," Dan replied, biting his thumb, seemingly reflecting on it all for a moment. "But not right now. Upon arrival I was told you were only allowed to consult me for half an hour and that the hearing would continue afterwards."

I felt my stomach clench, and for a moment I was afraid that those few chunks of sandwich would come back up again, but I managed to get a hold of myself. "I'm not sure I can do this, Dan, I'm so scared," I said, quelling the urge to desperately cling on to him like a little child.

Dan held me by the upper arms again, his hands soft and firm, his big brown eyes locking onto mine. "You must be strong, Jennifer . Think of your son, think of Oliver."

He was right, I had to keep my composure.

"Everything will be okay in the end. You need to have faith that justice will prevail," he added solemnly.

I nodded, stroking the sides of my face with my hands, pulling myself together – I had to rise to the challenge.

There was a sharp rap at the door.

"Are you ready?" Dan asked.

I lifted my chin, looked him deep in the eyes and straightened my back. With a firm jaw, I confirmed I was prepared for whatever was coming next. "Yes."

We rose from the bed, as the lock of the steel door clicked open, revealing a tall male guard with startling blue eyes awaiting me with a pair of handcuffs. "The detective is expecting you."

Not waiting for the guard to ask the question, I turned and put my hands behind my back to be cuffed again, avoiding Dan's gaze during this humiliating scene.

The three of us headed downstairs in silence, where Dan and I were led to the same interrogation room I'd been in earlier. As the guard uncuffed me, he instructed us to sit down alongside one another, on two chairs at one end of the table. Moments later, Detective Armstrong entered the room, ending our muffled conversation, closed the door behind him and advanced towards us, sending a chill down my spine.

"Good afternoon," he said, shaking hands with Dan. "I understand you will act as a legal counsellor on behalf of Mrs Smits today?"

"Yes, I will."

"I gather you've recharged your batteries with a light refreshment," the detective turned to me affably, as if he'd whisked me off to a two star Michelin restaurant.

I nodded, my lips pulled into a straight line.

He grimaced. "Wonderful. Let's get going again."

The detective switched on the recorder and after verbalising all the details, turned his attention to Dan. "Your client, Mrs van Smits, is accused of involvement in the death of Sandra delaHaye and will be charged with manslaughter."

"So I've been led to believe," Dan responded in a business-like tone that I hadn't heard from him before. "Let's not get ahead of things, shall we?" Dan pressed on. "The DNA proof that you claim to have against my client is circumstantial. Why don't we first wait and see if there's unequivocally a match when we compare the DNA profile you found on the victim's bike with my client's."

My eyes flew open. What was Dan doing? He was hanging me out to dry. We already knew that Mason & McGant had somehow retrieved my DNA and that there was a match via the Databank with a sample my father had once handed in. So what was the point of going down this route?

Dan gave me a reassuring look. I sat back, trying to soothe myself –surely he would know what he was doing? I had no other option but to trust him right now.

The detective cast us a cantankerous look, noticeably displeased with Dan taking charge of the interrogation and spoke between gritted teeth. "We are indeed compelled to take a direct sample of Mrs Smits' DNA to complete the forensic evidence. But there's no doubt in my mind that our suspicions regarding Mrs Smits' involvement will be confirmed, given the family bond that has already been demonstrated." He rose from his chair. "I'll be right back."

When the detective had left the room, I turned to Dan, the bit of self-confidence that I had left in me was crumbling away in chunks. "Why did you bring that up? It's clear that they'll find a match when they collect my DNA – it will provide them with the evidence they need to corroborate their accusations." I felt like I'd been hurled out of the pot and into the fire.

"Granted," Dan said in a muffled voice, as if he was expecting the detective to be eavesdropping on us from the other side of the door. "I'm merely taking this route to buy us some time. Although the evidence they have is *prima facie*, from a legal point of view, nothing has been proven yet. By first having them run a full DNA analysis, we're creating an opportunity to garner all the evidence to the contrary."

"Right," I muttered, feeling flustered by the legal terms Dan was throwing at me, but there was a voice in the back of my mind whispering that we were heading down the wrong path.

There wasn't any time to elaborate on Dan's plan and give his approach more consideration, as the detective entered the room again, accompanied by a younger officer, carrying a test tube with a cotton swab, asking me to open my mouth. As I stood up and complied, I thought to myself, another umpteenth degrading gesture, while the man briskly scraped the inside of my cheeks with the brush. Detective Armstrong towered over us, as if to check the officer was doing his job properly.

"That should do it," the junior officer declared as he finished, sliding the specimen into the tube and retreating into the dimly lit corridor.

We all sat down on the wooden chairs again, the inside of my mouth felt dry and cottony. The detective leaned back and folded his arms over his big belly protruding over his grey trousers, and the buttons of his dated, white shirt looked set to pop open. "I took the liberty to discuss the death of Mrs DelaHaye at length with Mrs Smits this morning. Although I presume there was nothing new to you, or was there?" the detective said with a condescending sneer. "What we haven't done yet though is review the death of your husband, Oliver Smits."

I shot a nervous glance at Dan, but his eyes remained riveted on the detective. What was this all about?

"Please enlighten me on what the afternoon of your husband's death looked like?"

My thoughts went back to that fateful day, when my life changed forever. I took a deep breath and started recounting the events. "We had decided to go away for a long weekend, just the three of us. Oliver had booked a bungalow at one of those holiday parks in the south of the country."

"You were leading a busy and hectic life," the detective interrupted. "Where did you find the time to do so?"

I shrugged. "Things weren't too perky between Oliver and me for a few months. We figured spending quality time together with our son, far from the turmoil of everyday life, would help us rekindle things."

The detective's eyebrows shot up. "Did it?"

I furrowed my brow. "Friday had been wonderful. We'd taken a refreshing dip in the swimming pool upon arrival at the park in the afternoon, and Tim had been enjoying himself in the paddling pool." I fought back the tears that were stinging my eyes as my mind relived the last moments of the three of us enjoying happy times together. "In the evening, when Tim was asleep, we ordered sushi and relished it on the couch while watching our favourite film." I smiled at the thought of how Oliver, craving for sushi, had managed to persuade a courier in the nearest town to deliver our order all the way to the holiday park for an obscenely large surcharge.

"Sounds wonderful," the detective scoffed with mock enthusiasm. "What about on Saturday, the day your husband died?" he queried, a harsher tone to his voice now, clearly eager to press ahead.

I coughed and shifted in my seat. "We decided to head to the indoor pool again. We were enjoying ourselves and had agreed that Oliver would watch Tim so that I could read my book for a while. But after just a few moments I looked up and realised that Tim was no longer there – Oliver had been distracted and Tim had wandered off."

"You must have been fuming with rage," the detective said, trying to rile me.

"What kind of father doesn't keep a close eye on his two-year-old, near a swimming pool?"

"I wasn't best pleased," I said euphemistically. The anguish over loosing Tim that had tormented me in those moments came flooding back, but I pulled myself together. "Fortunately our panic was short-lived and there was no harm done. We located Tim just a couple of minutes later in the sandpit," I said, trying to dismiss the incident.

"Then what? The pair of you were all lovey-dovey again?" the detective asked.

I glanced at Dan, who gave me an almost invisible nod.

"No," I answered truthfully. "We had an argument, and Oliver decided to go for a stroll around the holiday park." I looked straight into the eyes of the detective. "It was the last time I saw him alive."

The detective was still leaning back, elbows resting on his belly and fingers interlocked, as he twiddled his thumbs. "Right," he muttered. "So, let's summarise. The relationship between you and your husband has been in dire straits for months – you keep nagging your husband about not being at home enough and it regularly ends in heated arguments. Then …" The detective slammed his hand onto the table "… Wham! Out of the blue you find out your better half is romantically involved with another woman."

I straightened my back and interrupted him. "I didn't know that when he died," I exclaimed, biting my lip, writhing in suppressed fury, but Dan waved his hand, urging me to calm down.

The detective ignored us and carried on summarising. "You decided to go away for a weekend to patch things up, full of hope that your husband would see the attractive woman in you that he once fell in love with, but it didn't have the intended effect. Things turned sour and Saturday evening ended, once again, in a bit of a ding-dong." The detective slowly leaned forward and planted his hands on the table. "You're claiming you had a good time together on Friday evening, but I have the idea that maybe things weren't quite so rosy," he said with derision, narrowing his eyes. "Did your husband confess to you that he wanted to choose Sandra over you, and break free from the shackles of marriage?"

I was shaking my head fiercely to indicate that wasn't what happened at all, but the detective rested back in his chair and continued undisturbed. "Who knows, maybe Oliver decided that weekend he was going to leave you for good and wanted to build a life with his mistress. Who's to say you're speaking the truth, Jennifer. Oliver can't corroborate your account of events, can he?" The detective brought a finger to his lips and looked up, pretending to be in contemplation. "Oh, wait. Sandra can't anymore either."

My jaw dropped open and I shook my head, trying to swallow the lump that had formed in the back of my throat. "It wasn't like that, honestly it wasn't," I whimpered, hearing my voice skip. I looked desperately at Dan, but his gaze remained straight ahead.

"So your brutally murdered husband was discovered a day later by an unsuspecting hiker, at the base of a steep hill – a giant gaping hole in his head. His lifeless body was drenched in blood, while the pounding rain and roaring winds thrashed him relentlessly for hours."

I closed my eyes, picturing my beloved husband lying there all by himself the entire night, exposed on those hard rocks in unforgiving weather, and felt a desperate longing to change history and run over to save him.

"What did you hit him with?"

I opened my eyes and snapped to attention. "I didn't hit him, honestly," I muttered.

"I want to notify you that as we speak, a new and vigorous team of investigators is scouring the crime scene again. We *will* find the murder weapon." The detective seemed to recall something and slowly leaned over to us. "Oh yes, the red knickers he was wearing when he was found, which had belonged to Sandra and that you dressed him in: was that a symbolic gesture towards your husband?" The detective started musing again. "Come to think of it, it may have been a warning from you directed at his mistress. You just wait, you trollop. You're next." A contented smile formed on the detective's lips, he seemed to be enjoying painting this picture of me as a raging, jealous killer. "Did you stumble upon the knickers as you searched through the pockets of his jacket that weekend? You must have gone ballistic when you learnt your husband didn't take your final attempt at reconciliation seriously." He gave a snicker and shrugged. "In any event, there are several plausible explanations."

"It didn't happen like that, it really didn't," I said in despair, trying to conceal my tears. "I did *not* kill my husband! It wasn't until months after his death that I discovered his deceit and the affair with Sandra."

Dan raised his hand. "Listen, Detective Armstrong," he interjected, his lips pulled into a straight line. "We find your train of thoughts immensely entertaining. You should seriously consider becoming a screenwriter for a day-time soap opera." He folded his arms and squared his shoulders, his face all business-like in a heartbeat. "But if you can't come up with any solid evidence against my client, I'd like you to end this so-called interrogation right now."

The detective raised his finger. "Oh, right, the evidence supporting all this – I was just about to get to that. We discovered a hair, right in the centre of Mr Smits' head wound." The man shot me a penetrating look, as if he wanted to make sure he'd caught my attention. "We've got you bang to rights, lady. The hair transpires to be from you."

An ominous stillness fell amongst us as I tried to wrap my brain around what had just been said.

"I'd like to talk to my client in private for a moment," I heard Dan say formally, his body all stiffened up. Dan's self-assured attitude from before seemed to have vanished in an instant.

"As you wish," the detective said, rising from his chair.

Dan waited for the detective to leave the room before turning towards me, his head still bowed. A long pause filled the air with silence. He rubbed his chin, then his eyes slowly raised to meet mine, shocking me with the look of anxiety on his face. "I'll be honest with you, Jennifer. This isn't looking good."

It felt like an imaginary rope was being tightened around my neck. The detective had me hauled me into a corner, like a rat in a trap.

"Finding your DNA on all parts of Oliver's body was in line with expectations, that goes without saying. Except for *in* the wound. You said you never saw him alive again after you'd been quarrelling?" Dan asked tentatively, worry lining his forehead.

I raised my hand like in court. "I swear," I said imploringly. "You do believe me, right?"

"Yes," he replied, but for the first time I saw a flash of doubt cross his face and it felt like my world was shattering to pieces.

"But I can't seem to find a straightforward explanation for the presence of your DNA at the trauma site." Dan leaped up, started pacing up and down the room, his lips pressed tightly together and his gaze averted, firing questions at me. "When did you first see Oliver after his death?"

I summarised the events of that fatal weekend to the best of my recollection. "The police showed up on the doorstep of the holiday bungalow that Sunday morning. They informed me of Oliver's passing and then took me with them in their police car to the station, where he was laid out on a table in a cold room, covered by a white sheet."

"Did they let you see him?"

"Yes, they did."

"Was there anyone accompanying you in the room?"

"No."

"Had the coroner already examined him before you went to see him?" Dan asked.

I shook my head, thinking back on how I'd managed to persuade the young female police officer to allow me to have a moment with Oliver by myself.

"That must be it," I exclaimed and jumped up, as this little glimpse of hope – a justification for this piece of evidence against me – presented itself. "I wanted to touch him, hug him one last time. I ran my fingers through Oliver's hair and before knowing it there was blood all over my fingers. That's when I knew he had a major head injury. That must have been the moment when my DNA ended up in the wound."

"Thank goodness. Yes, that must be it," Dan said, an unconcealed sense of relief flitting across his face. "Okay, we've got our work cut out with this – that woman completely disregarded the protocol and she may be unwilling to admit it. But if need be, we'll question her under oath. She'll need to come clean and ultimately will confirm you were with Oliver before any forensic analyses were carried out."

I gave a big sigh of relief and lowered myself onto the chair next to Dan again.

"It's a stick to beat them with, but we're not out of the woods yet. That's just step one," said Dan. "The other missing part of the jigsaw is how Mason & McGant managed to put your DNA on the luggage rack of Sandra's bike."

I shrugged. "I really don't know, Dan. I've been racking my brain over it."

Dan looked me in the eye as he held my hands, our knees lightly brushing. There was a gentleness and familiarity in his touch that made me feel safe, in spite of the predicament I was in. "I know we've been over this before but I just want to make sure ..." Dan said tentatively. "You really weren't with Sandra that day?"

"No, I really wasn't," I said, in a drained voice. My mind was going round in circles trying to come up with an explanation that made sense. "You know I broke into Mason & McGant twice with Sandra at night," I said, for the first time admitting it had indeed been trespassing rather than just a visit. "Do you reckon they somehow collected my DNA during one of those nights?"

Dan sunk his teeth into his bottom lip, his gaze wandering off, and shook his head. "I highly doubt it. The place must be swamped with hairs and other bodily material. Suppose someone would go looking for traces of you a few hours after you went in, it would be impossible to establish which hair belonged to you. No, it can't be that." Dan released my hands and started drumming his fingers on the table. "You said you met Sandra on a few occasions. Where was that?"

"A cafe, restaurant. Those kind of places."

Dan kept shaking his head in vexation, his finger held up to his lips. "No, it's too farfetched."

Out of the blue he slammed his hands onto the table, scaring me out of my wits, and leaped up. "Damn it!"

Then he turned to me and grabbed my shoulders, towering over me. His forehead creased with worry. "Think hard, Jennifer. It is of pivotal importance that we find out."

I felt the immense pressure – my future was hanging in the balance. "I really don't know, Dan," I whimpered.

Slowly, Dan retreated and proceeded to pace up and down the room, hands clasped behind his back. His eyebrows drew together in an anguished expression.

"You must have had another moment of contact with Sandra, there is no other way. I have a strong inkling that if we ascertain where it was, it will ultimately be the key to your acquittal."

"Did she lend you any of her clothes? Perhaps you got cold on one of those nights at Mason & McGant and she offered you her coat?"

I tried to recollect if any such thing had occurred but soon concluded it had not.

Dan continued throwing suggestions at me. "Did you perhaps borrow her bike? Or maybe you just sat on it when you went for a coffee with Sandra?"

Desperation was taking hold of me. "Absolutely not, I never sat on her bike, I never even so much as touched her. I haven't even been to her home ..." My voice trailed off.

There was a click in my mind – all the pieces of the puzzle fell into place, suddenly exposing the big picture. The devious stratagems, the lies and deceit, the calculated coverup defied all imagination. I slapped a hand over my mouth and my eyes popped wide open. "How could I have been so stupid?" I whispered.

Dan's voice sounded far away. "Jennifer?"

I slowly pushed myself out of my chair and started pacing the room, my arms dangling lifelessly on either side. "So it was him all along. It's all starting to make sense. That man – just like me – had a legitimate reason to be outraged with Oliver and Sandra. They hadn't just deceived me with their affair, but him too. Besides, as a partner of Mason & McGant, he had to prevent Oliver from blowing the lid on their 'arrangements' with the DFI. That bastard must have made a boatload of cash with that scam."

I looked at Dan, who had a bewildered look on his face.

I continued rambling. "I wasn't able to see the light all this time – he played his role of grieving husband far too convincingly when I visited him in their home that day."

Dan gawked at me and was shaking his head. "Jennifer, you have to take me with you. I'm not following."

I narrowed my eyes and started bobbing my head as the logic of the events increasingly started to seep into my brain. "It must have been my coat …Yes, of course it was," I exclaimed. That innocent-looking woman plucked my hair from my coat in a supposedly trivial act," I reasoned out loud. "She told me he had requested it – she probably didn't even have the faintest idea why she needed to brush my coat." I gave a wry smile, my fists clenching. "It was the perfect moment for him to seal the deal against me – it was the final nail in my coffin. And I just handed it to him on a plate when I decided to pay him a visit – he hardly had to make any effort. That rat must have been laughing himself silly."

"Jennifer," Dan said, gently tugging at my sleeve and snapping me out of my train of thought. I came to a halt and looked at Dan – it dawned on me he didn't have a clue what I was referring to.

I straightened my back as I delivered the message. "Roderick," I said. "It is Roderick delaHaye, Sandra's husband, who killed Oliver and Sandra."

As Dan's mouth dropped open, I filled him in on my *rendezvous* with Roderick, who was a partner at Mason & McGant as well as Sandra's life partner, in that exclusive, cold-hearted penthouse, where I had fallen for his trap – hook, line and sinker.

37

The next morning, I was gazing out of the tiny window, which formed my only connection to the outside world. The people on the streets hurried about, heading to school or work, just following their everyday routines. They had no notion of the privilege they had as autonomous citizens being able to go their merry ways. In the far right of my field of vision, a small boat glided smoothly through one of the countless canals of the city. The freedom of the vessel contrasted sharply with the utter lack of it I was experiencing up here in this tiny cell.

After I'd shared with Dan the ins and outs of my visit to Sandra's husband a few weeks ago, he told me it was Roderick who had put him on hold after finding out we'd been going through the secret files, something I'd never known. I, in turn, had never mentioned to Dan that Sandra was Roderick's wife and that I'd recently met him. And so it transpired that we each had a missing piece of the puzzle in our possession, without knowing it.

Not long after my epiphany, Detective Armstrong had re-entered the interrogation room and told us that questioning for that day was over. I spent the remainder of the day on this wretched bed in my cell, right in the heart of the city. The detective had expedited an application for my remand, to give them more time to collect further evidence against me, and, if granted, I would be transferred to a nearby maximum-security prison at the end of the day, so I was told. The thought of being incarcerated among criminals who had a long tally of Lord-knows-what kind of horrific crimes, filled me with terror.

During the night, I'd tossed and turned on the uncomfortable mattress, drifting in and out of sleep as I kept hearing snippets of conversations, shouts and bellows coming from the corridor, and only managed to get a few hours of sleep, until the unforgiving spirals poking into my back roused me again. The unpredictability of the season had brought a cold night, and the threadbare grey blanket offered insufficient comfort. I must have dozed off again after hearing the first birds chirping outside, announcing a new dawn, only to be rudely awakened by a prison guard shortly after, announcing it was time for breakfast.

I tried to freshen up at the basin as best as I could, and smooth out the creases in my skirt. There was no mirror in the cell – presumably for safety reasons – but I didn't need one to know I looked scruffy and ghastly. I only managed a few nibbles of the boiled egg and washed it down with two or three swigs of tea. The rest of the food was collected by the guard later in the morning.

It felt like I'd been in this confined space for hours, left to the mercy of my thoughts, which ranged from despair and despondency to tentative optimism for a good outcome. Dan had asserted he'd be able to gather the evidence against Mason & McGant and present it to the police as soon as possible. Meanwhile, I had no idea what was in store for me – more interrogations or perhaps an immediate transfer to the high-security prison.

I snapped to attention as I heard the noise of clattering keys coming from the hallway and spun around.

The door swung open and to my astonishment, there was Detective Armstrong standing in the doorway, his hands tucked casually in the pockets of his jeans.

"I have some good news for you, Mrs Smits. You are free to go."

My jaw slackened. "What?" I asked, my head tilted.

"We're releasing you from custody. You're as free as a bird."

"But what …" I stammered, shaking my head as if to make sure I wasn't dreaming. "How's that possible?"

"That boyfriend of yours brought us a pile of irrefutable evidence, giving us some fresh insights." His gaze softened as he held out his hand to me. "We realise we've made a mistake, I'd like to offer you my sincere apologies. You have been fully exonerated."

As the detective squeezed my extended limp hand, I was still feeling dazed. I couldn't wrap my head around what was happening.

He let go of me and gave my shoulder a nudge. "Let's head this way."

I looked around searchingly, but the guard with the handcuffs was nowhere to be seen. I started walking, trying to catch up with the detective who was already ahead of me.

As we approached the end of the corridor, I laid eyes on Dan who was waiting for me, his hands folded across his chest and a big grin on his face.

The detective came to a halt and addressed me. "I hope you'll make a swift recovery from your ordeal. We'll be in touch," he said, raising one hand in the air as a goodbye gesture before using it to open the door to another corridor. I stared after him as he briskly walked off until the door automatically closed and he vanished from view.

I turned around.

Dan uncoiled his arms and spread them open, his mouth grinning even wider.

I leaped forward and hugged him, the comforting warmth of his body making my senses tingle with happiness.

Dan stroked the back of my head that rested against his chest, and we stood there for a moment, his familiar eau de cologne having a soothing effect on me. I gently moved back and looked up to Dan, his face a mere inches away. "I am so incredibly grateful to you," I said softly. "What on earth have … ?" I shook my head. "How did you manage to get me out?"

Dan ran a hand through his hair. "I sat down with Detective Armstrong this morning and submitted to him all the evidence you and I collected – the sound recording you captured at the DFI, the overview that Oliver had already prepared months ago and the information I managed to extract from TelExact." A laugh broke from his chest. "The icing on the cake was a string of transactions from a covert account held by Mason & McGant with a bank on the Cayman Islands, wired to that Joe guy, the scientist at the DFI."

I was gobsmacked and impressed, and jabbed my fist in his chest. "So you've been pulling a few strings eh?" I said, laughing a hearty, genuine chortle.

He waved his hand airily. "Last night I reached out to one of the back-room boys in the finance department at our firm, who's an old friend of mine. I knew I was taking a huge risk, but I figured I could trust him. After hours of digging through endless accounts and payments, we stumbled upon a transaction from one of the partners of Mason & McGant to the crook at the DFI. This enabled us to build the foundation of our case that the firm – or more precisely Roderick delaHaye – paid Joe de Smet at the DFI for his services."

I looked away, letting the information sink in, noticing some guy with scruffy hair at the far end of the corridor screaming and hollering, the two guards holding him attempting to calm him down. My arms dropped to my sides as the corners of my lips rose in a light smile.

Dan held my hands. "The case is not yet a done deal, but Detective Armstrong intimated that they are going to turn Mason & McGant inside out. It's just a matter of time before they indict Roderick."

I sunk my teeth into my bottom lip and searched his face. "Do you think Roderick has been operating this scam by himself at Mason & McGant all this time, or would more partners have been involved?"

Dan wrinkled his nose. "I'm not sure, but you know what they say – one rotten apple spoils the whole barrel. In any case, it's out of our hands now. The police are dedicating all of their resources to the investigation – I'm sure they'll work out all the intricacies. But if you ask me, Roderick was the mastermind behind all the forgery and bribery. He must have discovered Oliver was on to him and lost his cool."

"Yes, you're probably right ..." My voice trailed off, as my mind played back memories of the first time Detective Armstrong rang me and turned my world on its head. "But there's one aspect we haven't fully addressed yet. Remember I told you about the pair of red knickers Oliver was wearing when they found him?"

Dan lifted his shoulder in a half shrug.

"Those knickers belonged to Sandra. Roderick must have slipped them on Oliver after his death," I said and winced as I visualised that bastard tugging on Oliver's lifeless body, trying to cram his heavy, unyielding legs into a degrading garment. I ground my teeth and clenched my jaw so tight it hurt.

"Why do you think he would have done that?" Dan asked.

"I reckon Roderick must have found out by then that Oliver had been having an affair with his wife. Perhaps the knickers were a sign or a warning towards Sandra, or maybe he just wanted to leave a final act of disgrace on Oliver's body."

I felt tears welling up, but managed to subdue them and rolled my shoulders to ease the tension in the nape of my neck. "I can't believe this nightmare is over," I said, looking at Dan, breathing off an easy laugh.

He flicked a defiant lock of hair back from my face and fixed it behind my ear with a lopsided smile. "Yes it really is over. Detective Armstrong informed me right before releasing you that they have apprehended Roderick in his home and are about to interrogate him. So you have nothing left to worry about now, that man should be going behind bars for a very long time. And besides," Dan said, flashing a cheeky grin as he slowly inched himself closer, "I'm here to protect you now," he whispered before pressing his lips gently onto mine, releasing a thousand butterflies in my stomach. I leaned into his kiss, enjoying every spark it kindled, until he slowly retreated.

"Come on, I already got your handbag, let's leave this miserable place behind," Dan said jauntily and swivelled around, invitingly holding out an elbow.

I tucked my arm through his and together we ambled out of the building towards Dan's car. As we got outside I came to a halt, tilted my head upwards, closed my eyes and breathed in the crisp fresh air. The light wind was rustling the leaves in the treetops overhead, birds cooing on the branches. I opened my eyes, my head still tilted up to the blue sky, mesmerised by a string of white clouds being swept forward. I let out a big sigh of bliss and looked down again, nudging Dan to indicate I was ready to continue.

As we got to his car, Dan opened the door me. "I'll take you home."

During the five-minute drive to my beloved neighbourhood, we remained silent, surrounded by the comforting hustle and bustle of the city, a symphony of clanging tram bells, flashy scooters shooting by and bikers yelling angrily at speeding cars. I smiled and stretched my legs – I couldn't wait to hold Tim in my arms again. The thoughts in my mind were still all over the place and it would surely take me some time to lay the ghost of these troubling times to rest, but, all in all, the jumpy feeling I'd been suffering from slowly abated. I looked at Dan, whose eyes were on the road, and suddenly realised that I'd been vindicated with Dan's aid as well as by the chart that Oliver had made before his death. It seemed a bizarre twist of fate that these two men in my life had, together, contributed to my release.

When we arrived home, I rummaged through my purse, looking for my keys. Just before I opened the door I paused, the key hanging in the air, and I looked back at Dan a little uncertain. I didn't know exactly how things stood between us, but I wanted to keep him with me. "Would you like to come inside?"

He nodded and flashed me one of his wonderful smiles. "I'd love to."

After slipping out of our coats, I hung them on the rack and was about to lead the way to the living room, but noticed through the window that the house was far from empty. Tim jumped up from the couch, pointed his little finger to me and called out, "Mummy!" I dashed inside and as my little baby flew into my arms, I sank to my knees and held him tightly, the scent of freshly shampooed hair flowing into my nostrils. "Oh darling, I will never leave you again," I whispered into his blond curls, as tears filled my eyes. Only now did I fully realise how different my life could have turned out if it weren't for Dan's help.

My little champ wiggled himself out of my arms – oblivious to the dire situation I'd been in – after which I cast a bewildered look around the room, the atmosphere thick with a solemn silence. My parents and my three girlfriends had formed a semi-circle around me, staring meekly at me. I threw my arms out, a bemused look on my face. "What are you all doing here? Is this a surprise party?" I joked, and the mood in the room instantly shifted to jolly and cheerful, chatter filling the air.

My mother held me in her arms for a while, stroking my hair. She released me, still keeping me close to her with a regretful look in her eyes. "Oh, darling, Dan filled us in yesterday on everything that's happened. I can't imagine the hell you've been through. Why didn't you share all of this with your father and me?"

I sloughed off a lame shrug. "I'm not sure, Mum," I said truthfully. "I didn't want to bother you or put you in harm's way – it was too complicated."

She nodded and took a few steps back, making space for my friends to console me. "Hun, I'm so, so sorry for how I've let you down. When push came to shove, we weren't there for you," Lindsey said, squeezing my shoulder. "I can't believe what a terrifying ordeal you must have been through. Dan told me the police have been giving you the third degree." A mixture of ache and guilt flashed across her face as her voice broke.

Frederique stepped in. "I feel so awful about all of this – we dropped you like a rock when you needed us most. Can you please forgive us for not believing you and sticking up for you?"

Karen stood with slumped shoulders, her arms folded across her chest and bobbed her head.

I wrapped my arms around the three of them and gave them a group hug. "Of course," I said, my voice muffled by Lindsey's white blouse. "You are my darlings …" I released my grip and looked them in the eye, one by one. "All of you. I should apologise for my behaviour too. You were concerned for my safety and all I did was shoo you away."

"Thank goodness for Dan who came to your rescue," Frederique said, gesturing towards Dan, who was engaging in a lively conversation with my father. She leaned in and lowered her voice as she gave me a wink. "If I were you I'd make sure not to let that man walk – he's a keeper."

I smiled, let my hands glide off my friends' shoulders and walked over to Dan. I laid a hand on his arm. "Dan, could you help me pour the drinks?"

"Sure."

We popped into the kitchen, where we were out of hearing distance from the others. "How did you pull this off? All my family and friends are here," I asked, bouncing on my toes.

He waved his hand airily. "Oh, it wasn't that hard. I had your phone, remember? Your mother filled me in on all the important people in your life. I kept them updated on how everything was going and indicated I was hoping to get you back home today. Everyone was incredibly relieved and delighted and wanted to give you a warm welcome."

I stepped closer and held his face in my hands, gazing into his beautiful, longing eyes. "Dan, you have done so much for me. How can I ever thank you for this?"

He gave me one of his gorgeous smiles. "Take me out for dinner?"

I chuckled and then gave a mock-serious face. "I will make a reservation at the best restaurant in Amsterdam."

Dan slid his arms around my waist, pulled me gently towards him with a teasing look. I closed my eyes and tasted his warm lips on mine, my senses tingling. We'd been through so much together in such a short time that the intimacy felt intuitive and familiar.

I opened my eyes and gazed up at him, his firm hands still lingering on my hips. "Would you mind getting a bottle of Moët out of the wine cooler?"

He gave me a wink and released his hands. "Of course."

As I heard the sounds of Dan rummaging around the kitchen, my gaze wandered through the room, filled with my loved ones chatting amiably while Tim scampered around between them, and it suddenly hit me how incredibly blessed I was to have all these wonderful, lovely people in my life. With a blissful smile on my face I sauntered to the mahogany cupboard, to fetch the crystal champagne glasses that Oliver and I had received as a wedding gift and always reserved for special occasions. Well, this is as special as it gets, I thought to myself, as I rejoined my family and friends, ready to toast my freedom and the next chapter of my life, with Dan by my side.

ACKNOWLEDGEMENTS

I'd like to thank all my reviewers of the Dutch version of this book that helped shape the story, Elsbeth Hamberg, Emmy Troquete, Hanneke Verbiest and my lovely sisters Valerie and Fleur Brouwers.

My thanks to my dear neighbour Beth Hutchings for being the first reviewer of the book and connecting me with editor and translator Sarah Fencott. Beth, without your enthusiasm and willingness to help me move the book further, Double Deceipt would never have existed.

Finally, the friendly and professional, creative and skilful Sarah Fencott. Thank you so much for our collaboration. Without your help and input, I'd never have been able to finish Double Deceipt. I've learned ever so much from you and had a wonderful time working with you.

Finally my beloved husband Chris and our wonderful three kids. Thank you so much for supporting me in my endeavours.

Dear reader, I really hope you enjoyed reading my book!
Would you please leave a review on amazon? It will only take a
few moments and would help me pursue my ambitions as a writer.
Thank you!

About the Author

Julienne Brouwers is married, has three children and lives in The Hague in the Netherlands. She has previously written two books in Dutch. This is her first thriller in English.

If you'd like to leave a message or get into my email list, please email to juliennebrouwers@gmail.com